THE GUID'ANTONIO VESPUCCI MYSTERIES
BY ALANA WHITE

The Sign of the Weeping Virgin

"Meticulously researched and pleasingly written."
Kirkus Starred Review

OTHER FICTION

Come Next Spring

Mark Twain Award Master List
Missouri Association of School Librarians

NONFICTION

Sacagawea: Westward with Lewis and Clark

"Intriguing and Well-Written."
Kirkus Reviews

DISCARDED

A **GUID'ANTONIO VESPUCCI** MYSTERY

The Hearts of All on Fire

ALANA WHITE

atmosphere press

© 2022 Alana White

Published by Atmosphere Press

Cover design by Matthew Fielder

No part of this book may be reproduced without permission from the author except in brief quotations and in reviews. This is a work of fiction, and any resemblance to real places, persons, or events is entirely coincidental.

atmospherepress.com

For my Husband Once Again and Always

HISTORICAL NOTE

In 1473, when *The Hearts of All on Fire* takes place, Florence was one of five major powers that dominated Italy's patchwork of independent city-states. High on the northern cuff of the boot-shaped peninsula were Venice and Milan. An oligarchy on the Adriatic Sea with a Doge appointed for life, Venice's lifeblood was maritime trade—spices, slaves, precious metals, and luxurious silks—an enterprise threatened by the steady advance of the Ottoman Turks who, by 1460, had in the name of *jihad*, holy war, made significant inroads in Europe.

West of Venice lay Milan, stronghold of the Sforza dukes. Shifting alliances and family quarrels plagued the ducal succession. Relations between Milan and Venice were hostile, with each government aspiring to extend its frontier at the other's expense.

Far down south, at the ankle of the Italian boot, King Ferrante ruled Naples. The elder of Ferrante's two sons, Prince Alfonso (also titled Duke of Calabria), was a professional soldier with an eye to using Neapolitan military superiority to make his family's house, the House of Aragon, dominant in Italy.

North of Naples lay the Papal States, presided over in Rome by Pope Sixtus IV. While building and decorating the Sistine Chapel and expanding the Vatican library, Sixtus IV immersed himself in politics. Uncle to a slew of nephews, dedicated to nepotism on a grand scale, he made no fewer than six of them cardinals. For his favorite, Girolamo Riario, Sixtus IV wanted nothing less than a lordship in the Papal States where the Pope ruled in name only. While giving lip service to papal authority, local families governed the towns of that sprawling province, towns the Pope meant to bend to his will.

Set in the sunny heart of Italy, in the lush, rolling hills of the Arno Valley between Venice and Milan in the north and

Rome and Naples in the south, Florence was a Republic whose citizens had clung to the trappings of a democratic form of government since the late thirteenth century. Not for them a king, lord, or duke. To prevent any one man from wielding power, the government changed with breathtaking frequency as members of duly elected committees were replaced by men who qualified and had their names drawn from a "hat." Ironically, what the fiercely democratic-thinking Florentines had created for themselves was a government that changed so often, Italy's four other major powers sought one Florentine man or family to deal with, while considering Florence easy prey.

The Florentine government's wobbly design kept the Republic weak at home, too. Over time, within the city walls a select political class had come to rule, dominated by several hundred families. By the mid-1400s these families, in turn, were ruled by about five hundred men at whose core the Medici family stood boldly front and center, acting from their palazzo on Via Larga as the *de facto*, or unofficial, leaders of the Republic. Why did foreign powers and Florentine citizens turn to one family for leadership? Because dealing with one family—one man, one faction, one voice—was the only recourse when faced with a government that, for the most part, changed every two months. Animosity and disagreements escalated between these five powers for decades, none with more deadly results than the friction between Rome and Florence that eventually exploded into a bloody assassination in Florence Cathedral in April 1478, signaling the death of innocence and forever changing the course of Italian history.

ITALY
IN THE LATE FIFTEENTH CENTURY

CAST OF CHARACTERS

1473

The Vespucci

Guid'Antonio Vespucci ~ Florentine investigator and doctor of law.

Maria del Vigna ~ Guid'Antonio's wife.

Amerigo Vespucci ~ Guid'Antonio's nephew and secretary, who later sailed west, twice for Spain, and twice for Portugal. The adventurer for whom America is named.

Antonio Vespucci ~ Amerigo's older brother and a rising notary in the Florentine government.

Mona Elisabetta and Nastagio ("Stagio") Vespucci ~ Amerigo and Antonio's parents. Mona means "madame," a title of respect.

Brother Giorgio Vespucci ~ Scholar, teacher, cleric. Amerigo's "other" uncle and Guid'Antonio's kinsman.

Marco and Piero Vespucci ~ A close Vespucci cousin and his father.

Simonetta Cattaneo Vespucci ~ Marco Vespucci's wife and Guid'Antonio and Amerigo's kinswoman by marriage. Simonetta is the golden-haired inspiration for Sandro Botticelli's *Birth of Venus* and other paintings.

Domenica Ridolfi ~ The Vespucci family cook.

Cesare Ridolfi ~ Domenica's adolescent son.

The Medici

Lorenzo de' Medici ~ Leader of the Medici family and its decades-old political regime in Florence.

Giuliano de' Medici ~ Lorenzo's younger, only brother.

Clarice Orsini ~ Lorenzo's Roman wife.

Piero ("the Gouty") and Cosimo de' Medici (at the time of his death named "the Father of his Country") ~ Lorenzo and Giuliano's father and grandfather.

Giovanni Tornabuoni ~ Lorenzo and Giuliano's uncle. Manager of the Medici branch bank in Rome and Depositor General of the Apostolic Chamber.

Duke Galeazzo Maria Sforza ~ Medici family supporter through his father and grandfather. Father of Caterina Sforza, the indomitable blonde beauty known to history as "The Tigress of Forli."

The Pazzi Family & Their Supporters

Little Francesco ("Franceschino") de' Pazzi ~ Banker, merchant. Manager of the Pazzi family bank in Rome.

Guglielmo de' Pazzi ~ Franceschino's brother, also Lorenzo and Giuliano de' Medici's brother-in-law through Guglielmo's marriage to their sister, Bianca de' Medici.

Pope Sixtus IV ~ Head of the Roman Catholic Church (1471-1484).

Count Girolamo Riario ~ The Pope's favorite nephew and his right-hand man in Rome. Married to Caterina Sforza to seal a political union between Milan and Rome.

Antonio Maffei ~ A priest from Volterra making his way as a scribe in the halls of the Vatican.

Others

Maestra Francesca Vernacci ~ A doctor of the house at Spedale dei Vespucci (the Vespucci Hospital) in Florence, along with her physician father, Dottore Filippo Vernacci.

Palla Palmieri ~ Florence's Chief of Police

Luca Landucci ~ Apothecary and proprietor of the Sign of the Stars.

Francesco Nori ~ Manager of the Florence office of the international Medici Bank headquartered in Florence. Before that, the local Medici Bank manager in France.

Bartolomeo Scala ~ Humanist scholar and Chancellor (secretary) of the Florentine Republic.

Angelo Poliziano ~ Poet, scholar, keeper of the Medici library. Later, tutor of Lorenzo de' Medici's sons and daughters.

Marsilio Ficino ~ Humanist philosopher, writer, teacher.

Leonardo da' Vinci ~ Craftsman apprentice at Verrocchio and Company, Florence's busiest workshop, owned and operated by sculptor/painter Andrea del Verrocchio.

Princess Eleanor of Aragon ~ Daughter of King Ferrante of Naples and the first duchess of Ferrara through her marriage to Duke Ercole d'Este.

Orlando Niccolini ~ Wealthy merchant and manager of one of Florence's most successful wool shops, Spinelli and Spinelli.

Mona Caterina Niccolini ~ Orlando Niccolini's wife.

Andrea Antinori ~ An apprentice at Spinelli & Spinelli.

The Caretto Family ~ Chiara Caretto, her grandfather Jacopo Caretto, and her uncles Salvatore and Fenso.

The Veluti Family ~ Orlando Niccolini's *inamorata*, Elena Veluti, and her kin, Baldo and Beatrice Pacini.

In Ognissanti (All Saints) Church

Abbot Roberto Ughi ~ Abbot of Ognissanti Church

Brother Battista Bellincioni ~ Almoner of Ognissanti Church

One

FLORENCE ~ SAINT JOHN'S DAY
THURSDAY, 24TH JUNE 1473

The meadow on All Saints Street hummed with music and voices raised in lively conversation, for it was late afternoon and Guid'Antonio's festivities honoring the city's patron saint had lasted for too long now. Wine poured, eyes met and held, anticipation was the order of the day. From the trestle where he sat with his nephew, Amerigo, and a handful of other men, Guid'Antonio observed the young people dancing in the grass, the maidens pink-lipped and rosy-cheeked, their partners' cotton tunics stuck to their chests with sweat. Fingertips lightly touching, they were oblivious to the meadow's sultry heat, deaf to every sound but the melody of lyres and lutes, blind to all but gossamer gowns, averted glances, and parted mouths. For them, there was no tomorrow and no consequence, only hot, rushing colors and pounding blood. Guid'-Antonio saw those colors now, gold and red exploding against his eyelids.

"Woolgathering, Dottore Vespucci?" the cloth merchant

beside Guid'Antonio said. "Having your way with those pretty boys and girls? Thee and me, Dottore, thee and me." The merchant leered at the dancers, wetting his lips.

Amerigo reared back, aghast. "You go too far, *Signore*! How *dare* you say such a ridiculous thing?"

"I say what I think. You don't?" the merchant said.

"No! Not—"

Guid'Antonio touched Amerigo gently on the arm, aware of the discontent rustling up and down their festival table. All day long, the cloth merchant's words had oozed with familiarity in Guid'Antonio's ear, as if they shared an intimate friendship.

They did not.

Woolgathering? No. And certainly not lusting after the joyful young people jumping and leaping in the grass, only aware of the afternoon shadows slowly gathering in the meadow, while his case involving the death of a girl from the Black Lion district nattered in his head. A ten-or-eleven-year-old girl violated, strangled, and buried in a hole just beyond the city walls, her fate unknown if not for the dog that smelled her rotting flesh in the darkness before dawn last Sunday morning. A dog digging in the dirt and retrieving a scrap of cloth crusted with blood, then howling at the girl's door until a night patrol followed the awful sound and arrested the child's grandfather. Shaken from sleep, the old man proclaimed his guilt to the world. All this on a hot June night when there was no moon, and there were no stars.

God wanted her found, Guid'Antonio thought. *But why this child? For that matter, why this dog?* Something about this odd resurrection gave him pause, causing him to wonder, *And finally, in the grand scheme of things, why me?* Well. Tomorrow, accompanied by Amerigo, he would begin a routine investigation in preparation for the grandfather's hearing late next week.

†

He turned toward the wheezing cloth merchant. Orlando Niccolini's watery blue eyes set in a broad, flushed face were rheumy, their rims red and inflamed. His summer tunic fit him poorly: the cotton luxurious, but far too loose, its white folds a shroud enveloping his body. Odd for an employee of a prestigious cloth manufacturing shop, but then to Guid'Antonio, Orlando Niccolini seemed a bit odd all around.

"I was only thinking," Guid'Antonio said. "If you consider that gathering wool, well then—" He shrugged amiably. "So be it."

The merchant sneezed and swiped the mucus dripping from his nose with the back of his fist. "The Devil take this cold and shove it up his ass!"

Guid'Antonio's table went silent. "Until then, God bless you," Giuliano de' Medici said, his brown eyes gentle beneath a cap of glossy black curls. From his leather scrip, Giuliano withdrew a lace-edged handkerchief and offered it to the older man, who honked noisily into the exquisitely embroidered letter *M*.

"Thank you for your kindness," the merchant said, catching his breath.

"Keep it, please," Giuliano de' Medici said. "It is a gift."

Amerigo, with a wicked gleam in his eyes, murmured, "It is now."

Guid'Antonio smiled along with the others. Nineteen-year-old Giuliano de' Medici was in the bloom of life. Kind, as the cloth merchant had said. Respected and loved all around town for his easy nature, although grudgingly by a growing number of men who were beginning to question how it was all Italy and most of Europe considered Giuliano and his only slightly older brother, Lorenzo, the true leaders of the Florentine Republic, no matter who sat in City Hall.

Amerigo fidgeted, his back stiff with discontent. "Soon the horses will arrive for the *palio*, while here we sit, waiting for our last course. Where's our little servitor-in-training with our salads, hmmm?"

Guid'Antonio followed his nephew's impatient gaze across the meadow to the broad thoroughfare separating the meadow and the River Arno. There in sunlit Piazza Ognissanti vendors hawked figs, tangy oranges, and savory pies to dyers and tin workers who had long since had their fill. Children shrieked with delight, fleeing the dogs playfully nipping at their heels. Lace-makers and knife grinders traded friendly insults and bets, anticipating the moment horses and riders would gather at the starting line for the *palio*, the most anticipated horse race of the Florentine year. All in all, it was a hot, spirited, and increasingly restive Saint John's Day crowd.

Much like Amerigo himself.

Guid'Antonio took a large drink of wine. "Our salads will arrive in time for the race, don't worry," he said. "When this meal is finished, you may fly off with your friends like a thrilled little bird. Meanwhile, please notice many of our guests haven't finished their trout. They are not worried about horses." Quite the contrary. Everyone in the meadow seemed happy to eat and drink and flirt all day long and far into the night.

"I am anxious, I confess," Amerigo said.

Giuliano de' Medici laughed, the light sound of bells ringing on a summer breeze. "*Tutti, per la salute!* Everyone, to your health." He raised his cup, his cheeks feverish with Chianti and heat.

"Here, you! Get away from me!" the cloth merchant screamed.

Giuliano flinched. *"Mi scusi?"*

"Not you—her!" Flailing his arms wildly, the merchant

shot out his foot and kicked the dog snuffling beneath the table for scraps. Sad-eyed and small, with scruffy ginger fur, the dog yipped and hunched away, her nipples so full and ripe, they dragged the ground. Around her neck she wore a makeshift collar, a frayed brown string.

Indignantly, Amerigo said, "She wasn't hurting anyone, *Signore*. She's hungry and having pups this very day, perhaps." He tossed the dog a chunk of rosemary bread from the silver basket at his fingertips. Waddling over, casting a wary eye at the row of boots beneath the table, the dog snatched the bread and scurried away as quickly as her short legs could manage.

The cloth merchant laughed. "Boy, you are too soft-hearted. Whose bitch is it?"

Guid'Antonio squeezed his toes in the tips of his boots. "Ser Niccolini. Clearly, the dog belongs to no one, like countless other strays."

Niccolini spat into Giuliano's lacy handkerchief. "Then someone should throttle her," he said.

"No, they should not," Guid'Antonio said.

Breathing deeply, he sought calm in the sound of laughter drifting from the table in the meadow where Maria, his wife for two-and-one-half years, sat entertaining guests. Jumping up to whisper something in the ear of a friend, she appeared as free as the wind. Not yet twenty and olive skinned, his wife was breathtakingly lovely in the shifting colors of her iridescent *festa* gown; from her raven hair done up in a cap of pearls to the rubies adorning her ears, she glowed. Feeling his gaze, she glanced his way, blowing him a kiss before flouncing back toward the other women, a blush ripening her cheeks.

Guid'Antonio smiled, his belly feeling a little trill.

"Ser Niccolini, I am no boy," Amerigo was saying. "In March I celebrated my nineteenth birthday."

"Years do not make the man," Niccolini said.

"*Madre di Dio.*" Amerigo smacked his forehead.

Seated on Amerigo's right, Medici banker Francesco Nori said, "We know they do not, *Signore*. We have proof with us here, *n'est-ce pas?*" He smiled blandly along the table at the other man.

Madonna. Guid'Antonio slid his eyes toward Orlando Niccolini, wondering how the cloth merchant would take Francesco Nori's insult, thinly veiled and capped off in French, a language Francesco had learned while overseeing the Medici family bank in Lyons for two decades—this, before King Louis XI tossed him out three years ago with the warning never to set foot on French soil again. Since then, Francesco had managed the Medici Bank's branch office in Florence.

The merchant's stubby fingers flew to the stiletto at his belt. Francesco followed suit casually, not too hurried. "Francesco! Are you suggesting I'm not a man?" the merchant yelled.

"*Moi?*" Francesco grinned wickedly.

"Francesco, please," Guid'Antonio quickly cut in. "No such thing, Ser Niccolini. You're nothing if not a man who appreciates a good jest now and again, even at his own expense. Am I correct?"

"No—" The scowl on the cloth merchant's face deepened, but he withdrew his fingers from the hilt of his blade. "I mean—yes! As for you, Francesco Nori, you would do well to remember you work not only for the Medici Bank, but for me, privately, as well."

Francesco raised his hands with an air of dismissal. "I remember it daily."

"See that you do!" the merchant said, his face red with agitation.

Giuliano de' Medici leaned around Niccolini's back, his dark eyes questioning and uneasy. *Guid'Antonio, what ails Ser Niccolini?*

Besides the summer fever? I have no idea, swear.

He did not know Orlando Niccolini well. He had invited the cloth merchant to join his holiday table only because Lorenzo de' Medici had requested it as a personal favor. "Business related," Lorenzo had claimed. "He will feel flattered to sit beside Giuliano, Florence's darling boy. You know Niccolini directs Spinelli and Spinelli's daily operations."

Yes. In his role as the Spinelli family's wool shop manager, Orlando Niccolini oversaw the transformation of fleeces imported from England and Spain into finely woven and brilliantly dyed cloths. "Our bank holds the Spinelli account. We want to maintain the *status quo*. He'll feel flattered to sit alongside you, too, of course, Guid'Antonio," Lorenzo had said, his thousand-candle smile warm on Guid'Antonio Vespucci, his friend and a longtime Medici family supporter. Guid'Antonio had not minded extending the invitation so very much. It was a favor between colleagues. Between him and the two fledgling leaders of the Medici political regime in Florence.

"Ser Niccolini, you seem—" *Confused*, Guid'Antonio thought. "Fatigued," he said.

Niccolini's scowl deepened into harsh lines around his mouth. "No more so than any other man who slaves for a living here in Florence."

"If you're ill, you should consult a doctor," Guid'Antonio said, wondering exactly when this day had started its descent straight to hell.

The merchant's glance darted here and there. "Why? What have you heard? I'm not so ill as that! I have pressing business to attend. Immediately, no matter this is Saint John's Day! Tonight bonfires will blaze and fireworks dazzle in Piazza della Signoria. Will I be there? No! I'll be in Pisa waiting for passage abroad."

Francesco Nori's eyes twinkled. *"Bon voyage, Signore."*

Beside Guid'Antonio, Amerigo shifted restlessly on the

bench. "Uncle Guid'Antonio, you know this afternoon Ser Niccolini is leaving town to board a galley bound for England tomorrow, and yet—" He anchored his hair from his face.

"Where are our salads?"

Guid'Antonio gestured sharply toward the crowded thoroughfare. "Where is peace and quiet? Do you see horses on the horizon? No. Our salads shall arrive, and then the horses, all in good order."

Orlando Niccolini sneezed loudly. "What kind of salads are they?"

"Mushroom." Carefully, Guid'Antonio straightened his dinner napkin, only half-listening to the conversation springing up around him again. Did he give a fig about the bonfires and fireworks happening in Piazza della Signoria tonight? No. Even the celebrated *palio* did not stir his blood. How many horse races had run in Florence since spring? Six? Ten? When was Florence *not* observing one holy day or another? His home town constantly danced, jousted, and bent its head in prayer, celebrating Carnavale, Easter, May Day, and Saint John the Baptist. At the same time, wedged like leaves of parchment into an already fat manuscript, came San Zanobi, Ascension Day, the Feast of the Holy Spirit, the Blessed Trinity, Corpus Christi, and a deluge of baptisms and wedding banquets.

This made his head throb.

All he wanted was to bid his guests *"Arrivederla,"* walk Maria home and fall with her into bed, his legs wrapped around her hips, his tongue licking her belly and full round breasts. In his mind's eye, he watched himself rise and stride to her in the meadow, watched her ripe blush deepen to scarlet as he took her hand. At home in their apartment, her eyes would feast on him from beneath feathery lashes until their bed jiggled in a fury of pleasure and sweat.

The noise of tambourines and stringed instruments yanked

him to the present.

    His watchful wolf's eyes went to Maria's table. One place remained empty. Where was Maria's guest, the cloth merchant's wife, Caterina Niccolini? Glancing over, lips tilted in a smile, Maria lifted her shoulders in an understanding shrug before pivoting to her neighbor. She had no idea why Caterina Niccolini had failed to join her as one of Guid'Antonio Vespucci's special Saint John's Day guests, a place of honor for which some people would kill.

Two

PASSIONE

Dancers danced, musicians played, wine flowed from fountains and the taps of wooden barrels.

Orlando Niccolini pressed close, his breath sour on Guid'Antonio's cheek. "Fleece shipped to us from the Cotswolds hasn't been the best quality lately. I have got to question our suppliers there. Can't let those English cheat us any longer. Well! No rest for the weary," he said. "Who knows better than you? Doctor of law, Lord Prior of the Florentine Republic, and our ambassador to northern Italy, too. Dottore Vespucci, our city salutes you." Niccolini lifted his wine, smiling vacantly all around.

Silence fell over the table with the weight of a sodden blanket. Every man there except Orlando Niccolini knew the situation. While spring had seen Guid'Antonio in Milan attending a series of important social events as one of several ambassadors from Florence, his secret mission had been to bargain with the duke of Milan for the purchase of Imola, a town up north near the Adriatic Coast, before it fell into the hands of Pope Sixtus IV. Armed with the duke's vow he would sell the town to the Florentine Republic rather than to Rome, from Milan Guid'Antonio had ridden fast to Imola to tell the mayor and town council about the transaction and assure them they had nothing to fear from Florence except, perhaps, higher taxes, Ah, me. He had been home two months now, and still the promised contract had not arrived at City Hall bearing the duke of Milan's signature and seal. Remembering this made Guid'Antonio feel as if he were standing barefoot on burning coals. His failure in this assignment—his first as an ambassador—would mean failure for the Florentine Republic.

Failure for him.

Failure for his house.

No news at this point is needless worry, he told himself.

And yet the lack of it is killing you, whispered the imp in his ear.

†

He adjusted the cuffs of his cream-colored tunic, cotton embroidered with the Vespucci family emblem, *vespe*, wasps, as befit their name. *Beware my sting.* "Thank you for your kind words, Ser Niccolini."

Amerigo tiptoed in. "Ser Niccolini, surely you know my uncle is neither a Lord Prior nor an ambassador at the moment, but we're busy in court. Tomorrow morning early, we'll be at the jail looking into the Jacopo Caretto incident." Amerigo gestured lightly with one hand. "He's the man who—well."

Incident. Violated. Killed. The murdered girl and her grandfather.

"Ah! The wool beater from the Santa Croce quarter." Niccolini tilted toward Guid'Antonio. "You have that case, Dottore?"

"Yes." A fly flew across Guid'Antonio's face. He swatted at it and watched it vanish, quivering, into the air, as if it never had lived.

"Pray the man has good reason for what he did, else his actions blacken my name," Niccolini said.

Francesco Nori gasped, drawing back. "Good reason? For killing a child? *Mon Dieu.*"

"Reasonable motive," Amerigo said.

The lines around Francesco Nori's eyes deepened into a frown. "The girl was his granddaughter. I don't recall a crime so . . . so repugnant in Florence before now. What reasonable motive could there be?"

Guid'Antonio spread his hands. It sickened him to think of anyone committing such monstrous deeds. Still, it was not his place to judge, but to remain objective in all matters pertaining to the law, always. The girl's grandfather, Jacopo Caretto, had confessed; for him, there would be no trial in court, only an oral statement from Guid'Antonio, who had been appointed to examine Caretto's degree of guilt, then offer his opinion regarding the punishment he believed the man should receive. In other words, exactly how guilty was Caretto for the crime of violating and murdering his granddaughter.

"I'll begin by searching for precedents and convictions in other cases involving children," Guid'Antonio said. "The magistrates will hear my opinion next Friday and sentence Caretto. As you say, Francesco, nothing like this has happened before in Florence—at least not within my memory."

"The court always considers extenuating circumstances," Amerigo said. "Which could be difficult in this case, since Caretto won't speak in his defense."

Francesco Nori cocked his head to one side, addressing Guid'Antonio. "But you give the court your opinion first regarding his sentence," he said.

"Yes. According to my investigation. But the magistrates

aren't bound to accept it."

A young acquaintance approached the table just then with the heavy-bellied ginger dog fast on his heels. *"Festa felice a tutti,"* Angelo Poliziano said. "Dottore Guid'Antonio, Amerigo said I might join you as the day wound down. There's no place at your table, but—" Angelo indicated the wooden stool in his hands. "If I may sit across from you and your guests?"

More wine. More talk. Still, Guid'Antonio liked Angelo Poliziano. Three years ago, Angelo had arrived in Florence as a boy of fifteen with nothing but the clothes on his back and his translation of the second book of Homer's *Iliad* from the original Greek into Latin, along with a letter to Lorenzo de' Medici promising to translate all the *Iliad* for him. Since then, the youth had lived in Palazzo Medici with Lorenzo, Giuliano, and the rest of the Medici family, studying and teaching Latin, philosophy, and Greek at *Studio Fiorentino,* the University of Florence.

"Of course you may," Guid'Antonio said.

"Grazie molto." Angelo bent to pet the little dog, Angelo's shining black hair feathering across his face, his long, delicate fingers ink-stained. "I think you've had enough to eat, little mother. Shoo." The dog shambled away, happily soliciting handouts.

"Ciao, Angelo," Giuliano de' Medici said. "We're discussing the wool beater and his granddaughter. The court has appointed Guid'Antonio to investigate and recommend sentence."

"Ah!" Angelo said. "Caretto's silence is the talk of the town. He won't say a word about what happened."

"He hasn't yet," Guid'Antonio said. Since Jacopo's arrest last Sunday morning, he had been isolated in a cell in the downtown jail with his mouth shut as tightly as if his lips were sewn together with needle and thread.

"Word is he was so addlebrained the night the guards came across the girl's remains at his door, he confessed to everything then and there," Francesco Nori said.

Guid'Antonio steepled his fingers, his eyes sweeping the meadow. There was no talk of violence there, only people enjoying themselves enormously. "Not her remains," he said. "The night patrol found her sleeve matted with blood and broke down his door. But, yes, he was so shaken that not only did he confess, he told the authorities where to find the girl's corpse. He thought the hammering and kicking was his granddaughter's ghost come to haunt him. Avenging spirit or no, all I'm meant to do is investigate the circumstances surrounding him and the girl and recommend suitable punishment. Which is ground we have already plowed."

Beside Guid'Antonio, Orlando Niccolini made a sour laugh. "My so-called wife, Caterina. Late, as always," he said, his eyes narrow on the woman hurrying off the thoroughfare and on across the meadow, her countenance shadowed within her hood, her voluminous brown cloak flicking around her heels.

Maria's missing guest. Halfway across the lawn, Mona Caterina Niccolini flipped the woolen fabric from her face and scanned her surroundings. Her glance settled on Guid'Antonio. Nodding, she turned away, stepping toward Maria's table, but quickly whirled back around, her eyes wide on Angelo Poliziano, seated on the wooden stool with his back to the meadow, waving his hands excitedly in the air. "Titus Lucretius Carus! A dissertation tomorrow at *Studio Fiorentino*! Amerigo, Giuliano, you simply must attend."

The merchant's wife went pale as a winter's day. She seemed about to cry out but caught herself back when a young woman skipped toward Guid'Antonio's table, a silver circlet crowning her flyaway golden hair. It was Simonetta Vespucci, Guid'Antonio and Amerigo's kinswoman by marriage.

"Giuliano," Simonetta Vespucci said, her smile deepening the dimples in her bright pink cheeks. "Come dance?"

"*Grazie*, Simonetta! I shall!" Leaping up, Giuliano de'

Medici bounded from the trestle and ran with Simonetta to their circle of friends as fast as his kid boots would take him, as if he were Zephyrus, the Greek god of the west wind, and Simonetta his blonde nymph, Chloris, the goddess of flowers.

"Ah, me," Angelo said, leaping up from the wooden stool and claiming Giuliano's vacant seat. "*La Bella Simonetta's* glance could calm a storm."

"Her glance may calm a storm, yet provoke a tempest in her husband," Amerigo said, nodding toward the wine barrels where Marco Vespucci stood swilling wine with his bravos. Simonetta's husband had hovered all day at the taps, singing boisterously, drinking Chianti, cup after cup. Now, patches of scarlet blotched Marco's petulant face, and his tambourine was limp in his hand.

Guid'Antonio groaned. "Amerigo," he said, "don't create trouble where there is none. Giuliano de' Medici and Marco Vespucci have been friends since they were boys."

"Let's hope they remain so," Amerigo said. "I would hate to see them fighting over Simonetta like two stags over a fecund doe."

"A fecund doe? Please, Amerigo." Guid'Antonio shook his head, grateful no one at the table seemed to have overheard the damning words issuing from his nephew's lips.

Caterina Niccolini remained isolated in the grass. Some of the color had returned to her face. Still, a lengthy moment passed before she made her way woodenly to Maria's table, where she shed her bulky cloak, her expression apologetic as she claimed her seat and greeted her hostess.

Guid'Antonio wondered about Caterina. A shadow of uncertainty—not quite fear, something close to alarm—had flickered in her eyes when she noticed Angelo Poliziano at Guid'Antonio's table. She and Angelo weren't lovers, surely. Angelo was eighteen, young enough to be her son. Guid'Antonio laughed silently to himself. Angelo was an engaging youth, and Caterina Niccolini was not in the grave. No longer wrapped in heavy fabric, her figure and face were pleasing, though she was a woman of at least thirty years. Whatever the truth, watching the dancers twirl around the meadow, watching Marco Vespucci with his hot glare on his fetching wife and Giuliano de' Medici, watching Caterina with her mouth close to Maria's ear, watching them all, Guid'Antonio had the unsettling feeling that on this feast day the meadow was a cocoon of false safety and comfort.

Too much heat, too much wine, too much *passione*.

†

Infine! Finally.

Heralded by the blast of trumpets, here came Guid'Antonio's little servant, Cesare Ridolfi, marching before a phalanx of whip thin young men ferrying covered silver trays aloft in their hands. In the meadow, the music fluttered and stood still. *"Grazie a Dio!* Our long lost salads!" Amerigo said.

All eyes followed Guid'Antonio's young servitor costumed in scarlet hose topped with a lavender vest whose grey silk ties fastened over a daringly short purple tunic trimmed with foamy lace at the neck and wrists. Orlando Niccolini fastened on him. "There's a pert boy."

Amerigo gave a fond chuckle. "He runs our house."

"He's how old now—twelve?" Francesco Nori said.

"And has ambitions above his station?" Niccolini snorted. "His ass would feel my belt."

Containing his anger by the sheer force of his will, Guid'Antonio reminded himself Orlando Niccolini was ill and soon this day would end. He reminded himself the Florentine Republic had sent him to Milan and Imola as a nod to his cool head and calm tongue. "Ser Niccolini, Cesare's mother has been with us since I was a boy," he said. "He was born in our house. He's a member of my family and deserves your respect."

Niccolini sucked his wine. "I meant nothing by it. Why haven't we seen that little Adonis before? Actually, I have seen him flitting about in the market."

"Because," Amerigo said, "he chose to focus on preparing and serving the salads for our Saint John's Day table."

Not exactly. Cesare's mother, Domenica Ridolfi, was the Vespucci family cook. Cesare had helped Domenica shop for fruits and vegetables in the outdoor markets since he could walk, but today was the first time the youngster had served food at a public Vespucci family event. For his debut, Guid'Antonio had allowed him to prepare and serve a salad for the head table, only. *Better to practice on me*, Guid'Antonio had thought. All the remaining guests had been served by other servants: roasts, breads, salads—everything.

Cesare placed a silver tray, rectangular with finely wrought handles, on a walnut side table. "Dottore Guid'Antonio," he said, fluttering his eyelashes, one hip cocked, his hand planted at his waist. "Cesare Ridolfi at your service."

He has been admiring Donatello's fetching bronze David in Palazzo Medici again, Guid'Antonio remarked to himself, a smile on his lips. "*Grazie*, Cesare," he said.

"It's about time, too," the cloth merchant complained. "Once this meal is over, I'm riding alone to the coast. I must reach Pisa before nightfall and sail from Livorno in the morning."

Cesare's violet eyes swept Niccolini. "Then I shall whisper a prayer to Saint Christopher to send you safely on your way. Dottore Guid'Antonio, I apologize for any inconvenience. The food, the service—everything must be perfect, and the kitchen is a riot of cooks and cutlery today. It has been all week."

"You're here now," Guid'Antonio said indulgently.

Cesare moved along the trestle, serving the salads, first to

Angelo Poliziano, now blissfully seated at the table, then to Orlando Niccolini, and on down the way. "Our Giuliano is where? He should have been *exactly* there at the end of the bench."

"He's twirling in the meadow with Simonetta, enjoying himself immensely," Amerigo said.

Niccolini sniffed the salad on his plate. "What kind of mushrooms are these?"

With a smooth turn of his wrist, Cesare filled Francesco Nori's wine cup. "Baby Cesare and wild greens caressed with a hint of *Aceto Balsamico de Modena*, the mushrooms purchased in the market by my own hand."

Cesare stepped back, tossing Angelo a quick look, a smile slipping across his lips. "With Giuliano de' Medici gone and the angel from Montepulciano in his place—" Angelo shook back his hair, smiling, a pink flush flaring along his cheekbones. "—We still have five salads for five men seated at our table in the drowsy afternoon heat. Dottore Guid'Antonio, do you like it?"

"*Magnifico.*" Guid'Antonio smiled at Cesare and lifted his cup toward Maria. *Here's to you in a very few moments, please, God, please.* Maria smiled back, tilting her head. *And to you, my love.*

Cesare beamed. "For you, I do my best. And for you, too, *Signori*," he said to Guid'Antonio's other guests. "*Buona festa a tutti voi.*"

"*Grazie, grazie,*" Guid'Antonio said.

Cesare swept a low bow. And then with his spine as straight as Giotto's bell tower in downtown Florence and his chin held high above the collar of his tunic, he marched back along All Saints Street toward the Vespucci Palace accompanied by the loud blare of trumpets.

Orlando Niccolini swiped a bit of mushroom from the corner of his mouth. "I only wish I could taste it." A glum expression spread over his face as his eyes shifted and found his wife, Caterina. "Always tardy, my darling spouse. But then, in her defense, she has been in the countryside, visiting her ailing mother. Caterina is a good woman, she just isn't good enough."

Guid'Antonio, raising his fork to his mouth, paused.

"Not good enough for what?" Amerigo said.

"For giving me a son. Or any child who lives."

Angelo Poliziano's eyes rounded in shock, as if he could not believe such a hateful comment had issued from the other man's lips. Slowly, Francesco Nori put down his cup and rested his elbows on the table, his dislike for his client palpable in the heat closing in around them.

Guid'Antonio swallowed his mushrooms. If Caterina Niccolini was cuckolding her husband with Angelo Poliziano, who could blame the lady?

"Lorenzo and Giuliano de' Medici aren't the only ones dipping their pens in more than one well," Niccolini said.

Guid'Antonio dropped his fork on the table. "Jesus God, Ser Niccolini! You would be wise to hold your tongue when it comes to slandering our friends."

Niccolini held out his hands. "Aren't men born to satisfy themselves in bed? Isn't it natural for a man's wife to give her husband children? Else what is she for?"

Guid'Antonio felt as if a hand had grabbed his throat and squeezed hard. He was not a father. At age thirty-seven, he could claim no boy or girl of his own. Five years ago, his only child, a son, had died as a newborn, along with his first wife, Taddea, who had bled to death in their marriage bed, screaming without cease as she struggled to bring the baby forth. With a Herculean effort, he squashed the urge to slap the merchant off the bench.

Blissfully unaware of the profound stink of disapproval perfuming the air, Niccolini said, "As for me, I have a girl set to bring forth my first child, please Christ's mother, a boy. My Elena Veluti is fourteen, her belly ripe as a watermelon. Damn the timing of this trip to England, but the Virgin Mary bless the outcome! I was with Elena today, and she's *una donna vera*, a real woman."

Guid'Antonio and Francesco Nori glanced with disapproval at one another. *Poor unfortunate girl.*

Niccolini shoveled mushrooms into his mouth. "Heaven knows I would rather be here with Elena than in England—" Groaning, he clutched his stomach and struggled for air. "But business—" His mouth gaped and he dropped his head in his hands. "Oh, God!" he moaned, his body shaking violently.

"Ser Niccolini?" Amerigo said. "What is it?"

Guid'Antonio stared as the wine from the wool merchant's cup saturated the family's white *festa* cloth with a spreading garnet stain. Bowels squeaking and roaring, Orlando Niccolini slumped face down in the chopped mushroom salad on his majolica plate, where chubby cherubs armed with bows and arrows romped around the rim, frolicking among lush, painted peonies and roses, grinning as if they knew a wicked secret.

THREE

DEATH IN THE MEADOW

"Orlando?"

Guid'Antonio reached toward the merchant's shoulder and pulled back his hand. The man was lifeless, drool dribbling from his mouth onto his plate.

Amerigo and Francesco scrambled from the bench. "Good God!" Amerigo gulped. "Is he dead?"

The cloth merchant's arms rested on the table. Reaching over again, Guid'Antonio felt for a pulse in the merchant's wrist. No beat, no flutter. Guid'Antonio stood up, alarm building in his chest. "I think yes." The dancers in the meadow slowed, glancing around, unsure. Gradually, the music broke off, and there was a deepening murmur as everyone studied one another, their confusion mounting.

"What happened?" Francesco Nori said.

"I don't know," Guid'Antonio replied, perplexed, irritated, and upset.

In the meadow, Maria rose slowly to her feet, all the color drained from her face. Caterina Niccolini, staring at her husband, stood beside Maria, dazed. One palm rested on the bodice of her gown, the other flat on the trestle, as if Caterina meant to steady her heart and her person.

Giuliano de' Medici bounded quickly from the circle of dancers, his hand light on the jeweled knife at his belt. Straight shoulders, broad back. "He's dead—?"

"Yes."

"What happened?"

As if Guid'Antonio should know. Well. Usually, he did. He made an ambivalent gesture. "His heart?"

"Apparently, lately he has given it a brisk workout," Amerigo said, an eyebrow arched.

"He has?" Giuliano de' Medici said.

"He left a girl with child," Francesco Nori said beneath his breath.

"—Oh," Giuliano said, letting Francesco's comment sink in.

As one, their glance slipped to Caterina Niccolini, who stood transfixed beside Maria, her eyes round hollows above bloodless cheeks and lips. "Now what, Guid'Antonio?" Giuliano said.

If only he had a silver penny for every time Giuliano or Lorenzo de' Medici had asked him that question, he would be as rich as King Solomon, if not in wisdom, then in coin. "Amerigo," he said. "Tell Maria and Caterina to stay where they are. Ask everyone else to do the same. We need to get him on the ground." He cast Angelo Poliziano a sidelong look, noticing how Angelo trembled, as frightened as a rabbit with a hawk circling overhead. Or like a young poet who had witnessed his *papa's* murder in a hill town in Tuscany when he was a boy.

"Angelo," Guid'Antonio said. "Find the *beccamorti* and send them here, *per favore*." The *beccamorti* would fetch the dead man and take him to his next destination in life's uncertain journey.

"Of course!" Angelo was on his feet so quickly, he almost tripped. He crossed himself, shaking his head at those who would interrogate him as he ran past their tables toward the street.

Guid'Antonio and Francesco maneuvered the merchant from his bent posture over the table, fumbling and unfolding and lifting the man's dead weight, then Giuliano de' Medici hefted him into his arms and got him onto the grass. The merchant stared up at them with eyes as vacant and unseeing as a dead fish. Bits of Cesare Ridolfi's mushroom salad glistened on his lips. *Unbelievable*, thought Guid'Antonio. *Dear God.*

Alert and curious, the little ginger dog hastened from the tables situated along the meadow's edge, wagging her wiry tail and wafer hips. Eagerly, she licked the cloth merchant's face. "Shoo!" Francesco Nori said. "No, wait. Here." His manner was easy as he handed her a bit of roasted chicken. "Though I wouldn't mind if you had your way with him, as you will."

Guid'Antonio glanced at his friend, his curiosity pricked by Francesco's spiteful comment—Francesco was not a spiteful man—as he plucked a dinner napkin from the table and knelt to wipe an explosion of food and spittle from Niccolini's lips. He closed the merchant's eyelids and, rising, motioned for Amerigo to escort Caterina and Maria forward. Huddled in her cloak, Caterina Niccolini clung to Amerigo, her body sagging, her pace that of a much older woman. Her knees buckled when she reached the table, and she would have fallen if Amerigo had not caught her by the arm.

"Mona Caterina." Guid'Antonio hesitated, not knowing what to say under such unusual circumstances. "I am truly sorry," he said.

"He's dead," she replied, her mouth slack.

For the third time, yes. Guid'Antonio nodded. "He is. I'm—"

"I wasn't expecting this," she said.

Giuliano de' Medici touched his breast. "Certainly not, *Signora*! Death comes as a thief in the night, when we least expect it. That is why we must live as if every moment is the last of life, yet prepared to stand without alarm before our Divine Judge." Giuliano's expression was devout, his eyes as soft and luminous as that of a deer in a woodland forest.

The air around them shimmered and stood still. "—Yes," Caterina Niccolini said. "*Salute*, bless you." Tentatively, then: "Dottore Vespucci, what do you think caused my husband's death?"

Guid'Antonio considered the question carefully. "He was suffering from catarrh," he said. Sneezing, fever, chills. "Otherwise, has he been ill?" Amerigo poured wine from a jug and offered Caterina the cup.

She sipped the purple liquid, and a little color spread across her cheeks. "Ill?" she said.

Yes? Or no? Guid'Antonio studied the woman more closely. It was an easy enough question for her to answer, surely.

"—No," Caterina said after a moment. "At least not as I am aware."

Guid'Antonio's brows snapped together. "Are you not his wife?" he said, thinking, *Did you not share the same bed?*

"Guid'Antonio," Maria intervened, her tone reproving. "Go gently, please."

"I mean not as I could tell," Caterina said. "He was not on his death bed. Nothing beyond catarrh, as you say, causing him misery these past few days. He purchased an infusion. Holly leaves and honey. Also, clover, mashed and boiled. Sadly, neither eased his coughing."

"Nor his sneezing," Amerigo said.

"When?" Guid'Antonio asked.

Caterina's shoulders lifted in the folds of her brown summer cloak. "Today is Thursday. So, this past Monday, or Tuesday perhaps."

Two or three days ago. I don't know. Perhaps. "Where?" Guid'Antonio said.

"Where what?" Caterina asked.

His lips curved in a slow smile. "Where did he acquire the infusion?"

"The Sign of the Stars."

Ah. The Sign of the Stars was Luca Landucci's apothecary shop. Guid'Antonio often visited Luca to purchase herbs and medicaments for the family and sometimes to engage the druggist's assistance with particularly . . . tricky . . . inquiries conducted outside the eyes or understanding of the public.

"The *beccamorti* are here," Giuliano de' Medici said, indicating the two men approaching them from All Saints Street, bearing a leather litter.

"Mona Caterina," Francesco Nori said. "These men will take your husband home and assist you with arrangements. I'll accompany you there."

Guid'Antonio held up his hand. "No—"

Caterina, her face ashen, appeared not to have heard. "Thank you, Ser Nori," she said, her eyes dull as the litter-bearers maneuvered her husband's corpse onto the leather and wood stretcher, sweat beading their foreheads.

"Which way?" one of the men asked, gasping for air.

"The Niccolinis—the lady lives near here," Francesco Nori said. "Just off Piazza Trinita on this side of the river." He indicated the Arno, nodding to Caterina, and the pair started away, about to follow in the faltering footsteps of the *beccamorti*. On both sides of the river, church bells pealed, marking the ninth hour after dawn, some lusty, some mellow.

"Mona Caterina. Francesco. Stop," Guid'Antonio said.

Four

WHERE WAS GOD?

The *beccamorti* halted.

Caterina drew up, her spine stiff. Slowly, she turned to Guid'Antonio, her hands clenched so tightly, the skin of her knuckles shone. "Yes?" she said, the word a puff of air on her lips.

"I'm sorry," Guid'Antonio said. "The *beccamorti* must take your husband to my hospital, instead."

She stared. "Why? When he is already dead."

Guid'Antonio looked at her, blinking. "For an official pronouncement of death. Also, his death was unexpected. Such situations require—" He paused, unsure whether Caterina Niccolini would understand the Latin word, *autopsia*. "He must be opened and examined," he said.

Maria gasped, her expression one of profound horror. "Cut open? Why in God's name would you do that?"

An edge flared in Guid'Antonio's voice. "Not me, Maria."

The litter-bearers cast one another a tired look and lowered their burden to the ground.

"It is a formality, *Cara*," Guid'Antonio said.

"He was ill," Maria said. "This formality, as you call it, will accomplish nothing but prolong Caterina's suffering. Please don't do this." Her lips quivered.

Beside her, Caterina's body shook. *"Autopsia?"* she said.

"A seeing with one's own eyes," Giuliano de' Medici explained, his manner tender toward Caterina Niccolini.

"It is the law when there is an unexplained death," Guid'-Antonio said, tired of repeating himself.

"I've never heard of such a thing," Maria said.

"Of course not."

Maria lifted her chin. "It is God's law that concerns me. Surely, He does not approve of the desecration of our bodies."

"It isn't often done," Francesco Nori said. "But Guid'Antonio is correct: in an event such as this, it is necessary."

Caterina looked at her husband on the litter. "I — I'm only . . . " She floundered, tears leaking from her eyes. "Where was God?"

A moment passed then. "I beg your pardon?" Guid'Antonio said.

Caterina shook her head, making a gesture of acceptance. "May I go home now, Dottore?"

"—Of course. Amerigo, you'll accompany the *beccamorti* to the hospital." The Vespucci family's hospital, Spedale dei Vespucci, sat just up the street on the left, a stone's throw past the Vespucci palace and the Church of All Saints. House, church, hospital: all strung along the west bank of the Arno like beads on an expensive chain.

Amerigo's eyebrows stitched into a frown. *What about the horse race?*

With an effort, Guid'Antonio reminded himself his nephew was only nineteen. "Do this and then you may go to Palazzo Rucellai and watch the horses with Bernardo and all your other bravos."

"Or come home with me," Giuliano de' Medici said. "If you can tolerate Lorenzo's impatience. Which I'm sure is mounting, given the delay. Of the race, I mean," Giuliano added hastily, his face going pink. "Not because of—" He gestured toward the dead man on the litter and the *beccamorti*, who stood waiting with their arms folded over their chests, their arms and faces dripping sweat.

"Amerigo," Guid'Antonio said. "You need stop at the hospital only long enough to tell Maestra Francesca what happened here. She will understand and send her findings to court, as she has done for me many times before." Francesca Vernacci, along with her father, was a *medico* at the Spedale.

Francesca. Her name on his tongue filled Guid'Antonio with a tangle of emotions. Bitterness. A sudden, strong feeling of something a long time cherished, and then stolen. He had not glimpsed Francesca in the market, nor had he ventured inside his hospital since his homecoming from northern Italy. He did not intend to see her now. Their love affair had ended three years ago in an eruption of harsh words and disappointment. Six months later, he had signed the marriage contract binding him for life to Maria del Vigna.

A deep purple flush crawled up Maria's neck, and her voice changed, became breathy, just as it always did when anyone mentioned in her hearing the name of the maestra of the house at Spedale dei Vespucci. "Why that woman? Her father oversees your hospital. Surely, she doesn't—" Maria swallowed hard, as if envisioning Francesca Vernacci with knives and saws in her hands, blood splattering her hospital gown.

"For me, she does," Guid'Antonio said. "Francesco, will you escort Maria home along with Caterina? Since it is on your way."

"Of course," Francesco Nori said.

"You're not coming now?" Maria blinked questioningly.

"No. I need to speak with them"—Guid'Antonio indicated

the musicians and servants standing awkwardly around, wondering what to do next—"then I'll follow behind you and our guests."

"Of course you will," she murmured as he draped her black velvet cloak around her, extinguishing the shimmering colors of her brocade gown, and arranged her hood around her face. No matter the air was hot as Hades. The display was the thing.

"Wait for me by our fountain," he whispered in her ear.

She softened. "I shall." She glanced at Orlando Niccolini's corpse and back again. "Be safe."

Guid'Antonio gave her a light smile. "I always am."

The *beccamorti* and Amerigo led the way across the lawn toward the street, where even the children and dogs had fallen quiet, everyone there sobered by the knowledge that something had gone terribly wrong in the meadow. Maria, Francesco Nori, and Caterina Niccolini fell in behind the *beccamorti*, their boots and sandals in the grass heavy and slow. Behind Caterina and her escort came Giuliano de' Medici, along with Simonetta and Marco Vespucci, then the remainder of Guid'Antonio's festival guests.

All along All Saints Street people moved aside, opening a path for the cortège. Some drew their attention respectfully from Caterina, making the sign of the cross as the procession passed, walking along the left side of the borgo, where lay Guid'Antonio's home, then the church, and close beyond that, the hospital. Others gawked at the mystery of Maria and the other young women walking a *fuori*, outside the house, shrouded from the eyes of the townspeople in velvet cloaks cut from fifteen to twenty *braccia*, armlengths, of cloth, their bodies bound with silken ties from the hollow of their throats to their sandaled toes. What wondrous beauty must lie behind the hoods falling about these well-married women in thick, dark folds, secreting from the world their freshly-washed tresses caught up in braids laced with ribbons, obscuring their faces, their skin glowing like pearls.

✝

In the street, the sudden white light of the sun pouring down on the thoroughfare momentarily blinded Guid'Antonio. He blinked, steadying himself. All around him the stink of horse manure and human sweat soured the air, along with the stench of cat piss and overripe cheese. A sea of ironmongers, belt-makers, and ruddy-faced peasants fastened their attention on Giuliano de' Medici as he passed, taking his measure in his gauzy white tunic, dove grey hose, and ankle boots of worn Spanish leather. Despite the seriousness of the moment, Guid'Antonio's lips twitched in a smile. Those were Lorenzo de' Medici's boots, given to Lorenzo as a gesture of friendship by the king of Spain. Giuliano the Beautiful, in borrowed boots so close to hand, jostling shoulder-to-shoulder with the *popolo minuto*, the Florentine poor who engaged in trades outside the guilds. But then Giuliano and Lorenzo often walked the town's streets and alleyways, armed only with gem-encrusted knives, whether together, with friends, or alone.

The Vespucci garden gate lay close by on the left. Guid'Antonio watched Francesco Nori and Caterina Niccolini pause as Maria slipped into the garden and closed the gate, its iron hinges screeching in protest. Guid'Antonio winced, his eyes moving to Amerigo and the *beccamorti* as they trudged on across Piazza Ognissanti to the hospital. Meanwhile, Francesco Nori and Caterina Niccolini walked east toward the river with the little ginger dog tagging along, her eyes lifted adoringly to Caterina, Francesco supporting the woman's bent form, their destination the house where Caterina now would live—alone? Or with family? Guid'Antonio had no idea at all.

Giuliano, dropping back from the others to walk with him, said, "Francesco has taken our grieving widow under his wing. He's a good man."

"That route leads him home, as well," Guid'Antonio said.

"But, yes. He is one of the best." An honorable man, a trustworthy friend. A family man devoted to his wife, Costanza, a Medici family kinswoman. A man devoted both to the Medici family and to his growing collection of Spanish pottery from Majorca.

On the lip of Piazza Ognissanti, Guid'Antonio and Giuliano kissed one another farewell. "I'm sorry your *festa* ended so cruelly," Giuliano said. "Sometimes Fate ruins our plans."

"How well I know," Guid'Antonio said.

Giuliano's sigh was heartfelt. "I'll tell Lorenzo what happened. Will someone inform the girl?" The fourteen-year-old expecting the dead man's baby.

Guid'Antonio had not thought of doing that. "No doubt someone already has," he said.

"True. This news will travel fast." With a nod and a wave, Giuliano vanished into the crowd. Just like that, a snap of the fingers: disappeared.

Guid'Antonio believed Giuliano and Lorenzo de' Medici should have bodyguards, lest they come to harm. Since the sickness and death of their father three years ago, several attempts had been made on Lorenzo's life. On Florence. As far as convincing the brothers they should watch closer for discontent, Guid'Antonio had tried once and failed. "I refuse to walk in fear in my own town. I am not a coward," Lorenzo had said. And whatever Lorenzo de' Medici said—well. In one way or another, anyone who pushed the first citizen of Florence against the grain got pushed back, hard. "I do not believe God means us harm," Lorenzo had said. And, as always, Giuliano had agreed with him.

God? No. But what about Evil's wicked henchmen?

✝

From where Guid'Antonio stood at the gate, he admired Maria seated alone in the garden. His wife was a vision of loveliness with her face tilted toward the sun, a woman as appealing as any woman, anywhere, her eyes drowsy and half-closed, her hands limp in the lap of her gown, her velvet cloak crumpled on the woven rush seat of a nearby chair.

He opened the complaining gate and stepped into another world, one perfumed with the heady smell of basil, lavender, and lemons in terracotta pots near the kitchen door, their scent mingling with the robust odors of the last few days' sauces and grilled meats. From within the kitchen came the clanging and clattering of pots and pans, with Cesare Ridolfi and his mother, Domenica's, happy, argumentative voices raised overall. Guid'Antonio envisioned a mountain of dirty dishes, soiled napkins, and wine-stained tablecloths to launder, though he doubted Cesare would set his delicate hands to those humble tasks. No, that young man preferred featherfooting about the marketplace, selecting this, avoiding that. "Spare no expense, Dottore Guid'Antonio Vespucci will see to our account."

And yes. He always did.

"Guid'Antonio. I heard you at the gate," Maria said.

"How could you not?"

She laughed, her dark eyes drawing him forward. She touched his face, his lips. She pressed her body against his. He bent down, kissing her deeply, fondling the curve of her back, sliding to the swell of the luscious *culo* he knew so well, lifting her with his hands.

She kissed the silver hairs peeking from the neck of his tunic, her eyes glistening with sudden tears. "Poor Caterina! One moment, her husband so full of spirit, of life, and the next—it would grieve me so were I in her stead."

"Nothing bad is going to happen to me," he said.

"I adore you," she breathed, her cheeks hot with a fresh blush of red.

He bunched up the skirt of her gown. "And I you," he

murmured into the delicate flesh of her neck. Life, so precious, so . . . temporary. He wanted to forget death now. He did not want to remember how those bony knuckles rapped on your door without warning and would not quit, no matter how hard you prayed, no matter what promises you made to God and to yourself. He wanted to drink Maria in. "Let's go upstairs," he said.

"Guid'Antonio!" she scolded, but she was pleased, as he meant her to be. "It's early, and not time for bed."

"And yet I'm ready," he said.

Gently, he kissed her, his mouth moving from her neck to the ruby earring fixed in her earlobe and on inside that private place. *There.* He wanted to tumble with her in the garden grass and push her gown to her thighs in a rustle of brocade and silk, while the fountain, a stone lion with its jaws open wide, shot golden droplets of water into the air.

At the same time, a disturbing, but familiar, sensation seized him, a prickle of loneliness and fear. As they hurried up the stone staircase to the apartment they shared, the sensation passed, only to give way to disquieting memories. His mind betrayed him, urging him back through the garden gate and up Borg'Ognissanti. Past All Saints Church and over Piazza Ognissanti he ran, on through the doors of his hospital, where, in a gown of plain white woolen cloth his former lover, Maestra Francesca Vernacci, lived and worked with her father among the dying and the dead.

Five

WHAT IS REAL, WHAT IMAGINED?
FRIDAY, 25TH JUNE 1473

The gate shrieked like an animal in pain when Guid'Antonio slid back the bolt the following morning. With one thrust of his fist he forced the bolt in place and strode south along All Saints Street with Amerigo, who smothered a fierce yawn. Like his nephew, the Unicorn district was stretching to life. Washed by a late-night rain, the ochre buildings off Piazza Ognissanti shone, their canvas awnings dripping moisture onto wet cobblestones. Sleepy stock boys unlatched wooden shutters and set out their masters' wares, while a parade of farmers from the countryside drove rattling donkey carts through the city gates, their wagons piled high with shimmering vegetables and fruit.

Tentatively, Amerigo cut his eyes to Guid'Antonio. "How long will we be at the jail?"

"However long it takes to review Jacopo Caretto's record of arrest and study similar cases," Guid'Antonio said. "I've only now and Monday morning to consider him and his granddaughter. And, no, I haven't forgotten about Angelo Poliziano's dissertation at *Studio Fiorentino* later today. You'll be there, never fear."

Amerigo grinned. "*Bene!* Uncle Guid'Antonio, you should have seen the race! When it finally happened, it was *magnifico!*" Amerigo kissed his fingertips, happiness rising off him in waves.

"I'm glad to hear it. Who won?"

"Lorenzo's horse."

A chuckle escaped Guid'Antonio. "No surprise there." Medici money purchased and trained the best horses in the land. From many lands: France, Constantinople, Spain.

"Exciting, still," Amerigo said. "Afterwards, Cousin Marco Vespucci, Giuliano, and I sang and danced with all Florence in Piazza della Signoria. The bonfire was glorious, until the wind and rain sent us scampering. *Mama!* Now, my head's pounding like a festival drum, and my mouth feels like raw wool."

Guid'Antonio sidestepped the boy sweeping the entrance to a wine and cheese shop, exchanging a nod with the child as he did each weekday morning. "What do you expect when you carouse with your bravos until dawn?"

Amerigo's hand flew to his breast. "I woke you? Oh, no! Christ, that gate's a real pain!"

"Christ has nothing to do with it," Guid'Antonio said. "The bolt and hinges need oiling, a task you've vowed to perform, oh, a dozen times now, although truly, I'm not counting."

A contrite Amerigo said, "This afternoon, I swear."

"See to it. But honestly, I was awake when you came in."

☦

He had slept poorly Thursday evening, by turns unsettled and lightly dreaming until, eyes flying open, he had lain as still as a dead man on the feather mattress, forcing even breaths in darkness lit by a solitary flame. What was real, what imagined? Everything in the shadows around him felt threatening. Reaching out, he touched Maria. Beneath the summer sheet, her body pulsed with vitality, with warmth. The puppy cradled between them popped up, staring at Guid'Antonio through a thicket of russet curls.

Guid'Antonio pressed his finger to his lips. "Shhh, *Orsetto*, Little Bear. Go to sleep, little boy."

A gift from the mayor of Imola, the five-month-old ball of fur sitting up in bed, yawning, had arrived by courier from northern Italy a few weeks ago, along with a note from the mayor thanking Guid'Antonio for his friendship during his brief stay there. A man as wise as he was congenial, the mayor had not mentioned the alarming downturn events had taken on the blustery spring morning they had met to say farewell.

They were standing in the center of town, Guid'Antonio's crimson cloak whipping in the wind, when the clatter of hooves striking stone assaulted their ears. Back-lit against the sun, a rider on a black stallion harnessed in scarlet leather had appeared on the lip of the square, backed by a company of mounted men-at-arms. All around the piazza, people hurried into the Cathedral or scattered into nearby alleys, tugging children by the hand, abandoning pails of icy well water and baskets of cherries and eggs.

Beside Guid'Antonio, the mayor of Imola gasped a mouthful of cold air. "God help you, my friend! Rome has caught you here."

Rome? Guid'Antonio's heartbeat slowed. "Who is it, exactly?" he said.

"Girolamo Riario! I warned you that prick has been sniffing around here, now he thinks he rules the land."

Alarm bells sounded in Guid'Antonio. A fruit peddler until his uncle's election as Pope Sixtus IV less than two years ago, Girolamo Riario was not only the Pope's favorite nephew and now the commander-in-chief of the papal armed forces, he was also a shiny new lord, thanks to the hamlet his uncle had bought him—an impoverished hamlet, but an attractive one, given its proximity to Imola and the fact it came with the elevating title of "Count." As power-mad as his uncle, Girolamo Riario was the principle weapon in the Pope's arsenal aimed at increasing his influence by cobbling together a family enclave on Florence's northern border—an arsenal Guid'Antonio Vespucci had been mandated to disarm.

From the corner of his vision, he watched Riario glance past deserted carts piled with golden pears, fennel, and *salame*. Little points of light, Riario's eyes slid past Guid'Antonio and darted back again. His brow rose, and his mouth lifted in what looked like a smile, as if he were realizing, little by little, he might know the man standing in the cold heart of the piazza with a crimson cloak flaring from his shoulders. Languidly, Riario rode across the square, saddle creaking, reins jangling, stopping so close, Guid'Antonio felt the stallion's hot breath on his cheek. "Count Riario," he said. "Good morning."

Riario flipped his bobbed hair from his face. Pale, pudgy hands, prissy mouth. "Ah! You know me," he said. "The morning definitely is good and getting better all the while. I arrive from Rome and find Florentine Dottore Guid'Antonio Vespucci in the center of things, laughing with the mayor, who never has laughed with me."

A wave of heat rushed over Guid'Antonio when he heard his name on Riario's lips. "How do you know me?" he asked, smiling easily.

"The same way you know me. We are well-known men."

"I know you only because the mayor mentioned your name to me just now. You are Pope Sixtus IV's nephew come from a small fishing village via the Vatican," Guid'Antonio said.

Riario's brown eyes flattened. "I know you because when

friends in the Vatican speak of that upstart Lorenzo de' Medici's supporters, yours is the first name on their lips. They falter, mentioning your eyes. Such an unnatural, pale grey shade. Ghostly!" Riario pretended to shiver. "Dark hair shot with silver, crimson cloak, and, *ecco qui*, here you are, magically, in northern Italy."

"What friends?" Guid'Antonio said.

Riario huffed a laugh, darting his finger at Guid'Antonio, exposing the fur beneath the frothy cuffs of his green velvet tunic, soft *pancie* harvested from the underbellies of white fox pups. "What are you doing so far from home, Dottore?"

"After you, Count Riario," Guid'Antonio said.

Riario spat air. "I'm here to have a look around for my uncle, as well as for myself. I shall be here often, now I'm lord of a nearby town. And recently married." Riario's tongue snaked across his lips. "To a beautiful girl you have met on occasion."

Guid'Antonio did not take the bait. "Both village and bride recently acquired by the Pope and presented to you as gifts, along with your title," he said.

Beside him, the mayor cringed and made a whimpering noise. *Have you lost your mind, Dottore?*

Riario's expression soured. "Do you always have the last word?"

Guid'Antonio smiled. "Pray so. I'm a lawyer."

Riario huffed. "Your turn," he said.

"I'm here on business for a client."

Riario laughed without humor. "I'm sure you are. Well! When you arrive home in the City of Flowers, tell Lorenzo de' Medici hello from Count Riario. Meanwhile, dine with Rome this evening. This unexpected encounter can only get more interesting."

"*Mille grazie*, no. My horse is saddled and waiting in the stable."

"You're leaving now," Riario said. "I just happened to catch you here at the exact moment—?"

"I am," said Guid'Antonio.

"Surely, the gods are laughing," Riario said, as amused as if he were one of the gods, himself. "If I had not ridden in when I did, I never would have known you were here. But now—oh, my." His lips curled in the semblance of a smile. "I won't forget you, Dottore. Nor shall my uncle, when he learns Guid'Antonio Vespucci, Medici man to the core, was here on business for a client." Squealing with delight, Riario wheeled his horse from the piazza and set off with his troops thundering behind him, mounts lifting their tails, hooves squishing in their own piss and shit.

The mayor's shoulders sagged. "There he goes down the old Roman road that cleaves us in two. How fitting! Someone should remind him if it weren't for the Pope, he would still be a grocery clerk selling raisins and oranges on a Savona side street, instead of the Vatican's second-in-command."

"Will you?" Guid'Antonio said.

"Me? I wouldn't dare. Dottore Guid'Antonio, after today, no matter what happens to our town, the Pope will have his eyes on you."

Guid'Antonio combed his fingers through his hair, dark brown streaked with silver, more and more of it, daily. "He already did," he said.

☦

Last night, the puppy had not snuggled down until Guid'Antonio slipped from bed and stood gazing, naked, across tiled rooftops stretching like a flaming orange sea across the Santa Maria Novella quarter of Florence. Dazzling stars. Silver needles of rain. With an effort he could push the disturbing encounter with Girolamo Riario and the elusive contract for

Imola into the shadows, but he could not banish the pinch in his gut caused by the death of the cloth merchant at his holiday gathering. Had the fellow choked on a bit of mushroom salad? It didn't seem so to Guid'Antonio. Well. No doubt Maestra Francesca Vernacci's autopsy would reveal everything.

Back in bed, he had fallen into a rough sleep with the palm of his hand cradling the puppy's furry head, until the high-pitched scream of the garden gate jerked him awake, alerting him to the sound of his nephew tiptoeing through the grass, humming to himself.

✝

Now, without breaking his stride, Amerigo glanced over his shoulder toward the meadow where the cloth merchant had drawn his last breath. "I am sorry about Ser Niccolini. He died in your arms."

"In my care," Guid'Antonio said.

Amerigo brushed back a lock of hair that had fallen over his face. "In Florence, that amounts to the same thing."

"Thank you for reminding me," Guid'Antonio said.

Amerigo's eyebrows rose. "One moment so vigorous, the next, so dead."

"Remember, I was there."

The Vespucci Hospital lay directly ahead on their left. Water stains streaked the Spedale's face like rusty orange tears. Straightening his shoulders, Guid'Antonio walked through the shadow the hospital cast over the thoroughfare. As usual as he passed the entrance, the atmosphere around him shifted, became cooler and still. Though open at the moment, at night the doors were closed and bolted with strict rules to keep them shut until the bells tolled dawn. That is, unless the housekeeper, Lena Barone, asleep on her cot, recognized a certain soft knock and opened the doors a notch to let Guid'Antonio Vespucci slip across the foyer and up the curving stone stairs to Francesca's bed, where he would throw off his dark brown leather *farsetto* and brown cotton tunic, stripping off in turn his hose and boots to stand before her, naked. That had not happened in three years, and it never would happen again.

Quietly, Amerigo said, "Do you suppose Maestra Francesca has finished butchering our dead *festa* guest?"

Stopping abruptly, Guid'Antonio peered into his nephew's eyes, eyes filled with curiosity, looking back at him. "Butchering? Amerigo, you know the law. All shall be performed with the utmost care. Show Orlando Niccolini some respect, and the lady of the hospital, too, *per favore*. Nothing huge, just a tiny favor, that is all I ask. Now, come along. At this rate, we'll never reach the jail." Pulling his crimson cloak close around his shoulders, Guid'Antonio stepped back into the light of All Saints Street, his stride brisk, his eyes fixed straight ahead.

†

The spindly byway they entered was so narrow, their shoulders brushed the walls. Rotting garbage, sewage, the musky bouquet of stale wine and sex, a thin ribbon of crystalline blue sky high above their heads. In small niches plaster statues of the Virgin Mary were draped with cornflowers and wild purple hyacinths. Amerigo wrinkled his nose, booting a pair of men's pink hose and a daisy garland from his path. "Praise God, Mary's flowers may be wilting, but they are still fragrant."

"Yes," Guid'Antonio said, forging a path through a shifting sea of fishmongers and butchers displaying fresh fish and pig's heads alongside fruit dealers and sellers of poultry and wild game. Armed with axes and knives, two police sergeants, burly men garbed in drab brown with bands of yellow cloth knotted around their upper arms, kept an eye out for the pickpockets and thieves who flooded town before, during, and after a *giorno festivo*.

"Why do you have only today and Monday morning when Jacopo Caretto's case isn't being heard until next Friday?" Amerigo said.

Guid'Antonio fanned his face, too warm in his crimson cloak, a daylight spectacle for everyone to see. Sometimes an emblem of power, sometimes a liability. "Because I promised Maria I would take her to the country Monday afternoon and relax," he said.

"Relax? You?" Amerigo burst into laughter.

Guid'Antonio scowled. "Can't a man spend time alone with his wife without drawing attention to himself?" Three perfectly good workdays whiling away time at the family villa north of Florence. To walk in the gardens and take slow baths scented with rose water and oil of lavender. To make a baby, please Saint Margaret and the Virgin Mary. "I'll arrive home on Thursday in time for Friday court," he said.

"That's cutting the cloth close."

Resigned, Guid'Antonio said, "I made a promise, one I wouldn't dare break."

Mud sucking at their boots, they entered a piazza so small and close, it was not much more than the shadowed heart of three alleyways come together. They were halfway across when an old peasant drove his milky-eyed donkey into a snail vendor's cart. The live snails the vendor had spent days gathering in the mountains poured from his pail and bounced across the square.

"Ha, ha!" cackled a woman hawking eggs and baby chicks, stomping the snails with her rough, bare heels in a half-crazed dance. "There!"

"Here's trouble," Amerigo said beneath his breath.

"Paulina! You old whore!" the snail vendor yelled. "And

you, Tommaso, you witless lout!" The vendor flew at the peasant and his blind donkey, pounding the animal's scarred nose with his knotted fist. "You'll pay for this! You and that hag—in court! *Guardia!*" The vendor waved his fist at the guard lounging nearby, resting his back against the wall of a used clothing shop. "Don't just stand there, arrest them!"

"Come along, Amerigo." Guid'Antonio was starting toward the alley on the far side of the square when a street urchin playing dice in the dirt jumped up, snatched an egg from the woman's basket, and hurled it at the vendor. "What will you do when they can't pay the fine?" cried the child. "Drag them by their ears to the Stinche?" A dank, dark prison meant for heretics, sorcerers, and witches.

Worse and worse, thought Guid'Antonio, pausing to see what happened next.

The egg smashed the vendor's chest. "You motherless brat!" the vendor yelled, scraping at the slimy egg white and thick yellow yolk oozing down the front of his threadbare shirt. "By then, they won't have ears! Nor will you, you alley rat! *Guardia!* Stop laughing!" The snail vendor lunged for the boy, who stuck out his tongue and raced past Guid'Antonio and Amerigo toward the alley. All around them, people cheered the youngster as he fled the square, laughing and thumbing his nose at authority.

"Thief! Robber!" the egg seller shrilled, her feet stomping a jittery dance.

The guardsman drew back his arm, his short ax poised for flight.

"No!" Guid'Antonio roared.

The guardsman hesitated a moment before his ax sliced the air. The boy, glancing back, dodged the blade whistling toward him and scampered into the nearest byway, but not so fast that a hank of his hair, flying wildly around his face, missed being chopped off so close to his scalp, the skin bled.

The boy's frightened scream echoed down the alley. The ax handle, its blade embedded in the wooden placard signaling the presence of a tavern down the lane, quivered and fell still.

The piazza held its breath. After a moment, people stirred, muttering among themselves. Amerigo stared at Guid'Antonio in horror. "Christ, if you hadn't called out—"

"That boy would be dead."

"Just because Palla's men wear his armband of authority, they think they can get away with murder." Palla Palmieri, the chief of police of Florence and the surrounding territory. Amerigo glared at the guard. *"Bastardo!"* he said.

"That was a street boy," Guid'Antonio said. "An orphan. If he had been killed, who would step forward to see he received justice in court? No one."

"Just now, you did," Amerigo said.

"Instinct," Guid'Antonio said.

The guard smirked, his shoulders raised in a careless half-shrug. *Would I have hung from the gallows if I had killed that gutter rat? No.* Guid'Antonio swallowed his wrath. In Florence, a man must choose his battles with care, else he would find himself fighting from sunup to sundown. With a dip of his head to the crowd, he signaled Amerigo to accompany him down the byway where the scalped boy had disappeared.

Six

CITY OF HEAT AND LIGHT

In silence they made their way through the corridor and out an arch that lead into Piazza della Signoria. Open to the sky, the ochre buildings circling the vast piazza shimmered with heat and light. Amerigo tipped his face to the sky, inhaling gulps of air. "I swear, I do believe warmth has healing powers. I wouldn't want to stay long in that damp, dark hole."

Guid'Antonio nodded, troubled by the sudden explosion of violence in the piazzetta. Here in the sunny heart of Florence, where scholars debated the immortality of the soul and merchants from England and France negotiated wool shipments worth thousands of florins, there was no sign of the terrified, bleeding boy. Did warmth have healing powers? He hoped so.

Drenched in sunshine, he and Amerigo started across the piazza, briefly greeting acquaintances here and there. Diagonally across from them, on the far eastern corner, stood the Palazzo della Signoria, Florence's City Hall, the fortress-like home of the Florentine Republic. Guid'Antonio craned his neck to see the *vacca*, the great bronze bell of the City Hall watchtower. Arnolfo di Cambio's crenellated tower spiked the sky like a fist, one so tall, Guid'Antonio's stomach flipped. He stopped, averting his gaze.

"Are you all right?" Amerigo said, hovering by his side.

"It's nothing," Guid'Antonio said.

But of course, it was something, this lightheadedness he experienced occasionally in tight spaces, or when he glanced up too fast. When he forgot and turned his head abruptly one way or another. The nausea always passed in a moment. It did now, emboldening him to risk a second look up the soaring tower, which never failed to draw his attention as if by some mysterious force. Forty years ago, enemies of Lorenzo and Giuliano de' Medici's grandfather, Cosimo de' Medici, had locked Cosimo in the tower's cramped cell known as the *Alberghettino,* the Little Inn. Had one of the richest and most influential men of his time, not only in Italy, but in the world, gazed down on his city from the narrow slit of the cell's solitary window, fearful he was about to be executed for treason by men who wanted Florence for themselves? Instead of exile, one opposing faction had suggested throwing Cosimo to the pavement far down below.

Amerigo followed Guid'Antonio's upward gaze. "Those were dangerous times."

"Dangerous then, dangerous now," Guid'Antonio said.

They started walking again, Amerigo rubbing the morning stubble on his cheek, nodding toward the stone arcade adjacent to City Hall, where the government received foreign dignitaries. "Look there," he said.

A group of boys were frolicking in the arcade, flirting among themselves, each trying to snatch a favorite boy's feathered cap. A light breeze lifted an older youth's blue *berretta* into the air. Another boy, leaping up, caught the cap, laughing and prancing until the cap's owner thrust out his foot. The cap whirled into the piazza where, from one merchant and monk to another, it traveled the square, soaring and dipping like a small blue bird.

"Just think," Amerigo said, matching Guid'Antonio's quick pace. "Yesterday gilt castles on carts pulled by caparisoned horses paraded here. Last night after the *palio*, we set torches blazing along the walls. We had rockets, fireworks, wheels of fire, and singing and dancing until—" Amerigo's mouth twisted into a grin. "Well. Until I met you in the garden a while ago."

"And from there, we have not got far," Guid'Antonio said.

They were almost off the square when they were hailed by a familiar voice. "*Mattina*, Dottore, Amerigo!" It was the painter, Leonardo da Vinci. A tall youth of twenty-one, Leonardo was dressed in a snug purple tunic and leggings dyed a deep rose color. His hair, long and carefully curled, was a remarkably fair hue, even among all the sunny heads in Florence, his smile as warm as the sun shining down on the piazza.

Another delay. Inwardly, Guid'Antonio groaned, but he could not nod pleasantly and keep walking toward the jail. Leonardo da Vinci's father, Piero, was a Medici man and had been since the days he first drew up deeds and contracts for the first truly powerful Medici family boss, Cosimo de' Medici, who had, of course, come down from the Little Inn, survived exile, and returned to Florence two years later not only unscathed, but more formidable than ever. Besides, Guid'Antonio liked Leonardo. He couldn't, wouldn't, brush him off, particularly not here in the piazza, with eyes watching all around.

"Leonardo, you're away from Verrocchio's early today," Guid'Antonio said. After completing his apprenticeship with Andrea del Verrocchio, Leonardo had remained at Verrocchio and Company, rather than open his own *bottega*, as his contemporaries Sandro Botticelli and Domenico Ghirlandaio had done.

"Only momentarily," Leonardo said. "I'm on my way to order a few travelers' checks. Next week, I'm riding to Vinci to deliver some legal documents for my father. It's not all business, though. The countryside brings me joy." He smiled happily.

"Fishing and singing," Amerigo said. "Giuliano and I are going this weekend."

Guid'Antonio inclined his head in the direction of the jail. "Amerigo—"

Leonardo's blue eyes shone. "Singing, Amerigo, yes! For the most part, though, I plan to visit my grandfather while wandering the hills and practicing drawing from nature." Leonardo indicated the *libriccino*, or sketchpad, not much bigger than a pack of playing cards in his left hand.

"Dottore—" Leonardo addressed Guid'Antonio lightly, but with a low note of uneasiness in his voice. "No doubt you have noted the monk lingering in the shade of the arcade while those boys lark about. He's eyeing you closely."

"Yes," Guid'Antonio said. A moment ago, he had glimpsed the heavily-garbed fellow lurking in the corner between the arcade and the church of San Pier Scheraggio alongside City Hall, the man's form one with the shadows, or so he thought.

Amerigo flicked his attention in that direction, a flash. "Wiry, hawk-nosed, the usual crude sandals and leather pouch. From his hateful expression, I don't believe he's there to beg bread from one of the bakeries behind the loggia."

Guid'Antonio turned, his manner casual. From the depths of his hood, the monk's eyes bored into him, hot with contempt. In the next instant, he thrust his thumb between two fingers at Guid'Antonio. Then, grinning, he sprang back, bolting toward the river with the folds of his robe rising and falling around him like frenetic black wings.

"That's bold!" Amerigo started to give chase.

"Leave him," Guid'Antonio said, plucking him back by the sleeve.

"But he insulted you! He gave you the *fico in mano*, the fig!—people saw him do it!"

"I said desist, Amerigo. We have drawn enough attention today." Thrust into the violence in the piazzetta, and here, now, with Leonardo and the fleeing monk. Running one hand through his hair, he added, "Not to mention yesterday."

Leonardo made a sympathetic noise down in his throat. "Your dead *festa* guest."

"Yes."

"Do you know what happened?"

"Not yet," Amerigo said, scowling as he reluctantly turned back toward his companions.

"An *autopsia*," Leonardo said. "I heard. May I—"

"No, you may not," Guid'Antonio said. "Amerigo, if we chased everyone who showed us interest, we never would get anywhere, including the jail. Anyway, that fellow had wings on his feet. He's long gone."

"He is now," Amerigo said. "Interest? He wanted to wring your neck."

"No."

A shadow of concern crossed Leonardo's face. "He did have the air of the devil about him, Dottore Guid'Antonio."

"And yet, he ran," Guid'Antonio said. "He's a coward."

In his sketchpad, Leonardo made a quick drawing. "Here's his likeness," he said, handing the drawing to Guid'Antonio.

With a few strokes of his pen, Leonardo da Vinci had captured the man's shadowy features deep within his hood. The rendering suggested a young man with eyes set like hard black stones in shaded hollows above narrow cheekbones. Lips clamped in a tight line, his expression was filled with contempt and loathing. Leonardo had seen him as Guid'Antonio and Amerigo had seen him, and more.

Unaccountably shaken by the image, Guid'Antonio thanked Leonardo and handed the drawing to Amerigo, who unbuckled his satchel and slid it inside for safekeeping. *Just in case,* thought Guid'Antonio.

"Dottore Guid'Antonio?" Leonardo said.

"Yes."

A tinge of pink suffused Leonardo's cheeks. "Word in the shops is your family wants a new fresco for the chapel you're building in All Saints. I would be honored if you would consider me for that labor."

"All right, Leonardo," Guid'Antonio said. "I'll mention it to the others."

"*Grazie.*" The painter smiled, pleased to have got this far.

Guid'Antonio and Amerigo had started off the square when Guid'Antonio wheeled around. In the arcade, the boys were still flirting and teasing one another, laughing and dancing about. Nowhere else in Italy had he seen such open playfulness among young men. No doubt one day soon one or more of these adolescents would stand before the Officers of the Night defending himself against the charge of performing indecent sexual acts of a nonviolent nature. And if found guilty as charged? Such a one might see himself riding backwards on a donkey through the streets, while spectators taunted him and cheered. He might see his family's home torched. He might see himself hanged by the neck until dead, or slapped with a modest fine, his actions dismissed with a wink and a nod. His fate would depend less on the strict law of the land than on the mood of the magistrates conducting hearings on any given day.

"Boys will be boys, no matter the cost," Guid'Antonio said beneath his breath.

"And men will be men," Amerigo said.

✝

Chased by the roar of the lions caged behind City Hall, those mighty, mangy, symbols of the Florentine Republic, they hurried down Stationers' Street, Guid'Antonio inhaling deeply. Here in the Black Lion district of Florence, the tangy smell of lemons for sale scented the air, along with goats' milk soaps and oils scented with lavender, almonds, and black currants. On down the street the Bargello, headquarters of Florence's major criminal court and the main seat of capital punishment in the city, stood open to officials, notaries, and *tavolaccini,* messengers who kept records of fines and deposits.

"Mother of God—" Amerigo clutched his ears, shielding them from the cries of a man two police sergeants were roughing into the courtyard of the jail. "Now what?"

A robust young fellow with a crossbow slung across his shoulder stepped into the street. It was Maurizio Maso, who served as the officer over Police Chief Palla Palmieri's two hundred crossbowmen quartered just off Piazza della Signoria.

"*Mattina*, Maurizio," Guid'Antonio said. "What's this?"

Maurizio huffed a laugh. "*Mattina*, Dottore! You would have thought the moon was full last night. The cells are cramped with everything from men drawing knives on one another to fornicating in church. That one's wine temper led him to slash his wife's face with a razor. He'll have his reward when he sees himself bumping along *Via dei Malcontenti* in the prisoner's cart, then hanging from a noose at Justice Gate."

Amerigo wiggled his fingers. "Or not. You know as well as I in Florence punishment is as fragile as glass."

The image of the razor slicing through warm flesh bloomed in Guid'Antonio. Blood bubbled and laced the woman's cheeks in fine, bloody threads. "May justice be done," he said.

"*Festa* madness prevails," Maurizio said. "The day is still in its infancy, and already we've had a disturbance in the courtyard."

"There are often disturbances in the jail courtyard," Guid'Antonio said.

One corner of Maurizio's mouth twisted in a smile. "Not caused by our police chief. A messenger arrived, and *subito!* Palla Palmieri scrambled downstairs from his office and flew off on his horse as if Satan had set fire to his tail."

Guid'Antonio and Amerigo flicked a glance at one another. Palla Palmieri had raced from the jail for an emergency, rather than dispatching members of his police family? "Do you know where Palla was bound?" Guid'Antonio said.

"The Unicorn district." Maurizio lifted his brow. "Isn't that where you live?"

A ripple of unease passed over Guid'Antonio. "Yes. Do you know what sent him there?"

"Sorry, no." With a nod to them both, Maurizio sauntered toward City Hall singing one of Lorenzo de' Medici's carnival songs. "If you like your biscuits big, that's all right. You can have two at the same time, one you hold, the other you slip into your mouth."

"We just came from All Saints," Amerigo said. "Surely, this can't have anything to do with us." Hesitantly, he added, "Should we turn back home?"

Can't. Surely. Guid'Antonio considered the commitment he had made to appear in court one week from today, prepared to give his opinion in the case regarding Jacopo Caretto and his granddaughter. He considered the toil required to be fair in all things, always. They had just come from the Unicorn district and everything there had been calm. "No," he said, and stepped without further comment into the courtyard.

Seven

THE GIRL IN THE WELL

Sunshine filled the Bargello's enormous *cortile*, or courtyard, with warmth and light. From the *Sala delle esamine*, the examination chamber where suspects and witnesses were interrogated, to the courtroom and the offices of The Eight on Public Safety, lawyers, secretaries, and notaries hurried about retrieving documents and questioning petitioners who had come to file for leniency for some father, son, or husband jailed while awaiting trial or execution. Everyone fell under the scrutiny of Palla Palmieri's police *famiglia*, heavy-lidded, tight-lipped men armed with axes and knives.

Inside the entrance a familiar figure in a scarlet gown with long, loose sleeves noticed Guid'Antonio. Registrar Gino Frescobaldi motioned him and Amerigo forward, stepping lightly from the booth where he was questioning anyone who made it past the guard posted at the gate, registering their names, districts, and their reason for coming today.

"Dottore Vespucci, Amerigo, *buona mattina*," Gino said, his smile as jovial as if he were welcoming them into his home, rather than police headquarters. "Did you have a fine holiday?" Gino's sunny expression dimmed, and he crossed himself. "*Mi dispiace!* I heard about the merchant who died during your *festa*. All Florence knows about that unfortunate incident. Terrible to contemplate."

Amerigo's gaze was solemn. "Terrible to see."

Gino went up on the toes of his red soled hose. "Yes! Well, Dottore—whom are we hunting today?"

"Not whom, what," Guid'Antonio said. "And that's the record of arrest for Jacopo Caretto, the wool beater Palla's night watch arrested early Sunday morning."

"Caretto! And that unfortunate girl." Gino made a spitting sound through his teeth. "Whenever was a man so vile?"

"That is a question for the ages, I am sure," Guid'Antonio said.

"Do you wish to interrogate Caretto? If so—"

"Not now, no. Only his record of arrest. But Gino—"

In his mind's eye, Guid'Antonio watched Palla Palmieri's lithe, brown-clad figure swoop down the stone steps from his office on the jail's first floor and fly swiftly as a sparrow across the courtyard into Stationer's Street, sending everyone leaping from his path as he mounted his horse and raced toward Borg'Ognissanti. *As if Satan had set fire to his tail*, crossbowman Maurizio Maso had said.

Gino stood a little straighter in his hose. "Yes, Dottore?"

"Maurizio Maso said Palla left just now for my parish. Do you know why, and why in such a hurry?"

"As if Palla would tell me? No." Gino laughed and snapped his fingers for a clerk. "Caretto's record will be in the pending files upstairs in Palla's office."

A young man appeared before them. Gino gave the youth Jacopo Caretto's name and date of arrest. "You'll find those documents toward the middle of the stack on the police chief's desk." The clerk bowed and hurried across the courtyard, threading his way past the messengers and couriers crowding the stairs.

"Where will you be, Dottore?" Gino said.

"In the *cancelleria*, where else?" All documents relative to the administration of Florentine justice were stored in the chancery office just off the courtyard.

"Reviewing precedents, yes," Gino said. "I don't believe you'll find many cases involving the violation and murder of a child."

Guid'Antonio tipped his head to one side. "We shall see."

☦

In the chancery he flung off his crimson cloak and hung it from a wooden peg. The chamber was hot, and here in private, he was glad to be rid of the extra cloth. In its isolated corner of jail headquarters, this small office always made him feel as if he might suffocate. Here, there were no frescoes by Giotto, Fra Angelico, Botticelli, or any other painter. The ceiling was as plain as the thick stone walls. In the center of the room there stood a trestle and two benches. Only the one door opened off the courtyard, but opposite the door three windows looked out onto the street. Fixed with iron bars, the windows, whose wooden shutters were kept open during the day, afforded the chamber with a fair amount of natural light. Candles and torches were forbidden in the chancery, where a single spark could destroy a trove of irreplaceable ledgers and loose papers.

Amerigo slipped his satchel from his shoulder. Unlatching the buckle, he searched for his pen, found it, and placed it on the trestle with several sheets of paper he removed from a leather binder embossed in gold with his initials: A di N V. Amerigo di Nastagio di Vespucci. "So!" he said. "Where shall we begin?"

Guid'Antonio thought for a moment. This investigation

would have been considerably easier had the child—or anyone of any age—been found strangled on a side street. People would have been questioned, suspects arrested, charges filed. The manner and circumstances surrounding Chiara Caretto's death and the discovery of her body were so unusual, he recalled nothing like it before. Her makeshift grave dug up, a piece of her bloody clothing retrieved by a dog. Sighing heavily, he swept his hand toward the shelves. On them were thick, leather-bound ledgers, metal strongboxes fixed with locks, and folios tied with narrow ribbons of red silk.

"Begin with the most current volume of the *Condempnationes*," he said. The *Condempnationes et Absolutiones* contained lists of people accused of various crimes and their sentences, with details of the incident in question, the victim, and the place and date of the event. To date, the *Condempnationes* included two complete volumes, 1400 to 1424 and 1425 to 1449. Volume Three picked up in 1450, but moved only so far as December 1470, almost three years ago. Proceedings from that time forward languished on the chancery shelves in wicker baskets. Who knew when one notary or another would find time to add those pages to the working ledger, which, combined with the first two, made a history of crime and punishment in Florence since the turn of the century.

"Volume Three," Guid'Antonio said, taking a seat. "As far as it goes. No need to sift through the baskets. I'm certain nothing resembling this has happened in recent years. We certainly would remember if that were so."

Amerigo hefted *Volume Three: 1450 – 1470* onto the lectern by the windows. "What am I looking for?"

Guid'Antonio considered his nephew's question for a moment, moving forward in his mind and circling back, at the same time pouring wine from a lidded jug into two pottery cups and opening his satchel—plain, no initials—and withdrawing his working journal and a pen. On the trestle table stood a small container of sand. And oh, yes, ink. "Wrongful deaths involving children," he said. "Also, cases of girls taken by force. Boys, too, come to that."

Amerigo made a sound of dismay. "As often as we've scoured these records, have we ever seen the likes of Jacopo Caretto and his granddaughter?"

"No. But we've never searched for anything even remotely the same. Also, incest," Guid'Antonio said.

"*Incest?* God's toes, Uncle Guid'Antonio—"

Guid'Antonio held up his hand. "We have no idea what will come out in that regard. Just—let's begin."

While Amerigo trailed his forefinger down the ledger's fragile pages, Guid'Antonio made notes for another case he had agreed to take, a private one on behalf of a nun battling her mother and father's families for an inheritance she considered her birthright. When her mother married her father, she had brought with her a dowry of five hundred florins. Recently, both of Sister Piera's parents had died, and now her mother's two brothers, as well as her father's family, were pursuing the money like hounds after a hare. Dowry battles were complex and very often favored the male claimants, no matter which side of the family they came from. Such complexities made dowry disputes interesting—which was why he had taken this one on.

"Uncle Guid'Antonio?" Amerigo said.

He looked up. "Yes?"

"Sometimes, I do not like this employment. Here are two boys, aged seven and eight, forced by the same man with damage to *il sesso*, as reported by the surgeon who examined them. For this, the sodomite was given fifty lashes in the Old Market and fined. Fifty and a fine?" Amerigo frowned. "I thought the law said such a heinous crime as this merits the death penalty. When bodily damage occurs."

"You know the magistrates have the final word in everything," Guid'Antonio said, glancing back at his notes regarding

Sister Piera's claim.

"But those boys were apprentices trusted into their master's care."

"When was this?" Guid'Antonio said, massaging the tightness between his eyes.

"February 1460."

"And that is it so far?"

"No . . . here," Amerigo said after a length of time that seemed to Guid'Antonio to last a dozen years. "An entry that is relative to the murder of a child. Eight years ago, the tenth day of April 1465. A young woman, the daughter of a slipper maker, Zanobi Gherucci, was tried for killing and throwing into a well the little daughter of Bernardo della Zecca, a goldsmith, for the sake of stealing the pearl necklace and certain silver ornaments the child wore about her neck."

Amerigo shook his head. "A *woman* did this? Impossible, surely."

Guid'Antonio put down his pen. "Nay. I know that case. Zanobi Gherucci still has his slipper shop across the river." Despite Gherucci's pleas for mercy, his daughter had been hauled away in the prisoner's cart and beheaded at Justice Gate, a spectacle that had drawn a large audience from the four quarters of the city. The murderer had been cut from decent cloth; why would she kill anyone for a few small pieces of jewelry, let alone drown an eight-year-old girl? "The devil was in her," people had whispered as the blade cut the killer's head from her neck. "Satan took her for his whore."

"What else?" Guid'Antonio said.

Amerigo let the ledger fall close with a thump. *"Niente."*

"Nothing? That's it?"

"In *Volume Three*, yes. There is murder, yes, but nothing that fits our needs. Next?"

Guid'Antonio drummed his fingers, a restless tap-tap-tap. Where was the registrar's clerk with Jacopo Caretto's record of arrest? He swallowed a drink of wine and thumbed toward the shelves. "Retreat to *Volume Two*."

"Not yet," said a voice at the door. Oily. Insinuating.

It was not the clerk, but Palla Palmieri's *secretario*, Sebastiano Spini, who stood poised in the doorway, dangling a solitary sheet of paper from his thumb and index finger. "Dottore, I believe you requested this?"

"Sebastiano, *buona mattina*," Guid'Antonio said to the other man, whose skeletal face always wore the same cold expression of contempt, no matter whom he addressed. "If that's Jacopo Caretto's record, yes, I did. You surprise me, venturing all the way downstairs on such a small errand as this."

Sebastiano glided into the room and released the paper, his lips crimped in a smile as the document floated onto the table. "In fact, the small nature of it drew me here. I must see for myself if the clerk remained in the arms of Bacchus after a week of holiday revelry. Tuscany's only doctor of law, the inestimable Guid'Antonio Vespucci, involved in a case involving a wool beater and his granddaughter?" Sebastiano smirked. "Your participation is one for the ages, surely."

"Among the many invaluable lessons my uncle has taught me, the most important one is that no case is trivial," Amerigo said, scowling at him.

"The one sheet is all you have?" Guid'Antonio said.

"The one sheet is all there *is*. For now." Sebastiano's damp lips tilted at the corners. "It is up to you to add the rest. And I must not keep you from it." With a slight bend of the head, Palla's secretary turned and swept across the *cortile*, the fabric of his robe twitching in a jaunty rhythm with his bony hips.

Amerigo growled. "What is wrong with that whip thin prick?"

"Not everyone likes me." Guid'Antonio raised his palms. "Difficult to believe, I know. Now, get on with *Volume Two*, whilst I read about Jacopo Caretto."

Amerigo sighed heavily, a puff of dust making him sneeze as he put away *Volume Three*, hefted *Condempnationes Volume Two: 1425 - 1449* onto the lectern, and began turning the pages. "God bless you," Guid'Antonio said, closing his eyes, clearing his head of Sebastiano Spini before reviewing Jacopo Caretto's arrest record as written in brown ink in Police Chief Palla Palmieri's small, neat hand.

> *Case #421946. Jacopo Caretto, 60 yrs. or so, Black Lion district, S. Croce quarter. Florence, Before light Sunday Morning, 20th June 1473. Sergeants Alesso Caccini & Ruberto Ricasoli, Night Patrol. The two Sergeants returned to police headquarters in the early morning hours with Jacopo Caretto in tow. Later, under oath in Criminal Court, Caccini & Ricasoli described the eerie sounds they had heard in Caretto's neighborhood toward dawn, a panting sound accompanied by howling and a low, whimpering moan. Coming upon a dog guarding a bloodied piece of cloth outside the door of a ramshackle house, they cast aside the wretched dog squatting there and forcefully entered the darkened quarters. Therein they roused an aged man (who later identified himself as Jacopo Caretto) and told him what they had found. Startled by the two men who had beaten in his door, believing he was haunted by an evil spirit, he cried out the fabric was the torn sleeve of a cotton camicia, the kind of long undergarment many people wear, belonging to his dead granddaughter, and the dog was the cur she had rescued from the street. Ranting like a madman, he confessed himself the girl's killer—*

Guid'Antonio sat back on the trestle bench. So. It was true Caretto confessed because—and only because—he was yanked from sleep by the sound of the pounding on his door and believed his granddaughter's ghost had come to haunt him. *Scared witless*, thought Guid'Antonio. Sipping his wine, he continued reading Palla's report.

> *—he confessed himself her killer. Later, in my presence, still babbling and almost incoherent, Caretto admitted defiling his granddaughter since she went to live with him at age six or so and then strangling her last week, squeezing his hands around her neck until she was dead. This latter happened on the night of Wednesday, 16th June 1473, four days before Caccini & Ricasoli discovered the blood-stained cloth. On that Wednesday, as the midnight bells tolled, Caretto covered the girl's body with rags, hefted her over his shoulder, and buried her in a hole outside the Santa Croce quarter, near Justice Gate. Given the man's ready confession, there was no cause to apply torture. He has no prior record of arrest.*

Something rustled in the back of Guid'Antonio's mind. He imagined a dog squatting beside a torn sleeve, as if protecting, or mourning, the ruined fabric; in other words, the girl. He recalled the questions he had asked himself on Saint John's day, while woolgathering, as the cloth merchant had said. *God wanted her found. But why this child? For that matter, why this dog? And: why me?* Regarding the howling dog, he had his answer: it was the dead girl's pet, a stray she had rescued from the street, according to Jacopo Caretto. Unaccountably troubled by this sad little detail, he returned his gaze to Palla Palmieri's statement, carefully crafted with a fine point metal pen.

> *Since his arrest Jacopo Caretto has refused to speak, neither explaining his behavior toward the girl, nor in any other way. Questioning the prisoner's neighbors in the Black Lion district in the Santa Croce quarter yielded little*

information. The girl was ten or eleven and had lived with Caretto in Black Lion for six years or so, as Caretto claimed. People say she was, in fact, his granddaughter. As for Jacopo Caretto, they describe him as man of good character. All denied witnessing any suspicious conduct on his part in the days preceding Caccini & Ricasoli's discovery.

Awaiting consideration for punishment in the Court of Criminal Justice on Friday, 2nd July 1473, when Florence's infamous, silver-eyed Doctor of Law Guid'Antonio Vespucci will offer the court his lofty opinion regarding Caretto's degree of guilt and how he should be punished. Following thereupon the magistrates will do as they damn well please.

Palla Palmieri
Chief of Police
Florence, Monday, 21st Day June 1473

Lofty and infamous, both? Guid'Antonio smiled, as he knew Palla meant him to do. He and the police chief weren't intimate friends, but they understood one another's stance regarding the law—fairness, always—they respected one another, and so, they got along.

Eight

WISHES

Beyond the chancery windows horsemen clattered down Stationer's Street toward the Cathedral, their voices a heated rumble beneath the sounds of squawking chickens and squealing pigs. Guid'Antonio sat at the trestle, thinking. His *designo*, or oral presentation, was scheduled for one week from today. Not much time between then and now to determine his recommendation regarding Jacopo Caretto's fate, particularly since he was traveling to the countryside with Maria after Orlando Niccolini's funeral this coming Monday, just two days from now. Die or live? The question sent a shiver down Guid'Antonio's spine, never mind the court ultimately would decide the matter for itself. The responsibility—the mystery and morality of it, combined—fascinated him.

    He shared Palla's police report with Amerigo, who remained buried in the dusty years 1425 to 1449, then asked, "What more have you found?"

    Amerigo's tone was sober. "You said incest, and here it is. A brother and sister, the sister had a child. Under torture, the brother denied everything; the sister stated she didn't know the father's identity. They both disavowed everything and were released. Then there's a father and daughter. After the father confessed, he was beheaded."

Guid'Antonio jotted a note in his journal. "When was this? And where? Was the father beheaded, I mean."

"August 1435. Here in the jail courtyard, his body displayed in public view and then burned."

A father and daughter. Forced on the part of the girl? At her father's trial had she said something or nothing? No doubt she would not have been present. "That is all it says?"

"Yes."

"What else have you?"

Amerigo stretched the muscles in his neck. "Nothing for us, or so at first I believed. But now . . . here." He thumbed back through *Volume Two*, no quick task, since the ledger was thick at four hundred pages, at least. "In January 1425, a merchant, one Antonio Rustichi, was brought before the court to answer charges he forced a serving woman, a slave. The woman's employer reported the incident. Rustichi was fined one hundred *lire* and required to pay an additional forty *lire* in court costs."

"A slave from where?" Guid'Antonio said. After the Black Death, the Florentine government had sanctioned the buying and selling of slaves provided they were not Christian. Russians, Greeks, Turks, they were captured from the Black Sea, Greece, North Africa, and many other foreign lands, then sold to slave merchants in Venice and Genoa for the cost of less than one of Maria's day gowns.

"Who knows? Anyway, what does it matter?" Amerigo said.

"It is another detail. What else?"

"Rustichi paid the fine and was released."

A fine for forcing a woman who was a slave, and case

closed. "I specified children," Guid'Antonio said.

"Yes, but when Jacopo Caretto killed his granddaughter, she was apparently eleven, or so. At that age, she may have been a child no longer. If you understand my meaning." Amerigo flushed a dark rose color.

Guid'Antonio's pen stopped on the page. *A little girl. A child*, the clerk who had described this case to him had said. It had been nineteen-year-old Amerigo, rather than Guid'Antonio, a man grown and twice married, who had understood immediately and fully what Chiara Caretto's age meant in the grand scheme of things. At thirteen, she might have married, had she been allowed to live. At fourteen, she might have had a baby. But what did her age have to do with this case? Something? Nothing? "Let's see what *Volume One* allows," he said.

†

Before switching to *Volume One: 1400 – 1424*, Amerigo removed a packet of bread and cheese from his satchel and helped himself to a small meal, offering Guid'Antonio a portion and washing his own down with a hearty swallow of wine. "So—1413, good God, incest, again! One Antonio di Tome had relations with his cousin, by whom he had a child, and also with his niece."

Guid'Antonio sucked olive oil from his fingers. "This Antonio produced children with both women?"

"That isn't clear. Another time in a fit of anger over gambling losses, this same brute slashed a painting of the Virgin Mary." Amerigo crossed himself, a soft prayer on his lips. "He also defaced a coin upon whose image the Virgin's face was engraved."

"That has nothing to do with incest," Guid'Antonio said.

"No, but it certainly is interesting."

Guid'Antonio let loose a weary breath. "Tome's sentence, please?"

Amerigo squinted. "The writing here's impossibly crabbed. For his crime of incest, Tome was sentenced to be burned to death in a cage—ah! But the sentence was changed to decapitation."

"Leniency, then." Guid'Antonio scribbled another quick note in his journal. "So, child murder—the little girl thrown down the well—warranted execution. Incest with cousin and niece? Execution. Incest between brother and sister, never mind, they deny everything and are released. Incest between father and daughter, execution. Assault on the boys, a public lashing and fine, on the slave woman, a fine, no more. A hefty fine, though, because she worked in a good household. Probably, too, because her outraged owner brought the charges."

Outraged because another man had her, thought Guid'Antonio.

Amerigo leaned toward him, a quizzical expression on his face. "—And?"

"Don't commit incest," Guid'Antonio said. "It is a crime against the Church and heavily frowned upon by the authorities."

Amerigo closed the ledger with a thud and heaved it back onto the shelf. "I mean, what is next?"

Guid'Antonio sprinkled sand on his notes and blew off the dust, watching the slipper maker's daughter throw the goldsmith's little girl to the bottom of a well. Had the child struggled? Had she realized what was happening and that she was about to die? Had Chiara Caretto fought her grandfather as he extinguished her last breath? "I'll speak with Caretto and determine his motivation," Guid'Antonio said.

"He won't talk."

"Yes, he will." Guid'Antonio closed his journal and snicked home the latch.

"To me his motive seems clear," Amerigo said. "What do

men of his ilk usually want when they—"

"I don't believe it is that simple," Guid'Antonio said. "Nothing ever is."

"Well, I'm off to *Studio Fiorentino*," Amerigo said, shaking himself as if he were Guid'Antonio's puppy waking from a nap.

"No, you are off to Santa Croce," Guid'Antonio said. "I want you to nose around the Black Lion district and see what you can learn about Chiara and Jacopo Caretto. Mingle, speak quietly with people, particularly Jacopo's neighbors. They would tell me nothing if I ventured there. I'm staying here. I need time alone."

Dismayed, Amerigo said, "Santa Croce? Why? You know Palla's men visited Caretto's neighbors straightaway."

"And for their efforts gleaned nothing other than the usual bland answers," Guid'Antonio said.

Petulantly, Amerigo said, "Why would those dyers and soap-makers answer someone like me? They're liable to slit my throat and rob my purse, instead."

Guid'Antonio looked sharply at his nephew. "Someone like you? Oh! From a wealthy, well-known family, you mean. While they're poor workers living hand to mouth." He rose from the bench, towering over his nephew. "You can't run to Santa Croce fast enough when that quarter is hosting a tourney. Moreover, you've undertaken missions for me in scenarios much darker than this. Ask nothing. Charm the ladies, the pretty fruit vendors and lace-makers. Flutter your lashes, or whatever it is you and your bravos do to work your magic on the ladies. Oh, yes, I've seen you do it. Only learn in a roundabout way the truth about the wool beater's disposition. His interaction with them, generally. They'll tell you more than they ever would dream of telling Palla's men or me."

Amerigo's face tightened. "They'll recognize me in the

piazza. They know you have this case—everyone does. You know as well as I, those people are thick as fleas." He shuddered. "They won't malign one of their own."

Guid'Antonio's temper jumped to a boil. "You're not so famous as that, Amerigo Vespucci. Also: may I remind you Maria's family lives in Santa Croce? You would do well to keep your dim thoughts regarding that quarter and its occupants to yourself."

Guid'Antonio's thoughts flew back three years. Had his house kept its low opinion of the Del Vigna family to itself when he married Maria? No. The Del Vignas were unimportant in a town built on marriages arranged to move a man up the social ladder, not down. Maria's father was neither notary nor merchant, nor even a tailor, but a saddler whose occupation afforded him minor guild status. A union with Maria del Vigna would stain the Vespucci family's honor, ruin them in every way. That had not happened, of course. Guid'Antonio's household had underestimated his worth, his rising reputation in affairs of state, his growing connection with the Medici family.

Although . . . that was then, and this was now.

What would his family have thought if he had spoken the name of the woman he truly wanted for his second wife? A woman with even less social standing than Maria, a woman for whom he would have risked everything—and might have lost everything, too.

His brusque words struck Amerigo to the core. "By all that's holy, Uncle Guid'Antonio! You know I love Maria! I wouldn't speak ill of her or her family. They are now our family, too."

Before Guid'Antonio could reply, a young messenger, a boy pink-cheeked with excitement and importance, materialized at the chancery door. "*Buon giorno*, Dottore! Praise God I found you here." He dipped a quick bow. "Palla Palmieri is at your hospital and said for you to come there fast."

Guid'Antonio's breathing slowed. "Did Palla say why? Quickly, now."

"Has someone in our family been killed?" The words rose, high and reedy, from Amerigo's lips.

"No, no!" exclaimed the boy. "It concerns the man who died yesterday in your garden."

"Good God," Amerigo said, his relief an elevated note in his voice. "Him, again?"

The boy retreated a step. "I don't know why, Dottore. All I know is Palla—Chief Palmieri—is waiting for you along with Maestra Francesca Vernacci." Francesca's name rolled off the boy's tongue as if its syllables were made of velvet. "She is one of the doctors there."

"I know who she is," Guid'Antonio snapped. Fingers trembling, he rummaged in his scrip and handed over a silver penny. "Tell Palla I'm on my way. Go on!"

"*Grazie!*"

Guid'Antonio and Amerigo slipped their papers and pens into their satchels, slung the leather straps over their shoulders, and hurried out into the harsh white light of the courtyard. Over Amerigo's protests, Guid'Antonio persuaded him to return Jacopo Caretto's record of arrest to Palla's upstairs office, rather than go home with Guid'Antonio, then to proceed to the depths of the Black Lion district in the Santa Croce quarter, where Jacopo Caretto lived. *A più tardi. Stai attento.* Until later. Take care. *Surely, if the situation were dire, Palla would not have sent a mere boy to fetch Guid'Antonio—?*

A short distance from the jail Amerigo peeled with long strides toward Santa Croce, while Guid'Antonio hurried in the opposite direction toward home. Head bent, fists clenched, he wished he were going anywhere other than Spedale dei Vespucci. Footsteps darting here and there through one alley after another, he wished he could shed his heavy crimson cloak. He wished a lot of things. He wished he never had asked Francesca Vernacci to marry him. Three years ago, almost to this very day. Their anniversary of sorts. He laughed, smarting with the heat of embarrassment, wishing that rather than whispering, "You would suffocate me," she had laughed with happiness and said, "Yes! *Ti amo*, Guid'Antonio!" He wished she had wrapped her slight arms around his neck, her lips as soft as silk against the pulse fluttering in his throat, as she had done so many times before.

Nine

AUTOPSIA

Francesca's eyes locked with his, then slid away, toward the stone trestle where the cloth merchant, Orlando Niccolini, lay with a linen sheet draped over his stubby legs. Sewn with fine black thread, a puckered seam shot from Niccolini's groin to his sternum. Maestra Francesca Vernacci had rummaged in the man and sewn him together again, leaving his cock limp and grey between his legs.

On the floor near the sink, the brass, iron, and steel instruments Francesca had used on Orlando Niccolini—a fine-toothed saw, tongs, a hammer, and an assortment of knives—soaked in a bucket of water clouded pink with blood. Around the surgery walls, cupboards and shelves housed mortars and pestles, lidded and labeled pottery jars, kettles, pans, and scrapers for removing infection from putrid flesh. Lit torches in iron brackets enveloped the chamber in a shadowy orange and yellow glow.

"*Ciao*, Maestro Vernacci," Guid'Antonio said as they acknowledged one another, then glanced from her to Palla

Palmieri. "What have you?"

Palla, trim in brown tunic, hose, and boots, regarded Francesca, his expression grim. A flaxen curl had escaped the gauzy coif framing Francesca's face. Beneath the folds of the gown falling from her shoulders to the floor, her spine was straight, her body slim. Plain, the white woolen gown, its only embellishment the seal of the Vespucci Hospital sewn on the left shoulder, a white lamb and gold cross on a red background. Guid'Antonio's seal on her one way, or the other.

Silence spooled between them, a single breath hushed before drawing in air again.

"Maestra Vernacci?" Guid'Antonio said.

"Dottore." She tucked the stray curl into place, and it leaped out again. Flustered, she touched the thin slash rippling her right cheek, as neatly stitched by her father's hand as the slit she had made in Orlando Niccolini. Guid'Antonio's stomach roiled. Francesca's scar was the result of an accident he had caused long ago, when she was a child of seven years, and he a fool of seventeen.

"Guid'Antonio," Palla said. "Close the door."

Guid'Antonio did as the police chief asked.

"Maestra?" Palla said.

Francesca's luminous green eyes drank Guid'Antonio in. "Ser Niccolini died from mushroom poisoning."

"What?" He took a step back. "That's—no."

"Death Cap does not lie, Dottore. I examined his stomach contents and consulted my medical books to identify the mushrooms I found in his gut. There were two kinds: Death Cap, with its telltale foul odor, and what appeared to be Baby Cesare, or some similar, mild mushroom." Removing a bowl from the counter, Francesca tipped the contents toward him, plucking a bit of gore from the bowl with tweezers. "See how the texture is different?"

Guid'Antonio held up his hand. "Yes." Death Cap was a

toxic mushroom found in Tuscany and God only knew where else. He stared at Niccolini's corpse. The merchant had forked one bite of Cesare's mushroom salad into his mouth and fallen face down in his plate, dead.

"Guid'Antonio, you served your guests mushrooms at your *festa* yesterday, correct? And Orlando Niccolini was there," Palla said.

"You know he was."

"Did everyone partake of salad?"

"I assume so. But—"

"But what?" Palla said.

"Not everyone had the same kind. Cesare Ridolfi, who works in my kitchen, well, all over my house, served my table with special salads he prepared for the occasion. Other servants delivered food to everyone else. Cesare is—"

"I know who Cesare is," Palla said. "Frisking about the market like a colt the moment the sun rises in the east. Just to be clear: Orlando Niccolini was at your table?"

Just to nail me down.

"Along with several other men. Yes," Guid'Antonio said.

"Yet only he is dead."

"Pray God, yes. I was with Amerigo just now. And I've heard from no one else. Still—" Guid'Antonio reached for the door. "Maria—"

"Guid'An—Dottore." Francesca spread her arms and curved them back again, as if she possessed the wings of an angel and would protect Florence from evil by cradling the city to her breast. "Slowly, now," she said. "If anyone else who attended your *festa* had succumbed to the poison, by now my father and I would know it, as would the entire Santa Maria Novella quarter."

An odd sense of calm settled over Guid'Antonio. And— since he knew as much about poisonous mushrooms as anyone else in Florence, in other words, *a lot*—he said, "Death Cap requires at least one day to kill a man, less for a child or woman. Yet Niccolini took one bite and was dead."

"At last we're getting somewhere," Palla said.

Guid'Antonio did the math. Niccolini had eaten his salad mid-afternoon yesterday. This morning, Maria had been smiling, content with their lovemaking when Guid'Antonio climbed from their sweat-soaked bed. A short while ago, Amerigo had walked with long strides away from the jail toward the Black Lion district, discontent, yes, but assuredly not ill. "Maestra Francesca. Your father's aware of your diagnosis and agrees with it?" Guid'Antonio said.

Irritation clouded her face. "My father was here during my procedure. He's at a guild meeting at present, but if you must, you may confer with him later today."

Guid'Antonio had not realized he was holding his breath. He released it, stepping away from the surgery door, and later it frightened him to think how easily he had turned away from home. "No need," he said. "So—the question now is how it is Orlando Niccolini barely tasted his salad and was immediately dead."

"Oh, there are many questions," Palla said. "But we have one very important answer. Maestra?"

"He died instantly because his liver was sick," Francesca said.

†

A brass candelabra set with costly beeswax candles, generous Saint John's Day gifts for Francesca and her father from the Vespucci family, burned on the counter by the sink. Carefully, Francesca leveled the flaring flames over the corpse. "When I undressed Ser Niccolini, I noticed his flesh bore a yellow tinge. My examination revealed a fatty liver. Not only fatty but also thick and inflamed. He was dying well before yesterday."

"His sick liver hastened the Death Cap's lethal effect," Guid'Antonio said.

"Yes. At your table, how did he seem? Confused? Fatigued?"

Guid'Antonio nodded. Niccolini's odd behavior made more sense to him now than it had on Saint John's Day. How many married men would boast about his lover at a holy day celebration? Especially when his wife was near. *A baby*, Niccolini had said. The cloth merchant and the girl, Elena Veluti, were expecting a child. "Still, he was sailing for England," Guid'Antonio said.

"England?" Palla's interest quickened. "When?"

"After finishing his salad he meant to ride to Pisa, spend the night there, and set sail today from Liverno."

"Odd, if he was ill," Palla said.

"He seemed a man equally animated and melancholy. Some business to do with inferior fleece and ill-spent funds," Guid'Antonio said.

Palla huffed a laugh. "Not a new story in Florence. So! What else? He was a liver-diseased fellow of—" He glanced at the corpse on the table. "About sixty years, and—?"

Guid'Antonio told him what little he knew about Orlando Niccolini. The man was a prosperous cloth merchant in the employ of Spinelli and Spinelli, whose thriving wool shop he managed. "He lived here in the Santa Maria Novella quarter."

"Which district?" Palla said.

Guid'Antonio waved his hands helplessly. "All I know is he attended Mass at All Saints along with his wife, Caterina. He was not a friend," Guid'Antonio said.

Palla cocked his head. "Then how did he come to attend your family celebration on our town's most popular holiday? A cloth merchant, though a successful one, it seems. One well enough esteemed by his employers for them to trust him with traveling on business to foreign lands."

"At Lorenzo de' Medici's request," Guid'Antonio said.

Francesca had turned to the counter, her hands working deftly as she threaded needles with gut and tucked them away for future surgeries. She turned back around, a smirk on her lips. "That explains it," she said. *"Parla Lorenzo."* Lorenzo speaks. *And you act accordingly, bowing to his every word and whim.*

Guid'Antonio's face warmed. "Lorenzo has business dealings with Spinelli and Spinelli through Niccolini," he said to Palla Palmieri. "The Spinelli relationship is one Lorenzo wishes to maintain."

Palla tapped his lips. "Let's go back and back. Where, exactly, was he seated? Niccolini, I mean."

"Beside me."

"A cloth merchant?" An amused smile touched Palla's lips. "How so, Dottore?"

"Again, at Lorenzo's request," Guid'Antonio said.

"Beside *you*?" There was something frightened about Francesca now. "You were extremely fortunate yesterday. If that has not yet occurred to you," she said.

"It has." Yesterday afternoon, every man seated at his table had been near enough to death for the angels at the Gates of Paradise to shake their hands.

The atmosphere sobered, became more tense.

"Who else was with you?" Palla said.

Guid'Antonio told him. *Medici banker Francesco Nori, Amerigo, Guid'Antonio, the cloth merchant, and Giuliano.*

"Giuliano de' Medici?" Palla said.

"Yes."

"Good Christ, Guid'Antonio," Palla said, his calm demeanor slipping. "Four men from Florence's leading families, plus one cloth merchant seated with you at Lorenzo de' Medici's request."

"Yes."

Palla scratched his cheek. "I wonder what our Lorenzo will say when he hears of this. Of his only brother's close brush with Death Cap."

"I would be afraid to venture a guess," Guid'Antonio said.

"Who else was at the *festa*?" Palla asked.

"The usual friends. Family. About fifty people. My wife, Maria. Simonetta Vespucci and Marco, who is her husband and my kinsman."

"I know who they are," Palla said. "But not Nastagio and Antonio—?" Amerigo's father and slightly older brother, Nastagio and Antonio Vespucci, Palla meant.

"No. They entertained guests at home in our courtyard. More people could be accommodated if we divided ourselves accordingly."

"Lorenzo de' Medici was not there?"

"No. He was home entertaining Princess Eleanor, along with his mother and other friends of the family." Princess Eleanor of Aragon had spent the week in Florence while traveling from Naples—where her father, King Ferrante, reigned—to Ferrara for her marriage to Duke Ercole d'Este.

"And the lovely Neapolitan princess is leaving when?" Palla said.

"Early morning Saturday," Guid'Antonio said. "At least, that is the plan."

"Hmmm," Palla said, circling around again. "Everyone knows Giuliano and Simonetta are, shall we say, fond of one another. And then, there's Marco, the husband. A volatile situation, at best."

The word *vendetta* stomped through Guid'Antonio's head. Revenge. "Marco is Giuliano's friend," he said.

Palla smiled. "Of course he is."

Guid'Antonio fell silent, wondering where the police chief would take them next. Back to the salads, unless he missed his guess.

"What other mushroom was served yesterday?" Palla said. "Along with the Death Cap."

"Baby Cesare, as Maestra Francesca guessed."

Francesca raised her brow. *Guessed?* But she made no comment.

"How was your salad prepared? By your boy, Cesare Ridolfi," Palla asked.

"With a little olive oil and a drop of white wine vinegar from Modena. Chopped," Guid'Antonio said.

Palla turned to Francesca, a question on his lips.

"The poisonous mushroom in Niccolini's gut was chopped, yes," she said. "Only a trace amount along with the Baby Cesare mushrooms, but enough to kill him, nonetheless."

Palla frowned. "Death Cap has a foul odor. Niccolini would have recognized it, or at least have found it too distasteful to eat."

"In addition to the sick liver, he had a cold," Guid'Antonio said. "Sneezing, fever, chills. According to his wife, he had gone to the Sign of the Stars for a remedy to clear his head." *I only wish I could taste it,* Orlando Niccolini had said, shoveling the Baby Cesare and Death Cap mushrooms into his mouth.

"How did he die, Guid'Antonio?" Palla said. "He ate some salad and—"

Guid'Antonio watched Orlando Niccolini's hands strike the table as he slumped forward. Saw his wine spill across the pure white linen cloth. "He grabbed his middle, then thrashed about and fell into his plate. Within a moment, he was dead." A sick liver. Who knew? Soon, all Florence would, surely. Guid'Antonio rubbed his forehead, easing the tension gathering there.

"This must have been upsetting to your surviving guests," Palla said.

"You have an amazing gift for understatement."

"I learned it from you, my friend."

"Upsetting to me, too," Guid'Antonio said. "But above all to Niccolini's wife, Caterina." They crossed themselves.

"When did your servants—Cesare and the others—offer the salads to your guests?" Palla said.

"At the end of the meal, of course," Guid'Antonio said.

"Did all the food and wine served yesterday come from your house?"

"This is beginning to sound like a trial," Guid'Antonio said. Palla grinned. "Not yet."

"Yes, all the food served came from our house. Our kitchen. Where else?" Cesare Ridolfi, his mother, Domenica, and Domenica's brother, Gaspare, had been preparing for the Saint John's Day feast since Easter, airing table linens, borrowing and cleaning silver, making lists for the marketplace. Fish, flowers, fruit. Mushrooms.

"Let's talk about Cesare," Palla said. "Has he served such gatherings before?"

A premonition of troubled days ahead whispered in Guid'Antonio's breast. "No." He hesitated, but it must be said: "This was something new for him, for his coming of age, one might say. Our salads—the ones he served my table—came from his own hands. He bought the mushrooms in the market and prepared them especially for me. Again, other youths accommodated my remaining guests."

"When Niccolini died where was Cesare?" Palla said.

"He had returned to the kitchen." Returned in spectacular fashion, strutting down All Saints Street accompanied by the music of trumpets, fluttering his fingers in giddy greeting here and there. In fact, Cesare Ridolfi had drawn considerable attention to himself while leaving the *festa* in the moments immediately preceding Orlando Niccolini's death.

"Where does this lead us?" Guid'Antonio said, although, of course, he had the answer.

"I'm keen to ask your perky *servitore* how well he knew

our dead cloth merchant," Palla said.

"My house, my kitchen," Guid'Antonio said.

Palla smiled sadly. "Yes."

Francesca stepped in. "Palla, along with my autopsy report, I'll file a certification of death with your office. Dottore," she added, turning to Guid'Antonio. "I'll let our frowning Abbot Ughi at All Saints Church know to expect Niccolini before evisceration becomes necessary."

"That message should please Father Abbot," Guid'Antonio said. "Like any message coming from you."

They shared a smile, rare these days. Roberto Ughi, the cold, dour abbot of Ognissanti Church, avoided Francesca Vernacci as if she carried the plague. In Florence, there was *one* female doctor. Why must she live and work in *his* parish? Ughi had chastised Guid'Antonio about Francesca on more than one occasion. The hospital belonged to Guid'Antonio's house. Could he not do something about Dottore Filippo Vespucci's wayward daughter?

No.

Palla bowed to her. *"Grazie di tutto."*

"As always, you are welcome," she said, adding to Guid'Antonio, "and welcome home to you, Dottore."

"*Grazie*, Maestra, I'll see you have the usual two florins for your examination," Guid'Antonio said, his eyes capturing hers an instant too long before he accompanied Palla down the surgery steps and across the hospital foyer, hastening to question Cesare Ridolfi.

Ten

THOSE EYES

Those eyes. Pale grey, like a wolf challenging her to look into him for more than a moment. And if she dared meet his gaze?

The surgery was quiet now. Alone in the silence, Francesca stood at the sink with a towel in her hands, watching the last of the dead cloth merchant's gore swirl down the drain, her cheeks pulsing with heat. If only she could dismiss Guid'-Antonio Vespucci from her mind as easily as she placed needles and knives on the marble counter along with forceps and pliers, dried them, and put them away. He was a disturbingly handsome man, whether standing before her just now in his crimson cloak, or in his hip-length brown tunic after removing his leather vest and tossing it to the floor.

The first time he had come to her bed, he had been newly widowed, Francesca the comfort he had turned to in the wake of his grief when his first wife died in childbirth, along with their baby. Francesca had been a virgin, eager to feel his mouth on her throat and belly. She had loved him since she was a girl, and he was the dark, chestnut-haired boy older by ten years whose family owned the hospital where she and her father worked and lived. That first night, he had been gentle yet probing, their bodies shuddering as he ran his fingers through the mass of tangled blonde hair between her legs. Beneath him, when her hips arced, she bit her teeth into his neck. He exploded inside her, and fire ignited her limbs. She wept, and he caressed her with rapid kisses, until she could scarcely breathe.

She could scarcely breathe now. She was part of the shadows, caught in a silence so deep, it hummed in her veins. The hem of her gown stirred. It was her cat, *Gatto*, winding around her ankles, now those intruders had flown. "In a moment, my sweet," Francesca said.

Steadying her hands, she draped the sheet over the length of Orlando Niccolini's corpse, scooped *Gatto* into her arms, and nuzzled his robust body close to her neck and cheek. The cat was so warm, so comforting. He purred noisily before angling from her arms and leaping to the tiles. Flipping his tail, he stalked toward the surgery door and peered at her over his shoulder, loudly meowing. *You're mine. Now, let me out of here.*

Francesca shook her finger at him, a half-smile on her lips. "Don't go far, *Signore*."

Her notebook of receipts—medicinal balms, ointments, unguents, and salves—was stored on a wooden shelf by the sink. She had placed the notebook as high as she could reach. Memories of the flood of 1466 haunted her, even after seven years. That January, although there had been no rain, the snow in the upper Arno Valley had melted, and the river overflowed its banks. Icy water had surged through Florence, drowning stabled mules and horses, gushing into workshops and houses. Benches from as far away as Piazza Santa Croce floated down All Saints Street. Filthy river water poured inside the hospital, where she and her father scrambled alongside

Guid'Antonio and his kinsmen, struggling to move patients from their beds and maneuver them up the foyer stairs, then rescue medicines and surgical instruments from the ground floor. The stench. The loss. The mud and debris, dead animals and fish rotting everywhere. *The Flood.* Her belly squeezed in on itself as it always did when these memories tangled her in their ropy net. Surely, such a disaster would not happen again.

On tiptoe, she retrieved the thick notebook, reaching as well for the pottery jar containing her latest experiment. Cradling the jar and journal to her breast, she closed her eyes, the unbidden heat of loss and desire for Guid'Antonio flaring in her again. She remembered their happiness. She remembered their joy. She remembered the touch of his lips on her neck like a heartbeat in the blood.

†

10 June 1470, three years ago. He had liked to lie beside her with her bedchamber windows wide after they made love, admiring the sky, the heavens. That Tuesday evening, gazing at the blanket of stars with the musky sheet tangled at the foot of her bed, he had whispered in her ear, "Tonight Lorenzo was unusually somber. He's only twenty-one, and yet lost time is his greatest regret. Poems are abandoned, books forsaken, while he is busy addressing the demands of the Republic. I don't want to lose more time than necessary with you, my precious girl. When the shops open this morning, I'll choose the velvet and pearls for your marriage gown. I'll speak with Domenico about a silver *ghirlanda* for your brow." Domenico Bigordi, the jeweler and painter whose hair ornaments for prosperous Florentine girls were so popular, people had begun calling him Domenico "Ghirlandaio".

I am not prosperous, Francesca thought. *And I am no longer a girl.*

Leaning over, Guid'Antonio kissed her scarred cheek, his lips as light as down. "*Ti amo tanto.* I love you so much," he said.

She had moved away from him then, only a hair's breadth, but he felt it. A shadow flickered over his face, coloring his pale eyes a deep smoky grey. "Francesca. You claim you love me, too. For the last eighteen months—almost two years—" His voice took on a note of wonder. "No—" Adamant, now, vigorously shaking his head. "No more lost time, my lovely girl. On Saint John's Day two weeks from now, we'll marry along with dozens of other couples." He smiled tentatively at her. The instant she had distanced herself from him, his demeanor had grown wary. "As is the custom."

"I have never told you a falsehood," she said.

He frowned lightly. "Yes, that's why I've spoken with your father. He's delighted. My notary and he agreed on the dowry straightaway." He relaxed into a smile, as if her father's blessing settled everything.

"You spoke with Pippo? When?" And with a notary as well. Fast!

"Yesterday. While you busied yourself at the Sign of the Stars."

Busied herself. At Luca Landucci's apothecary shop, she tended patients neither sick enough nor poor enough to receive free care at Spedale dei Vespucci. For this service, she collected precious coins to help support herself and her father. "You had no right," she said. "I am not an eleven-year-old girl. You should have told me."

"I'm telling you now."

She wanted to pound his chest with her fists. "Guid'Antonio," she said, scooting quickly up on the mattress, catching him off balance, "we've discussed this before." *But you have never mentioned velvets and wedding ornaments. You have never slipped behind my back and spoken with my innocent father, who had no idea you and I have argued about this to the breaking point. As if my feelings are as unsubstantial as air.*

Neutrally, he said, "*Cara*, remind me." He arranged himself beside her, pushing hard against the chestnut headboard, rattling it with his weight. He was a strong-willed man accustomed to having his way. He would have his way now.

She touched the silver tangle of hair on his chest, her fingers resting there. No longer a boy, but a man, that same delicate silver lacing his temples and his black eyebrows. Eyebrows at the moment knit in a distinct, hard V. "The poor people who come here depend on my father and me for their care," she said. "Filippo's fifty-two this year. And he's ill. I'm the only female physician in Florence. I've attained the dream I've carried since I was a child, and I never would have, if it were not for him." She had not been allowed a university education—she was not a man. Still, women and Jews could study medicine with a university-trained physician, then undergo a practical exam administered by the Guild of Doctors and Apothecaries and receive a license to practice. *This* she had accomplished with her father.

"If it were not for him, I would not be here," she said.

Her gesture encompassed not only the hospital where she lay in bed with Guid'Antonio, but also Luca Landucci's Sign of the Stars and the pharmacy at Santa Maria Novella monastery. From the monastery's Dominican friars, whose order had grown herbs and flowers in their infirmary garden for over three hundred years, Francesca purchased medicinal plants, along with lavender and roses, and made from them balms, medications, and sweet-smelling lotions.

Her gesture included the courts in the city jail, where she was paid for her professional opinion in cases against those who had gravely wounded others, and to make judgments regarding the cause of death under suspicious circumstances.

It included *Studio Fiorentino*, where she attended disputations on a variety of medical topics with her father. This latter she had done with Pippo since she was a child. Medicine—*this hospital*—was her world. Guid'Antonio knew that.

She had always been . . . different.

He knew that, too.

He made a guttural sound down in his throat, and she could almost hear his thoughts.

You would not be here if it were not for me. This is my hospital, not your father's. My great-grandfather founded it over a century ago. My influence made your father Provost and head of the College of Physicians within the Guild of Physicians and Apothecaries. Because of me he is the administrator here. When you were a motherless child twice over and followed on his heels to Studio Fiorentino, *I watched with compassion. When you earned your surgeon's license and later, when the guild recognized your medical skill by bestowing the honorary title of physician on you, I congratulated you and kissed you, while others called you "witch." Some still do. That includes Abbot Roberto Ughi. If it were not for me, you would have been married to some minor notary or cloth merchant a dozen years ago, when you were eleven or twelve. That or married to Christ and living behind cheerless stone walls in a nunnery somewhere, perhaps not even in Florence.*

Drawing a deep breath, he said, "I assured your father you could care for patients here with him and at Luca's during the day, then come home to me."

She cut her eyes at him, surprise fluttering in her chest. How many Florentine men had ever permitted a wife or daughter to leave the house they shared to do *anything*, other than make a heavily cloaked, escorted visit into the neighborhood markets and shops for ribbons and laces and, perhaps, a few artichokes in season? None that she could name.

She chose her next words carefully. "Widows and orphans

seek me in the loneliest hours of the night, not only during the full light of day. They need me constantly."

"How about what I need?" he said.

Looking at him then, she saw an extremely wealthy man, a widow of thirty-four with no heir. His family honor, the palace on Borg'Ognissanti and its far-flung holdings—villas, wine, silk farms—remained shaky until he sired a boy. She said, "I am twenty-four. What you need is a young wife, one who can bear you a dozen children. You need a connection with a house as important as yours."

"I had a young wife. She died. Now, I want you," he said.

Want. A small word armed with muscle and intent.

"Spoken like a true Medici man," she snapped, her arms tight across her chest.

He leaned against the headboard, rattling it repeatedly, his smile slow with a dangerous edge. The candle burning in a saucer on the small cabinet beside him flared before settling to a low, erratic flame. "Meaning?" he said.

"Meaning you live for Lorenzo and Giuliano de' Medici. For power and prestige."

"I believe in them," he said.

"You believe in yourself."

"I believe in and live for my family," he said, stiff-lipped. "For Florence. For you, no matter what you believe. And so, yes, for Lorenzo and Giuliano de' Medici, since they and Florence are one and the same, given their father is dead, leaving them the heirs to our city and government."

"With Lorenzo only twenty-one, as you say, and his brother a boy of sixteen or seventeen years."

She slumped down on her pillow and stared at the ceiling, high overhead and plain. She possessed neither a bed canopy trimmed with fringe sewn with gold thread, nor a summer coverlet of silk imported from Persia through Venice, items surely not uncommon in the bed chambers in Palazzo Vespucci, a few steps down the street. "You would suffocate me," she said.

He could not have looked more stunned if she had jumped from the mattress, grabbed a poker from the hearth, and cracked him over the head with it. "That's enough," he said, scrambling from the bed. "I'm leaving."

As if in a dream, she watched him pull into his hose and tie the strings at his waist, watched his tunic float over his shoulders and settle around his hips. Rounding on her, he gestured sharply with his hand: *Finito!* It's finished.

"You accuse me of loving power, while what I am doing is fighting for Florence," he said. "You have the balls—yes, Francesca, *the balls*—to say you refuse me for my own good and for the good of your father." He laughed shakily. "This is as practiced as if you were fingering your rosary. What you want is this hospital, with or without me or him. You don't love me. You never did. Don't look for me in your bed again."

Unable to curb the ugly words spewing from her mouth, she said, "How dare you bring my father into this! Your wife and son were barely in the grave before you came to me. Anyone can be replaced."

He had stared at her in disbelief. "Do it, then," he had said.

With that, in a flash of rich brown and black leather, he was gone.

✝

In the surgery, Francesca stood motionless, faintly aware of the pottery jar and notebook in her hands. After Guid'Antonio's departure that night, he had not returned to her bed. Within six months he had married Maria del Vigna, a sultry, sixteen-year-old with dark olive skin whose family lived in *Bue*, the Ox district of the Santa Croce quarter. Not a wealthy girl from an esteemed Florentine family, but a saddler's daughter. On the surface, the Del Vigna girl appeared as remarkably different from thin, pale-haired Francesca Vernacci and Guid'Antonio's first wife, blonde-haired Taddea, as nighttime was from day.

"Francesca," a voice behind her said.

She whirled from the counter, emitting a small cry. The pottery jar slipped from her fingers and shattered on the tiles. Before her, with a scruffy leather satchel over one shoulder and a loaf of bread in his hand, stood a thin man wearing sandals and a modest cloak of dark blue cloth. His face bore a hint of wrinkles, and his thin hair was going grey.

"Father! You startled me," Francesca said, her limbs as light as air. "I wasn't expecting you now."

"Obviously," Filippo Vernacci said. Fingers trembling, he placed the satchel and bread on a table close to hand. *"Perdonami, Cara,"* he said, smothering a cough. "Forgive me. I thought you heard me on the landing. Instead, look what I've made you do."

They stared at the jar in pieces on the floor, its contents mixed with pottery shards.

Francesca bit her lip. The ruined ointment represented her new receipt for reducing fevers and headaches. Mandrake oil, opium, balsam, and witch hazel, ingredients gathered and prepared with equal love and care. She had worked on the ointment for over a year and had intended to administer it as necessary, monitoring her patients closely, adjusting the preparation according to her observations.

"That's the ointment whose ingredients and measurements you're testing for our *Ricettario fiorentino—mea culpa.*" Filippo pulled a handkerchief from his cloak, wiped his mouth, and tucked the bloodstained cloth back inside his pocket.

Blood. Again. A worm of fear uncoiled in Francesca. She had thought her father's health improving, now the dampness of spring had given way to summer. "Don't worry, Pippo," she quickly said. "I have the ingredients recorded, and I have time to begin fresh. Every physician, surgeon, and apothecary in Florence knows your College will take years to assemble all the receipts submitted for the *Ricettario*. No offense to you," she quickly said.

The Physician's College suspected sick people faced grave dangers due to the variety of preparations and practices one healer or another used in medical treatments. Thus, her father, whose position as Provost of the Physician's College meant he was bound to enforce medical standards, had decided to systemize the preparation of medicines in the city, countryside, and district. The *Ricettario fiorentino* was a noble project. Its publication would bestow tremendous honor on those whose work it included, and Francesca burned for acceptance.

"No offense taken," he said.

She found the surgery broom and began cleaning the floor. "That pot is easily replaced, and all the ointment requires is patience." *Days. Weeks. And several more florins.*

Filippo picked up the surgery bell. "No need for you to sweep. I'll summon Lena." Lena Barone, the hospital cook, laundress, and cleaning woman who slept downstairs, just outside the patients' ward in the foyer, ready to summon Francesca or her father if anyone required aid after nightfall, when the doors were closed and bolted.

Francesca glanced from her task. "Pippo, no! Not while Ser Niccolini is on the table. Lena is excellent help, but she's squeamish."

"After all these years?"

Francesca grinned. "Yes."

Filippo rummaged in his shoulder bag, located his spectacles in their calfskin case, and pushed the fragile wire rims onto his nose. Behind the round eyeglasses, his gaze appeared watery and dim. "You seemed distracted when I came in," he said.

She glanced at Orlando Niccolini. "Death Cap."

"Indeed, but that's not all that's worrying you, is it?" her father said.

"Of course it is." She retrieved a dustpan, frowning to herself.

"I bumped into him and Palla in the street just now," Filippo said.

Him. "—How did he seem?" she asked.

"Rattled beneath his usual calm air. Where were they going in such a hurry? This time, I mean."

She told him everything.

"Ah," Filippo said. "His house, his kitchen. His little *servitore.*"

"His big embarrassment," she said, dumping the sticky waste into a wooden pail, huffing a sour laugh. "Given a guest died from mushroom poisoning at his house, he'll need to work hard to maintain his self-appointed role as the savior of this town. Of this Republic. I'm surprised he let down his guard for a moment, even with you."

Filippo tilted his head. "Francesca. Guid'Antonio carries all the weight of his house and this hospital on his shoulders. Such rancor is unlike you."

Ashamed, she turned her face away.

He sank into a chair, sighing heavily. "Look at me."

"Yes, Papa?" she said.

"I'm disappointed to hear you speak so spitefully about someone who treats you honorably, unlike many others in this town. Someone who has been your friend since you were a child, when he visited the hospital with his father, always bringing you a smile and a plaything from the market. Someone you laughed with for years before he left for school in Bologna. And after."

Francesca rubbed at the ache in her temples, heat rising in her cheeks. Only a few doors separated her bedchamber from her father's. He was not deaf, and he was not a fool. Never had they spoken of the sudden rupture between her and Guid'Antonio Vespucci, of the forgotten dowry and disappointed notary. For Pippo to nudge against it now was like a knife twist in her ribs. "I was cruel just now," she said. "I'm grateful to know you find it unlike me."

"I love you, child. I only want you to treat yourself, and him, kindly."

Child. She smiled despite herself. As for the other—

Another attack of coughing shook him, splattering more blood onto the cloth he raised to his mouth. He shook his head, unable to speak. "Papa!" she said. "Please! I'll get you to bed."

Fear pumping in her breast, she assisted him to his chamber, chatting with forced cheerfulness about the hen she would purchase in the marketplace today on her way home from seeing patients at the Sign of the Stars. Carrots, sweet yellow onions. She would cook a thick broth for their evening meal.

After helping him remove his cloak and settling him in his bed, she slid his spectacles from his nose and watched him swallow the syrup of quince and cordials she held in a cup to his lips. A bit of the liquid drooled from his mouth and onto his chin. Still, he managed to keep the better part of the medicine down. Relieved, she plumped his pillows, noting how his eyelids drooped, weighty with approaching sleep.

"Papa?" she said, licking over the dryness of her lips. His eyes shuttered and he fell back on the pillows. "Papa?" She lay her ear against his lips and listened to him breathe. A light rattle, but he was drifting into sleep. Wearily, quietly, she remained with him until she was certain the medicine had soothed him completely.

†

In the surgery, moving with practiced care, she gathered the cloths stained with Orlando Niccolini's blood and added them to the pail. *We will survive this cough,* she told herself, pouring fresh water over her hands, scrubbing them with soap, drying them with a clean towel. *Holy Mary, Mother of God, Pippo is the one person I have in all the world. Please, please heal him. No. Three,* she reminded herself. *If I am brutally honest, I have three.* Breathing deeply, she crossed herself.

Unlike most other *medicos* in Florence, Francesca and her father kept a written record of patients. She opened the journal and in a clear script wrote: *Orlando Niccolini, abt age sixty, Died Saint John's Day, Thursday, 24 June 1473, Examination Friday, 25 June. Liver Disease, Death Cap—*Her hand paused mid-sentence.

Those eyes. Pale grey, like a wolf challenging her to look into him for more than a moment. And if she dared meet his gaze?

She did not know, but she was fearful, nonetheless.

Eleven

DEATH BY CESARE RIDOLFI

Standing outside his garden gate, Guid'Antonio heard the sound of laughter and loud voices, punctuated by a puppy's shrill *yip, yip, yip!* His courtyard. His *Orsetto,* his Little Bear. He looked over his shoulder at Police Chief Palla Palmieri, the corner of whose mouth rose ever so slightly. "Chaos everywhere," Palla said.

"Welcome to my house." Guid'Antonio prepared to force the gate, but the bolt slid back smoothly, and the hinges remained silent. *Thank you, Amerigo.*

"Dottore Guid'Antonio—*ciao!*" Cesare ran to him, a smile wreathing his face. "You're home from the chancery early today. Will wonders never cease?"

"Apparently not," Guid'Antonio said, aware of Palla lingering behind him in the street.

Happily, the boy said, "Our house has been a hive of activity today."

"So I see." In the garden, hired women sat at a trestle dipping cloths in a mixture of salt and water, polishing silver, gossiping among themselves. Barefoot laundresses bustled about, draping damp linen tablecloths and napkins over rope lines strung across the yard. Rude, jolly remarks, red, raw hands.

"Cesare," Guid'Antonio said, "I'm home early because Palla Palmieri and I have questions about the salads you prepared for my table yesterday." Beyond the water fountain, *Orsetto's* high-pitched bark ripped the air. "Orsetto! Puppy! Stop that!" Guid'Antonio called. He waited and was ignored.

Cesare's smile waned. "The chief of police of Florence is at our house to discuss our food?"

"I am." Palla, stepping off the thoroughfare, closed the gate. Slight though he might be, Palla had a sure air about him, and his expression was dark and keen. In the courtyard, the women fell silent, ears stretched toward the two men and the boy.

"*Signore* Palmieri," Cesare replied with an abbreviated bow.

"Cesare." Palla tipped his head to one side, his attention fast on the boy.

Cesare's violet eyes flashed. "What questions can there be? Everyone at the table was enjoying my salads, until that cloth merchant—" He waved his fingers carelessly, as if to say, *Until Orlando Niccolini chose that moment to die and ruin everything.*

Palla leaned close. "You seem a heartless boy."

Cesare drew back a pace, almost stumbling over *Orsetto*, who had come bounding from behind the water fountain, chasing the wasp buzzing and diving at his button nose, the puppy quivering with joy. "Heartless?" Cesare echoed. "Me?"

"*Orsetto!* No—!" Guid'Antonio swatted at the wasp, missed, and scooped up the dog, holding its wriggling body close.

"*Maledizione!*" Cesare grabbed a hoe, smacked the insect, and crushed its tiny corpse into the grass with the sole of his boot. "There!" He dusted his hands, straightened his shoulders, and cocked a lopsided grin at a younger boy peeking around the clothesline, smiling adoringly at him.

"That *vespa* probably came in with the *chamomile*," Cesare explained. "I gathered an armful during the night. Early this morning after the rain, I spread the flowers on yon table to dry in the heat of the sun."

On the trestle by the kitchen, tiny flowers with daisy-like white petals and bright yellow centers lay scattered beside a pair of shears. "You collected the flowers after the bonfires and dancing in Piazza della Signoria?" Palla said. "During the night?"

Cesare's face flickered for a moment. "—Yes."

Palla's gaze narrowed almost imperceptibly on him before shifting the short distance to the kitchen door from whence there came the clatter of pots and pans and a woman shouting, "Livia! Take care with the fire! The broth's boiling over! You silly girl, you've burned yourself! Mary, Christ's Mother, where is the salve!"

"*Orsetto,*" Guid'Antonio said, "that romp with a wasp could have caused you no end of trouble." He patted *Orsetto's* plump, puppy belly before setting him in the grass, where the little fellow scampered after the cat sauntering across the yard, whisking its tail, ready to whirl and smack *Orsetto* silly. Turning to Palla, Guid'Antonio said, "The woman in the kitchen is Domenica Ridolfi. She—"

"I know who she is," Palla said. "The kitchen's busy today."

"Yours isn't?" Cesare asked.

Palla returned his attention to him. "Especially around holy days, yes? Everyone's frantic, in one way or another. Haste makes waste, if you are not careful. What will you do with the dried *chamomile*?"

Cesare ignored Palla's question for one of his own. "I thought this was about the *festa* meal."

"It is. But now you've roused my curiosity about your little flowers. Several of which are caught in your hair," Palla said.

Cesare screwed up his face, swiping his fingers at the petals caught in his curls. "I shall grind them into fine powder. Mixed with wine and heated, its properties are relaxing, producing sleep."

"Huh," Palla said. "From time to time, I could do with something to help me sleep the night away."

Cesare arched his brow. "Residing as you do in the jail amongst killers and thieves, I would think you would prefer to remain wide awake, always."

"Not so many killers now, but then, the day is young," Palla said, smiling guilelessly at him. "After you, Guid'Antonio?" he added, gesturing toward the kitchen.

"*Tanti baci,* Many kisses." Cesare eased toward the gate.

Guid'Antonio plucked him back, grasping the strings of the apron the boy had donned to protect his cotton shirt. "The kitchen is this way, my little *Signorino.*"

†

"Livia, no! Stir the broth with love! Keep sloshing it about, and you'll scorch yourself again. *Con amore, Signorina!* That is the secret to good cooking. Has your mother taught you nothing?" At the sound of footsteps, Domenica Ridolfi swung around from the hearth, rosy-cheeked and smiling, the plum wine in her pottery cup sailing merrily from rim to rim.

On the hearth, savory chicken broth seasoned with onions and sage simmered in an iron pot. Skillets and pans crowded the kitchen counter, freshly scrubbed with sand in the wake of the holiday celebration, along with more silver serving jugs and trays, many borrowed from the Rucellai, the Medici, and the Ginori families. Baskets of ripe strawberries filled the table near the curtained portal that separated the kitchen from the *saletta*, the informal dining room where Guid'Antonio and his Vespucci kinsmen dined when they weren't entertaining guests in the more spacious *sala*, or in one of their private apartments.

"Guid'Antonio!" Domenica said. "Here's a . . ." Her voice trailed off when she spied Police Chief Palla Palmieri at Guid'Antonio's shoulder. "Surprise. You're home early."

"Buon giorno, Signora," Palla said. And he was amiable enough.

"'Giorno," Domenica replied, glancing at Guid'Antonio: *What have you got us into this time?*

"Domenica, Palla has some questions regarding our *festa* salads. Specifically, those Cesare served my table." Guid'Antonio flicked his eyes toward Livia, the kitchen girl. "Privately, that is."

"Go home now, Livia," Domenica said. "Return later today."

In the garden, the cat squalled, and *Orsetto* raced into the kitchen. *"Sì, Signora."* Livia hurried to the back door that opened into the serpentine alley leading from the house, the puppy nipping at her heels.

"Watch him, Livia!" Guid'Antonio called. "Don't ever let him out, we'd never find him." Strike out on his own and that little dog would end up in a stew pot, or lost in the byways of Florence, maybe even killed for sport. Guid'Antonio pictured his jaunty puppy carried off, happily wriggling and licking the face of a thief, or in a well in a forgotten piazza, struggling to keep his nose above water. In the instant before Livia slammed the door, *Orsetto* jumped back, his fuzzy rear narrowly missing the bucket of chicken bones beside the kettle bubbling on the hearth.

Palla laughed.

"Careful, *Orsetto*!" Guid'Antonio said. *Good Lord.*

A strand of thick black hair had escaped Domenica's coif. In one motion, she swiped at the sweat streaming down her cheeks, tucked the damp lock into place, and swallowed deeply from her cup, carefully watching the police chief of Florence. "Has someone complained about the food? I'll put my kitchen up against any in town, including the Medicis." She slipped Guid'Antonio a side look. "You do know they have a kitchen sink with water pumped to it from their well."

Guid'Antonio placed his crimson cloak on the trestle bench, grateful to have the weight off his shoulders. "You've reminded me often," he said.

"First things first, *Signora*," Palla Palmieri said. "Are you prepared to swear under oath that Cesare Ridolfi, and he alone, prepared the salads he served Guid'Antonio and his guests in the meadow yesterday afternoon?"

Guid'Antonio glanced quickly at Domenica, who had grown still, absorbing the sudden seriousness of Palla's tone and the import of the question he had posed concerning her only son. "You want my salad secrets! I knew it!" Cesare glanced uncertainly around.

"Be quiet, young man, or we'll continue this conversation at the jail." Palla addressed Guid'Antonio, shrugging lightly. "I've always wanted to say that to someone."

"Jail?" Cesare stared at Guid'Antonio. "Have I witnessed something? A crime—?"

"Just answer his question," Guid'Antonio said.

The woman who had been the Vespucci family cook for thirty years regarded Palla as if he had just asked her if she was certain Florence Cathedral was capped with a red brick dome. "Of course I'll swear it," she said. "Because he did. What is this?"

"You asked if anyone had complained about the food," Palla said, taking a winding path. "Orlando Niccolini would if he could."

"Oh! Him." Domenica wagged her head. "God bless his poor wife, Caterina Niccolini! All the wealth in the world couldn't prevent her husband's heart from betraying him in the end. It reminds us all we know neither the hour nor the day."

Guid'Antonio and Palla exchanged a look. His heart? Nay. "Reminds all who?" Guid'Antonio said.

"Why, the chicken sellers, the bakers, the candlestick makers—everyone in the market while I was making rounds this morning. They're gossiping of nothing else."

Merda. He had thought the news of Niccolini's death at the *festa* would travel like wildfire. And so it had.

"Before I forget," Domenica said. "Your kinsmen asked me to tell you to make a point of dining with them here at home tonight." She quaffed her wine, glancing from Palla Palmieri to her son and back. "Something about a fresco."

The fresco for the Vespucci family chapel, the one Leonardo da Vinci wished to paint when the time came. An Annunciation, probably. Guid'Antonio nodded. *"Bene."*

"*Signore* Palmieri, what is this about jail," Domenica said.

Amerigo blew across the threshold. "What happened? *Buon giorno, Signore* Palmieri." He dropped his satchel on the trestle bench beside Guid'Antonio's crimson cloak, sucking in his breath. "Uncle Guid'Antonio, after leaving the jail, I went to Santa Croce as you asked, then hurried to the hospital. Lena said you rushed here with Palla—"

"Orlando Niccolini did not die of natural causes," Palla said.

"What? Then how—"

"I'm coming to that," Palla said.

Stunned, everyone glanced at Guid'Antonio, who remained silent.

Excitedly, Cesare rose up on his toes. "What has Niccolini and how he died got to do with me?"

"That's what I intend to find out. Cesare, where did you get your mushrooms for yesterday's feast?" Palla said.

Cesare glared at him. "*Get?* You make it sound as if I stumbled across them in a back alley in Santo Spirito!"

To Cesare's dissembling, Guid'Antonio gave a curt, *"Answer him."*

Cesare thrust back his shoulders. "For yesterday's celebration, well ahead of that fabulous event, I ordered mushrooms for my especially tasty salads from the two most respected vendors in town. Uncle Gaspare and Livia purchased their own mushrooms to prepare salads for our other guests, but—" He shrugged. "Who knows where, and who cares?"

"What kind of mushrooms were they? The ones you purchased?" Palla said.

"Baby Cesare." Cesare glanced at Guid'Antonio and back at the police chief, his frown deepening. "I think probably you already knew that. Why are you asking me now?"

"Where did you store your especially tasty Baby Cesare mushrooms before preparing them?" Palla said, fixing him with a hard stare.

"My shopping baskets. Where else?" Cesare's gaze wandered to the wicker hampers and baskets in the far kitchen corner.

"Have you any left?"

"A few."

"Ah! Let's have a look." Palla smiled.

"Dottore Guid'Antonio—?" Cesare obviously sensed real trouble now, if he had not before.

"Show him," Guid'Antonio said, vaguely aware of *Orsetto* resting with his nose on the toe of his boot, yawning.

Palla poked in the baskets. "Beans, apples and, yes—a few mushrooms." He took one. "What kind is this?"

"Baby Cesare," Domenica said.

Palla, dipping into the basket again, turned this time with

a spongy grey mushroom in the palm of his hand. Sniffing it closely, he recoiled and took a quick step back. "Cesare," he said, and the solemn tone of his voice told Guid'Antonio that Palla took no pleasure in this, "what am I holding in my hand?"

"A mushroom. What else?" Cesare asked.

Guid'Antonio was only glad the boy did not say *What else, you fool?* In the hearth the broth bubbled, and the low fire danced in bright, shifting flames of yellow, orange, and blue. Guid'Antonio's heart sank.

"Take a whiff, my little man," Palla said.

Cesare sauntered around the table. Palla held the mushroom out in his hand. Cesare bent down and seemed to levitate. "Death Cap!"

Domenica grasped the edge of the trestle. "No!"

"Yes," Palla said. "*Signora*, Orlando Niccolini was poisoned with Death Cap and see what we have found." He slipped the offending mushroom into his scrip. "For safe-keeping," he said.

For proof, thought Guid'Antonio.

"No," Domenica said again, slumping onto the bench.

"Your son recognized it immediately," Palla pointed out.

"Of course I did!" Cesare exclaimed. "Death Cap is similar in appearance to Baby Cesare, but it stinks!"

"Madre di Dio," Amerigo whispered under his breath.

"Everyone listen and be quiet," Guid'Antonio said, his pulse slow in his chest.

"Death Cap is not foreign to the boy." Palla caught Guid'-Antonio's eyes with his own. "He put the smell with the name." Palla's brown gaze returned to Cesare. "Don't try to say so later."

Later? Here was a leap on Palla's part. Guid'Antonio watched and listened closely.

Cesare shuffled back. "Why would I deny it? I know

mushrooms! I myself question how Death Cap came to be in my basket! Moreover, why didn't Ser Niccolini reject his plate when he caught the foul odor?"

"Because he couldn't smell. He kept sniffing and blowing," Amerigo said. "Ugh."

"Ironically, but for that Niccolini would still be breathing," Palla said.

Amerigo agreed, adding. "Just not very well."

"And not much longer, " Guid'Antonio reminded the chief of police.

"I don't understand!" Cesare wailed.

"Nor do I," Amerigo said. "Death Cap doesn't act straightaway, and yet one taste, and Niccolini was dead. In fact—" Amerigo touched his stomach. "I—"

Impatiently, Guid'Antonio said, "Francesca's autopsy showed Orlando Niccolini was gravely ill with a sick liver. Apparently, Cesare handed him the only tainted plate. And so he died immediately."

"The only plate? Amazing!" Amerigo said. *"Grazie Dio."*

"Nay!" cried Cesare. "I did no such thing! I mean, yes, but—"

"Calm down," Palla said.

"It's a sick feeling to know one has touched the sleeve of death," Amerigo said, then frowned. "Why didn't Cesare smell it?"

"No one did," Guid'Antonio said. "In fact—the autopsy revealed only a small amount of the poisonous mushroom in Niccolini's gut. Finely chopped and mixed with greens, oil, and balsamic vinegar, which as we all know, is intensely flavored. However small the amount of Death Cap added to that plate, it affected Niccolini quickly because of his sick liver."

"Definitely not his heart, then?" Domenica said.

"No!" Guid'Antonio and Palla said.

"What about in the kitchen?" Amerigo pressed. "Before he

chopped it. Why didn't Cesare smell it then? Along with the one now in Palla's pocket?"

"Excitement," Guid'Antonio said.

Cesare gasped. "Excitement? You are going the wrong way—!"

Palla leaned down, his lips close to the boy's ear. "Alternatively, Cesare Ridolfi, how well did you know Orlando Niccolini?"

"Not well enough to murder him!" Cesare exclaimed.

Guid'Antonio massaged the back of his neck. Palla had been bound to ask this question sooner than later. But he did not like seeing Cesare cornered this way. Not proud Cesare, who believed himself as perfect as he imagined himself to be. Guid'Antonio remained silent.

Palla smiled. "Now, there's an interesting statement. But I believe you, little man. You killed Orlando Niccolini when you served him a plate laced with Death Cap you accidentally purchased along with the other mushrooms for your salads. Death Cap you carelessly added—"

"No!" Cesare wailed. "I know food! I know mushrooms! I ordered the sort known as Baby Cesare ahead of time from the two most reputable mushroom vendors in town—they would neither gather nor sell Death Cap!"

"How many mushrooms did you purchase?" Palla said, retreating a bit.

"The entire lot!"

"Cesare," Guid'Antonio said. *"Stai calmo."* Be calm.

Palla grunted, his eyes never leaving the boy. "And so like Orlando Niccolini's galley to England, that ship has sailed. Why question the vendors now? They have nothing left for me or my men to inspect."

Into the pulsing quiet, Guid'Antonio said, "However it happened, Cesare, you would do well to demonstrate some remorse, just a little, more or less. You could have handed that plate to any one of us at the table."

Everyone stared at the boy, who had gone pale, so astonished, he could say nothing.

Palla observed Cesare closely, his countenance somber. "This is a grave matter, Cesare Ridolfi. Because of your carelessness, a man died yesterday. Not just any man: an important cloth merchant. A friend of Lorenzo and Giuliano de' Medici seated at Dottore Guid'Antonio Vespucci's table. What do you think people will make of that?"

Sorrowfully, Amerigo said, "Make of it? They'll crow about how inept we are, unable to manage our own household. We're ruined."

Guid'Antonio looked at him, pained, thinking, *Amerigo, please.*

Cesare rallied, regarding Palla through glossy black eyelashes. "This is unfair! Why is everyone blaming me?"

"Because you bought the damned things!" Guid'Antonio said, giving way to anger.

"Nay! You're not listening! But for argument's sake—he would have died anyway! Dottore Guid'Antonio, isn't that what you said? His liver was sick!" Cesare gave Guid'Antonio a trembling look and crossed his arms, tapping his foot, waiting for affirmation.

Domenica's head snapped up. "My only living child, my hope, my salvation! Or so I believed! Instead of my angel, you are Satan!"

"Mama, no—"

Guid'Antonio despaired, thinking of himself in court one day defending Cesare against charges of extreme arrogance and disrespect, if not something worse. Something like murder. Frustrated to the breaking point, he said, "Enough, Cesare Ridolfi! Despite his illness, Ser Niccolini might have lived for years, a successful merchant sailing to Lyon, Bruges, and London. Instead, because of *you* he is dead on a slab in *my* hospital, poisoned by *you* before the eyes of the entire city. Do you understand what it means to be *dead*?"

"I believe I do, since all my family are in the grave except Uncle Gaspare and my mother," Cesare said. "And yet, I'm only twelve."

A gust of pure fury swept Guid'Antonio. "You amaze and disappoint me with this—this selfish attitude! You disgust me!"

Cesare seemed about to faint. Was he no longer Guid'Antonio's beloved boy? "What will happen now you have abandoned me?" he said, his voice hollow.

Amerigo hid a fleeting smile, while Domenica wept unabashedly. Palla said, "What will happen is I will charge you with the crime of accidental murder. With no time spent in jail, but a fine of six florins paid the court." Palla slid his gaze to Guid'Antonio. Everyone present knew who would pay the money in Cesare's name.

Domenica blew her nose into a linen towel. "*Signore* Palla, thank you. He never would survive in jail."

"Death by Cesare Ridolfi," the boy said lifelessly. "This is a black mark on my name."

Palla's temper flared. "Better than a noose around your neck. You killed a man! Pah! Guid'Antonio, I've lost all patience with this arrogant, bull-headed boy."

"Thee and me," Guid'Antonio said. "A black mark against *your* name, Cesare? This is a smear, a bloody stain on our house. A centuries-old house that because of you cannot offer an entertainment without killing a guest."

"My house, too!"

"We shall see," Guid'Antonio said, and Cesare gasped.

"Guid'Antonio," Palla said, "I will visit Niccolini's widow—her name is Caterina?—and explain everything, saving you the embarrassment for now. Wherever she lives—here in the Santa Maria Novella quarter, you said? Which district?"

"I—"

"Not Unicorn," Domenica said. "Back toward Santa Trinita Bridge. Just off the river. I know her from the market, from church, and so on."

Palla nodded. "I'll find her."

A few easy strides bore him to the threshold. In the garden, the voices of the hired women dropped before rising again. Palla stood still, the sun silhouetting his brown form as he gazed intently into the yard. And then he pivoted. "Cesare," he said. "I'm curious about your pretty little flowers."

Twelve

CHAMOMILE

Two spots of hot color marked Cesare's cheekbones. "You are?"

"I am," Palla said. "You claim you picked the flowers last night following the celebrations in Piazza della Signoria. Where and when?"

Cesare cocked a lopsided grin at him. "What does it matter?"

"Don't try to evade me," Palla said.

Guid'Antonio groaned. "For God's sake, Cesare, for once will you just give someone a straight answer?"

The boy rallied. "It was important I gather the *chamomile* during the most propitious phase of the moon."

"And that was last night?" Palla said.

"Yes."

"What phase was it?"

"New." Cesare pulled a frown. "You know that as well as I do."

"Who wouldn't?" Amerigo said. "What does that have to

do with anything?"

Palla threw Amerigo a look that said *Let me do this.* "Where?" he asked.

"Why?"

"Cesare!" Guid'Antonio said.

Palla held up his hand. "Cesare Ridolfi, is it your habit to prowl the countryside in the dead of night?"

Guid'Antonio and Amerigo shared the briefest of glances. At sundown the gatekeepers closed and barred the city gates. Until sunrise, Florence remained under strict curfew. Given that, *prowling the countryside after dark*, as Palla described it, was not only difficult to do, getting past the night patrols—getting caught slipping in or out of town—was a serious offense. Too much mischief occurred in the nighttime hours. Too much passion, too much death. Which made Guid'Antonio wonder how Jacopo Caretto, a man in his sixties, had managed it burdened with the dead weight of his granddaughter. Well. There were ways and ways. Who knew this better than Guid'Antonio Vespucci?

Cesare said, "I'm sorry you think me a prowler, *Signore* Palmieri. In fact—" He gave the police chief a triumphant look.

"Yes?"

"I collected the flowers *this* side of the Prato Gate just beyond the meadow where we held our doomed Saint John's Day celebration." *So there*, Cesare's lofty expression said.

"After curfew." Palla closed the trap.

Cesare's eyes flickered with uncertainty. "Guilty!" he cried, covering his face with his hands. "Go on! Arrest me! That's what you want to do, if not for one thing, then another!"

"By the Virgin's girdle, a confession," Palla said, but hesitated. "Oh, never mind. If we charged everyone we caught out after curfew last night, we'd not see the end of it in court. Anyway, I understand the holiday spirit." He regarded

Amerigo, who shrugged sheepishly, acknowledging his own guilt and his appreciation for the police chief's leniency in this matter during holy day celebrations.

Palla considered Cesare appraisingly. "Just so you know, one of my men will visit the meadow later today to admire the flowers you say are found this side of the gate. *Signora, Signori*," he said, smiling all around.

Breaths held, everyone watched the police chief strike across the garden, whistling to himself. At the gate he slid back the iron bolt, stepped from the courtyard, and slipped the bolt home. They did not breathe easier until they heard him light-footing south along All Saints Street, where eventually he would turn east toward the River Arno and the house of Caterina Niccolini.

†

"He's a cunning man. I loathe him!" Cesare said.

"He is your mirror," Guid'Antonio said.

The boy whipped from the kitchen door. "He will say 'Death by Cesare Ridolfi'! The widow Caterina will believe him. She, the town—like you!—will think me a disgusting boy." He looked at Guid'Antonio, his shoulders slumped. "My reputation is ruined, my honor stained."

"*Your* reputation? *Your* honor?" Guid'Antonio said. "Unbelievable!"

Domenica slapped the trestle with such ferocity, the baskets of strawberries lifted from the table. "Cesare Ridolfi! You consider only yourself! You killed Caterina Niccolini's husband, you wicked boy! Because of you she's a widow and all alone in the world, with no one, neither husband nor child, to give her comfort! Though on some days you are anything but a comfort to me!"

She rushed him, seized him by the shoulders, and shook

him handily before yanking him up by the arm. "You'll stay in our chambers until I give you permission to leave! Darken this kitchen before then, and I'll throttle you soundly!"

"Madonna *Madre*! I have regrets! Please, let me have my final say." Cesare bowed his head, sniffling.

Domenica relaxed her grip. Eyes tight, she held onto him waited.

Cesare lifted his eyes to Guid'Antonio. "Dottore Guid'-Antonio?"

Everything in him resisted engaging with the boy. *"Sì?"*

"I'm as baffled as you by the death of Ser Orlando Niccolini. I would not serve a poisonous mushroom in any way, shape, or form. You've agreed so quickly to 'Death by Cesare' because for you it is the least worrisome course. The cloth merchant was murdered, and you know it."

Guid'Antonio stared at him, speechless.

"This is regret?" Amerigo said.

Guid'Antonio clenched his fists. "How dare you, you aggravating—I can't think what to do with you!"

Cesare's mouth turned down at the corners, and he cried harder. "I'm bereft and faint of heart, as ruined as the coliseum in Rome."

Jaw clenched, Guid'Antonio said, "All you should be is sorry."

"Not when I've done nothing wrong!"

"Devil take the coliseum!" Domenica said, tightening her grip on her son. "One day your self-importance will land you in such hot water, you will think you are dancing in the flames of hell!" She pulled him from the kitchen, Cesare as limp as a cloth doll, dragging his sandaled feet on the tile floor.

An extended sigh issued from Amerigo as he watched them go. "Bereft and faint of heart. He is, you know."

"He is also guilty of murder," said Guid'Antonio. "If accidentally, though." He blew out a deep breath, emotionally exhausted, feeling as fatigued as Cesare Ridolfi.

"Granted, but my God, this is a dreary business. Orlando Niccolini wasn't a particularly likable man, but still—" Amerigo crossed himself, shaking his head at this turn yesterday's events had taken.

Guid'Antonio strode to the kitchen doorway and stood there with his nephew, gazing into the courtyard. So calm, the garden, so fragrant the scent of Cesare's *chamomile* wafting on the breeze blowing off the borgo. The washerwomen were gone, tablecloths and napkins gently flapping on the rope lines, silver ewers and trays shining as prettily on the trestles as if they had just been delivered new from Verrocchio and Company. Later today, Domenica's brother, Gaspare, would return the silver to their owners, with warm thanks and tokens of friendship from Palazzo Vespucci.

"Those women had an earful," Amerigo said.

"Undoubtedly. I'm tired. Still, let's fetch some wine and cheese and sit in the garden. I need to know what you learned about Jacopo Caretto in Santa Croce. Come along, *Orsetto*."

†

They settled on the stone bench circling the fountain. "So," Guid'Antonio said. "Santa Croce this morning."

Amerigo plucked one of Cesare's flowers from the garden table. "As you suggested, I posed as a bravo exploring the shops, one who gossips, fingering this, sniffing that. People are more talkative about a local, Jacopo Caretto, I mean, when hoping to sell new boots and belts. By all accounts our wool beater's a hardworking man. Quiet. Honest."

That agreed with Palla's report. "And the girl? His granddaughter?"

"Friendly," Amerigo said. "A bit precocious, mayhap."

"Precocious?"

"Forward."

"Brazen?"

"Yes."

"With men?" Guid'Antonio said.

"Playful." Amerigo stuck the daisy behind his ear. "Always humming and twirling to the music piping in her head."

Not any more, thought Guid'Antonio. "Bold?" he said.

"Yes."

Forward. Precocious. Brazen and bold. The exact opposite of how he felt seated here in the garden. *Tired. Washed out. Stuck waiting for the contract for Imola from the duke of Milan. A contract that might never come. No!—he would not let himself think that. The official papers would arrive soon, please God and Mary.* "You found Jacopo's house?" he said. The Black Lion district in the Santa Croce quarter was an especially dense warren of byways and thin streets.

"*Certamente.*" Amerigo waggled his eyebrows. "I entreated a pretty miss to lead me there. It's close by Justice Gate, not far from Verrocchio's *bottega.*" Verrocchio and Company.

Guid'Antonio nodded, scooping *Orsetto* into his arms and kissing his nose. "One more thing—"

Amerigo darted a quick glance toward him. "Oh?"

"When, exactly, is the dissertation you want to attend today? The one Angelo Poliziano was raving about yesterday to you and Giuliano. Concerning Titus Lucretius Carus."

Carefully, Amerigo said, "When the bells ring for nones."

Mid-afternoon, then. "*Bene.* As soon as possible, I need you to deliver a message to Palazzo Medici. Lorenzo should hear of the circumstances surrounding Orlando Niccolini's death from me, rather than on the street. Before I see him, I need to speak with our family, decide where we are going from here. Be sure you are here later, Amerigo. You should be involved." *Death by Cesare Ridolfi.* Guid'Antonio sighed heavily.

"Of course!" Amerigo said. "I'll hurry home in time for the evening meal."

"*Grazie.*"

Together they retired to the *scrittoio*, the airless stone chamber off the garden where the Vespucci men tended family business. There Guid'Antonio jotted a brief note to Lorenzo de' Medici, thinking, *I would love to see the expression on Lorenzo's face when he reads this.*

Or not.

Death Cap.

Thirteen

RESPECT

That night in bed Guid'Antonio lay sweating on the feather mattress with the coverlet wound around his feet, Maria on one side of him, *Orsetto* on the other, the puppy a hot ball of fur snuffling with contentment. Exhausted and heavy-lidded, Guid'Antonio prayed for sleep. Instead, his mind roamed wildly over the events of the day and evening. *Murder. Palla Palmieri. Cesare Ridolfi. Not outright murder, no, but a terrible punch in the gut for the Vespucci family in the grand scheme of things. For their honor, for their reputation, for their house. And always, always, the delayed contract for Imola hovering in the air all around.*

What had begun as a relatively quiet supper in the *saletta* with his Vespucci kinsmen had become a heated argument concerning the future of their little *servitore*, with Amerigo's father, Nastagio Vespucci, demanding that Cesare, that *witless, silly boy*, be exiled for embarrassing the family—"We've worked too hard for respect in this back-biting town to let that fool destroy us now. I say we purge him like a sore"—while

Nastagio's brother, cleric and scholar Giorgio Vespucci, had insisted Cesare was part of the family. "If we make him an outcast, will people respect us then? No," Giorgio had said.

"That would do our reputation more harm than good," Amerigo said. "We must tread carefully here."

Throughout, Guid'Antonio sat quietly listening, drinking Chianti and sopping the chicken broth in his bowl with a chunk of day-old *festa* bread.

"What say you?" Nastagio finally said, eyeing Guid'Antonio, Nastagio's cheeks burning darkly red. "Your silence is thunderous."

Guid'Antonio wiped his fingers on a napkin and calmly addressed the other men. "I say we keep Cesare here, but in confinement. Close ranks and keep our heads low, but when asked, explain the situation honestly and openly."

Nastagio huffed his dissatisfaction, but acquiesced. "This will get worse before it gets better," he warned.

Steered by Brother Giorgio, the talk sailed into less choppy waters toward the chapel nearing completion in All Saints Church. Which Florentine craftsman should they commission to fresco the wall behind the altar—Domenico Ghirlandaio, perhaps, or their neighbor and friend, Sandro Botticelli? Guid'Antonio pushed back from the supper table. "Leonardo would appreciate our consideration."

"Piero da Vinci's bastard boy? No," Nastagio said, pouring wine into his cup and drinking it quickly. "Domenico and Sandro have more experience."

So, Guid'Antonio thought. *I will have my way regarding Cesare Ridolfi, and you will have yours regarding the fresco.* He left them to it, pausing only a moment in the doorway. "Nastagio, *ascolta*, listen. Leonardo da Vinci aside, Cesare Ridolfi may at times seem silly, but he is not witless. Anyone who thinks otherwise is the fool."

†

When a few moments later he entered the apartment he shared with Maria, she had been awake, sewing by candlelight. "I waited," she said, standing, smoothing the folds of her gown. "I'll pour fresh water into the basin for you to bathe. You're later than usual."

"*Grazie*, Maria."

By the light of the brass lamps burning near the washstand, she poured tepid water into a basin and took his cloak, lingering as he tugged his tunic over his shoulders. He rinsed his face and body, and she handed him a towel. As always, her dark, feverish eyes drank him in, as if she wondered what he had just done and what he might do next. What he did at that moment was reach down and pet *Orsetto*, who had raised his head from the hearth and wiggled over to him, wagging his tail. When Guid'Antonio wrapped Maria in his arms, *Orsetto* barked in protest. "Be quiet, puppy," Guid'Antonio said. "Maria. I have something to tell you. Many things, in fact."

"I would rather you had something to do." She laughed, biting his shoulder playfully, then sobered. "Something serious," she said.

"Yes."

Sitting beside him on the bed, she listened intently as he explained the manner of the cloth merchant's death, its aftermath, and the quiet dignity with which the Vespucci family must comport itself in the coming days. She pursed her lips in thought. "You were at the hospital today. That woman's examination revealed the poison." She shied from him a bit.

Guid'Antonio brushed a strand of shining black hair from her cheek. "Among many other places. Now, I am here with you."

"Cesare is responsible for the merchant's death?"

"Yes."

"Domenica must be sorely grieved. But you were in no danger?"

"—No."

"Praise God. I'm sorry for his wife," Maria said. "Mona Caterina. And for you. You're spent."

"Yes."

He had extinguished the nighttime candles then, and they had lain down, Maria removing her gown, *Orsetto* snuggling close to him. "You are mine here in this bed," Maria had said, so quietly, he was not quite sure he heard her correctly. "I have you, and I love you," she had added with more force.

"I am blessed," he had said, asking God please to let him sleep.

God's reply had been a firm, "No."

Maria twitched and *Orsetto* stirred, while all through the night Guid'Antonio's mind sang. Tomorrow morning, Saturday, would come early. Just after first light he was expected at the San Gallo Gate, where he would join Lorenzo and Giuliano de' Medici in bidding Princess Eleanor of Naples farewell as she continued her wedding journey north. This was a great honor. One that would be remarked by all—

A crash and a screeching noise jolted him from his thoughts. *Orsetto* sprang up, growling. *For Christ's sake, what now?* Guid'Antonio jumped from the mattress, his dagger in his hand. "*Orsetto*, hush." In the inky darkness, he strained his ears, glancing at Maria, who lay undisturbed in bed. Voices—no, one very familiar voice—echoed up the walls from the kitchen alley far down below.

"Go on, now! Shoo!" It was Cesare Ridolfi.

A wave of aggravation swept Guid'Antonio. At this unholy time of night, despite Domenica's warning for him to remain inside until further notice, not to mention the fact servants were forbidden to roam the house at night, Cesare was in the back alley chasing some animal scavenging for scraps. A lice-infested cat, a rat, or both.

Guid'Antonio stretched out in bed, his heart hammering in his chest. After a moment, he patted *Orsetto*, then woke with a shock. Beyond the windows, church bells rang, signaling terce, the third hour after dawn. Awake most of the night, he had overslept.

Leaping up, he rinsed his face and teeth before pulling into tunic and hose. He found his boots and belt, whipped his crimson cloak from a hook, and closed the chamber door with a soft snap, praying that somehow, miraculously, the Neapolitan princess had not yet departed Florence.

Fourteen

THE DEVIL'S DISCIPLE
SATURDAY, 26TH JUNE 1473

"Guid'Antonio, *buona mattina*," Giuliano de' Medici said, his lips warm on Guid'Antonio's cheek. "It's not like you to be late." He lowered his voice: "You look tired."

Guid'Antonio straightened the folds of his cloak, catching his breath. *If only you knew*, he thought. "I am," he said. "Bartolomeo, *ciao*—" He exchanged cordial greetings with Bartolomeo Scala who, as chancellor of the Florentine Republic, also was the secretary of state for foreign affairs. "Giuliano, I—" *feared*, he nearly said—"I thought Eleanor might be gone by now."

Instinctively he, Giuliano, and Bartolomeo looked toward the San Gallo gate, where Lorenzo de' Medici stood smiling up at Princess Eleanor with his hand on her mare's broad flank. Gazing down at him, Eleanor blushed, her soft, jeweled fingers working the thick folds of her gown. Black velvet in this heat, adorned with pearls, as befit the eldest daughter of the king of Naples, no matter the sun was blazing in the sky overhead.

Grinning, touching his heart, Giuliano said, "An abundance of kisses has been exchanged, along with lingering glances and vows of eternal friendship between our houses."

"Let us hope they mean it," Bartolomeo Scala said, fanning himself, sweating profusely in his chancellor's robes cut from fine red cloth. "As for arriving late—" He turned his attention to Guid'Antonio, his thin lips pursed beneath blue eyes and hooked beak. "Given the news from your house, I'm surprised you arrived at all. I would be in hiding."

Guid'Antonio touched his fingertips together for a moment—not quite an invocation. Obviously, his note to Lorenzo de' Medici concerning the cause of Orlando Niccolini's death had been passed along to the secretary of the Florentine government. "No, you would not," he said.

"Don't rub salt in his wounds, Bartolomeo," Giuliano said with a gentle glance at the other man.

Bartolomeo harrumphed. "I meant no disrespect."

"You never do," Guid'Antonio said.

Impatience was everywhere. Eleanor's horses snorted, stamping their hooves and swishing their tails, their liquid brown eyes rolling toward the farmers carting bawling calves and bleating lambs into town for Saturday market. Eleanor's armed guards shifted their attention to her blushing maids and ladies, whose mounts pranced, impatient for the road. Finally, Lorenzo stepped back, and Eleanor's entourage passed beneath the stone arch whose portal led north toward the road to Bologna, thence to Ferrara and her future husband, Duke Ercole d'Este.

The instant Eleanor vanished through the gate, Lorenzo whipped around and walked with rapid strides to the three men waiting for him on Via Larga. "Safely she entered our town, and safely she departs, praise Mary and all the Saints. Guid'Antonio, here you are." Lorenzo brushed his hair from his face before letting those dark wings fall back along his shoulders. Olive-complexioned and taller than the average man, twenty-four-year-old Lorenzo de' Medici was not handsome by any means, a hint of roughness about his face prevented that, but in no way was he ill-favored, gifted as he was with expressive black eyes accompanied by a ready smile, almost always.

"*Mattina*," Guid'Antonio said as they exchanged quick kisses on the cheek.

They fell into formation, walking four abreast as they made their way down the broad thoroughfare toward Palazzo Medici, several blocks away. "What if something had happened to the princess during her stay?" Bartolomeo Scala fussed, glancing sharply at Guid'Antonio while dodging a deep hole in the street. "She's King Ferrante's daughter, for God's sake! Not to mention the future duchess of Ferrara. We'd be caught in a war with them, one we could ill afford and could not possibly win."

"But it didn't, and we aren't," Giuliano said.

"Bartolomeo. You know as well as I Eleanor came nowhere near my *festa*," Guid'Antonio said, sharply aware of the eyes of everyone taking their measure as they passed: Lorenzo and Giuliano, *the Medici boys,* in unadorned tunics, tired boots, and snug leggings, while he and Chancellor Bartolomeo Scala paraded past with the hems of their fine red cloaks fluttering around their heels.

"Bartolomeo, my friend, you're finding trouble where there is none," Lorenzo said, waving a friendly greeting to shopkeepers and vendors here and there. High above their heads blue banners painted with golden lions rampant and *fleurs-de-lis* representing the Golden Lion district of the San Giovanni quarter flew from iron poles jutting from balconies like long black tongues.

"She'll tell the world we're a town of poisoners," Bartolomeo said.

A frown darkened Lorenzo's features. "Eleanor knows naught about Guid'Antonio's dead cloth merchant. We read poetry and listened to music. When we gossiped, it was of other things. Anyway, how could she speak ill of us, when her father is not only the king of Naples, but the lord of violence? It is us she prefers."

"It is *you*," Giuliano said, with an affectionate cuff on his brother's arm.

"It is true she enjoyed her respite here." Lorenzo grinned.

My dead cloth merchant, Guid'Antonio thought. *There you are.*

They stepped from the center of the street, making way for a farm wagon loaded with baskets of fragrant peaches fresh from the country. The farmer smiled, calling, "*Mattina*, Giuliano! Your angelic face lifts my heart this morning, as always!"

"*Mattina*, Giusep'!" Giuliano caught the peach the man tossed him and pulled a silver penny from his scrip, offering it to him.

The farmer doffed his cap. "God bless you and keep you well."

"And you," Giuliano said, catching up with the other men.

Lorenzo inclined his head to Guid'Antonio. "I'm glad you're here. I'm sorry for the trouble in your house. Cesare seems a well-meaning boy—I'm sure he regrets this misadventure. What do you mean to do with him?"

Misadventure? Guid'Antonio blew out his breath. Perhaps the family should have let the town take a vote. "He's confined to the house for now," he said.

Bartolomeo snorted. "*Buona fortuna!* Everyone knows— well. Never mind."

"I won't," Guid'Antonio said.

Giuliano wiped peach juice from his mouth. "That little cherub isn't going to like having his wings clipped."

"I am still the boss," Guid'Antonio said. And laughed.

"Last fall I almost died from eating a toxic mushroom." Bartolomeo drew air deep into his chest, as if to convince himself he was not a ghost wafting south along Via Larga.

The others exchanged a quick, amused glance. How many times had they heard about Bartolomeo Scala's close brush with Thanatos? Last September, the former impoverished miller's son from Colle di Val d'Elsa in southwestern Tuscany, who now knew all the nooks and crannies in a town teeming with secrets, had won a hard-fought battle with death when he mistakenly ate a poisonous mushroom. Fortune had smiled on him, and on Lorenzo and Giuliano, too. Now forty-three-years of age, Bartolomeo had been the Medici family's personal conduit to City Hall since attaining the office of secretary of the Florentine government a decade ago. If he died, it would be no easy matter for the Medici political regime to arrange a replacement for him in Palazzo della Signoria. City Hall.

"Such dreary conversation," Giuliano said. "Death. Fatal accidents. All the more reason to celebrate life and give thanks while we may. We're alive, *Gentiluomini*, and we are Florence." They all smiled agreement.

A sound from the San Marco Church gardens and monastery on Guid'Antonio's left took his attention, and he turned to see a monk in the black and white robes of the Dominican order shuffling through the gate onto the street, breathing heavily, sweat dripping from his brow, a muddy trowel in one hand.

"*Buon giorno*, Brother Matteo!" Lorenzo said, hailing the monk with good cheer.

"And to you, as well!" Brother Matteo waved, his manner effusive and content.

Guid'Antonio's smile deepened. Why wouldn't Brother Matteo's raspberry-pink cheeks stretch almost to bursting and his eyes crinkle with gladness at the sight of the two young men whose family had rebuilt and restored San Marco, saving it from complete ruin? Within that holy place, paintings from Fra Angelico's hand enriched the monk's cells, the corridors, the cloister, and the chapter house. In the library a multitude of shelves housed priceless illuminated manuscripts. Guid'Antonio had gone there often to absorb the brilliantly painted parchment and papers. All this, a short distance from Palazzo Medici—directly ahead of them now, where the San Lorenzo marketplace and church lay just around the corner.

Beside him, Lorenzo's pace slowed, his hooded brown eyes settling with disapproval on the small figure of a man who had just emerged from the front gate of the Medici Palace. "What is that prick doing at my house?" Lorenzo said.

†

That prick was Francesco de' Pazzi, trailed by his brother, Guglielmo, Francesco bouncing on the balls of his feet as if he needed to piss on the corner of Via Larga and Via dei Gori, a true crossroads of sorts, with Florence Cathedral and the baptistery in view not too far up the street. Quietly, Giuliano said, "Lorenzo, we knew Francesco was in town. Remember, he is our kinsman now, given Guglielmo's marriage to our sister. We must treat him with respect."

"I don't like him," Lorenzo said.

Francesco de' Pazzi cocked his head, his pale blue eyes as round as coins as the foursome approached the gate. "Well, well, well. If it isn't Via Larga's golden lion and his little brother come home from bidding our visiting royalty farewell," he said.

Strained smiles and effusive greetings were exchanged all around.

"Chancellor Scala," Francesco said, shivering with amusement as he swept Bartolomeo up and down. Red robe, Red hose. "I heard in Rome you were elected one of our nine priors a few months ago. One of the highest ranking men in the land. For a while." Francesco snickered. The Nine Lord Priors served terms of eight weeks before new men took their place. This, in an effort to maintain a democratic government by preventing anyone from gaining too much power at any one time. *Ridiculous,* thought Guid'Antonio, *but there you go.*

Bartolomeo's solemn expression pulled into a scowl. "The instant my term expired, I donned this robe to wear each day as I have done for the past ten years as Chancellor of the Florentine Republic."

Francesco ignored the comment, addressing Guid'Antonio, instead: "If it isn't the leading saint of All Saints Street. Dottore Vespucci, whatever are you doing here?" As part of Princess Eleanor's handpicked farewell delegation, he meant.

Guid'Antonio looked straight into Francesco de' Pazzi, someone he knew as a volatile, combative young man with no love for the Medici family. Francesco's blond hair was lanky and long, his complexion deathly pale. Both he and his brother Guglielmo wore grey velvet tunics decorated with the Pazzi coat of arms the sculptor and painter Luca della Robbia had designed for their family chapel in Santa Croce: two scowling dolphins and five small crosses surrounding a garland of lush foliage, fruit, and even some small insects and reptiles. The latter images were very fitting, Guid'Antonio thought. "I was invited," he said.

"I might ask the same of you, Franceschino," Lorenzo said. "Why so far from the lie factory today?" *Roma.*

Francesco de' Pazzi's nostrils flared. "Little Francesco." Lorenzo's use of the diminutive form of his name was a sharp slap at the other man's small stature. Franceschino danced back from Lorenzo, raising his hands in an odd gesture of defense. "I do still call this home. My family has done for—oh, centuries. Is that reason enough for you?"

Two red patches blazed on Lorenzo's cheekbones. Before he could reply, Guglielmo de' Pazzi swooped in. "Lorenzo *mio*!" he said. "I brought Bianca here to visit Clarice. Bianca wanted to come, since Clarice isn't well. Your mother sent word she is in bed burning with fever." Bianca de' Medici, one of Lorenzo and Giuliano's three sisters, had been wed to Guglielmo de' Pazzi these last few years.

They all crossed themselves, silently praying for Lorenzo's wife, Clarice Orsini, who was expecting their third child, and also for themselves. In Florence—hell, everywhere—despite prayer and coral amulets to protect them and safeguard their newborns, many, many women died giving birth, along with their babies. "Thank you, Guglielmo," Lorenzo said.

Guglielmo swallowed a deep breath of air. "Of course! Meanwhile, we—my brother and I—are going to Santa Croce for a game of *calcio*—"

Lorenzo stared at his quivering brother-in-law for one brief moment before turning from him to Franceschino. "But you must admit you're seldom in our town."

Guid'Antonio squared his shoulders. Dark-robed clerks and notaries were hurrying back and forth through the Medici Palace gate, acknowledging with curious smiles the half-dozen men gathered there, the visitors' eyes all on Lorenzo de' Medici. Many were here to conduct business in the international office of the Medici banking empire on the palazzo's ground floor, if not hoping for the privilege of speaking with the family boss himself. A favor here, a favor there. It would not do for them to feel the winds of uncertainty and discontent whistling around the six men caught as if in a spider's web on Via Larga.

Before Guid'Antonio could speak, Guglielmo exclaimed, "My brother missed Easter, but Saint John's Day brought him home once more, praise God and all the saints."

Franceschino snapped a glance toward Florence Cathedral. "I ached for the Duomo." He fluttered his eyelashes, wispy and disturbingly pale. "For the length and breadth of Santa Maria del Fiore." He touched the sleeve of Giuliano's tunic. "For my beautiful, good friend."

Guid'Antonio marveled, listening to him. What a terrific liar Francesco de' Pazzi was! No wonder he had done so well down south, not only as manager of the Pazzi family branch bank in Rome, but also as manager of papal finances. Whatever the reason Francesco presently was in Florence, it was no secret he had left in the first place so he would not have to lay eyes on Lorenzo, whom he loathed. Why? The Pazzi family fortune equaled that of the Medici, or might even surpass it. At any rate, Franceschino was without question Lorenzo and Giuliano's foremost business rival, both in Italy and abroad. Guid'Antonio had long ago concluded Franceschino was not jealous of Lorenzo and Giuliano's money—he had no need to be—but of their birthright, through their father and grandfather, so that now in the eyes of Italy, even in some parts of the world, they and Florence were the same.

Lorenzo de' Medici was prince of this city.

Francesco de' Pazzi was not.

A sly grin curled the corners of Franceschino's lips. "Speaking of Saint John's Day—Dottore Vespucci, I hear I'm blessed to have survived it. Had I attended your *festa*, I might not be standing here—" Francesco performed his peculiar little dance, holding his fingers before him in the sign of the cross.

"A man died on Thursday," Guid'Antonio said. "I'm sorry to hear you take his death so lightly." *Moreover, you were not included,* he thought, but did not say.

"Lightly? Nay! As you point out, that cloth merchant is no longer in the world. I understand how you, more than most, might take that especially hard, since he was killed by your servant." Francesco snickered maddeningly.

Before Guid'Antonio could reply, Giuliano de' Medici said, "I was at the table until I left to dance with Simonetta. Our

Angelo took my place."

Arms akimbo, Franceschino said, "Angelo Poliziano? That hooked-nosed parasite? Praise God you're safe! It seems you and all our good dottore's guests—besides the unfortunate cloth merchant—escaped death by a hair! Life is fickle that way, yes?" He grinned like an imp.

"Angelo Poliziano is not only one of Italy's foremost scholars and poets, he is my friend," Lorenzo said. "Part and parcel with my family."

Franceschino spread his hands. "Perhaps he will write something entertaining about Dottore Vespucci's Death Cap."

Guglielmo de' Pazzi appeared about to weep. "We must be going. The game will be underway in Santa Croce."

Franceschino ignored him. "Dottore Vespucci, you're not long from Imola, yes? Count Riario told me in Rome how he found you there hot on the heels of your visit to Milan." He grinned.

†

An icy sheet of silence descended over Guid'Antonio, but only for a moment, the blink of an eye, nothing more, all his senses aware of the fleeting glance between his friends. If Girolamo Riario had told Little Francesco de' Pazzi about Guid'Antonio's encounter with him in northern Italy, there was no way in hell Riario had not told his uncle, the Pope, as well. Of course, Riario had promised Guid'Antonio he would do exactly that, and Guid'Antonio's companions knew it from the report he had made the moment he arrived home. *I know you because when friends in the Vatican speak of that upstart, Lorenzo de' Medici's, supporters, yours is the first name on their lips,* Riario had said. *They falter, mentioning your eyes. Such an unnatural, pale grey shade. Ghostly! Dark hair shot with silver, crimson cloak, and,* ecco qui, *here you are, magically, in northern Italy.*

Guid'Antonio sketched a vague gesture with one hand. "I'm surprised the count thought to mention me to you," he said.

Franceschino, plucking a loose thread from the cuff of his tunic, affected indifference. "He knows we're both sons of Florence. Incidentally, I've glimpsed your little dog at your heels while I've been in town. Guglielmo tells me the mayor of Imola sent him to you as a gift of friendship. *Orsetto*. A *Lagotto Romagnolo*. Such a pretty little truffle-hunter. You should take care, Dottore, lest he disappear."

Guid'Antonio remained very still. "What do you mean?"

Franceschino shrugged. "He is unusual in these parts and would fetch a good price on the market."

"If any man harms a hair on my dog's head, I will kill him," Guid'Antonio said.

Franceschino quivered. "Oh! Careful, you! You'll be accused of showing some emotion. It was lightly meant."

"Yet I am deadly serious," Guid'Antonio said.

Franceschino clapped his hands. "With that stony pronouncement, we'll be off to Santa Croce." Again, he touched Giuliano. "Come along! How entertaining to boast on our side the town's finest athlete." He smirked at Lorenzo: *You notice, I did not mention you.*

Do you think I care?

"Lorenzo," Giuliano said, "is there something you wish me to do? If not, I'd like to play *calcio* with Francesco and Guglielmo."

Guid'Antonio could almost see Lorenzo's mind churning. Like it or not, the Pazzi brothers were his and Giuliano's kinsmen by marriage. Giuliano de' Medici and Guglielmo de' Pazzi were close friends, often riding and hunting together in the countryside around Florence, singing, drinking wine late into the night at one or another of the Medici or Pazzi villas. Four years ago, along with several other men, Guglielmo had accompanied Lorenzo and Giuliano to Milan for the baptism of Duke Galeazzo Maria Sforza's firstborn son. What had their sister, Bianca de' Medici's, marriage to Guglielmo Pazzi been meant to do, if not ease tensions between the two families? Medici and Pazzi children and grandchildren down through the ages. *Now there,* Guid'Antonio thought, *is an interesting concept.*

"Of course. Enjoy yourself, Giuliano," Lorenzo said.

Giuliano hugged him. *"Grazie!"*

The threesome departed, Giuliano and Franceschino's arms linked around one another's waists, chatting amiably as they ambled along Via Larga in the direction of the Cathedral.

"Giuliano," Lorenzo called. "Take care on the field. Watch yourself."

Giuliano glanced over his shoulder. "I shall."

Bartolomeo Scala turned quickly toward Lorenzo. "Now Franceschino de' Pazzi and Girolamo Riario are friends? There's a disturbing discovery."

"Obviously, they are," Guid'Antonio said.

Lorenzo huffed. "I doubt they know the meaning of the word. Franceschino's like a fly buzzing around, looking for a pile of shit to land in."

"He found it," Guid'Antonio said. "Down south in Rome with Riario and the Pope. The Pazzi Bank manages Sixtus IV's money—it makes sense Franceschino encounters Riario in the Vatican, often, no doubt. Who knows what mischief they may get up to while there?"

"Some flies have a sharp sting," Bartolomeo Scala said.

"And I have tough skin," Lorenzo informed him.

"But why would Riario mention seeing me in Imola to Francesco de' Pazzi?" Guid'Antonio pressed. "And that he 'found' me there? That turn of phrase suggests to me Riario knew I was in Imola, perhaps came there for that very reason, and yet, with me he feigned surprise. I don't like it." As for

Orsetto—a muscle twitched in Guid'Antonio's jaw. He had meant what he said. Harm *Orsetto* and feel a dagger in your ear.

Lorenzo made a dismissive gesture. "As you say, business has thrown Pazzi and Riario onto the same twisted path."

"But—" Guid'Antonio started, thinking, *You are not listening to me—*

"Who knows what they find to moan about?" Lorenzo said. "Don't worry about your contract, Guid'Antonio *mio*. Milan is our friend now as always. We will have Imola, thanks to your efforts there. Perhaps the papers arrived this morning. Meanwhile, I have a mountain of correspondence to tend. King Louis wants an ambassador from Florence, as well as a new guard dog, not to mention—Guid'Antonio, will you go to Paris for me?"

"No," Guid'Antonio said, glancing at the same time down the street toward Giuliano and his companions, still arm-in-arm, laughing easily with one another. Following their progress, he felt a small, unpleasant sensation, pinpricks on his skin. A tall marble column dedicated to the memory of Saint Zenobius, the first bishop of Florence, stood near the baptistery in Piazza San Giovanni. Before turning left with Franceschino and Guglielmo toward Piazza Santa Croce, Giuliano brushed the column lightly with his fingers.

Guid'Antonio held his breath. Would the monument crowned with a cross burst into bloom with greenery and flowers? Centuries ago, a rotting tree had done so on that very spot. That miracle had happened one snowy winter morning when the casket transporting the saint's relics from San Lorenzo Church to Florence Cathedral brushed against the dead elm. While alive, Zenobius had resurrected dead people—did it not make sense his corpse could breathe life into a ruined tree?

Guid'Antonio listened to Bartolomeo and Lorenzo's farewells to one another with half an ear, watching Giuliano's figure dwindle as he entered the shadow of the Cathedral. Something dark stirred in Guid'Antonio then. Half-formed. Disturbing. In the years ahead, he would clinch his fists, questioning if things might have come to a different end, if only he had screamed, "Giuliano! Come back! Take my hand! Don't trust him!" But he didn't.

He didn't.

When he glanced down the street a second time, the cross atop the Saint Zenobius monument remained barren of fruit and flowers, and Giuliano de' Medici had disappeared.

$\mathcal{F}$IFTEEN

AUTOPSIA DEL CANE

Saturday afternoon, Guid'Antonio and Amerigo were in the *scrittoio* when Cesare skittered in from the garden. Face flushed deep pink, breathless, he slammed to a stop. "Dottore Guid'Antonio, *permesso*! I thought you never would come home today!"

Amerigo whipped around from the wall lined with pine cabinets. The letter opener he had been about to return to his leather satchel clattered to the floor. "What do you mean, rushing in like a demon? I thought you meant us harm!" Flustered, Amerigo retrieved the sharp blade.

"I had no choice; this is no time for polite entries. I have news!" Cesare said.

Guid'Antonio rubbed the bridge of his nose, a fatigued, busy man. The wooden trestle bench in the family office was hard as marble, the chamber close and dim, with only one small window high overhead. Beneath his tunic, sweat dribbled through the hair on his chest like a line of ants.

He locked his eyes on Cesare Ridolfi. "You are supposed to

be in your room, *Signore*, not here, and certainly not in the alley last night."

"You heard me?"

"I hear everything."

The boy shook his head. "No matter. The finger of fate pushed me into the kitchen for a midnight repast, then beckoned me into the alley."

Amerigo snorted, arranging his satchel across his body. "You do have a flair for the dramatic."

"Thank you." Cesare edged toward the trestle. "Dottore Guid'Antonio, what I also have is proof. *Evidence*."

Guid'Antonio sprinkled sand on the numbers he had entered in the thick ledger of accounts. Ten florins for the *festa* musicians? Sweet Lord. "Proof of what?" he said.

Cesare leaned in: "Orlando Niccolini's death was no accident. Our cloth merchant was murdered!"

Guid'Antonio slammed his fist on the table. The ink bottle jumped. Cesare jumped. *Orsetto*, curled at Guid'Antonio's feet, sat up, startled.

"We have danced this dance!" Guid'Antonio roared. "You made a grievous error! Accept your guilt and move on! You've been excused from killing a man, escaped execution by Palla Palmieri's kindness toward our house." With a lightning gesture of his hand, he dismissed the boy. "Return to your room! We're working."

"But not much longer," Amerigo said. "I have—"

Cesare interrupted him. "Excused? For something I didn't do! I have been humiliated in the eyes of Florence, my honor impugned! I have nothing but what you give me, Dottore—foremost, a home with my mother and uncle and my service to you. What if on Saint John's Day I had killed you? No! I accept the fact I served Ser Niccolini, but I never will believe I purchased deadly mushrooms! Death Cap was not put in that salad by my hand, and I can prove it, but you won't help me." He wept.

Amerigo pursed his lips, his eyes on Guid'Antonio, who was thinking, *God help me.* For all Cesare's pompous airs and graces, until Thursday, he had been a steady, if fragile, boy, one bereft of family, other than Domenica and Gaspare. And Guid'Antonio. His head throbbed. He wanted Orlando Niccolini's death buried and forgotten, along with Niccolini the day after tomorrow. He wanted to rise and move forward, not take a step back. "What proof?" he said.

Cesare swiped the tears from his eyes. "There is a dead dog in our alley. When I went to the kitchen during the night, my nose caught the smell of something foul. The sweet, stinking smell of death! I searched a pile of rags and found the dog there."

Amerigo grunted lightly. "Dead dogs abound in Florence."

"Sadly, too! Dottore Guid'Antonio, this is the same ginger dog begging at your table Thursday afternoon! She was hungry, as always, but she was not sick. No! She was as healthy on that day as on any other."

A ripple of unease moved through Guid'Antonio. The little dead dog in the alley was the dog Orlando Niccolini had kicked with his boot? "And now she's dead," Guid'Antonio said. "Does it occur to you that you may be tiptoeing in the wrong direction, Cesare Ridolfi?"

"No."

Guid'Antonio closed the ledger. "She was hungry as always, you say. You knew this animal?" he said.

"Yes. From our kitchen scraps, she has been well fed."

"From your hand, you mean."

"Yes! She has dropped by our house often, importuning for food. She attended our *festa*. And then last night, I found her in the alley, stiff as a pine board." Cesare placed his hand over his heart, his expression imploring. "Come see, that is all I ask. If you disagree evil's afoot, I'll never mention my innocence again. I swear."

"Given those terms, perhaps you should accept his offer," Amerigo said, stretching and yawning.

"Have you moved the dog's body?" Guid'Antonio asked.

Cesare swiped at the air. "Am I a fool? I know better than to touch anything at the scene of a crime, having watched you work since the moment I was born."

The trestle bench screeched as Guid'Antonio pushed back. "Show me."

"*Grazie, grazie, grazie!*"

"Don't overdo it." Guid'Antonio locked the ledger in the cabinet, slipped his keys into the scrip at his belt, and scooped *Orsetto* into his arms.

"I could take a look and save you the trouble," Amerigo said.

Cesare's shoulders slumped.

"No," Guid'Antonio replied. "I want you to return to Santa Croce."

Cesare perked up.

Amerigo's hands went to his hips. "But I was there yesterday morning."

"Yes, but I want to know why Jacopo Caretto's granddaughter lived with him. Are both her parents dead? Probably. Is there—was there—no sister or aunt, no female to take her in? Also, ask around about the monk watching us in Piazza della Signoria yesterday morning. He fled toward the river. Begin with the taverns and inns around there. He ran for a reason. Who is he? Where is he from? Here or elsewhere?"

Amerigo squeezed his eyes in irritation. "When I wanted to pursue him, you called me back. You said—"

"I know what I said. That was then. This is now. Why was he lurking in the shadows? I don't like secrets. Cesare, let's go. *Arrivederci*, Amerigo. You've a busy afternoon ahead."

That was before the troubled feeling he had experienced when Giuliano de' Medici vanished in the shadow of the dome this morning. A premonition of dark days ahead, as vague and as insubstantial as a spider's silken web.

✝

In the kitchen, Guid'Antonio placed *Orsetto* in his padded basket near the alley door, noting with consternation that the door to the alley was ajar. From the palace, that narrow lane led to byways that were narrow, dark, and soggy with damp. He glanced at the kitchen girl, Livia, who was frying trout in an iron skillet on the hearth. Beside Livia on the trestle a bucket contained more fish, alongside straw baskets piled with lemons and loaves of bread scented with the fragrance of rosemary and black olives, fresh from one of the market ovens.

Cesare raised his brow, glancing from the alley door to the girl, and then to Guid'Antonio. Would he leave the kitchen vulnerable to strangers upon returning from market as, apparently, Livia recently had done? No.

"Livia," Guid'Antonio said.

Wide-eyed, twisting her hands in her oil-splattered apron, timorously the girl said, "Yes, Dottore?"

She feared him, the master of the house. He stepped back. "You have been to market. Did you return via the alley door?"

She sniffed and wiped her finger across her nose. "Yes, Dottore."

"Was it bolted? Who let you in?"

"Gaspare, but he has gone now to—" She hesitated. "To do something or other."

"Bolt it behind you from now on," Guid'Antonio said. "I'm serious, Livia. Do you understand? Anyway, it would be safer for you to come and go through the garden."

"Yes, Dottore."

With renewed urgency, Cesare said, "Dottore Guid'Antonio, *andiamo*."

Turning to go outside with Cesare Ridolfi, Guid'Antonio glimpsed *Orsetto's* golden eyes peeping at him from the rim of the small wicker basket. Smiling, Guid'Antonio closed the door and stepped into the alley, where a horrible stench hit him with such force, he gagged.

†

He crouched down. Beneath a pile of rubbish and rags lay the dog who had attended his *festa*, her corpse beneath his fingers stiff, her collar—that ragged brown string—loose around her neck. Once, she had belonged to someone, whether for good or for ill. He smothered his nose with his hand. The stink was sickening, the rags, the decaying dog, near the kitchen door. How was it Livia had not smelled the dead animal when she returned from market? He blew out a long breath. About herself Livia wore the aura of garlic, lemons, and fish.

Eyes narrowed on the dog, he watched Orlando Niccolini kick her, hard. He listened to Amerigo reprimand the merchant. He saw Niccolini fall face down in his mushroom salad, dead. And now this dog had come to this ignoble end. Odd, at best. And sad.

"What now?" Cesare said.

Guid'Antonio stood. "Fetch a blanket. Bundle her in it and take her to our hospital. On the way say nothing to anyone. Ask Maestra Francesca to perform an autopsy and determine the cause of death. Explain this dog was at my *festa*, and so on."

Cesare's mouth dropped open. "An autopsy on a *dog*? That's bold! What an excellent idea!"

"If she will," Guid'Antonio said. Francesca could say "No" to this peculiar request. He would not blame her, if she did. "If she demurs—" He tugged his ear. What then?

"She won't." An angelic smile lit Cesare's face. "Not when

I say this comes from you, her favorite."

"Blanket *now*!" Guid'Antonio said. "If *Orsetto* is still in the kitchen don't let him slip by you as you go in. He would be off like a shot past me to Siena, or God only knows where."

Cesare drew himself up. "I never would make such a mistake. Where will you be?" he asked.

"Out here waiting for you to return with a blanket. And then in All Saints on my knees praying for the Virgin Mary to restore my sanity."

Cesare shifted uneasily on his feet. "Are you sure you will be all right here?"

"Why wouldn't I be?" Guid'Antonio snapped. "Go now. Go."

†

Drawing sweet, foul air into his lungs and chest, he waited for Cesare to return with the blanket to collect the dog, alive to the prickling sensation someone was watching him. Removing his handkerchief from his pocket, he held the fabric to his nose, feigning indifference while straining to hear the sound of breathing somewhere near.

The alley remained quiet, fetid, and sad.

Forcing himself to relax, he craned his neck. High above him overhanging roofs wavered toward one another, leaving only a thin ribbon of sky overhead. The stone walls of the buildings alongside him crept toward him, squeezing him in. Swaying slightly, he braced his hands against them. *I am in the lane behind my house*, he told himself. *Beneath my feet the world is solid and whole.*

Carefully, he withdrew first one hand and then the other, fighting the sickness gnawing his gut until, gradually, the nausea washing over him eased. He gulped air, rank as it was, knowing better than to move too quickly. Stooped, still feeling trapped, he considered that what Maestra Francesca Vernacci would do was think him a fool. Today, finally, she would have proof. But if God was kind, Guid'Antonio would have proof, too. Proof the ginger dog had died not from mushroom poisoning, but from Orlando Niccolini's brutal kick in the stomach.

Proof of "Death by Cesare Ridolfi."

†

"And?" Guid'Antonio said.

"She agreed."

Amazing. "*Bene.* Good," he said.

†

He was about to retire to his *studiolo* later that evening when he caught a whisper of footsteps beyond his apartment door. A soft knock, a hushed voice, "Dottore—?"

He glanced at Maria, who was sleeping quietly with her back to the room. "Shhh, *Orsetto*." Lightly, he slipped across the floor and released the latch, his dagger ready in his hand.

One of the kitchen boys, Poggio Bernini, stood before him in the hall, his countenance ghostly in the yellow light of the torch in his hand. The boy recoiled, his eyes fastened on the knife. Poggio had dressed with such haste, he had his thin tunic on inside out, the seams showing, his hair tangled around his head. *Orsetto* backed up on the mattress, a warning rumbling in his throat.

"Shhh," Guid'Antonio said. The dog curled down on the sheets, watching him closely. "Poggio—" Guid'Antonio eased into the hall, lowering his weapon. "What's wrong?"

"I heard someone at the garden gate," whispered the boy.

"I was asleep, but lightly, and leaped from bed. It was the devil, I supposed! But then he spoke. Not the devil, praise God, but a messenger from Palazzo Medici. The fellow loomed over me and asked if you were home." Poggio shivered, still frightened by the stranger's appearance in the dead of night.

"—And?" Guid'Antonio said.

"I asked him how was I to know your whereabouts, whether daylight or dark, but he thrust a letter at me and swore if I didn't deliver it to you immediately, Lorenzo de' Medici himself would box my ears. So—here I am."

Guid'Antonio's name on the missive was a deep scrawl forged with thick black ink, as if Lorenzo had written it with his fist clenched. This was not the usual delicate script taught Lorenzo by the finest tutors in Italy. Guid'Antonio turned over the folded parchment. An explosion of red wax embossed with a *fleur-de-lis* bled raggedly onto the page.

Trouble.

"Is the messenger waiting?" Guid'Antonio asked.

"Nay. But I'm to say that while this is a matter of extreme urgency, Lorenzo cannot discuss it with you until Monday. He'll be in Ognissanti that morning for the funeral of the cloth merchant, Nicco—Nicco—"

"Orlando Niccolini."

"Yes! Our Lorenzo's wife is ailing, 'else he would see you now at Palazzo Medici."

Now? Good Christ. Behind Guid'Antonio the moon cast a wash of silver light through the chamber windows; the rising sun was a long way off. "Then goodnight and thank you," he said. "Poggio. I'm sure you understand none of this is grist for the mill."

The boy drew up, indignant. "Of course not! I serve this house. I serve *you*. Cesare Ridolfi is not the only one who does, no matter what he believes. *Buona notte.*" Poggio bowed, holding the torch aloft as he padded down the dark hallway.

At the top of the steps, he touched the wall and vanished in a flare of yellow light.

Guid'Antonio closed and bolted the chamber door. *Extremely urgent*, Lorenzo's messenger had said. Outside the windows, a cat yowled. Maria stirred lightly, and *Orsetto* jumped from the bed. Guid'Antonio caught his breath before ghosting into the *studiolo* with the puppy traipsing at his heels. By touch he found the candle on his desk, set it aflame, and with one quick slice of his dagger, he broke Lorenzo de' Medici's crimson seal.

Sixteen

DEVIL'S DANCE
BEFORE DAWN SUNDAY, 27TH JUNE 1473

Sometime after midnight, Lorenzo had made his signature with such force, the ink had seeped through the parchment, speckling the document with black fluid: *"A dì XXVII di giugno 1473, Il Tuo Lorenzo."*
Your Lorenzo.
There was that, at least.
Hands sweating, heart pounding hard, Guid'Antonio added Lorenzo's hastily scribbled note to his letter chest, then locked the chest with the key he slipped into the leather pouch at his waist. *Orsetto*, sprawled across his feet, watched sleepily for a moment as Guid'Antonio unlatched his journal and dipped his pen, writing with shaky fingers.

> *Catastrophic news tonight. Lorenzo has heard from his uncle Giovanni Tornabuoni, manager of the Medici bank in Rome and Depositor General of the Apostolic Chamber, that instead of selling Imola to us, Duke*

Galeazzo Maria Sforza has tucked his tail and run to Pope Sixtus IV, agreeing to sell the town to him, instead. This on the heels of my negotiations with Sforza last spring, all now gone to hell, leaving me with a profound feeling of sickness in my gut. Adding insult to injury, whereas we had agreed to pay Sforza a whopping 100,000 florins, the Pope is paying the duke less than half that amount. Good God, why would Sforza agree to such as this? Also, the Pope informed Tornabuoni he expects a loan from Lorenzo for the required 40,000 florins. Unbelievable!

Guid'Antonio's jaw tightened.

For my government this Judas kiss means not only the forfeit of an important land boundary but also the possible loss of vital trade routes, including those with access to the Mediterranean lands east of Italy. For L. de' Medici and me it is a cut to the bone. For him: Florence and Milan—the Medici and Sforza families—have been friends since the days of his and Galeazzo Maria Sforza's grandfathers. When Lorenzo was twenty, he traveled to Milan to stand as godfather to Sforza's first born son. Now Sforza is willing not only to embarrass Lorenzo in the eyes of all Italy, but also to rip a hole in the fragile web of Italian politics. Alliances here shift constantly. They just did.

For me: my ambassadorship, my mission to Milan and Imola, was a tremendous honor, placing me securely in the circle around the Medici family. I have prayed for more: more respect, more honor, more prestige. I believe it is true as Ermolao Barbaro wrote, "The interests of the State and the individual are one and the same." Now, not only Lorenzo, but I, too, have been betrayed by that fool, Duke Galeazzo Maria Sforza, who, since the death of his father, rules Milan. Why? I do not like being in the dark. Not about this, not about anything.

Sensing Guid'Antonio's disquiet, *Orsetto* licked Guid'Antonio's bare toes, quivering and sighing before settling back down. *My good boy,* thought Guid'Antonio, bending to pat the puppy on the head. *Sleep and dream of chasing rabbits in sunny, far off fields, so long as when you're awake, you remain with me.*

When had he fallen in love with this little comet of crimped, reddish-brown fur whose birthplace was northeast Italy? Guid'Antonio relinquished a smile. The answer was easy: from the moment the puppy had arrived in a crate from Imola, a gift from the mayor there.

He had not been smiling following his disturbing encounter with Girolamo Riario in the middle of the town square that frosty spring morning. After Riario had departed with his men-at-arms, his shrill laughter bouncing off the stones all around the piazza, Guid'Antonio had ridden hard to tell Lorenzo—City Hall—all that had transpired. Stopping only once for a fresh horse, he had galloped into the night past vineyards, rolling hills, and thrashing plane trees, past reeds twisted into makeshift crosses, then placed in fields by farmers as charms against evil. Devils and demons rode on the wind, bent on stealing souls, coming in the guise of hounds, stooped old women, and conniving cats. Guid'Antonio believed none of this. What he believed, what he *understood*, was how ambitious, "new men" bent on gain—men like Girolamo Riario and Pope Sixtus IV—could not and would not tolerate being thwarted by anyone, let alone a Florentine lawyer who was in the eyes of Italy a new man himself, given his family history harked back only a century. Well. Perhaps a few decades more. What he could not *guess* was how furious Sixtus would be when he discovered the extent of Guid'Antonio Vespucci's part in the plot to deprive him of a town he wanted for his family. What he did not *like* as he traveled south down Via Emilia toward Florence was the unsettling feeling something had shifted in Imola's town square that blustery spring day, had moved toward malevolence and death.

In the hours just before morning, he had ridden his horse into a storm. Lightning flashed, and thunder rumbled nearby. "*Felice.* You're safe in my hands," he had whispered, urging the skittish mare gently along in the rain. Slowly, the storm had rolled away, giving way to mist in the hills and vales of Tuscany, and dawn had melted into the hard, white light of day. As they crested a rise, he lowered the hood of his rain cloak, soothed by the gathering warmth of the sun. Below him, luminous and quiet, lay a walled city of fifty-thousand souls whose river adorned her like a silver bracelet. His eyes feasted on Santa Maria del Fiore, Saint Mary of the Flowers, the Cathedral crowned with Brunelleschi's magnificent red brick dome, his heart rising with joy.

Florence.

Home.

Felice tossed her head, shoulder muscles straining, hooves dancing, as if sensing contentment and rest not far down the road. Not so, Guid'Antonio.

I won't forget you, Dottore.

Kneeing the horse into a gallop, Guid'Antonio had ridden swiftly into the unknown.

†

The edge of a headache flirted across the base of Guid'Antonio's skull. Still, he continued writing in his *ricordo*:

> *I am absolutely certain Franceschino de' Pazzi knew yesterday on Via Larga that Imola has been stolen from us by Rome. Behind his hand, he was laughing at me, at Lorenzo. So warped by jealousy, he welcomes any loss for*

the Medici family, for it is Lorenzo who has led the charge to acquire Imola, no matter the ultimate cost to our Republic from the hands of Pope Sixtus IV.

What had Lorenzo said when Guid'Antonio had told him about his encounter with Riario? "Sing and it shall pass. Milan would never betray us to Rome."

Wrong, Lorenzo! Because of Imola, Rome and Florence were poised for a devil's dance; never had Guid'Antonio felt anything with such conviction in his bones.

Deeply troubled in spirit, he signed his journal, letting the leaves sigh through his fingers to the beginning, where the title page spoke a brief tale.

> This is the Second Book of my Life, Guido Antonio Vespucci, son of Giovanni di Simone Vespucci and of Antonia Ugolini, in which I shall continue writing all my personal records. In the name of God and his virgin mother, Mary, may this second book, as the first, be to their honor and to the honor of my family. This second volume begun 5 June In the Year of Our Lord 1466.

Fourteen sixty-six seemed a lifetime ago, although it was just seven years in the past, on the occasion of Guid'Antonio's thirtieth birthday. A lot had happened in these pages.

Sifting forward:

> I record how on the 5th day of January, 1469, on the 9th hour, my Taddea Canigiani passed from this life, to me so joyous and happy these past four years and six months. May God have received her soul, as I certainly believe because of her kindness and the great honesty and the grace of her ways. She was 20-years-old. I buried her in our tomb in All Saints with our dead babe, Simone, in her arms.

Guid'Antonio swallowed hard over the lump in his throat. A little over three years ago, beside the word *babe*, he had drawn a cross, a quick, insubstantial shadow. Now he wondered if he ever would open his journal and pen the words,

Book Three, in which I shall continue writing all my personal records. In the name of God and his virgin mother, Mary, may this third book, as the first and second, be to their honor and to the honor of my family.
Praise God & Saint Margaret,
I have a baby boy.
I have a daughter.

Seventeen

SATAN'S HOOVES
SUNDAY MORNING, 27TH JUNE 1473

Abbot Roberto Ughi touched his finger to his forehead and his heart, then to one shoulder, and the other. "Go in peace," he intoned, casting his frosty blue gaze over the All Saints Church congregation. All, all were guilty of something wicked on this suffocating Sunday morning, the abbot's narrow look said.

Rivulets of sweat dribbled down Guid'Antonio's back. *Peace?* Lorenzo de' Medici's midnight note regarding Galeazzo Maria Sforza's unexplained betrayal of them, of their homeland, had Guid'Antonio in knots. It was a long while until tomorrow morning, when, apparently, Lorenzo hoped his wife, Clarice, would be out of danger and Lorenzo could address the situation in person. Which left Guid'Antonio wondering who else had received a note from Lorenzo in the dead of night. He shook himself, attempting to free his mind from wandering.

"*Andiamo*, Antonio," he said, addressing the nephew standing in the church at his right shoulder. "Let's go."

Yes: rather than Amerigo, it was Amerigo's twenty-two-year-old brother, Antonio Vespucci, who was with Guid'Antonio this morning. Instead of doing as Guid'Antonio had asked him to do yesterday afternoon, willful Amerigo had returned to Santa Croce to inquire into the murdered girl, Chiara Caretto's, family situation, but then he had taken it upon himself *not* to investigate the monk whose fearsome black eyes had watched them with such sizzling hatred in Piazza della Signoria—at least not immediately. Why? Because, as Amerigo had explained in a scribbled note he left in the Vespucci kitchen, he, Giuliano de' Medici, and Guglielmo de' Pazzi were riding to Fiesole for one of Marsilio Ficino's popular Saturday evening lectures on Plato.

The three would return to Florence sometime Sunday. Today.

Guid'Antonio growled down in his throat. This evening he and Amerigo would meet at the Red Lion tavern for supper, at which time they would discuss the past week's events, as was their habit. Burning with anger, he thought, *Discuss events is the least I will do when I see you this evening, my wayward young nephew.* He did not like being disobeyed by Amerigo, whom he paid handsomely as his secretary and assistant. He did not like being ignored. He did not like people doing things by halves.

†

Before the miraculous old painting of the *Virgin Mary of Santa Maria Impruneta* propped on the altar, he paused with Antonio to make the sign of the cross. Early last week the painting had been carried in a winding parade from the village of Impruneta and placed here for the Saint John's Day celebrations. Kneeling before the image of the Blessed Virgin Mary, after lighting candles the people of Florence had prayed for bountiful fruit and grain, for good health for them and their children, and for peace, rather than war. Christ's Mother had granted their prayers in the past; perhaps she would do so again.

But it was Giotto's Crucifix in Ognissanti that offered Guid'Antonio hope. *Pray to that,* he thought, his eyes fixed on the cross suspended in the air in the chapel to the left of the transept. That flat, painted crucifix was taller than most men—twice over, in fact. In the shadows of All Saints Church, the gilt decoration shone like gold, illuminating the high, vast space as if the sun were shining upon Christ's flushed lips and Mary's sapphire robes. Even the wrinkles around the Virgin's eyes and mouth had been tenderly rendered by Giotto's brush in this, his tribute to Christ's crucifixion as a human triumph, with the image of Him risen painted above the dying man on the cross.

Subdued and hopeful, Guid'Antonio pressed toward the church front through a sea of sword-makers, welders, masons, and bow-makers, breathing in the thick stew of human sweat, incense, and spent candle wax. A curtain gathered along a rope divided the length of the sanctuary: during Mass men stood on one side, women and children on the other. From beyond the drapery, beneath a chorus of crying babies, came the sound of feminine voices, vendors, embroiderers, and slaves in simply-cut, calf-length shifts dyed a simple light blue or warm white, side-by-side with prostitutes wearing green cowls with bells on their heads, wealthy girls and young wives like Maria in heavy, hooded cloaks.

☦

Outside in Piazza Ognissanti, the world shone. Guid'Antonio shaded his eyes. In the middle distance, the Arno's surface, flat for the lack of a breeze, appeared shiny and hard, like a gold coin. "Antonio. Do you see Maria and your mother?"

Antonio Vespucci swiped beads of sweat from his forehead. "They're attempting to brush past our almoner, butter ball that he is. Though I believe my mother could match Brother Bellincioni in girth. Fair warning, Uncle Guido. She has been in a particularly foul mood since the death of the cloth merchant. She is embarrassed for the family."

"Who isn't?" Guid'Antonio said. "Maria!" He waved.

The two women hurried into the piazza, Maria blowing a stray wisp of hair from her cheek. "*Buongiorno di nuovo*, good morning once more, my love," she said, smiling.

"It's hot as Satan's hooves out here," Elisabetta Vespucci fussed, tilting her double chin toward Antonio, who dutifully kissed his mother's cheek. "Domenica could roast a chicken on these stones."

"Pray she has done so in our kitchen," Antonio said. "I'm starving."

Irritably, his mother said, "When are you not? You're like your brother, Amerigo, who could eat a horse raw." Scowling, she added, "Where is he this morning?"

Guid'Antonio's mouth folded down. "In Fiesole with Giuliano de' Medici and Guglielmo de' Pazzi," he said.

Without a break, Elisabetta spun on her heel, motioning, at the same time, for them to accompany her down the borgo toward home. "*Sprigati! Andiamo!*" Hurry up!

"Dottore Guid'Antonio!" a familiar voice called.

He glanced over his shoulder. Behind him in the piazza, Dottore Filippo Vernacci waved an urgent greeting. Maestra Francesca Vernacci was with her father, her hood pushed from her face, her demeanor grave. Guid'Antonio waited, his heart slowing as Francesca and Filippo made a path across the crowded square toward him and his family.

Elisabetta's face sharpened. "What could be so important those two would dare delay us in the street?"

"Mama, I wager we'll soon find out," Antonio said.

She snorted her displeasure. "Maria! Come along! Surely we may walk the short distance home alone."

Maria's black-eyed gaze slid from Guid'Antonio to the frail man and tall, somber woman in a plain white cloak approaching with the summer heat shimmering all around. "I'll wait here." She edged closer to Guid'Antonio, so they touched shoulders.

In a rush, Dottore Filippo Vernacci said, "Good morning, forgive me. Us. But—" Seized by a fit of coughing, Filippo tugged a crumpled handkerchief from his cloak and covered his mouth, his eyes red, with dark circles beneath.

Deeply concerned for him, Guid'Antonio said, "Filippo, take your time, please."

Elisabetta tapped her foot on the pavement. "Surely this— this *whatever it is* may be addressed later."

"Father," Francesca said, her voice strained. "We should go. Leave this—"

Brusquely, he waved her away. "Let me breathe."

People were watching.

Francesca's glance shifted from her father, and Guid'Antonio's eyes unexpectedly met hers. "It is I who must speak with you, Guid'Antonio," Francesca said. "That is—Dottore," she amended hastily, her face flushing red. "Not here in the square. In the surgery."

The dog?

Yes.

The autopsy, thought Guid'Antonio with a deep intake of breath. Now, what?

Maria stiffened, cutting her eyes at Francesca Vernacci, this bold, beautiful woman up close, a woman who addressed her husband with easy intimacy, then blushed crimson, understanding her mistake and realizing she could not retrieve it. Too late!

"Now, Maestra Francesca?" Guid'Antonio said. Around them, the atmosphere became expectant and still.

"Yes."

Guid'Antonio glanced at Maria, who made a small, wounded noise and turned away from him, her hood shadowing her face. He hesitated. "I'll be with you shortly," he said, nodding to Filippo and Francesca, taking Maria gently by the arm.

†

"Shameless! Why you keep a connection with that woman is beyond me!"

Elisabetta Vespucci's mantle blew around her like an ill wind as she sailed before her companions along Borg'Ognissanti, glancing over her shoulder at Guid'Antonio, her face blotchy with heat, her eyes accusing. "Allowing her to—" Elisabetta waved her arms and bumped into a flower cart, almost toppling it. "To *exert* herself in *our* hospital, defying propriety and all expectations of—" She paused for breath. *"Womanhood."*

Elisabetta Vespucci was only two years older than Guid'Antonio, but what a dried-up old dragon she seemed! Not yet forty, and the mother of five sons. Not quite able to dampen the ill will he felt for this judgmental, spiteful woman, he said, "I'm certain it is. Beyond you, I mean."

"Not entirely," she retorted smartly through gritted teeth. "I know more than you think."

Measuring each word carefully, he murmured, "Mona Elisabetta, what are you saying?"

She pulled a face, her eyes glinting with malice. "Rather than in our hospital that witch should live in a shanty in Santo Spirito and cast stones! Instead of the white coif she wears on her head, she should wear bells!"

Guid'Antonio had had enough of this. "Mona Elisabetta—"

Antonio gasped. "Mama! Take care what you're saying! The implication Maestra Francesca is a whore and a witch—and, anyway, people are listening." He flicked his eyes toward Guid'Antonio, two red spots of color flaring on his cheeks.

Maria kept her gaze pinned ahead. "Mona Elisabetta," Guid'Antonio said, blazing with anger, his mind screaming at him not to engage. "Francesca Vernacci is neither whore nor witch. In fact, if I had to assign—"

A torrent of words poured from Antonio's lips. "Mama, Maestra Vernacci is not a woman, she's—she's different." Palazzo Vespucci lay just ahead. By the garden gate, Antonio stepped aside, waiting for the family to enter before sliding home the bolt. "I would say God has put her where He means her to be."

At the water fountain Elisabetta whirled and flipped back her hood. "God and Guid'Antonio!" she hissed. "Different? She is unnatural, you mean! If her father couldn't buy her a husband, he should have bought her a nun's habit, instead!"

She did not want a husband. She did not want me. "Mona Elisabetta, Francesca—Maestra Vernacci—is the only female physician in Florence," Guid'Antonio said. "My great-grandfather paid for the construction of our hospital, and if I want to allow her to work alongside her father within those walls, then that is how it shall be."

"And isn't he the ghost of himself these days?" Elisabetta said. "What will happen when he finally coughs himself to death, leaving both his daughter and our hospital bereft? It will be the nunnery, or worse, for her then." She leaned slightly toward Guid'Antonio: "Since under no circumstances may she remain there, a woman alone."

"Of course she can't, Mama," Antonio said. "Even to think it—" He laughed lightly. "Have you gone off your head?"

Elisabetta slapped at him. "Your uncle Guid'Antonio is capable of everything and nothing, as he demonstrates time and time again! Watch your tone with me, young man! By the Virgin, your father will hear of this!"

"Both Nastagio and Mary will agree with me," Antonio muttered beneath his breath.

"If I were either of you," Guid'Antonio said, his words clipped, "I would take care where my tongue leads me."

Elisabetta looked startled, then deflated. "Men," she said, but with less vigor than before. "I'm weary. I'm hungry. I want Domenica's broth and a long nap."

Antonio accompanied his mother to the kitchen, flicking back an apologetic glance. *I'm sorry.*

Guid'Antonio drew a steadying breath, turning to his wife. "Ignore her, Maria. Please. I don't know what she wants from me."

"If that woman had beckoned you with one finger, you would have gone," Maria said, her voice bereaved.

That woman, again, again, and again. "Maria," Guid'Antonio said. "Asking me to come to the hospital has to do with a case. Or rather a development. I don't know how, but I do know it is important. Else, she never would beckon me. Who would? Except you. And immediately, I would follow."

His wife's eyes flickered uncertainly. She was considering his words, deciding how to feel, how to react, how much to show him. "The cloth merchant?"

"I'm certain of it. Yes."

Maria nodded, still clearly unappeased when it came to the matter of Maestra Francesca Vernacci. "Elisabetta Vespucci is a difficult woman," she said. "And it isn't what she wants, it's what she fears."

"From me?" He floundered, a man capable of everything and nothing.

"She's afraid you will falter, and we will lose everything. This week, it's Cesare." She gestured helplessly. "I don't know."

"*Cara*, you don't need to know," he said.

He ran his finger along the tender hollow of Maria's neck, his lovely young wife, standing beside him on this sweltering Sunday morning. "I have to go," he said. She lifted her chin dutifully, and he removed her cloak, placing the heavy bundle in her arms.

"You'll come home straight from the hospital?" she said, searching his eyes, hers filled with questions and a trace of fear.

Where else would he go? Today was Sunday. "Yes," he said. "And later to the Red Lion to meet Amerigo, as always."

Maria clapped her hands. "Good! I'll begin packing our things for Peretola, so we can leave immediately after Orlando Niccolini's funeral tomorrow morning." She closed her eyes for a moment. "A week alone with you. Heaven, Guid'Antonio."

Four days, he thought. And then, court, where he would stand before the magistrates in the case of Jacopo Caretto and his granddaughter. "I love you, Maria," he said.

She smiled fetchingly. "Then go. And take this with you." She cupped his face in her hands and roughly drew him down, kissing him deeply on the lips, one hand leading his to the fullness of her breasts. "When you return, I'll be upstairs, waiting," she said, slipping her tongue into his mouth.

†

Guid'Antonio was at the garden gate, calming his mind and his heart, when he sensed a nearby presence. "*Mattina*, Dottore Guid'Antonio! I am ready to go!"

Poof! And in a twinkling the imp was here. "Cesare," Guid'Antonio said. "How do you always know—how are you *always*—oh, never mind." By now probably half of Florence knew he was on his way to his hospital for the results of a dog autopsy.

"So strong is the connection I feel to you," Cesare replied, his hand on the latch.

Guid'Antonio pulled him back by the sleeve. "You are venturing no farther than the walls of this garden until I say so, *Signore. Mi capisci?*"

Cesare tapped his foot in the grass. "If you don't want to be seen with this criminal, we can slip down the back alley. We can—"

"We are slipping *nowhere.*"

"*I* found the dog," Cesare answered, his gaze unflinching, his eyes a darker violet than the foxglove growing in the fields. "*I* took her to the hospital and, withstanding Maestra Francesca's stony gaze, obtained this examination. This is my life! As one accused of murder, this is my right."

"As the guilty party in the death of Orlando Niccolini, you have no rights, *Signore.*"

Cesare opened the gate. "Come along. Trust me."

Eighteen

CANNELLA

The ginger dog lay on the stone trestle, her belly sliced open and mended with thread. Gently, Francesca Vernacci lowered a sheet over the dog, then washed her hands with soap and dried them briskly with a towel before turning to Guid'Antonio. Her green gaze flickered, and then her expression smoothed. "Death Cap," she said. "This poor dog died from mushroom poisoning, much like Orlando Niccolini."

Guid'Antonio felt as if he had been hollowed out by one of Francesca's steel blades, and the air seemed too thick to breathe. *Much like.* "What do you mean?" he said.

"I know!" Cesare interrupted, socking his palm with his fist. "This dog was murdered in cold blood, like that man at our table! But who would want to harm her? Especially in such a cruel way?" He shook his head sorrowfully. "As much as this wounds me, I cannot entirely mourn her death, since it proves my innocence."

Guid'Antonio rubbed his temples, a dull ache beginning to form. Glancing away from Francesca, he said, "Cesare. What roundabout logic could possibly lead you there?"

Cesare's mouth trembled, and his eyes grew damp. "I wouldn't serve the cloth merchant or anyone else a poisonous mushroom, nor would I hand any mushroom to a dog! In fact—I'm innocent twice over!"

"If you missed one mushroom, you could miss another," Guid'Antonio said. "With this mushroom, we have three so far, and we are spinning our wheels." The Death Cap in Orlando Niccolini's gut, the one Palla Palmieri found and took with him from Cesare's kitchen basket, and now, this one consumed by the little ginger dog. Three, at least.

Cesare came up on his toes. "You are not listening—!"

"Neither are you," Francesca said, her face suffused with heat. "Both of you be quiet and give me room to explain. As I said, this dog died from mushroom poisoning much like Orlando Niccolini. You will be happy to know there is more to my examination. More proof in your favor, Cesare Ridolfi."

Cesare's irritation gave way to happy laughter. "I knew it, my angel!"

"Let's hear it then," Guid'Antonio said, frowning.

"Along with the Death Cap in the dog's stomach, I found bread and a bit of grass," Francesca said. "But while Orlando consumed a salad of Death Cap and greens dressed with vinegar and olive oil, there was neither oil nor vinegar in the dog's stomach."

"Amerigo tossed her a bit of rosemary bread in consolation after Niccolini kicked her," Guid'Antonio said. "And Francesco Nori gave her some chicken. But as you say, she had no oil or vinegar."

"Niccolini kicked her?"

"He did."

"Not a nice man."

"No."

"She did not eat any of the salad I prepared!" Infused with

joy, Cesare bolted to Francesca and hugged her around the waist. "Maestra, bless you, bless you, I adore you like my mother!"

Awkwardly, Francesca patted Cesare before disengaging and fussing with the folds of her gown. "In addition," she said, clearing her throat, "the Death Cap the dog ingested was not finely chopped. Rather, it was in large chunks, which is further evidence she did not have any of the salad Cesare prepared Thursday for your table, Guid'Antonio. Dottore."

"Madonna, I am blessed!" Cesare said.

Guid'Antonio looked at the dead dog on the table, his mind reeling, reaching out, and drawing back. "She ate the Death Cap elsewhere," he said.

Francesca nodded. "Yes, though somewhere near. The timing of her death argues for that. And remember, Cesare found her in your alley. My examination indicates she had been dead for about one day before his discovery. Which indicates she had the poisonous mushroom at about the same time Orlando Niccolini ate his salad."

"But," Cesare cut in, "her murder followed the timing Death Cap *usually* takes to work its black magic. She died in the alley in great pain."

Francesca nodded again. "Sadly, yes."

"She could not have crawled there to die from somewhere else?" Guid'Antonio said. His house, his kitchen—even his alley.

Francesca appeared sympathetic. "Possibly, but as I say, not from very far."

Essentially then: the dog had expired after one day, whereas Orlando had died immediately because of his sick liver. Otherwise— *Otherwise what?* The connection slipped away.

From his scrip, Guid'Antonio withdrew three smooth stones and placed them at the foot of the surgery table. "The Death Cap that killed Orlando Niccolini was chopped and dressed with vinegar and oil. Francesca—Maestra, your autopsy shows the dog had none of that." He pushed one stone aside. "Cesare, the single Death Cap mushroom Palla found in your kitchen basket and put in his pocket was whole and plain. Unused by either you or the killer. The question is how it got there."

He pushed aside another of the three stones, leaving one remaining; this last one, he took in his hand. "Where did this poisonous mushroom come from—the one that killed the dog?"

"Something I wonder is why she ate it," Francesca said. "Given the foul odor."

"Her puppies were hungry," Cesare pointed out.

Guid'Antonio agreed. Apparently, by the time the dog appeared at the *festa*, she had already consumed several chunks of the Death Cap. She simply had not exhibited any adverse symptoms yet. "Speaking of the puppies, where are they?" he said.

Francesca glanced toward a rubbish bucket lined with an old cloth bag. "I removed them during the autopsy. There were three."

"Poor things," he said.

"Yes."

Cesare looked from one of them to the other. "It is sad." Gently, he patted the little bundle beneath the sheet. "First, her little girl misused and murdered and now she, too, is dead. And yet, her passing proves my salvation. I did not kill the merchant. Someone else did."

Guid'Antonio's heart landed in his gut with a mighty thud. "What do you mean, 'her little girl'?" he said.

"Chiara Caretto. The one whose grandfather you're—"

"I know who Chiara is! Was," Guid'Antonio said. "Are you telling me this is the dog who found Chiara's sleeve and took it to her house?" To her home. Putting up such a howl, the night patrol had come running and arrested Jacopo Caretto.

"*Cannella.* Yes. You didn't know this?" Cesare asked.

"I certainly did not," Guid'Antonio said. *Cinnamon.* Now the dog had a name, the name Chiara Caretto had given her, apparently. He had witnessed the reddish-brown—ginger, cinnamon, or whatever the hell color she was—dog scrounging for food around the festival tables. But he had not connected the dog with the dead girl—why would he? And what did it matter, anyway? *Why this girl? Why this dog. Why me?*

"Cesare," Guid'Antonio said, his frustration mounting. "How could you possibly know this animal?"

Cesare's expression turned earnest. "How could you not? Since losing Chiara, *Cannella* has been a ward of the streets, wandering everywhere, seeking handouts. She was a sweet girl and made many friends outside her own Black Lion district."

Including wandering into my kitchen alley, Guid'Antonio noted to himself. *After making friends like Cesare Ridolfi.* "Amazing," he said.

And Cesare solemnly replied, *"Sì."*

"What will you do now?" Francesca asked.

Over, and over, and over again from one person or another.

To Guid'Antonio, Francesca appeared tired, her fair skin puffy around the eyes, her thin shoulders slumped beneath the fabric of her gown.

"He will tell the world I'm innocent! Palla will absolve me," Cesare cut in, shimmering with joy. "Thank you, thank you!"

"No, I will not," Guid'Antonio said. "Palla will consider whatever happened here mere happenstance. Don't forget for a moment he found a deadly mushroom in your basket, presumably put there by you. He will *not* absolve you, and he will *not* reopen this case. The end."

A thick silence gathered around them. "I repeat, I know

food, and I'm no fool! And yet I'm ruined," Cesare cried, hanging his head. "I may as well jump off the Ponte Vecchio and drown."

Guid'Antonio and Francesca locked gazes for a moment, neither smiling, nor looking away. Cesare Ridolfi might be overdramatic occasionally, but no better time for that than today. "No need," Guid'Antonio said. "At least not yet."

Cesare peered at him, an expression of hope on his face. "You're going to help me. *Grazie, graz—*"

"Be quiet," Guid'Antonio snapped. With Francesca's diagnosis, everything had changed. "What choice do I have?" he said. "Someone committed murder at our house, and if it weren't for this dead dog, he would have gotten away with it."

He ran his hands up his face, fighting to contain a storm of emotions. One poisoned salad, one man, dead. How could the killer be sure Cesare would serve Orlando Niccolini the poison—if, in fact, Orlando was the target. Maybe that was an accident—maybe Orlando *wasn't* the target. Whatever the case, the killer had been willing to risk the life of every man at Guid'Antonio's table. And whoever the killer was, he remained free. *He could have killed anyone of us, including me*, thought Guid'Antonio. *He still may do exactly that. But I will not go easily.*

"Francesca," Guid'Antonio said, "I'll begin by asking around. By making quiet enquiries and trying to gain a sense of what happened on Thursday. Cesare, Friday you told Palla that rather than gather the mushrooms for my table, you planned ahead and ordered them from two vendors. Where?"

"The market in San Lorenzo and the lesser one in Piazza Sant'Elisabetta, by the Cathedral," Cesare told him. "Lovely women! I knew the demand would be high because of the holy day celebrations. Wednesday morning I brought the mushrooms home and Thursday, I prepared them."

"You're sure you emptied both vendors' baskets? That is what you said."

"Yes. Praise God, it was enough."

"Praise God you left none for the next customer," Francesca said.

Cesare leveled her with accusing eyes, his jaw firm. "Maestra Francesca, that was not fair. Those women and I know mushrooms. We are professionals in our way as much are you are in yours." He bowed.

Francesca glanced at the floor and up again. "Of course you are. Forgive me."

"Nessun problema."

Guid'Antonio tapped his finger against his lips. "What are their names? Your two lovely women."

Cesare told him, grinning happily, "You're on the case! You defend all manner of men and women. Now, you're defending me!"

"I am seeking answers," Guid'Antonio said. "Don't forget, I prosecute people, too, and send them to the hangman. Or worse." His thoughts slipped again to Jacopo Caretto, who had admitted his guilt concerning his granddaughter, and now was refusing to speak on his own behalf. What punishment did Caretto deserve? Guid'Antonio had four days to make his decision. Four days, and now a killer was on the loose, possibly still in Florence and possibly planning to strike again with no one to stop him except Guid'Antonio Vespucci, who had honestly intended to take a trip to the countryside with his wife tomorrow morning. A wife who at this moment was waiting for him at home, waiting and packing for their journey. When he thought about telling her their time together would have to wait, his skin went cold.

Cesare piped up again, "You prosecute people when they've performed terrible acts and deserve to be castrated, drawn, and quartered. I have complete faith you will prove my innocence and restore my good name."

Francesca's slow sigh held the weight of fatigue as she

motioned toward the surgery table. "Shall I dispose of *Cannella*?"

"Please do," Guid'Antonio said. "This little dog has told us a lot at your hands. An autopsy on an animal. Will wonders never cease? Thank you." His voice was warm, his smile one between friends.

Her fingers fluttered to her cheek, the white scar, that brand, of sorts. "This is your hospital. If you asked, I would be obliged to autopsy a frog squashed by the hooves of an ass at the gate of Palazzo Medici."

His face stung as if she had slapped him, hard. "That isn't true, and you know it," he said, aware of Cesare's attention flitting between them.

"Do I?" She shrugged carelessly.

"Don't mention the dog to anyone," Guid'Antonio said, his voice pinched. "Secrecy is everything. I don't want to tip the killer we are on to him. Cesare, this directive includes you."

"I shall be as quiet as a mouse," Cesare said.

"Of course I won't," Francesca said. "I'm a doctor, bound by oath not to discuss my patients, except with police authorities. And, from time to time, with you, Dottore. Lest you forget, I'm married to my profession."

Guid'Antonio laughed dryly. "Not a chance."

Streaks of hot color reddened her cheeks. "I'll send Palla a report on the dog. Poison is poison, after all."

"Again, that man will point his finger at me!" Cesare said. "Dottore Guid'Antonio, we must act fast!"

"There is no *we*," Guid'Antonio snapped. "*You* will stay out of my way and remember you have been blessed so far. Which brings to mind that in the eyes of the public, you must remain guilty, else the killer realize we are onto him now."

"What!" Cesare huffed but quickly calmed himself. "I see it is necessary," he said.

"Then act accordingly. Maestra Vernacci, where is your

father? He seems alarmingly ill."

"Improved, he claims," Francesca said. "He's in bed resting, but plans to ride to Castellina in Chianti tomorrow morning to visit a dear, sick friend for a few days. I'm worried about him."

"As am I," Guid'Antonio said. "I'll offer a prayer to Our Lady for his health." He hesitated. "Maestra, who else might have known about Ser Niccolini's sick liver? Did Niccolini himself know, I wonder."

"He told me once his physician is in Santa Maria Nuova," she said. "Find him, and perhaps he can tell you more."

†

She waited in the surgery motionless as Guid'Antonio and Cesare clattered down the foyer stairs and emerged onto Borg'Ognissanti, their footsteps turning toward home. Carefully, she scooped *Cannella* into the threadbare sack containing the three ginger puppies bound for the town dump, their combined weight as light as a feather in her hands. Hot tears stung her eyes and dampened her cheeks as she pressed the lumpy little bundle against her breast. "I'm sorry for you, little mother," she whispered. "For your little girl, and for your lost babies, too."

A lost dog. Unloved and missed by no one. It mattered, still.

Nineteen

ORSETTO
MONDAY, 28TH JUNE 1473

In the shadows off Borg'Ognissanti, obscure in a robe of coarse black cloth, the monk waits, as still as a cat taking measure of its prey. Peering from the folds of his hood toward the Vespucci garden gate, his eyes smolder with hate. A few people remain in the street, hurrying to the Monday morning market, to the money-changers' green-clothed tables in Orsanmichele, and to God only knew where else.

Patience!

Antonio Maffei has waited over a year to savor the taste of revenge on his tongue.

He can wait a few moments more.

He will torment the man who lives in the palace just across the way, cut deep into his soul. This, with a profound feeling of gratitude to Francesco de' Pazzi, or "Little Francesco," as he sometimes is called. "Vespucci will be gone from home early Monday," Francesco had said. "He adores his silly little dog. *Orsetto* is his name and he is, you might say, Guid'Antonio

Vespucci's Achilles' heel."

At Francesco's house last Thursday, how the wine had flowed! Antonio Maffei had not intended to remain in Florence for so long. No, he had come to town as a diversion on his way from Volterra to Rome, had craved a taste of the Saint John's Day celebrations in Florence as much as he had needed to exchange a traveler's check for cash at the Pazzi branch bank. There he had been delighted to encounter Francesco de' Pazzi, a man of importance Antonio knew from the Vatican, and then to be honored with an unexpected invitation to dine Thursday at the Pazzi palazzo situated in the shadow of the Cathedral dome.

Honored, yes! But, after all, Antonio Maffei is making his way as a scribe in the Apostolic Chamber. He has walked the Vatican's vast halls in the bulky shadow of Pope Sixtus IV, and he counts the Pope's favorite nephew, Girolamo Riario, as a friend. Well—as an acquaintance. And he is bound to them all by their mounting hatred for Lorenzo de' Medici, who is a menace, no—an outright killer—a murderer who must be stopped. *Permanently.*

Over supper on Thursday, Francesco had glittered with resentment when speaking of the Medici boys and their supporters, especially that silver-eyed devil, Guid'Antonio Vespucci, with his quiet insinuations and the holier-than-thou attitude exuding from his pores. Together at the Pazzi table, Antonio Maffei, Francesco, and even Francesco's uncle, Jacopo de' Pazzi, had flirted with possibilities. Kill, kill, kill! Do unto them! Eradicate! Erase! Remove!

All illusory, of course. An impossible dream. But still a low-burning, steady flame.

"Except that little dog is real, and he is big man Guid'-Antonio Vespucci's pride and joy," Francesco had said, his giggles turning sober. "You hate Vespucci for good reason. You are here in Florence, and there is no time like the present to punish him for the pain he has caused you and your family. Wounding him will be easy. A delicious, daring achievement that will not go unnoticed by our friends in Rome. I swear."

Antonio Maffei hates those cowards on Via Larga and all their accomplices, too. Big men, yes, when they have behind them a mercenary captain and troops hired to destroy a small, vulnerable town. And so in Ognissanti, he waits, twenty-three-years-old and about to prove himself to Rome, thanks to Francesco de' Pazzi. Already, Vespucci has walked from his garden onto the street with the sullen, dark-skinned young woman Antonio assumes is Vespucci's wife, along with a beautiful, but cocky and extremely argumentative boy, and another young man the monk has not seen before. Only moments ago, Guid'Antonio had sent the unhappy trio packing with horses and baggage toward the Prato Gate, while Guid'Antonio strode back inside the garden, closing the gate behind him, rather than proceeding on his way.

What the hell?

"A funeral," Francesco de' Pazzi had said. "A dead cloth merchant. Our insufferable dottore will leave home for that. He must! The man died while seated beside him, you know."

Antonio Maffei waits. The bitter look the woman had given her husband over her shoulder had said clearly there was trouble in Paradise. Good! Any moment now surely the gate would open once more and . . . there the devil is now, flinging a blue cloak over his shoulders—no crimson for a funeral, that blood red hue would be inappropriate, Antonio Maffei understands the signs and symbols of Florence's clothing as well as any other man, woman, and child living in this town of cloth and color. Antonio may hail from the small town of Volterra southwest of Florence, but he is not a fool. In one quick movement, that butcher of Volterran men, women, and children turns and calls, "No, you wait here, puppy boy, I'll be home soon. Come along, Amerigo." He slides the bolt home,

173

but he does not pause to lock the gate, does he, none of the family ever do, before turning left toward All Saints Church just off Piazza Ognissanti. Accompanying him, this "Amerigo" is the youth who had been with him Saturday in Piazza della Signoria, the one Little Francesco had said was the older man's nephew and secretary, laughing when Antonio told him how that hot-headed fellow had wanted to chase him down in Piazza della Signoria, only to be caught back by his cowardly uncle.

God is with me and my friends here in Florence and in Rome, Antonio Maffei thinks, grinning as he crouches in that blind alley, watching and waiting until the hem of Guid'Antonio Vespucci's blue cloak slips inside All Saints. Instead of entering the church, Amerigo Vespucci disappears on down the street. Casually Antonio looks this way and that—one of them wouldn't turn and come back this way, surely?

No. He crosses himself, growling with pleasure.

Quickly, he leaves the bleak, damp alley. Casually crossing the street, as if his presence in the Unicorn district is an everyday occurrence, he approaches the gate. Beyond it, all is quiet. With a quick prayer to the Virgin Mary, Antonio eases back the bolt, weasels inside the garden, and from his robe withdraws a small cloth and a juicy chunk of meat. The cloth is soaked with the juice of Dead Men's Bells, the beef rich with fat.

"*Orsetto?* Where are you, boy?"

And here the puppy comes from the flower garden where he has been digging in the dirt, bouncing along like a little ball, greeting him as a friend.

Antonio Maffei is not a friend.

He scoops the dog into his arms, smothering its face with the rag, until the dog's squirming slows and ceases altogether. Then he tucks the limp puppy beneath his robe and hurries out the gate.

This has been too easy.
He needn't have bought the beef.
Coins wasted.

Twenty

PARLA LORENZO

"Steal Imola from me? Does the Pope think he can collect forty thousand florins from the Medici Bank and shoo me away with a pat on the ass?" Lorenzo de' Medici swiped his hand through the air, his dark eyes flashing with anger. "Suffer the wrath of City Hall, as well as of all Florence? Not without a fight. Not easily. No!"

Parla Lorenzo.

Lorenzo speaks.

Loudly.

Guid'Antonio glanced around Piazza Ognissanti. Today was Monday, a bright, sunny day, the morning of Orlando Niccolini's funeral, the Mass finally over. By now, Maria, Cesare, and his nephew, Antonio Vespucci, were well beyond the Prato Gate and on the road to Peretola. He had told them farewell, left *Orsetto* playing in the garden, and then walked directly here, his mind firing in all directions as he strode down the borgo with his blue cloak flaring from his shoulders. At the church he and Amerigo had parted company, with

Amerigo continuing downtown to make inquiries about the monk who had watched them—him!—from the shadows on Friday with such blazing anger.

Now, standing in the piazza overlooking the river with Francesco Nori, Giuliano, and a very perturbed Lorenzo, Guid'Antonio understood this was not the moment to mention Francesca Vernacci's dog autopsy.

"Sixtus has the balls of an ox!" Lorenzo exploded. "And the duke—selling Imola to him? Can you believe this twist so late in the game?"

"Yes," Guid'Antonio said. This twist, that twist, too many twists to count. "Do you know why Sforza made this turnaround?"

"Not yet! I wish I could get my hands on that conniving bastard."

A worried-looking Francesco Nori addressed Lorenzo. "Big balls or no, Sixtus has us by the short hairs, since most of the Medici bank's assets are tied to the Vatican. He carries a big stick. He'll hit you with it if you don't loan him the forty thousand."

Lorenzo swore colorfully. His family had been bankers to the Papacy since the early part of this century, with over half its profits flowing from the Rome branch managed by Lorenzo and Giuliano's uncle, Giovanni Tornabuoni. As the Vatican's Depositary General, Tornabuoni worked under the Apostolic treasurer. The Medici Bank held the Pope's cash, collected his incomes, and covered his expenditures. Tornabuoni himself advanced the funds necessary to fill the gap between the income and outgo of the Holy Father, who lived dangerously far beyond his means.

"I will not be cowed, no matter the personal consequences to my family," Lorenzo said.

Guid'Antonio and Francesco traded a glance. The Medici wanted a cardinal attached to their house, and they wanted him named Cardinal Giuliano de' Medici. A high church office would offer lasting distinction for their merchant-banking family—a family lacking a king, duke, or lord, nay, not even a count. Refuse Pope Sixtus IV the loan for Imola and forfeit that dream, that legacy, for now and, perhaps, always.

"I thought Galeazzo Maria Sforza was my friend! With friends like him, who needs enemies?" Lorenzo railed, suddenly whipping around on his brother. "Why are you sighing like a distressed boy? Say what you mean to say, and for Christ's sake have done with it!"

Giuliano appeared discomfited. "People are listening."

All around Piazza Ognissanti, there was a low babble of voices, along with the sharp stink of people sweating in the sun as they made their way across the square, a shifty glance here, a raised brow there. "Let them!" Despite his defiant stance, Lorenzo modulated his tone. "Clarice still in bed and now this betrayal by Milan at the last hour. It is too much."

Dark smudges purpled the tender skin beneath Lorenzo's eyes. Obviously, he had not slept since hearing about Imola from his uncle. Well, Lorenzo was not the only one suffering. Guid'Antonio motioned them all a step closer in the piazza. "What do the midwives say?"

"Her fever has broken. Praise God."

Crossing himself along with the others, Guid'Antonio said, "Lorenzo, there is something—" but Lorenzo spoke over him.

"Guid'Antonio, the moment you came home from Imola you cautioned me about Rome. I should have listened. *Mea culpa.*"

Guid'Antonio chose his next words with care, thinking, *Well, but you didn't, did you?* "Given Francesco de' Pazzi's I-know-something-you-don't-know behavior Saturday morning, I believe he knows everything," Guid'Antonio said. "Sforza's betrayal, the cut-rate deal. And yet, he revealed nothing, preferring to taunt us on Saturday. That is worrying."

Lorenzo laughed without humor. "And that is putting it mildly. You were right when you said Franceschino's often in the Vatican—why did he not warn me Sforza and the Pope were scheming against me? Against Florence?"

"He doesn't like you," Giuliano said.

A look of surprise twisted Lorenzo's features, followed by a dark grin. "I don't like him either, as you well know. But what of his homeland? We have wanted Imola for a long while. Needed it to protect our boundaries and for trade. Francesco de' Pazzi knows this as well as I do."

Francesco Nori exchanged a friendly wave with a group of men passing by the river, saying beneath his breath, "He wants you to fail."

"At the expense of the Republic? I have a good mind to have City Hall call him in, question him while he is still in town."

"Lorenzo, no!" Giuliano said. "That would only add fuel to the flames."

"I am not scared of Francesco de' Pazzi," Lorenzo said. "Fuck him."

With a forced air of calm, Guid'Antonio said, "Best never to forget the power of the Vatican."

Giuliano lay his hand on Guid'Antonio's arm. "Truer words were never spoken." He looked around. "But where's Amerigo? I haven't seen him since yesterday, when we rode home from Fiesole with Guglielmo. I thought Amerigo meant to attend the funeral with you this morning."

He is where he should have been this weekend, hunting a fleeing monk, rather than disappearing into the countryside to hunt Plato with Guglielmo de' Pazzi and you.

"He is on an errand for me," Guid'Antonio said.

☦

Last night, Sunday, he had stared at Amerigo with eyes narrowed to slits as that wayward youth strolled, whistling cheerfully, into the Red Lion Tavern to join him at the corner trestle with their backs to the wall. "Why didn't you do as I asked and uncover our monk's whereabouts yesterday instead of riding to Fiesole and staying—well, until just now, apparently?"

"I didn't think it was that important," Amerigo had said.

"You didn't think—?" Guid'Antonio's displeasure with Amerigo increased. "Since when do you second guess me? Oh, I forget! It happens daily! Now—I want you to do as I asked and find that monk for me! The more I think about it, the more his behavior seems threatening. Do it tomorrow morning, while I'm at Niccolini's funeral, since it is far too late today." Guid'Antonio blew out his breath. "Do you still have the sketch Leonardo drew of him yesterday morning?" Saturday, in Piazza della Signoria.

Amerigo's cheeks flamed. "Of course. It's in my satchel."

"Good. Here's something more." Guid'Antonio told Amerigo then about the meeting with Maestra Francesca Vernacci and the results of the dog, *Cannella's,* autopsy. Unlike the Death Cap in Orlando Niccolini's stomach, the Death Cap the dog ate was neither chopped nor dressed with vinegar and oil. She had not eaten any of the salad Cesare Ridolfi had prepared.

Amerigo's jaw dropped. "Which means *Cannella* found—or was given the Death Cap—elsewhere. But where—how—and this suggests—"

"Yes," Guid'Antonio said.

"God's toes! And this was the dead girl's dog? Are Chiara and Niccolini's deaths related? If so, there's a coincidence of amazing proportions."

"Intertwined, perhaps. Soften your voice."

All around them men sopped crusty bread in bowls of thick

bean soup while the tavern owner, Neri Saginetto, bustled about, wiping spills from trestles with a bar towel and trading gossip with his customers. His black-eyed daughter, dimpled, seven-year-old Evangelista Saginetto, tagged after him, collecting food-encrusted pottery bowls and cups.

Amerigo shivered. "Niccolini, murdered. This changes everything."

"To put it mildly," Guid'Antonio said.

"What will you do?"

"We."

"Naturally."

Guid'Antonio raised his wine to his lips and drank his fill, signaling to Neri they were ready for their typical Sunday evening repast. "First, we will keep this quiet. We can't let the killer suspect we're onto him. No, rather let him think he's gotten away with poisoning Niccolini and, perhaps, also the dog. Also, don't ever forget that if Niccolini wasn't the intended victim, the killer may strike again."

"You think he may have meant to kill one of us?"

"Anything is possible," Guid'Antonio said, shifting on the bench as Neri Saginetto placed an oak board on the table laden with cheeses, figs, almonds, small pottery jugs of balsamic vinegar and honey, and aromatic, crusty bread, along with two plates.

"Where is that little bear of yours tonight?" Neri said. "You usually bring him with you on Sunday evenings. I miss his vitality, his constant good cheer." With a sweep of his hand, Neri refilled Guid'Antonio and Amerigo's cups.

Guid'Antonio laughed. "Vitality? Running around, jumping on everyone and begging for scraps?" On this particular Sunday evening, he had left the puppy at home with a very angry Maria. *You are going to Peretola. I am not.* He lifted his drink to Neri. *"Grazie."*

"You are welcome as always," Neri said. "Evangelista, go

to the storage room and fetch another *salame*. Slice some for Ignazio and Gianluca. They are at their usual place by the door. Enough for Piero, too. He's late arriving, as always."

Guid'Antonio slathered a piece of bread with thick, golden honey. "Amerigo, tomorrow, Monday morning, in addition to hunting the monk, while I attend Niccolini's funeral I want you to speak with the two women who sold Cesare his mushrooms. One is in the San Lorenzo market, the other in Piazza Sant'Elisabetta near the Cathedral. Go to them first; they hawk their wares early. Cesare swears he bought all they had when he purchased them Wednesday morning. I understand these women are reputable, but I would like to know where they got the mushrooms and if, perhaps, they actually had any left, once Cesare bought his lot. Also, ask Gaspare and Livia if they remember seeing any strangers in our kitchen on Thursday."

"Opportunity," Amerigo said.

"Yes." *And motive*, thought Guid'Antonio. *Those are the keys to finding our killer.*

He bent to pat Evangelista's pet dog. A large, handsome animal plucked from the street, *Biscotto*, Biscuit, was about five, two years younger than his mistress, his brown eyes gentle, his fur a light yellow shade. A sweet, good boy. What would Guid'Antonio have done if the dog on Francesca's autopsy table after church this morning had been *Orsetto*? Belly slit open. Dead. The puppy could so easily have darted into the alley behind the Vespucci kitchen and greedily gulped down the Death Cap, never knowing—Guid'Antonio swallowed over the lump in his throat. Without that little ball of fur, he would be lost.

Briskly, he said, "Amerigo, according to the note you left in the kitchen yesterday before haring off to Fiesole, you did speak with Jacopo Caretto's neighbors regarding his guardianship of his granddaughter, correct?"

"Yes," Amerigo said. On Saturday afternoon, venturing

deep into the Santa Croce quarter for the second time in three days, Amerigo had learned from one of the murdered girl's neighbors, a woman, that Chiara Caretto's parents and siblings had died from some sickness or other when Chiara was about six. Chiara claimed uncles and aunts, but none would take her in. "One aunt spoke for her, apparently, but the men in the family overruled her, saying that Jacopo, living alone, needed Chiara's help," Amerigo said. "In the end off to her grandfather's house she went, and there she stayed until he dumped her in her grave."

Help from a six-year-old girl. Is that what Jacopo called years of taking the girl into his bed? "Did you speak with this aunt?" he said.

"No, she's ill, or so her husband claimed. Anyway, not available at the moment. He seemed evasive when I pressed him about the girl."

Guid'Antonio sucked honey from his fingers. "Evasive? How so?"

"He pretended not to remember much about her. But the Carettos live together in the Black Lion district. He would have seen Chiara daily until she disappeared. After all, he is her uncle. He and Chiara's father were brothers."

"His name?"

"Fenso Caretto. A sausage-maker. Fenso's wife, the sympathetic aunt, is related to Chiara by marriage, not blood."

So. A kinswoman by marriage willing to take the child in, and her overridden by the rest of the family, including her husband. "Why did the others refuse to help her, I wonder," Guid'Antonio said.

Amerigo wiped a bit of cheese from his mouth with his fingers. "The neighbor I spoke with suggested the girl was a pretty little thing, as she put it."

They kept hearing that, didn't they? Jealousy on the part of the women in the family and throughout the Black Lion district. But not on the part of this ailing aunt. And all the while—

"Now," Amerigo cut in, pouring more wine into their cups. "Tomorrow morning, I'm to talk with Cesare's mushroom vendors, learn what I can about the monk, and speak with Gaspare and Livia about the people in our kitchen on Thursday. What else?"

Guid'Antonio circled back to Chiara Caretto. "Talk with the two patrolmen who arrested Jacopo. See if you can glean anything from them that isn't in Palla's report."

"All right, but where are you with him? If only that bastard would talk! At least then we'd know why he killed his granddaughter. And, maybe, whether her death had anything to do with Orlando Niccolini."

"I'll speak with him tomorrow morning after Niccolini's funeral," Guid'Antonio said. "I'm sure he'll talk then."

Amerigo tilted his head at him, his expression doubtful, but he made no further comment.

☦

Now, in sunny Piazza Ognissanti the Monday morning activity had quieted. Still, Guid'Antonio kept his voice low. "Besides the troubling news regarding Imola, there is more." Warned by his somber tone, his three companions listened closely as he told them everything he had told Amerigo last night at the Red Lion. The Death Cap the dog ate was plain, free of vinegar and oil, which meant she had not had any of the salad Cesare prepared for Guid'Antonio's Saint John's Day table. She had come by the poisonous mushroom some other way, and so on.

Lorenzo recovered first. "Also, as Cesare has protested all along, or so I hear, he wouldn't make the same mistake twice. He didn't accidentally kill the dog."

"No."

Francesco Nori looked bewildered. "You believe the killer's intended victim may not have been Orlando?"

"It is possible, Francesco. Whoever killed Niccolini added the chopped Death Cap to one plate only, a plate Cesare could have set before anyone at our table. Did the killer just hope it would go to Niccolini?" Guid'Antonio shook his head, genuinely intrigued. "Until I unravel the circumstances surrounding his death and how it was done, we must all look to ourselves."

"Who would give a hungry dog a poisonous mushroom, unless in an act of desperation?" Giuliano said. "Is Palla investigating?"

An act of desperation. Take note, Guid'Antonio. "Palla will have Maestra Francesca's report, but he will not spend a moment counting mushrooms and worrying how a dead dog got poisoned," Guid'Antonio said.

A cloud passed over Giuliano's usually bright features. "I was at that table."

Guid'Antonio cast back. Giuliano had been at the table, true, but he had not been there the entire time. Late in the day, he had flown off to dance with Simonetta Vespucci, and Angelo Poliziano had leaped into his place. What did that have to do with anything? Something? Nothing?

"Guid'Antonio," Lorenzo said, "if Palla won't pursue this killer—"

"I will," Guid'Antonio said.

Francesco Nori frowned. "I thought you were leaving town this afternoon with Maria. After the funeral. After we—" He waved his hand, gesturing toward the church. "—got the service over with."

"No. I put her on the road to Peretola with Cesare and Antonio earlier this morning."

"Without you."

"Yes."

"These are strange times," Lorenzo said.

"They are, indeed."

Lorenzo shook his head. "I'm sorry. Anyway, regarding Imola, Sixtus understands this is an impossible situation, one involving our government. For me, my bank, to loan him the money would be an act of treason. The Lord Priors would throw *me* out the windows of the Palazzo della Signoria. Besides, I don't want to."

"You'll deny him the forty thousand florins," Guid'Antonio said, remarking to himself how easily Lorenzo de' Medici left the subject of a killer in their midst to matters of state. *I will handle it*, Guid'Antonio had said. *I will do it. As always.* Or words to that effect.

"What choice do I have?" Lorenzo said. "Moreover, if I can find a way, I will block him entirely. He thinks he can outplay me? Over my dead body."

"He is the head of Christendom," Giuliano said. "He is the Pope."

Lorenzo leaned close to his brother. "And I am Lorenzo de' Medici."

"Block him how?" Guid'Antonio said, wondering, *And at what final cost?*

A slow smile curled Lorenzo's lips. "I'll think of something."

"The Pope will find the funds elsewhere," Guid'Antonio said. "In the end—" He spread his hands. *Someone will provide him with forty thousand florins.*

"I will make that difficult," Lorenzo said.

"He will know. And he is dangerous," Giuliano said.

Lorenzo agreed on both points. "He also will know Florence will not cower before him. Neither now, nor ever. Letting him have his way without a fight is the greater danger."

†

"Was I that cocksure when I was twenty-four?" Francesco Nori said, watching Lorenzo and Giuliano stride south, shoulder-to-shoulder, glancing back, waving, before they disappeared in a passageway leading from Ognissanti to downtown Florence.

"Yes," Guid'Antonio said.

Francesco spread his hands. "He thinks he's immortal. I worry about him. He's right when he says he has to deny the loan. But it's foolish to engage the Pope in a pissing contest."

"It isn't him I worry about, as much as about Giuliano," Guid'Antonio said, thinking, *He's too innocent for this world. He is my good, young friend.*

Francesco spoke heavily. "By now my office will have heard about Rome's request for the money to pull the rug out from under Florence. Gossip and speculation will rule the day. I don't look forward to it. And you? Where are you going?"

"To the widow Caterina Niccolini to offer my condolences for the loss of her husband. Pray for me, *per favore*."

Twenty-One

THE BELL

Guid'Antonio was considering how best to approach Caterina Niccolini in the matter of her husband's death when he spied Amerigo walking toward him in the hot white light of Piazza Trinita. "This is fortuitous. What have you?" he said.

Shading his eyes, Amerigo reported how after parting ways with Guid'Antonio before Orlando Niccolini's funeral earlier today, he had encountered Gaspare Ridolfi and Livia, the kitchen maid, in the Old Market purchasing vegetables and fruit. Neither Domenica's brother nor Livia had anything to add to Cesare's version of events regarding the mushroom salads served during last week's holy day celebration. Many people had been in the kitchen on Thursday, coming and going. But no, no strangers, no. Venturing then into the Golden Lion district of Florence, Amerigo had found Cesare's two mushroom vendors exactly where Cesare had said they would be, one in the sprawling San Lorenzo market around the corner from Palazzo Medici, the other in snug Piazza Sant'Elisabetta near Florence Cathedral.

"Your approach?" Guid'Antonio said.

"Friendly," Amerigo replied. Since he had to let the women believe like the rest of Florence that Niccolini's death was an accident caused by Cesare Ridolfi, Amerigo's manner had centered on the Vespucci family's dismay and natural curiosity regarding how such a terrible event had taken place. "Both women said yes, they sold all their mushrooms to Cesare Ridolfi on the morning prior to Saint John's Day. He had placed his order with them earlier in the week. No, Cesare had not suggested to either of them he might go elsewhere to purchase more mushrooms for his baskets. Also, they had said they had been as stunned as everyone else to learn the cloth merchant had died from Death Cap. Appalling, truly.

The more questions Amerigo had asked, the more both vendors had started to suspect there was more to his inquiries than mere inquisitiveness. To hear each woman tell it, theirs was a family business harking back to the days when Florence was part of the Roman Empire. Amerigo had not dare imply either had ever sold tainted wares.

"They know mushrooms," Guid'Antonio said. Like Cesare. The discussion ended there.

Amerigo held up the two woven baskets in his hands. "Meanwhile, we have more than enough mushrooms for the next dozen years."

"I assume you came and went via Piazza della Signoria," Guid'Antonio said. "Was the blue cap sailing around the square?"

Amerigo laughed. "Oh, yes! With the boys enjoying every delicious, tortured moment."

"Any sign of Brother Monk loitering there?"

"No. He's gone," Amerigo said.

Guid'Antonio straightened. "Gone? You sound sure. You found where he'd been staying?"

"I did. He had a pallet at *La Campana*, The Bell, a faded inn with an even more faded sign over the door, situated between Palazzo della Signoria and San Pier Scheraggio on *via della Ninna*." Lullaby Street. "I just came from there," Amerigo said. "I had only to poke my head inside a couple of inns in the area and show the proprietors Leonardo's sketch. Speaking of which, that drawing is beginning to look worn. Perhaps Leonardo will do another by memory."

Impatiently, Guid'Antonio said, "And?"

"And I spoke with the tormented woman at The Bell, showing her the drawing and inquiring cheerfully about the monk, as if I knew him as a friend. She shrieked, 'Monk? What monk?' before I had the words out of my mouth."

"Shrieked? Tormented how?" Guid'Antonio said, frowning.

Amerigo shrugged. "Worried sick about something or other from the moment I entered the door until I left—well, until she threw me out. When some dishes fell from a cupboard in the kitchen and crashed to the floor, I thought she would leap through the ceiling. I offered to see what had happened—it sounded to me as if the cupboard had somehow tipped, then righted itself—but she blocked the curtain and said it was the cat, knocking things around and breaking them all the time which, of course, we know they do. As for the monk, I told her I understood he was staying there and asked why she had implied otherwise." Amerigo nibbled a mushroom he removed from one of the baskets.

"—And?" Guid'Antonio asked.

"—And she said, "Oh, yes! That monk! He's gone.'"

"Gone where?" Guid'Antonio said.

"She didn't know, or at least she said she didn't as she pushed me out onto the street and bolted the door."

"You didn't insist on going into the kitchen?"

"Why would I?" Amerigo said. "Anyway—I'm not Palla Palmieri."

Guid'Antonio sighed. Hmmm. That had been a mighty big cat. "The monk's name?" he said. "You did ask?"

"Of course. She had no idea."

Guid'Antonio's frown deepened. "She's lying, obviously."

Amerigo's gaze followed a pretty *signorina* who was starting with her maid across the Ponte Vecchio toward the Santo Spirito quarter of Florence, the girl's mantle flowing behind her on the stones, her hood back, revealing her face—as yet, she was unmarried. "Ah, me," Amerigo said dreamily, before turning again to Guid'Antonio. "Lying or no, the landlady said her husband, the landlord, recorded the fellow's name but keeps the ledger under lock and key."

"Of course he does," Guid'Antonio said. "And of course he was not there." What did the name matter, truly? The monk could have given the couple a false identity.

"No. Or so the landlady claimed," Amerigo said.

Something was wrong here. Guid'Antonio knew it. Meanwhile: "The patrolmen you spoke with regarding Jacopo Caretto—did they have any useful comments?"

Amerigo gave Guid'Antonio a disconcerted look, as if saying, *It's only mid-morning Monday, and already I have been from San Lorenzo and Piazza Sant'Elisabetta all the way to Piazza della Signoria, thence to The Bell, and now have come here.* "I've not yet found the patrolmen," he said. "I haven't had time to go to the jail."

Guid'Antonio nodded. "All right, I want you to return to The Bell. If the landlord still isn't there, wait for him. I want the name the lodger gave them, even if it's a lie. Also find out if the landlord knows where the monk came from and where he was going. Let him know I sent you, and that I do not consider the monk a friend. Concerning Palla's patrolmen, I'm going to the jail later today to interrogate Jacopo. I'll read their arrest report again after questioning him, and also speak with them, if they are there."

Amerigo gasped as if he had been shot with an arrow through the heart. "Me? Return to the inn? Now?" With his boot he poked the ground.

Guid'Antonio folded his arms over his chest. "What is it?"

"I'm almost afraid to say."

"Too late."

"It is only . . . The Bell is in Piazza della Signoria. I'm supposed to meet Angelo at Palazzo Rucellai. Bernardo Rucellai invited us to come. Angelo is bringing a copy of Leonardo Bruni's translation of Aristotle's *Politics* from the Medici library." Amerigo squinted at the sun, watching it scoot across the sky, marking time. "I was only walking home for some bread and cheese to eat and to rid myself of these damned mushrooms when I saw you coming from All Saints. May I go back to the inn tomorrow morning? First thing, I swear!"

Tomorrow morning. Tuesday. Guid'Antonio scratched his forehead, considering Amerigo's request. Bernardo Rucellai was Lorenzo and Giuliano de' Medici's brother-in-law, married to their sister, Nannina, these last seven years. The monk was gone from Florence, if the innkeeper's wife could be believed. Wait one day? What harm could it do? "Fine," he said. "Go fill your mind with meditations on philosophy and poetry."

Straightening his blue cloak around his shoulders, Guid'-Antonio bid his nephew farewell and departed Piazza Trinita, veering left at the foot of the Ponte Vecchio and striding into the stinking air of the fish market along the Arno, then quickly left into the decaying piazza where his friend Francesco Nori had said the widow Caterina Niccolini dwelled.

Twenty-Two

CATERINA

Alarm flickered in Caterina's face when she saw Guid'Antonio at her door, as if she had been half-expecting him and now, confirming her worse fears, here he stood in the flesh. "Dottore," she said, exhaling a deep breath.

"Mona Caterina." He tipped his head.

Eyelids drooping, she allowed him entrance, one hand running tremulously along the folds of her black damask mourning gown.

Ruefully, he smiled. When had he ever intimidated anyone while wearing sapphire blue? He reminded himself the lady was newly widowed, her husband cold and bound for his tomb. Surely, she was consumed with sorrow and confusion. He entered the *sala*, the eyes of the house. "*Signora*, I wish to say—" He began his little speech.

But she was gazing past him toward the cemetery behind him in the piazza. There in Piazza Limbo in sad, small graves outside the Church of the Holy Apostles lay the remains of babies who had died before being baptized, infants whose souls would eternally haunt the edges of hell.

"You are alone," she said.

Who was she expecting? He resisted the urge to follow her gaze over his shoulder. Behind him, embraced by crumbling stone walls, the piazzetta where Caterina Niccolini lived was eerily silent, the atmosphere thick with the musky smell of incense and wax offerings that had burned within the walls of Santi Apostoli across many centuries. Where were Caterina Niccolini's friends at this desolate hour? Women from her *contada*, district, bearing food and words of comfort? One woman had brushed past him in the tight entry to the piazza, solemn-faced and in a hurry to leave this ancient place. One woman, only.

"I wish to say how sorry I am about your husband. For such a terrible thing to happen at my house because of a boy's careless mistake—" *Forgive me, Cesare.* "On my word, he is being punished."

Caterina's eyes—large and dark with long, silky lashes—widened, and for one moment, she seemed almost to crumple to the floor, overcome with emotion. "Punished? How, Dottore?"

"He is in exile at home."

"Oh—I see," she said. "Well—Police Chief Palmieri explained the circumstances. I don't blame Cesare," she added in a rush. "I didn't want him to go to jail. He's a boy, as you say, and Domenica's only son."

Guid'Antonio frowned—Palla had offered to send Cesare to jail? Well, why wouldn't he? Cesare Ridolfi had been blessed not to have spent time in a cell, or even to be hanged.

"Thank you for the candles for Ognissanti—for Orlando's mass," Caterina said. "He admired you greatly and would appreciate your family's thoughtfulness. Chianti, Dottore?"

Along with several stoppered bottles of wine on the credenza against one wall, there was a bold display of silverware, goblets, pitchers, trays. A tapestry decorated another wall of the small, but inviting, *sala*, the hanging purchased during one of Orlando Niccolini's excursions to Bruges, probably. A cloth fringed Turkey carpet covered the trestle where Orlando and Caterina had shared meals. All signs to those who entered here that this was the house of a prosperous merchant.

"No, *grazie*," Guid'Antonio said.

"Work beckons." She smiled.

"Always," he said, hesitating, tempted, after all, to accept her kind offer. After a bitter confrontation with Maria Sunday afternoon and then again this morning when he put her on the road to their villa, not to mention the worrying discussion with Lorenzo in Piazza Ognissanti a few moments ago, a drink of wine would go down well. Caterina's gesture toward the credenza had been graceful, her unexpected smile, engaging, and it struck him for a second time she was not an unappealing woman. No more than three years or so older than Francesca Vernacci, Caterina Niccolini was petite and slender, and he had caught a flash of keen intelligence behind her eyes when he explained the situation regarding Cesare's role in her husband's death.

But, no. He raised an eyebrow, as if about to say: "Goodbye—"

"Please thank Maria for the honey and roast veal. It was generous of her to remember me," said Caterina.

The comment was icy water dashed in Guid'Antonio's face. "Maria remembered you?" Recovering quickly, he added, "Of course she did."

Another smile lightened Caterina's features. "She sent gifts by Livia. Maria is such a thoughtful young woman. How is she?"

"Content," he said. Liar! Yesterday afternoon, Sunday, his wife had glistened with the devil's fury when he arrived home from the hospital and told her he was not going with her to

Peretola today but would join her there soon. Vague, vague!

"What? Why!? We've planned this for months! After Saint John's Day—you promised! It's that woman!" Maria had flared. "What did she want with you after Mass? And to keep you for so long—she is as bold as Mona Elisabetta claims!"

"Yes, she is," he had said.

Maria had knotted her fingers in the folds of her gown, the clothes she had been arranging for their trip forgotten on their bed. "Do you know how her face was ruined? People say it happened when she was a girl, but when I inquire, they turn away."

"Her face is not ruined," he had said coldly. *Francesca's face hit the edge of a jagged rock hidden beneath the water's surface in the silvery, shimmering creek in Peretola, where she and her father had come to visit my family. Her flesh ripped open, her fall my fault and mine alone for daring her to walk across the slippery stones. The same creek where you like to wade.*

"Where are you going?" Maria had cried when he turned away.

"To the *scrittoio*. Then to the Red Lion to meet Amerigo." *And then back here to go to bed with you, God help me in all His infinite glory.*

†

He had drawn to a halt in his conversation with Caterina Niccolini.

"Dottore?"

He shook himself lightly. "Forgive me, my mind was on your dear, departed husband. Such a tremendous loss."

"Yes. Has anyone else fallen ill?"

"Why would you think so?" he said.

She shrugged her shoulders gracefully. "Where there are

two poisonous mushrooms, there could be three."

Indeed. "You know about the second Death Cap mushroom, *Signora*?"

Twisting her brow into a frown, Caterina said, "When Palla explained the circumstances surrounding my husband's death, he mentioned the mushroom he found in Cesare's kitchen basket. Again, where there are two, there could be three."

"There was no third mushroom," Guid'Antonio said. Liar, again! Chiara Caretto's dog was dead, sliced open on the same table as Caterina's husband with that third Death Cap in her gut.

"Praise God for that," Caterina said, her fingers fluttering to the jeweled cross hanging from a gold chain around her neck. "My husband's final words were spoken to you. What was Orlando saying? He seemed so carefree."

He was saying you are a good woman, but you are not good enough. He was saying that his *inamorata*, whose name is Elena Veluti, was, or is, expecting his child, and how desperately he wanted a boy. *That* is the kind of man he was. "He was speaking of his voyage to London for Spinelli and Spinelli and how delighted he was to be traveling there. Though he did not like being away from you and Florence," Guid'Antonio said.

She smiled. "My husband was a sensitive man."

"Yes. Well. *Signora*, if in the coming days you require a lawyer, I'm happy to help." This house, Caterina's marriage dowry—or whatever of it remained—would be fair game for the hawks who would swoop down on her in the coming days. Niccolini kinsmen, brothers, male cousins from far and wide, surely.

Her smile widened. "*Grazie*. Orlando had no family. He's much missed, but he provided me the comfort of home and hearth for the rest of my days. God has been good to me."

"Every cloud has a silver lining," Guid'Antonio said.

He wished her good health and turned to leave, but paused to ask, "Who will handle his duties at the wool shop, now he's gone?"

She stared at him vacantly. "He had a young boy working with him. An apprentice or assistant... a youth named Andrea Antinori. Who can say what the Spinelli family will decide to do about filling Orlando's place?" *Nor is it for me to care*, her expression said.

"Did your husband and the Antinori lad get along?"

"Certainly. Orlando mentioned he was a good boy. And everyone loved Orlando."

Guid'Antonio smiled guilelessly "Of course they did."

For a moment, Caterina regarded him thoughtfully. "Life is strange, isn't it?"

Extremely. "How so?" he said.

"My husband would have died, anyway."

Cesare's words, exactly. "Given his sick liver," Guid'Antonio said. "Eventually. Yes. But who knows when? Did you know he was ill?"

"You asked that at the *festa*," Caterina said, a quick smile flickering at her lips. "My answer remains the same." *Not as I could tell.*

"I did, didn't I?" Guid'Antonio said, half-smiling himself. *"Signora, ciao."*

†

He was sharply aware of Caterina Niccolini lingering on her doorstep as he skirted the infants' cemetery and walked past Santi Apostoli, where red glass votives burned in a sea of darkness alongside the three flints that had been used to light the lamps in Jesus's tomb when he was buried in Jerusalem. Guid'Antonio felt Caterina's eyes on him until he stepped into the maze of *vicoli* that eventually would lead him to police headquarters in the Bargello and Jacopo Caretto's airless, dark cell. Turning quickly as he entered an alley, he saw her face vanish as she closed the door to her house, bolting the door with a soft little snick that did little to ensure safety.

Twenty-Three

JACOPO CARETTO

How did you transport your granddaughter's corpse beyond our city walls? Over your shoulder, yes, your confession states this. But how did you avoid the night patrols? What did you do to the little dog, Cannella, *to keep her quiet? Oh, yes, squirm with your chin resting on your knees on the hard dirt floor. I know the animal's name. She was the girl's pet. Did you lock* Cannella *away somewhere? Your mistake was not choking the dog to death, as you did your granddaughter. Had the dog not returned a remnant of her clothing to your door, it is likely no one ever would have known what happened to the girl.*

Why did you kill your granddaughter?

Jacopo Caretto, a rugged, pock-faced man with a muscular body beneath the fabric of his hose and tunic, kept his lips sealed and his sinewy arms crossed over his chest. Guid'Antonio watched him closely. Why would Caretto not speak in his defense? His expression had gone from mild curiosity to stony when Guid'Antonio stepped into his cell well after midday. It seemed the man did not care what happened to him. So be it. Jacopo Caretto would talk, or not. In court, Guid'Antonio would present his opinion in light of the research he and Amerigo had conducted Friday in the chancery office. Following Guid'Antonio's oral report, the magistrates would render their verdict. In time a court scribe would record these proceedings in the *Condempnationes, Vol. Three.*

Next case.

Enjoy your four florins, Dottore.

☦

In the jail courtyard, Guid'Antonio found Gino Frescobaldi, the registrar, and told him if anyone came looking for him, he would be in the chancery reviewing Jacopo's Caretto's record of arrest. "Have someone deliver it to me from Palla's office, please."

"Again?" Gino said.

"Yes." Guid'Antonio glanced around the courtyard. "Are you familiar with Alesso Cassini and Ruberto Ricasoli?"

"Of course. The two sergeants who found the girl's sleeve at her door. They're on patrol. Shall I send someone to find them?"

"No, no." Guid'Antonio did not truly believe talking with those two sergeants would reveal anything new. Still, he would look back over their report as recorded by Palla Palmieri, hunting an overlooked nugget here, a potential thread there.

☦

Case #421946: . . . . *Coming upon a dog guarding a bloodied piece of cloth outside the door of a ramshackle house, they cast aside the wretched dog squatting there and forcefully entered the darkened quarters. Therein they roused an aged man (who later identified himself as Jacopo Caretto) and told him what they had found. . . . believing he was haunted by an evil spirit, he cried out the fabric was the torn sleeve of a cotton camicia, the kind of long undergarment many people wear, belonging to his dead granddaughter . . . . Ranting like a madman, he confessed himself the girl's killer—and so on.*

Wretched dog. Sad, more like. There was absolutely nothing suggesting a link between the little ginger dog and Orlando Niccolini's deaths. Well: other than Death Cap. Guid'Antonio tapped his mouth. He would put the brave little dog aside for now, tuck her away for future reference. *Cannella.* A member of the Caretto family, one might say.

☦

At dusk, the Monday evening shadows in the streets began to lengthen. Guid'Antonio sat at the table beneath his apartment windows to eat his meal of hard rosemary bread and cheese and work with paper, pen, and ink. Today had been spectacularly long—had it really begun with Orlando Niccolini's funeral? No—with Maria and Cesare leaving for Peretola, then the funeral and the devastating news about Imola, then Caterina and Jacopo . . . Guid'Antonio was feeling every one of his thirty-seven years.

Two weeks ago—no, two months, just after returning from Imola—he had promised a friend he would write to Lorenzo de' Medici recommending him for the position of professor of civil law at the University of Pisa when, *if,* the *Studio* there reopened its doors in early winter. This relocation of most of the curriculum of the University of Florence to one of the Florentine Republic's subject cities was a pet project of Lorenzo, who meant in this way to correct the lackluster status of the *Studio* in Florence, when compared to schools in Padua and Bologna—the latter where Guid'Antonio had studied law—while also resurrecting education in Pisa. The Florentine *Studio* would concentrate on grammar and rhetoric, while civil and canon law, philosophy and the other sciences would transfer to their neighbor west of Florence.

New blood, enhanced reputation. Or so Lorenzo hoped. Tomorrow, Guid'Antonio would send a messenger with the letter of recommendation to Palazzo Medici. He sifted through written files.

Yawning, he surrendered to a fresh wave of weariness and lay down without removing his clothes. As happened frequently these days, worrying images pinched and poked his sleep. He saw Maria glance coldly over her shoulder and Francesca flailing in a stream, pink blood gushing from her cheek. The smell of sorrow in Piazza Limbo filled his nostrils, along with the dry scent of dirt sifting over the used, broken body of a young girl. He tossed and turned, aching for something missing, a void he could not name. And then at daybreak Tuesday morning, when he reached out to run his fingers though *Orsetto's* thick curls, he realized the puppy was gone.

Twenty-Four

DEAD MEN'S BELLS
TUESDAY, 29TH JUNE 1473

"Orsetto!"

Guid'Antonio sprang upright in bed. Where was Little Bear? Fear pooled in his stomach. Had he left the apartment door open? Probably *Orsetto* had slipped out sometime during the night . . . no. No! *His dog had not been there at all.*

In an instant, he was on his feet. Where had *Orsetto* been when Guid'Antonio quit his notes and fell into bed? Surely, the puppy was in the kitchen now with Domenica and Gaspare or in the courtyard digging in the garden or chasing a bee. He would find the mischievous little rascal there, and upbraid him for scaring him half to death.

†

No! No! Pale streaks of light were just now beginning to appear on the horizon, lifting darkness into light. The courtyard was silent, the gate latched for the night. No opening for a dog to slip off for an adventure. The kitchen was silent. A wail rose in Guid'Antonio's throat. Think! He had not seen *Orsetto* since the previous morning, when he put Maria on the road to Peretola. When he left for Orlando Niccolini's funeral Mass, *Orsetto* had been here in the garden, bouncing about. Think back, think!

He had kissed *Orsetto* on the head and set him by the fountain with a fond pat on the rear before throwing his blue cloak over his shoulders. Together, he and Amerigo had hurried along Borg'Ognissanti, Guid'Antonio to attend Orlando Niccolini's funeral, his nephew to locate the mushroom vendors in downtown Florence and then to the neighborhood around Piazza della Signoria to inquire about that damned monk. *Orsetto* could not have skipped out behind them; they would have noticed.

Someone had taken him.

Guid'Antonio's mind fired in all directions. The little *Lagotto Romagnolo* would fetch a good price on the market. And, and, and? Little Francesco de' Pazzi would not *dare* take him. He was a coward. Think, think! What else? He remembered that late yesterday morning in Piazza Trinita, Amerigo had told him he had located the inn where the monk they were seeking had stayed in Florence. *La Campana*, The Bell. The innkeeper's wife had been worried, "tormented" about something, Amerigo had said. First, she had indicated she knew nothing about any monk, but when pressed, suddenly she had realized that, yes, a monk had stayed there recently, but now was gone. *When some dishes fell from a cupboard in the kitchen and broke, I thought she would leap through the ceiling. She said it was her cat.*

An image of the monk watching him through the eyes of a viper in Piazza della Signoria sizzled through Guid'Antonio. The landlady had been in a panic. What if for whatever reason the monk had stolen *Orsetto* while Guid'Antonio was at

Orlando Niccolini's funeral mass and fled with the puppy to The Bell? He imagined the monk's horror when he heard Amerigo at the innkeeper's door, saw the monk rush into the kitchen with *Orsetto* and stumble into the cupboard. What had that wild-eyed man done to keep *Orsetto* quiet? Drugged him, undoubtedly.

What if by now he had ferreted the puppy far, far away, or left him behind, and—worse?

☦

Guid'Antonio hurtled from the garden, fear shrieking along his skin. Down Borg'Ognissanti, across Trinita, and into the gathering light of Piazza della Signoria he ran, gasping for air before running diagonally across the square toward the eastern corner between City Hall and the arcade, empty of cavorting young boys or any other sign of life in these painfully early morning hours. Breathless, with his hands on his knees, he glanced toward the river and back toward the church of San Pier Scheraggio. The public inn called The Bell was on the throughway called *via della Ninna*, Lullaby Street, Amerigo had said. There!

"Open up!" He pounded the door, then kicked it in with such force, the wood splintered.

A man and woman in nightclothes cowered in the shadows, as far as they could get from the madman who had broken down the door. The woman moaned in fear, liquid puddling the floor at her ankles.

"Where's my dog!" Guid'Antonio yelled.

"*Your* dog?" All the color drained from the landlord's face as he realized the man standing before him shaking with fury was Dottore Guid'Antonio Vespucci.

The man's reply told Guid'Antonio all he needed to know. "He was here, wasn't he? Don't lie to me! I'll break your neck!"

"Who was here?" the man said, flinching, then recovering slightly. "Who are you talking about—"

Guid'Antonio slapped him, hard. "The monk!" he yelled. "WHERE'S MY DOG?"

"I don't—"

Guid'Antonio slapped him again, harder. "Tell me or I'll kill you!" he shouted in the man's face. "He had better not be dead!"

"Husband, please!" the woman howled. "Tell him! This is too much! We hadn't counted on this."

"What had you counted on?" Guid'Antonio shouted, anger ripping like fire through his veins.

"He said—he said he would pay twice the nightly rate," the woman said, wiping her runny nose with her hand. "Instead, he didn't pay anything. He ran!"

Her husband panted, struggling to breathe. "He fled after a young man came asking about his whereabouts late yesterday morning. I swear!"

Amerigo.

While Guid'Antonio was in church, in the piazza, in Caterina Niccolini's house, *Orsetto* had been in this kitchen. The woman standing before him now had not told Amerigo that when Amerigo asked her about the monk yesterday morning. Guid'Antonio resisted the urge to knock the trembling woman to the floor. "Gone where!" he said.

The innkeeper shrugged. "I don't know. He could still be around. He mentioned family in Volterra. He said they are all dead."

Guid'Antonio took an involuntary step back, startled to hear the name of that unfortunate town on the innkeeper's lips. "Volterra," he said.

The man nodded. "Yes. Too, there was his dialect. His speech was different from here."

"We didn't know the dog was yours, Dottore, I swear on

the Virgin," the woman said. "The monk is gone, yes, but—" Whimpering, with shaking hands she pointed to the curtain separating the front room from the kitchen. "Have mercy! He—he left him here, he was in a hurry. He said the dog was a burden. We didn't know what to do with him—"

Since midday, Monday.

Guid'Antonio's throat tightened. *Please God, if you have ever granted me anything*—as if in a dream he walked into the kitchen and found the puppy's lifeless body on the floor wrapped in a bundle of cloth.

Guid'Antonio felt as if he were floating on air, his breath hushed. *"Orsetto?"*

Nothing.

Gently, he picked up the limp ball of fur and cradled the puppy against his breast. No heartbeat in the puppy's chest. An odd smell prickled Guid'Antonio's nose. *Fear.* Also the smell of the unguent, or poison, or whatever the monk had used to sedate *Orsetto*. To kill him, perhaps. *Orsetto* had been so scared.

He kissed the top of the puppy's head, patting the curls gently, the round little belly. Tears sprang to his eyes. *"Orsetto,"* he whispered. "My Little Bear. I'm so sorry. I love you, I love you, my little man." How could he have forgotten the puppy for even one moment? He had been distracted and worried these last few days, granted, but there was no excuse for this. He would never forgive himself.

And then he felt a soft, fluttering sensation beneath the palm of his hand. The puppy was breathing. Stunned, Guid'Antonio gently, rhythmically blew air into *Orsetto's* nose and mouth. After a moment, the puppy took several long breaths. *A miracle, praise God.*

Guid'Antonio raced from the inn, holding the dog close. A grey horse tethered to a nearby rung along the loggia wall snorted, dancing on its hooves. Cradling *Orsetto*, catching the grey and awkwardly untying its reins, Guid'Antonio leaped into the saddle and pounded across Piazza della Signoria in the direction of home, oblivious to the sleepy-eyed messenger boys jumping from his path. Francesca—the Spedale—was too distant. Wheeling the galloping horse toward the Red Lion district in Santa Maria Novella, he rode fast to Luca Landucci's apothecary shop, the Sign of the Stars.

Twenty-Five

THE SIGN OF THE STARS

"Luca!" The bell announcing visitors who entered Luca's shop jangled in Guid'Antonio's ears.

"Who's there?" A stout fellow rushed from the back room, slapping aside the curtain that divided the shop from the Landucci family's living quarters. "What do you mean running in here, yelling at the top of your lungs so early in the morning?" Luca stared. "Dottore! Why are you here?" The apothecary's gaze fell on the limp dog in Guid'Antonio's arms. He glanced up, his eyes stricken. *What's this?*

"Orsetto," Guid'Antonio said. "Poisoned." *Not Death Cap. Please, God, no.*

"Give him to me, quickly!"

A measuring scale and a small bronze statue of Hygeia, the Greek goddess of good health, stood on the counter. Luca swept the scale and statue aside, accepted the puppy in his arms, and carefully placed him on the counter's wooden surface, leaning close, sniffing *Orsetto's* nose and mouth. "Here's a distinctive smell."

THE HEARTS OF ALL ON FIRE

"Hurry!" Guid'Antonio said. "Give him something. Help!"

Calmly, Luca said, "First, I need to know what to give. *Orsetto*—yes, boy, look at me. Good boy. His eyes are not dilated. He's not drooling. He's sleepy." Tapping his fingers together, Luca added, "You say poison—what makes you think so?"

"What else?! Some bastard coward stole him, poisoned him, and fled town."

"Fled from where?"

"An inn called The Bell."

"Not Death Cap in your house, then," Luca said, lifting his brow.

"No! Luca—"

Calmly, the apothecary raised his hands. "I don't believe *Orsetto* has been poisoned, my friend. From the smell of his mouth, I think he has been sedated with poppy juice, or perhaps Foxglove, just enough to make him drowsy and remain still."

Foxglove, Fairy Thimbles, Dead Men's Bells. "Foxglove is poisonous," Guid'Antonio said.

"Too much of it, yes." Luca sniffed *Orsetto* again. "There is a distinctive stink about him."

"Fear," Guid'Antonio said. "My boy was so scared." Leaning down, grateful beyond measure, he patted *Orsetto* gently on the head.

"Time and love will take care of that," Luca said.

At the shop's stone sink Luca wet a cloth with water and bathed *Orsetto's* face, softly cooing the dog's name. Guid'Antonio stared, transfixed, as the puppy shuddered, blinked his eyes open, and closed them again. "What now?" Guid'Antonio pressed.

"Pray. But truly, Dottore, I believe your dog will be well."

Guid'Antonio felt weak all over, the lump in his throat the size of a chunk of coal. Was the scent of fear emanating from him now? He smoothed his hand over *Orsetto*, who was motionless beneath the small blanket Luca retrieved from the shelf beneath the counter. Guid'Antonio patted the puppy again, loving him with all his soul and heart. Complete alarm. Now, fragile hope. Swallowing hard, he thanked God for His grace, thanked God for everything. Thanked God and Luca Landucci. "What should I do for him at home?"

"Offer him water to drink. No food today. Tomorrow, something easy for him to digest. Have Domenica boil a chicken breast, perhaps." Luca studied Guid'Antonio quietly, his eyes roaming Guid'Antonio's hastily donned brown tunic, hose, boots. "A cowardly bastard took him, you say?"

"Yes! When I find him, he will pay. Not once, but many times over."

"He was right to run for his life," Luca said. "How did he know he was in danger of being found out? Why did he leave *Orsetto* at an inn?"

Gently, Guid'Antonio traced the back of his fingers along the puppy's little belly. "Amerigo went to The Bell yesterday seeking him because . . . well, never mind. I think that scared him and he ran. If not for Amerigo arriving when he did—" He drew a long breath, praising God for allowing him to move forward. "Luca," he said, still softly stroking *Orsetto*, "you mentioned Death Cap. If you had a mind to do so, where might you purchase it in Florence?" *Not from one of Cesare's two vendors,* Guid'Antonio thought. Amerigo's conversation with them had convinced him of that.

Luca replied cautiously, weighing his response with care. "Not on just any street corner, Dottore." *You are suggesting murder in the case of the merchant, Orlando Niccolini.*

All shall be revealed.

"Where, then?" Guid'Antonio said. He knew the answer but wondered if Luca would suggest other resources.

"From some demon peddler of weapons and drugs come

to town for the purpose, mayhap?" Luca said. "They appear like vermin on holy days. Sadly, such wicked people often are found mostly on the south side of the river, holy day, or no."

In Santo Spirito, that sprawling quarter on the Arno's left bank. "Not by any licensed apothecary?" Guid'Antonio said, sniffing *Orsetto* for the sheer pleasure of it, no matter the dog stank, wiping the puppy's face with the damp cloth and rejoicing when *Orsetto* stirred again, blinking blearily at him. "On the sly, I mean."

Luca drew himself up. "Dottore! We are trustworthy men enrolled in the Doctors and Apothecaries Guild. Death Cap serves no medicinal purpose." He calmed himself. "I worry for Niccolini's widow. It is always difficult to lose a spouse, but surely the loss of her husband is especially trying for Mona Caterina."

This sharpened Guid'Antonio's interest in that lady. "Especially trying how?"

With a glass dropper, Luca squeezed water from a pottery jug into *Orsetto's* mouth. The dog snuffled and choked a bit before back settling down. Again, watching this hurt Guid'Antonio, but he knew Luca's ministrations were for the best and well meant. "The lady Caterina is completely alone in the world now, as she has no children," Luca said. "Though not for lack of effort."

Guid'Antonio laughed lightly. "Luca, how could you possibly know this?"

The druggist was contrite. He should not have spoken of a patron's personal situation. But clearly he was affronted, perhaps most particularly by the word *possibly*. "Because," he said, lowering his voice, although they were the shop's sole occupants, "the lady has tried all manner of practices and potions. All came to nothing. And now—" Luca shrugged. "She's alone and thirty or so. Much too old to harbor dreams of a family, children, and grandchildren." He crossed himself.

"What practices? Did she share them with you? The practices, I mean."

Luca reddened. "Of course not."

The implication Caterina Niccolini was trying everything was plain.

"What potions?" Guid'Antonio asked.

"The usual," Luca said. "The most efficacious one made by bruising the fresh leaves of mandrake in a mortar and adding this and that." *The exact recipe is my secret*, Luca's raised brow said.

"Again, mandrake is poisonous," Guid'Antonio said.

To this, the druggist replied smugly, "Not in the right hands."

"What else did Caterina purchase?"

Luca sighed, plainly regretting ever taking this path, but said, "The cooked and cooled berries and bark from an elderberry tree. Ingesting this often helps in the birth of a boy. And before you say it, yes, elderberry is poisonous, that is why people should purchase any potion from a licensed apothecary." He smiled.

Here it was: children and the length people would go to in an effort to produce one or twelve of their own. As for practices to observe when struggling to plant seed, in that Guid'Antonio was well versed. His wife had seen to it. Prayers for a child every night before going to bed. Not too much wine beforehand. But if wine were consumed, it should come from Venice, since drinking wine imported from the Lion of the Adriatic would produce boys. Guid'Antonio himself subscribed to Leon Battista Alberti's insistence in his book *On the Family* that the woman must be fully aroused before the man shot home the bolt.

For a brief moment, thinking he would stand on his head and couple with Maria if she ever spoke to him again, he wondered if she ever had sought aid from Luca Landucci. Not that he would ask. "Did Caterina purchase the items in question herself, or did she send a maid?"

"Dottore Guid'Antonio," Luca began. "You know I cannot—"

Guid'Antonio stared at the other man with eyes as round and silver as the coins in Lorenzo de' Medici's prized collection in Palazzo Medici.

"—She came here herself." Luca's glance darted away. As if he had another confidence he would divulge only upon threat of death—and perhaps not even then.

On the counter *Orsetto* drew a contented breath. Guid'Antonio patted the puppy with care and felt its heartbeat, soft but steady.

"At any rate, the last time I saw Orlando Niccolini, he seemed hale enough, other than the sneezing and fever making him miserable here in the height of summer," Luca said. "I sold him several infusions."

"Yes." Guid'Antonio considered telling Luca about Niccolini's sick liver but decided to let that go. In the meadow on Thursday Caterina Niccolini had referenced the cold remedies her husband had purchased from Luca Landucci. Holly leaves and honey, also clover, mashed and boiled. "Well—" He spread his hands, his eyes questioning on *Orsetto* and then on his friend.

"You say you'll find the culprit who harmed him," Luca said. "In God's name, how?"

"I'll return to The Bell, the inn where he stayed while he was in town." Perhaps the landlord had noted the man's religious order or could say whether or not his robes were a disguise. He could ride to Volterra, as well; somehow, he would uncover what that devil had meant to happen here in Florence. Obviously, as Guid'Antonio had told Luca, Amerigo's unexpected visit to The Bell yesterday mid-morning had sent the excuse-for-a-man scurrying like the rat he was, otherwise—Guid'Antonio glanced at *Orsetto*. Otherwise, *Orsetto* would be far away or dead. "First, I'll take *Orsetto* home," he said.

"This day is young, Dottore. Go to the inn. I'll see to the pup. He's a stout little man. All shall be well." Luca smiled, ruffling the thick curls along *Orsetto's* side and the top of his head.

☦

Despite Luca's assurances, Guid'Antonio's chest felt leaden as he walked out onto Canto de' Tornaquinci, his soul dispirited, restless, and fueled with anger. Get his hands on the rat bastard who had taken *Orsetto*, and he would rip him limb from limb.

He was reaching for the grey's reins—eventually, the owner of the horse would have an apology and a few coins—when he heard a familiar voice call his name and saw his friend, Francesco Nori, hurrying toward him. "Guid'Antonio, bless my good fortune! I was on my way to your house—" the banker started, but then frowned. "Are you ill? You look pale."

"I feel pale," Guid'Antonio said. "And you appear agitated. What now?"

"I've come from the jail." The banker's face was flushed with excitement. "You know how in the middle of the night you wake tossing and turning, your thoughts chasing you relentlessly round and round—"

Guid'Antonio huffed a laugh. "Yes."

Francesco lowered his voice. "Yesterday after the funeral, when you told us Orlando Niccolini probably had been murdered, I kept wondering who might have done it. Last night I bolted up in bed, having sewn together theft and death."

Guid'Antonio studied Francesco closely. "Theft and death?"

Francesco leaned in: "Niccolini told me he caught an

employee at Spinelli and Spinelli stealing from the company. A young accounting apprentice. Niccolini found him out and meant to report the crime to Palla, who surely would have the boy's hand, if not his balls, as punishment."

Fraud. "The boy's name?" Guid'Antonio said.

"Andrea Antinori from the Santa Croce quarter. A youth not yet twenty."

Guid'Antonio considered this new information. Andrea Antinori was the apprentice Caterina Niccolini had mentioned when Guid'Antonio visited her yesterday following her husband's funeral. "Go on."

With escalating energy, Francesco Nori said, "It occurred to me if anyone had reason to kill our cloth merchant it would be the boy, especially if Niccolini had not yet got around to reporting him for stealing. Just shut Niccolini up and go merrily on his way. No one ever would know Andrea had been pilfering money from the shop. I hurried to Spinelli and Spinelli at first light this morning to see if, indeed, there is an Andrea Antinori in their employ. Yes! But no longer—Andrea did not return to work after the Saint John's Day celebrations.

"This made me doubly suspicious," Francesco went on, "so I hurried to the jail to find Palla and tell him what was afoot, and now to find you, since quite likely this solves the mystery of Niccolini's death, and we may all rest easy. There is no killer on the loose who may mean to slaughter one or another of us." Francesco shrugged a smile. "At least not this time around."

"And *had* Niccolini reported the alleged theft to Palla?" Guid'Antonio said.

"No! Palla knew nothing about it until I spoke with him a short while ago outside the jail, thank God he was there! He's on Antinori's tail even now, riding hard to Santa Croce where the boy lives."

"How could Palla possibly know where—"

Francesco touched his chest. *"Moi encore.* When Niccolini

told me about the fraud, he mentioned Antinori's dwelling."

"*Grazie!*" Guid'Antonio grabbed the reins of his borrowed mount and leaped into the saddle. Questioning the landlord at The Bell would have to wait. "Did Niccolini say where in Santa Croce?" Beneath him, the borrowed horse snorted and shuffled about.

"Where's Flora?" Francesco said, stepping away from the grey's sharp, shifting hooves.

"It's a lengthy story," Guid'Antonio said.

Francesco laughed quietly. "No doubt. Anyway, Antinori lives with his uncle Otto, who has a leather shop in Piazza Santa Croce. On the left as you face the church, the shop identified with the typical sign. Ride hard, and you stand a good chance of finding Palla there."

☦

Astride the grey, Guid'Antonio galloped in the direction of Florence Cathedral. After some moments of hard riding, he slowed the horse to manage the cobbled lane that twisted between Giotto's bell tower and Piazza Sant'Elisabetta before spilling into the noisome quarter of cloth-dying and leather- and wool-cleansing shops huddled around the Franciscan church of Santa Croce. Sweat-drenched construction workers toiled in the piazza, some pushing cartloads of earth and stone for the pilings beneath the columns of the new infirmary loggia, others with bundles of walnut planks for the wood-workers who would cut the wood with fine-toothed saws for the infirmary's cabinetry, rafters, and other furnishings.

Guid'Antonio glanced rapidly from the house where Maria's family lived on the far right side of the square to the church at the distant end of the great rectangle, the banging of hammers assaulting his ears. Santa Croce's unadorned brick facade gave no evidence of the magnificently sculpted tombs and rich frescoes painted in private family chapels by Giotto, Aretino, and other Florentine craftsmen. The last time Guid'Antonio had stepped inside that echoing space had been to admire the *Madonna delle Latte* Francesco Nori had commissioned Benedetto da Maiano to sculpt as a memorial for Francesco's late father. Around the back of the church, beyond the leather school and workshop, lay the warren of alleys and byways where Chiara Caretto had lived with her grandfather.

His gaze swept the wooden structures hugging the left side of the piazza where Palla Palmieri's brown-clad figure had just flown from Otto Antinori's Shoes & Belts, Palla's dagger bouncing at his hip.

Guid'Antonio rode toward him, the grey flicking her ears restlessly, shying from Palla's horse as Palla leaped into his saddle. "Andrea Antinori?" Guid'Antonio yelled.

"How did you know—Oh, never mind. Yes!" Palla's horse grunted, flighty, tossing its mane. "He's gone! But not far—a short ride into the country."

Guid'Antonio's horse wheeled. "His uncle told you this?"

Palla's lips tilted in a smile. "Remember, I am the chief of police. Apparently, Antinori's mother is a spinner in a nearby village. I'm riding there now, and, yes, I'm in a hurry!"

"With no sergeants at hand?"

"Why, when I have you?" Palla steadied his mount. *"Andiamo!"*

Guid'Antonio calmed the grey, intending to ride at once with Palla, but as he did so, movement on the far side of the piazza caught his eye. At the eastern side of Santa Croce's first cloister rose the small brick dome of the Pazzi family chapel. Guid'Antonio drew a sharp breath, startled to see Little Francesco de' Pazzi standing at the chapel entrance watching him without expression, his image as pale as a specter in a dream. The image changed. Now Franceschino was hanging by the neck outside the windows of Palazzo della Signoria, his hands tied behind him, his watery blue eyes bulging, blood gushing from his mouth. *I am not sorry!* he silently screamed. *I am not and I never will be!*

Uncertainty pulsed through Guid'Antonio. It had been a trick of the light, the image already fading into the shadows . . . and yet, it had been frightening. Not sorry? Not sorry for what? Shaking his head to rid it of cobwebs, he nudged the grey into a trot and caught up with Palla as he raced from Santa Croce.

Twenty-Six

ANDREA ANTINORI

They rode from Florence quickly, galloping from Santa Croce toward the river, then to Borg'Ognissanti, urging their horses through the Prato Gate, holding the middle of the road as verdant meadows, groves of firs, cypresses, laurel, and myrtle flashed by, along with battlemented towers abandoned long ago, relics of a by-gone age, when families fired arrows from slit windows, fighting to keep enemies at bay.

At the first village they came upon, Palla hailed a baker shoveling bread from the community oven. "The Antinoris," Palla said, jutting his chin. "Quickly!" Eyeing them with disdain, the baker indicated a sign with a spinning wheel sketched on it in white, along with an arrow pointing down a dirt road.

Riding alongside one another, not bothering to approach the Antinori dwelling with stealth—where would Andrea run to if, in fact, he were here?—Guid'Antonio and Palla traded a look. *Here we go again.* Guid'Antonio calmed himself, admiring the bright yellow *genestra* stretching out around them and the hawks circling their heads.

A stone cottage came in view, one whose door bore the image of a white spinning wheel identical to the wheel on the sign in the village. "This was too easy," Palla said.

Guid'Antonio grunted. "Something must be."

A grin crossed Palla's face. "By the way, my man found *chamomile* thriving in the meadow where Cesare said it would be."

This side of the Prato Gate. "Of course he did," Guid'Antonio said.

The Antinori cottage was modest but the ground well-tended, with a garden of dill, fennel, and mint and a riot of scarlet poppies and sweet-scented wildflowers sweeping around both sides of the cottage into the pine wood forest. They slowed their horses to a walk, Guid'Antonio wondering what manner of mischief they would find inside this house.

†

He dismounted behind Palla but fell in step beside him as they strode into the farmyard, sending chickens scattering in a storm of white feathers and a cat bounding into the lavender flowering around the edges of the vegetable garden. "Andrea Antinori!" Palla called, slamming the cottage door open, bursting in, knife drawn.

Two youths occupied the single room, both about eighteen years of age. Lying on a pallet on the floor, one was dark, his brown hair lanky and unkempt. The other, frozen and fearful with his back to the hearth and a bowl of steaming liquid in his hands, was lean-limbed, tall and fair, with blue eyes and golden curls. Shoulders slumping, he exhaled a breath of despair. "*Signore* Palmieri, I am he."

Carefully, Andrea Antinori sat the bowl on the trestle beside a host of woven baskets and a chunk of bread loosely covered with a thin white cloth. It struck Guid'Antonio forcibly that he had never seen such a terrified expression as the one on the face of this boy. Clearly, Andrea was guilty of something. Now, he was facing the chief of police of Florence.

"That same Andrea Antinori who is an accounting apprentice at Spinelli and Spinelli under the hand of the cloth merchant Orlando Niccolini?" Palla said.

"Yes," Andrea managed, his voice weak with the threat of tears, his eyes flicking from Palla to Guid'Antonio and back again.

"And this is?" Palla indicated the youth on the pallet. The young man stared at him, his dark eyes shining with fever and alarm. Despite the blankets weighing him down and the hot breeze wafting in the cottage windows, his body shivered uncontrollably.

A light sweat broke out on Andrea's upper lip. "This is Emilio Barucci, my—cousin," he said. "Let's go outside, please! Emilio has nothing to do with this."

"To do with *what*?" Palla demanded, once they were in the yard, his eyes as hard as stones.

Andrea extended his hands. "*Signore* Palmieri, Dottore"— he glanced at Guid'Antonio—"I know why you are here."

"You know who I am?" Guid'Antonio said.

"Who doesn't?" Andrea shrugged. "These last few weeks, Ser Niccolini spoke of little else. Of you. Of your Saint John's Day celebration. All Florence knows you, in any case, Dottore."

"Now we have that settled—" Palla cast a wry look at Guid'Antonio. "Andrea, you say you know why we're here. *Bene!* Let's move along to how you murdered Orlando Niccolini."

Andrea's mouth fell open. "Murdered him? No! I borrowed money from the shop, yes, but that's all. I never killed him! I couldn't kill anyone!"

"*Borrowed* it?" Palla laughed. "We know about the fraud, the theft. You stole money from the shop, and Niccolini was about to expose you."

Andrea recovered, speaking haltingly. "I was frightened, yes! I feared he would report me, though we had an agreement. Then he died suddenly, and—"

"And you ran," Palla said.

Andrea looked about to faint. "I came here to escape. I knew if it became known I had borrowed money from the wool shop accounts, the law—you!—would suspect me of foul play. I could hang! When I said I knew why you were here, I meant because of the money, not because I killed Ser Niccolini. In the end, my fears were correct."

"This is garbled," Palla said. "An agreement? Kiss my ass."

From the cottage there came a series of racking coughs. Andrea glanced toward the open door, his expression pained. Blinking back tears, he appealed to Guid'Antonio. "Everyone knows your servant, Cesare Ridolfi, accidentally poisoned Ser Niccolini. On that count, surely, I have nothing to fear. That was your official decision, was it not, *Signore*?" He looked at the police chief.

Palla flushed deeply. "That was before Orlando's notary told me about the money theft."

That was before I told you about the third mushroom found in the dead dog in my alley, and this became a case of possible premeditated murder, Guid'Antonio thought. "Andrea," he said, "putting Cesare aside, you say you borrowed the wool shop money. If so, running could be the death of you. Under our law, anyone who runs is guilty." *Of everything. The end.*

"So, we are going to discuss this?" Palla said, rolling his eyes. "Don't let me stop you. There's nothing quite so entertaining as a good, convoluted tale."

Andrea moistened his lips. "I needed time to figure out what to do. I knew if my transgression against the wool shop were revealed, people might suspect I killed Niccolini and forget Cesare Ridolfi."

"Precisely," Palla said, bowing to him.

"Slow down," Guid'Antonio said. "Andrea, you say *if* it came out. Niccolini stated unequivocally to his notary that he meant to report you. So . . . you can see this suggests you killed him to keep him quiet."

"No!" Andrea cried. "He changed his mind! He and I have a written contract! He found out about the money and threatened me with exposure, but then he swore he would say nothing to the Spinelli family. He would repay the coffers entirely from his own funds. In turn, I would repay him, slowly. I have been doing so from my earnings. He said he was keeping count."

"Since when?" Guid'Antonio said.

"These last few weeks." Andrea hung his head, fighting tears. "Forever now."

"That is when you first started taking money?" Guid'Antonio said. "In early summer?"

"Yes."

"How much?"

"Two florins."

"And how much have you repaid?"

"I had already spent one florin, but I returned the other one. I have been trying to repay the one spent, but it—it is difficult."

So, if what the boy said was true and he had been making payments to Niccolini, he remained less than one florin in debt.

Scowling, Palla said, "No doubt it is. Why would Niccolini protect you? Out of the goodness of his heart? You're talking in circles, my fair-haired youth."

"Because—" Andrea licked his lips, glancing away. "He liked me. He had no son of his own."

Hmmm, thought Guid'Antonio.

Palla laughed. "There are two Orlando Niccolinis, mayhap. Mine liked no one, except his young girl, from what I hear. Where is this contract? Speak carefully now."

"I don't have it," Andrea said.

Palla laughed. "Of course you don't."

Guid'Antonio watched and waited. Could Andrea's plight get any worse? Yes.

Grimly, Palla said, "Andrea Antinori, you are under arrest for extorting funds from the Spinelli family and for the murder of Orlando Niccolini. You are on your way to jail."

"No! No," Andrea cried, his eyes on the house, where his cousin lay ill. "I can't leave Emilio! I'm telling the truth, I swear on my mother! Orlando showed me the paper! I signed it in good faith, and he said together we would go to his notary, the Medici banker, Francesco Nori. Orlando promised he would sign it, too, but then—he kept delaying. Perhaps—perhaps you could find it in his papers? It has my signature."

"Palla," Guid'Antonio said. "We know Niccolini had not yet reported Andrea."

"Just so!" Palla said. "And Andrea knew it, too! He understood Orlando Niccolini was sailing for London, leaving Andrea with the sword of Damocles hanging over his head, so he poisoned him. Fear, Andrea Antinori! Fear Orlando would change his mind and reveal your thievery upon his return from England. Fear you couldn't pay, fear you would die in the Stinche or chained in one of our underground cells with rats nibbling your toenails."

Quietly, Guid'Antonio addressed Palla Palmieri. "How did Andrea administer the poison? Orlando ingested Death Cap at my *festa*. Cesare Ridolfi served the salads. This young man was nowhere near. I would have seen him."

Andrea stepped back, his downy cheeks flushed with heat. For the first time since they had come into the yard, he fell silent, though he seemed freshly alarmed.

"Andrea," Guid'Antonio said, "when did you leave Florence and ride here? Remember, we can speak with your Uncle Otto in Santa Croce."

"And will," Palla said.

Andrea drew a shuddering breath. "Saturday morning."

That was well after the news of Orlando Niccolini's death swept through town. If Andrea *had* somehow murdered the merchant, why would he not leave immediately after adding Death Cap to his salad? Andrea had not been in the kitchen, surely. Here was another question for Domenica Ridolfi, Gaspare, and the kitchen girl.

"How is not up to me," Palla said. "Andrea Antinori, I repeat, you are under arrest for fraud and the murder of Orlando Niccolini by Death Cap poisoning. Let the court unravel the details. Now, I mean to go inside and peek into those baskets." He smiled at Guid'Antonio. "I have been doing that a lot, lately."

†

Leather creaked as they rode from the farm, Andrea leading the way, hands bound with rope to the pommel of his saddle. Palla had searched the cottage for Death Cap and uncovered nothing. Meanwhile, Guid'Antonio had kept watch as Andrea saddled his horse, making idle conversation with the lad, or so he had let it seem. Why had Andrea taken two florins from the wool shop? To do so was exceedingly dangerous. Get caught, and his career as an accounting apprentice, any dream of accomplishment, would be shuttered forever in Florence. At the far extreme, he could hang. Andrea seemed a bright lad, far too bright to risk everything by stealing from his employers.

"Andrea, why did you take the money?" Guid'Antonio had asked while they waited for the police chief to return from the cottage. "You must have had good reason."

"My—my mother is ill," the boy said, his horse pawing the dirt, impatient to go. "I needed medical advice and medicaments to make her well."

His mother. Such a sad little lie. "Which doctor did you visit?" Guid'Antonio said.

"Yours. Maestra Francesca Vernacci. The best doctor in Florence."

Mine. "Of course," Guid'Antonio said. "Your mother is blessed to have such a son as you. Where is she now? Your mother?" Guid'Antonio glanced around the yard. The cottage had been deserted but for Andrea and his sickly, dark-haired cousin.

"The market in the village," Andrea said.

"Recovered enough to go there, then. Praise God in all His Mercy." Guid'Antonio crossed himself.

Hot blotches of color rose in Andrea's milky cheeks. "Praise Him." His eyes shifted toward the cottage, where Guid'Antonio envisioned Emilio half-awake on the narrow bed, shivering, covered in blankets.

"Do you fear for your friend?" Guid'Antonio quietly said.

"Yes! I should be here with him, not in Florence. I should have been allowed to tell him farewell."

"Who will take care of him now? He should not be alone," Guid'Antonio said.

"My mother will try," Andrea said, but he did not sound convinced.

†

"You noted the traveling bags snug in a corner by the hearth?" Palla said beneath his breath as they rode from the cottage with Andrea out ahead, a quiet pace, taking their time on the return journey to Florence. "The bags were half-hidden behind the spinning wheel."

Behind not only a spinning wheel, but a sturdy chair, and wooden blocks wrapped with strands of wool dyed rich purple and red. "I did," Guid'Antonio said. Clearly, once Andrea had fled his native city, he had meant to keep running with Emilio, God only knew where. Guid'Antonio and Palla had nipped that plan in the bud. That and the fact Emilio Barucci was far too weak to travel and obviously had been for several weeks now.

Hope. Faith. Both had shone in Andrea Antinori and Emilio Barucci's eyes, along with unrelenting fear.

Twenty-Seven

A FISHER OF MEN

Here is the truth about Guid'Antonio Vespucci: he spends most nights restless in bed or barefoot in his *studiolo* contemplating the flickering light of a solitary flame. Tuesday evening, with one hand fisted at his mouth and the other hand resting on his puppy asleep in his lap, he is moodily considering the last few days. First, Amerigo. He has not seen his nephew since yesterday in Piazza Trinita, on Monday, just before Guid'Antonio's visit to Caterina Niccolini. Since then he and his darling nephew have been ships passing in the night. According to Domenica Ridolfi, Amerigo did come home in the late afternoon today, seeking Guid'Antonio, but of course Guid'Antonio had been in the countryside with Palla Palmieri, while *Orsetto* had remained with Luca Landucci at the Sign of the Stars.

Amerigo said that according to their neighbors, the landlord and landlady at The Bell fled town this morning with only the clothes on their backs. He turned the place over but couldn't locate a ledger of names—he said you would understand.

Yes. Those villains had flown the instant Guid'Antonio had left the inn with his limp little dog in his arms. So much for questioning them further about the monk if, indeed, monk he be. Guid'Antonio could have had that ledger, could have ranted and railed at the landlord, threatened him, demanded more information. But he had been too rattled, his only concern, *Orsetto*. He burns with anger, second-guessing himself, cursing himself, and then sharpens his focus, willing himself to keep a clear head, feeling blessed to have his puppy with him, his little bear. A foul odor still oozes from *Orsetto's* pores, but he is sound. The little *Lagotto Romagnolo* had even licked a bit of bone broth from the bowl Domenica offered him in the kitchen before Guid'Antonio retired this evening.

Someone took him Monday morning, Guid'Antonio had told her. From now on, at all times, the garden gate must be bolted as people come and go. We've become lax. We cannot let people come and go as they please, not anymore.

Tenderly, he takes the drowsy puppy from his lap and places him in the padded basket at his feet on the *studiolo* floor, then sits back down in his chair, considering the monk and why he had taken *Orsetto*. According to the innkeeper, that miscreant hailed from Volterra, a small town southwest of Florence, whose citizens had good reason to hate Guid'Antonio as one of the Medici family's most devoted supporters. Last summer in June 1472, Volterra had been sacked when the *reggimento* sent troops to squash a rebellion that threatened the peace of Florence. For reasons still unclear, Florence's hired army had moved swiftly out of control, murdering innocent men along with the guilty, raping women and children. This horrendous tragedy had been born of a quarrel over the rights to an alum mine that in the end proved worthless. Walking the streets with Lorenzo and Giuliano after the sack, Guid'Antonio had witnessed human bodies in pools of blood. Slaughtered animals littered the streets, and the Bishop's *palazzo* lay in ruins. Anything the hired soldiers on both sides—Volterra's mercenaries also had run amuck—anything they had not destroyed had been leveled by a landslide.

After surveying Volterra, the Medici brothers had offered survivors words of hope. Florence would send food, grain, and wine. Together, they would donate 2,000 florins in private funds for the rebuilding of the town. Christ, have mercy, and that was that. Except Guid'Antonio understands the Volterrans despise Lorenzo for the death blow dealt their town—and yes, along with many others, Guid'Antonio had backed Lorenzo's decision to send troops there under the leadership of the duke of Urbino, Federigo da Montefeltro. All uprisings against the Republic must be crushed. But how could a foreign monk possibly know who had supported Lorenzo and who had not? Why strike at Guid'Antonio? Because the puppy was an easy target? A failed attempt, but an attempt, still, by a man Guid'Antonio would like to see roast in hell.

In the small, intimate space surrounding him, Guid'Antonio dips his pen:

> *Yesterday* Orsetto *was stolen, but on these pages I shall not mention the details; it is enough to say he is now home safe. In other matters, my investigation into the cloth merchant, Orlando Niccolini's, death has turned on its head. Death by Cesare Ridolfi? No. By whom, then? Today Florence's chief of police arrested Niccolini's apprentice for theft (the boy, Andrea Antinori, stole funds from the wool shop where he was employed) and also for murder. Andrea's motive, according to Palla Palmieri, was to prevent Niccolini from reporting him to the authorities. While Andrea admits to thievery, he denies killing Niccolini. And if Andrea did not kill him? Well. Who did?*
>
> *I am casting about like a boatman bobbing on the*

Arno in a high wind, lowering my net for fish who flip their tails at me and vanish in the depths.

In Piazza Ognissanti Monday morning, as we spoke of the possibilities surrounding Orlando Niccolini's death, Giuliano de' Medici was the first to say the salad laced with Death Cap could have been served to anyone at my table, whether accidentally or on purpose. Love and money. Money and Andrea Antinori. Love and money and Orlando Niccolini's fourteen-year-old inamorata, *Elena Veluti. No matter how far-fetched, I believe this tale circles around to the dead girl, Chiara Caretto's, little ginger dog. I believe in the end* Cannella's *hunger will see Orlando's killer hanged, be he Andrea Antinori or another.*

Murky waters. Slippery fish.

Tuesday evening, 29th June
In the Year of Our Lord 1473
Guid'Antonio Vespucci, Florence

Twenty-Eight

EARTH TO EARTH AND DUST TO DUST
WEDNESDAY, 30TH JUNE 1473

Wednesday morning Guid'Antonio began work early by walking to the Merchant's Court in Piazza della Signoria to endorse a few legal documents, thence to Palla Palmieri's police headquarters and straight to Jacopo Caretto's cell. Beyond the thick iron bars, the wool beater lay stretched on a narrow cot. Guid'Antonio nodded to the guard, who turned a key in the iron lock and knocked back the bolt. Caretto cast a sneering glance toward the cell door, peering at Guid'Antonio through greasy bangs.

The prisoner did not seem afraid. He did not seem remorseful. "Jacopo," Guid'Antonio said. "You've admitted killing your granddaughter. Your punishment is meant to be fair, according to the law. Remain silent and gamble with your life. Unless you relish hanging, you'll tell me the circumstances surrounding her death. In just two days' time, based on my recommendation, the court will consider your fate."

Caretto swung his legs from the cot and rose to his full

height, his eyes filled with bone-chilling contempt. In his sixties, Jacopo Caretto was a big man and strong, typical of the men who, under the eyes of a watchful foreman, beat fleece after it had been washed and returned to the shop, a task requiring more physical strength than skill.

"Fuck your recommendation!" Jacopo spat, looming over Guid'Antonio, his voice grating like an iron shovel scraping stone. Beyond the cell, the guard fingered his knife.

Guid'Antonio stepped slightly away from the prisoner, signaling to Palla's man there was no cause for alarm. "No need for me to present a motive?" Guid'Antonio said, thinking, *No matter how twisted it may be.* "There are two sides to every story."

The wool beater flipped his fingers at Guid'Antonio in an insulting manner. "Exactly, Dottore! My sons are in the *cortile*, recording our plea for leniency."

Leniency. "On what grounds?" Guid'Antonio said.

Caretto stormed toward him, but Guid'Antonio stood fast, a blaze of crimson in the airless chamber. "I'm a man of good character! She bewitched me!" Caretto screamed.

"How so?" said Guid'Antonio.

Jacopo burst into wild laughter. "You think you can trick me? Tell you more, and, yes, I could hang! That is not going to happen."

Amazing, how on fire and confident Caretto was today, compared with his demeanor on Monday, when he had been resigned and as silent as the grave. Now, however, his family had stepped forward in full support, breathing air into his sails. Moving in, closing ranks. Why? "Your sons are here now?" Guid'Antonio said.

"Didn't I just say so?" Caretto grinned. "That little bitch deserved what she got, and were she here, I'd stick it to her again!"

Guid'Antonio's fingertips tingled, and again he wondered how and why God had connected him to this man.

†

In the *cortile*, two men approached Guid'Antonio. "Nosing around my father again?" the older of them said.

"And you are?"

"Jacopo's son, Salvatore. And this is Fenso, my brother. We've filed a written appeal."

"So I hear."

"The court will consider our plea Friday when you make your *disegno*," Fenso said. Guid'Antonio's oral report.

"I cannot wait," Guid'Antonio said.

So, the smaller of the two men was Jacopo Caretto's son, Fenso Caretto, who was a sausage-maker in Santa Croce, according to Amerigo. That same Fenso Caretto whose wife had offered five- or six-year-old Chiara Caretto shelter when the girl's parents' died, only to see her sent to live with her grandfather, instead. As for the appeal for leniency, there was nothing unusual about this. The Court of Criminal Justice heard appeals more often than not. Still, Guid'Antonio wondered what secrets these men were harboring when it came to Chiara Caretto and their father. "An appeal on what basis?" he said. *I am a good man, Jacopo had said.*

There's a laugh, thought Guid'Antonio.

Fenso scowled fiercely. "The magistrates will consider our father's virtuous character and the poor reputation of the girl. Everyone knows the magistrates would prefer an acquittal or a fine when and where they can."

The girl.

Brazen.

Bold.

"What else?" These men's desire to strut like crows and

sing like larks was writ all over them. And there was always *more*.

Fenso opened his mouth to speak, but his brother hushed him. "Rest assured our father will leave court with nothing more than a slap of congratulations on the back," Salvatore said. "What man could fault him for acting as he did, since he had good reason? *None.*"

"Good reason?" Guid'Antonio said.

Salvatore grinned. "*Addio*, Dottore." With that he stalked toward Jacopo's cell with Fenso on his heels.

☨

"Guid'Antonio!"

He turned to see Palla hurrying down the stone stairs toward him in tunic, hose, and boots in his familiar brown colors. "You look thoughtful," the police chief said, puffing out his breath.

"Just surprised by my fellow men."

"Still?" Palla laughed.

"It happens from time to time," Guid'Antonio said. "I just spoke with Jacopo's sons. As surely you know, they have filed an appeal."

Palla inclined his head. "That is their right. Do you wish to see it?"

"Does it contain Jacopo's motive? In that case—"

"No. Apparently, that information they are saving for court."

"Good. I love surprises," Guid'Antonio said. "You were looking for me?"

Palla studied Guid'Antonio's face, his eyes dark with triumph. "This morning even *before* witnesses came forward to say they saw Andrea Antinori fighting with Niccolini the afternoon the merchant was killed, Andrea admitted to me he was lying about his innocence and confessed to killing Niccolini."

Guid'Antonio grew still. Andrea Antinori, suddenly confessing to murder? He could not imagine Andrea killing anyone, or anything. Nor could he imagine him fighting with anyone, let alone his employer. Even without Andrea's confession of murder, the testimony of witnesses to a fight between the two men could be enough to see the boy hang. "Where did this fight occur?" he said.

"Near the meadow off Borg'Ognissanti. Your *festa* was there. As was the cloth merchant a short while later, unfortunately for him."

"Why did witnesses come forward now?" Guid'Antonio said.

"Because word travels quickly in Florence. These observant, good people heard Andrea is in jail and stepped forward to report the incident." Palla leaned in toward Guid'Antonio. "It was an altercation so violent it ended with Niccolini slapping our fair-haired boy soundly across the cheek before scurrying down All Saints to your table. An altercation Andrea did not mention when we talked with him yesterday in the country."

Orlando Niccolini had slapped Andrea Antinori. Was he so sure of the boy he did not fear retaliation? Well. If every apprentice in Florence killed his master after being slapped or cuffed about the head, Florence would be a messy place, indeed. Also, the merchant knew that later in the day he was leaving town for England, where Andrea could not reach him. "It makes sense the boy didn't mention the exchange," Guid'Antonio said. "It could have harmed his plea of innocence."

"That's putting it mildly." Palla laughed and performed a little dance. "Case closed in the matter of Orlando Niccolini."

"Again," Guid'Antonio said.

The smile dropped from Palla's mouth. He glanced around

the courtyard, then at Guid'Antonio. "Yes! Meanwhile, I have spoken with Mona Caterina."

Niccolini's wife, again. "That's quick," Guid'Antonio said.

"Better for her to hear the truth about her husband's murder from me, rather than on the street." A touch of truculence appeared in Palla's face. "Now, everyone will understand Cesare Ridolfi is innocent and was all along. You should be dancing, too."

"Not yet," Guid'Antonio said. His gaze swept toward the far corner of the *cortile,* where Salvatore and Fenso Caretto had just emerged from Jacopo's cell. Catching Guid'Antonio's eye, Salvatore grinned maliciously before slamming Jacopo's cell door behind him with such force, the sound clattered noisily around the jail.

Palla narrowed his eyes. "The delightful Caretto brothers," he said.

"Yes." The pair sauntered from the courtyard, snickering as they looked over their shoulders at Guid'Antonio. Such open contempt for him in his crimson cloak. He would like to encounter them in the dead of night, in brown. "How did Mona Caterina react when you told her about Andrea's confession?" Guid'Antonio asked.

"Stunned. She believed Orlando's demise due to accidental death by Cesare Ridolfi. She said never in one hundred years would she have suspected her husband's apprentice killed her husband. In the end, she accepted the truth falling like rose petals from my mouth. She wishes this sad affair at an end as much as we do."

"She said all that, our Caterina?"

"She did. I assured her the court will view that slap as proof of Andrea's guilt. What more motive could a man have to kill? Considering Orlando was a man of substance in the community, Andrea Antinori will hang. Or see his head roll, who knows."

Whereas in the case of Chiara Caretto—and in light of the Caretto family's appeal—the wool beater might very well suffer no more than a monetary fine and a light tap on the wrist. No more than that for the dancing girl from the Black Lion district.

†

Guid'Antonio located Andrea Antinori's cell along the heavily guarded row not far from Jacopo Caretto. The wool shop apprentice sat huddled on the stone floor in a corner at the foot of his cot, knees drawn to his chin. Startled when the iron door groaned open, Andrea flinched as his blue eyes lit on Guid'Antonio. "You wonder why I'm here," Guid'Antonio said.

Andrea drew his mouth down at the corners, unwilling to speak, lest he weep, Guid'Antonio supposed. After a moment Andrea accepted Guid'Antonio's hand for help rising from the floor, and together they sat on the cot, a small distance between man and boy. "Why did you confess to killing Orlando Niccolini?" Guid'Antonio said.

"Did Palla Palmieri send you here?" Andrea said, his breath small gasps of air.

"No, he's happy to close this case as it stands. I'm here of my own accord, a man with nothing but time on my hands. One who will ask again why you confessed to killing Orlando Niccolini. You who yesterday were innocent."

Andrea stirred, fidgeting with the hem of his tunic. "Yesterday, I didn't understand the workings of the court. This morning, the police chief explained I would have to appear before the magistrates in the Court of Criminal Justice and answer one ruthless question after another before they even came close to believing I didn't kill Orlando Niccolini." Andrea smiled, a sweet, sad flicker. "This way, it's settled. In that, there is comfort."

There is? thought Guid'Antonio. *Hmmm.* "Recant your false confession of murder, and we'll see where that lands," Guid'Antonio said. "As far as the charge of fraud goes, I'll represent you in court, seek a lesser punishment than losing your hand or hanging. You will swear you took the money for medicine for your mother. Even Niccolini's widow has mentioned your good character." He cut his eyes at the boy. "Though at the time I suppose she didn't know you stole funds from the company."

"Ser Niccolini told her nothing. *Ever*," Andrea said.

"I'll approach the Spinelli family and ask them to request mercy from the court," Guid'Antonio said. "As for your good character, others at the shop may speak for you, along with your mother and your cousin Emilio."

This had the desired effect. Andrea jerked up, wide-eyed and fearful. "No. No! Respect my wishes, please!"

Guid'Antonio pressed on, certain now that Emilio Barucci, cousin or no, had something, if not everything, to do with Andrea's false confession. Andrea did not want Emilio questioned in court, that much was clear. "I'll tell the Spinelli family the things you told Palla and me. Niccolini replaced the stolen money from his own pocket, and you were repaying him, correct?"

"Yes. But—"

"But what?"

"I'm begging you to leave this!" Andrea said. "I took the money and I killed Ser Niccolini!"

"Why?" Guid'Antonio said.

"Because as Palla said, Orlando was going to expose me!"

"For what? For the fraud, perhaps, and what else?"

Tears leaked from Andrea's eyes. "I'll never say."

Perhaps yes, perhaps no, Guid'Antonio thought. "What were you two arguing about on Saint John's Day? You were seen on Borg'Ognissanti. Orlando slapped you." Circling around, around, and around.

Andrea gasped. "How did you know that?"

"I said you were seen. Why were you arguing? Was it about the money?" Of course it wasn't, or at least not entirely, but he asked, anyway.

Andrea was sharp. "Tell you that and you will know everything."

"I will know eventually, anyway."

"Please go. I'm weary of this."

"You?" Guid'Antonio exhaled a soft laugh. "How about me?"

Standing, making as if to leave, he hesitated, then turned, facing the boy. "How did you do it?" he said.

"Do what?" Andrea said, confusion clouding his face.

"How did you kill Orlando Niccolini? How did you make certain he had the poisoned salad—him, particularly, since you certainly were not serving them, but anyway, taking a breathtaking risk considering the other men at the table, then put another Death Cap in Cesare's basket while also tossing one into my back alley? Or *vice versa*, who knows? You would have to have been in my kitchen. Were you?"

Andrea moistened his lips, and Guid'Antonio imagined the thoughts whirring in the boy's head. Kitchen basket, more than one poisonous mushroom, back alley? Why did he insist on claiming a murder he did not commit?

Andrea said nothing.

"Why did you kill the dog?" Guid'Antonio said.

Andrea's voice cracked. "Dog?" He stopped abruptly. "You're trying to trick me!"

"I'm trying to help you," Guid'Antonio said. "A dog was found poisoned in my alley the day after Orlando died. Death Cap."

"I—" Andrea faltered. "I—why would you help me?"

"Because I have a kind heart." Guid'Antonio smiled at him

benevolently, thinking, and also, since you are innocent, someone else is guilty of murder.

Guid'Antonio's comment gave Andrea pause. After a moment, quietly, Andrea said, "The only way to help me is to accept the fact I killed Orlando Niccolini, and quit—"

Guid'Antonio inclined his head. "Quit what?"

"Bedeviling me! Either way, I will hang!" Bending his head like a penitent, he averted his face and stared at the cell floor. "God wills it, I believe."

Guid'Antonio sighed inwardly. Should he touch the boy? Yes? No? Stepping forward, he placed a hand on Andrea's shoulder, then motioned for the guard.

†

"A false confession?" Amerigo whistled beneath his breath. "By all that's holy, why would anyone confess to a murder he didn't commit?"

"That is the question," Guid'Antonio said.

They were in the Red Lion Wednesday afternoon, seated at their usual trestle with their backs to the wall. Brick masons, carpenters, and glaziers crowded the smoky, candlelit *taverna*, seated at wine-stained tables or standing by the hinged service counter, drinking Chianti and grumbling about low wages, while the taverner, Neri Saginetto, shook his head in sympathy and kept the *vino* flowing. Perched on a stool near the counter, Neri's daughter, Evangelista, sat contentedly dressing a doll with the remnants of silk and brocade Guid'Antonio had given her in May for her seventh birthday.

"Who is this Andrea Antinori?" Amerigo said, frowning. "Not one of *the* Antinoris, surely."

"Nay. Only some distant kinsman of that illustrious wine-making family. He's an accounting apprentice at Spinelli and Spinelli. Or was."

"And that is his connection with Niccolini," Amerigo said. "Yes."

"Niccolini slapped him?" Amerigo was aghast. "Men have killed for far less than that."

"Of course they have," Guid'Antonio said. *Passione.*

"No one mentioned this Andrea boy when I visited Spinelli and Spinelli Tuesday morning," Amerigo said.

"Why would they?" Guid'Antonio stirred the soup in his bowl, inhaling the hearty aroma of white beans, carrots, garlic, and chicken broth. When was the last time he had eaten? "Andrea had yet to be arrested then, so there was nothing for his fellow employees to say about him. Come to that, their silence regarding him suggests no one was looking askance at him for any reason."

Amerigo said, "Given the stolen money, Niccolini held in his hands the power to see Andrea's life destroyed. All hope of future employment as an accountant eventually earning ten florins a year ruined, if Orlando exposed him for fraud. Not to mention punishment in our courts."

"But he did *not* kill him," Guid'Antonio said. "Motive, plenty. Means? Somehow, he could have procured the Death Cap, after all he has lived in the country. Opportunity? At our *festa*—no. Everyone involved in our kitchen swears there were no strangers there on the day of our celebration."

Amerigo's eyes twinkled. "Maybe he disguised himself as one of our trumpeters."

"This is serious," Guid'Antonio said.

"Stranger means have been found," Amerigo said. "Remember—"

"Biscotto," Guid'Antonio said, greeting Evangelista's dog, who had come over and nudged Guid'Antonio's leg with his nose. "Yes, you are a fine boy." He patted *Biscotto's* head, admiring the animal's kind brown eyes and soft yellow fur.

Neri hastened over with more bread, a plate of cheese and

grapes, and a pot of honey. "*Biscotto!* Stop bothering our guests."

"You know I enjoy his company," Guid'Antonio said. "He's a good big boy."

"*Grazie.* Is *Orsetto* well?" The taverner screwed up his face, his eyes flashing a challenge. "If anyone tries to snatch *Biscotto*, I'll hunt him down and slaughter him in the street! Have you found the madman who took your boy? That monk, or priest, or whatever he was?"

As Neri spoke, Amerigo lowered his head, subdued, and Guid'Antonio smothered a groan. By now, everyone in Florence must know about the monk's attempt to steal his dog, not to mention how a crazed Guid'Antonio Vespucci had galloped across Piazza della Signoria on another man's horse to rush him to Luca Landucci at the Sign of the Stars. Amerigo, meanwhile, had spilled his heart to Guid'Antonio. He blamed himself for the incident, he would have *died* if any harm had come to *Orsetto* because he had failed to go to The Bell when Guid'Antonio first asked him to do so, and on and on and on.

Guid'Antonio put down his wine and answered Neri Saginetto. "Not yet. But I will." *One day*, he thought, *that bastard and I shall meet face to face. Up close. Personal.* An odd sensation came over him then, a sickening in his gut. The monk might be gone for now, or he might still be in Florence. If the latter were true, it would be impossible to find him; none of his ilk would expose him. Wherever he was he was plotting evil, his existence a thunder cloud in the distance, coming near.

Neri gave a lop-sided grin. "I have three silver pennies riding on you. No matter how long it takes."

"People are betting?" Guid'Antonio said.

"Of course!" Neri clapped his hands. "Your cup is empty." He poured Chianti for Guid'Antonio, then whisked away, calling, "Evangelista! Will you do something for your Papa—?

That's a good girl—"

Amerigo tucked a lock of hair behind his ear. "Thank God *Orsetto* is well. If I had searched for the monk on Saturday as asked, that lowlife might have been frightened and never have taken *Orsetto*. I keep thinking, what if—" Amerigo's voice trailed off, and he swallowed hard. "I wonder why he didn't hurt him. I mean—"

Guid'Antonio drew a steadying breath. "We have covered this ground. When you arrived at The Bell on Monday, he—whoever he is—panicked and ran. He's a coward, like all who bully and terrorize the innocents in their path."

"I am so sorry," Amerigo said. "I only wish when I returned there on Tuesday, I had found the ledger of names, for whatever it would have been worth."

"Apology accepted. Where were we now?"

"Andrea Antinori. Why didn't Orlando report him for stealing? Especially when Orlando was leaving Florence for London as soon as he finished his meal."

Guid'Antonio experienced a fleeting thought he could not quite contain. "I think he meant to hold Andrea's thievery over his head. For meanness. And for gain. Who knows what else? He held the boy in his power."

Amerigo took a bit of pecorino from the cheese plate and sniffed the fragrant cheese appreciatively. "Andrea could have hired an assassin to kill Niccolini," he said. "Perhaps—"

Guid'Antonio laughed lightly. "No, he could not. Keep in mind he had to steal money just to purchase medicine for—whomever."

"But then if, as you say, Andrea's lying, who is he trying to protect?" Amerigo said. "The true killer, most like."

"No," Guid'Antonio said. "But yes: Niccolini's killer is still somewhere feeling safe, thanks to the arrest of Andrea Antinori."

"So, we've gotten nowhere." Amerigo handed *Biscotto* a

bit of crust lightly spread with honey much the same golden color as the dog's thick fur. "After one week and two suspects, we're no closer to determining who killed our *festa* guest. Which way now?"

Guid'Antonio thought for a moment. "I want to know where Elena Veluti—Niccolini's *appassionato*—lives. When we leave here I want you to return to Spinelli and Spinelli, order some wool fabric, play the gossip."

"Why, when I've been there already? They'll think me a pest."

"Play to your strengths, my darling boy. With Orlando Niccolini dead and Andrea arrested, the shop workers will have plenty to talk about now, and they must know about the girl. Find out what you can about her family. No one much liked Niccolini. Nose into enemies, vendettas, grudges, debts. Who stands to replace him in the shop? Also visit the used-clothes dealers in our quarter and find out when Caterina Niccolini rented her mourning gown. The better dealers, since hers is a fine black damask. Did she hire the dress before or after her husband died? Find the date on the account."

"*Before* Niccolini died?" Amerigo's brow lowered. "Surely, you don't think Mona Caterina had anything to do with her husband's death. Surely she would not have been that stupid. What a giveaway!"

"I'm grasping at straws," Guid'Antonio said. "People make mistakes, Amerigo. Remember, I count on that. Also, find Niccolini's doctor in Santa Maria Nuova Hospital and confirm Niccolini's sick liver. Did Niccolini understand he might not have long to live? For God's sake, don't let Maestra Francesca know I sought a second opinion."

"I wouldn't dream of it," Amerigo said, keeping his face blank.

"*Grazie,*" Guid'Antonio said. "I would like to keep my balls intact."

"Thee and me." Amerigo finished his wine. "My head aches from all the bits and pieces and endless possibilities these investigations drag us through."

"Sometimes, rather than thinking, it's better to feel. To consider the *passione* at the heart of the matter," Guid'Antonio said.

Amerigo looked at his uncle as if he had just addressed him in Sicilian. "What will you be doing?"

"I'll be considering the case of Jacopo Caretto and his granddaughter. No matter our killer is on the loose."

"Why hurry?" Amerigo grinned. "You have three more days."

They departed the Red Lion past men sopping crusty bread in their soup, while Neri Saginetto bustled about with his bar towel, keeping an eagle eye on his daughter. *"Arrivederci, i Vespucci! Ci vediamo domani!"* "Goodbye! See you tomorrow."

"Uncle Guido," Amerigo said as they hurried up the steep stone stairway and into the bright light of Via Porta Rossa. "Why—truly—are you so certain Andrea Antinori did not kill Orlando Niccolini?"

"I feel it in my heart."

"Be serious," Amerigo said.

"I am. All right: Andrea Antinori wouldn't risk harming a dog, let alone kill it."

"You mean *Cannella*?"

"Yes." That suffering ginger cur from the Black Lion district of the Santa Croce quarter.

"Who would?"

"Find the answer to that, and we have our killer," Guid'Antonio said.

Twenty-Nine

ELENA VELUTI

Guid'Antonio was in the family office when Amerigo walked in from the courtyard after dark that evening. Amerigo's father, Nastagio, was seated on the trestle bench beside Guid'Antonio, having insisted the ever-elusive Guid'Antonio Vespucci give him a moment to review the plans for their chapel nearing completion in Ognissanti.

"Ah, good, Amerigo," Guid'Antonio said, moving his candle away from the large drawing spread out on the table. "You've been to Santa Maria Nuova?"

"I have," Amerigo said, "and, yes, Niccolini understood he had a sick liver. He lived in fear of dying, why that's important to us, I don't know, but according to his doctor, he was scared. Also, Caterina Niccolini rented her mourning clothes on Friday, the day after Orlando's death, not before."

Guid'Antonio nodded. "And Niccolini's *inamorata*?"

"According to the gossips at Spinelli and Spinelli, Elena Veluti lives with her aunt and cousin in the Green Dragon district in the Santo Spirito quarter."

Nastagio looked up from the detailed sketch of the chapel anchored to the table with a smooth stone at every corner, snapping a glance from Amerigo to Guid'Antonio and back again. Lightly sighing, he focused his attention back on the construction plans. Such exchanges between his son and kinsman were nothing new, truly.

"The names of the aunt and cousin?" Guid'Antonio said.

Amerigo sat down across from him. "Beatrice and Baldo Pacini. The woman's a wool spinner. Her son, Baldo, is a wool scourer. His shop boss died several months ago. Now, Baldo is unemployed."

"Where in *Drago Verde*?"

"Camaldoli," Amerigo said.

"Hmmm." A good number of workers in Florence's wool industry lived in the Oltr'Arno, a part of town separated from the *centro*, or city center, by the river Arno, whose bridges provided ready access back and forth. Wool weavers, spinners, scourers, washers, beaters—government officials had labeled many of the Camaldoli population *miserabili*, "wretched," during Florence's first taxation years ago. Elena Veluti, living there with her aunt and her cousin, Baldo, would have made easy prey for Orlando Niccolini, who apparently was her aunt's employer thorough Spinelli and Spinelli.

"What else?" Guid'Antonio said.

Amerigo yawned and rubbed his eyes, flexing his shoulders. "According to a fruit vendor in *Drago Verde*, Elena is thirteen or fourteen, with a belly growing daily. Orlando met her when he went to the Pacini dwelling to deliver and collect materials from Beatrice Pacini."

So, Elena Veluti truly was only one or two years older than Chiara Caretto, Elena's aunt a woman who, along with her niece and son, had come to depend on the good graces of Orlando Niccolini for their living. "Which dwelling?" Guid'Antonio said.

Amerigo told him, according to the loquacious fruit vendor. "Enemies, grudges?"

Amerigo yawned again. "No one at Spinelli and Spinelli seemed to wish Niccolini ill. He was off-putting, yes, but he was no fool, else he would not have been given such responsibility by the shop owners. As far as who will take his place as manager, the Spinelli family is looking outside the doors. No one there was in line to replace him, so no one had motive to wish him dead, not for a promotion, anyway."

"That's right," Guid'Antonio said. "Andrea was apprenticing as an accountant, not as a wool broker. And?"

"And," Amerigo said, "I saw our Francesco Nori this afternoon and took it upon myself to ask him if Niccolini had a written agreement with Andrea Antinori regarding repaying the funds he stole from the Spinelli family."

"You did?" Guid'Antonio had not got around to that. "And did our Francesco Nori have or know of a written agreement between the two men?"

"No."

Guid'Antonio grunted. On Tuesday that young fool Andrea had told him and Palla he had signed a contract with Orlando, but Orlando had put him off when it came to signing the contract and having it witnessed by Francesco Nori. Without that official document, Andrea could hardly demand Orlando make good his promise concerning their agreement if, indeed, they had one. "Thank you, Amerigo. You've done well," Guid'Antonio said.

A flush of pleasure colored his nephew's cheeks. *"Prego!* It's late. I'm tired. I'm going to bed."

Nastagio Vespucci rolled up the construction drawing, tied a scarlet ribbon around it, and slipped it lengthwise onto the office shelves. "Thee and me, Son, thee and me. Guid'Antonio, have you and I accomplished anything?" As Nastagio spoke, dark shadows played across his face in the flickering light of the small office.

Guid'Antonio tugged his ear. "As you and Brother Giorgio wish, Ghirlandaio's in, and Leonardo's out for the Annunciation. But let's do consider Botticelli for something later. He's a good friend and our neighbor."

Nastagio nodded, extinguishing the candle at his place on the table. "Fair enough. Are you retiring now?"

"No. *Buona notte.*" They kissed one another's cheeks, and Amerigo and Nastagio departed, father and son chatting amiably as they crossed the moonlit courtyard toward their apartments.

Now Guid'Antonio's mind raced in many directions. When he was certain his kinsmen had not paused by the fountain, talking, he slipped into his dark brown leather vest and black leather sleeves, blew out the remaining *studietto* candles, and ghosted into the street, careful to lock the gate behind him, his destination the Camaldoli neighborhood across the river deep in the Green Dragon district.

Thirty

DRAGO VERDE

A high, hot wind tossed Guid'Antonio's hair from his face as he crossed Ponte alla Carraia into the sprawling Santo Spirito quarter. Above him, scudding across the moon, bruised rainclouds threatened a downpour. He kept a quick pace, looking neither right nor left, aware of eyes boring into him as he crossed the river roaring angrily down below. At the foot of the bridge, he strode as far as Borgo Friano, then turned right. Swallowed in darkness, he edged the rough-hewn face of an ancient tower whose walls climbed toward God. Over his head green dragons rampant, tongues flaming with fire painted on banners of white silk, snapped in the wind, symbols of the Green Dragon district. At the far end of the street, Porta Frediano's massive gates, closed and bolted since twilight, guarded the road to Pisa.

Somewhere a baby cried. Guid'Antonio paused before quietly moving forward. At a shuttered workshop, he sensed movement. Suddenly, a dog lunged against the chain clipped to the collar around its neck, snapping and barking. A mastiff, fawn-colored, with a black mask across the muzzle and floppy ears. Huge. Compact. Swallowing his alarm, Guid'Antonio searched in his scrip, found the rabbit bone wrapped in waxed cloth he had brought from the kitchen, and tossed it to the snarling dog. The animal snatched the bone and plopped on the ground, growling with contentment.

Guid'Antonio blew a ragged breath. Dogs were everywhere in Florence, and it was best to be prepared to mollify them, especially when out and about in the dead of night. He thought of *Cannella*, Chiara Caretto's pet, abandoned after the girl's disappearance, hunting food, choking it down, willing to ignore the foul odor of the poisonous mushroom she had chanced upon in his alley. Chanced upon: it was chance, was it not, pinned to the hunger of her puppies, that had led to the arrest of Jacopo Caretto. Perhaps now *Cannella* was with God and her mistress. Some people would say so and take comfort in believing it. As for him—maybe yes, maybe no.

Heart pounding hard, he maintained a steady pace past the worn houses of barbers, weavers, trumpeters, and lesser notaries, his destination the bowels of the Green Dragon district, glancing left as he passed the monastery of Santa del Carmine and the Brancacci Chapel set off from the piazza. Within the walls of that chapel, Tommaso Masaccio's Adam and Eve, those wretched, wretched sinners, walked weeping from the garden, Adam's lamentations and Eve's silent howl fixed forever in fresco, their profound agony the curse of the knowledge of good and evil.

At the bulky church of San Frediano in Cestello, he bore left once more, slipping through a labyrinth of narrow corridors. Reasonably confident of his surroundings, he melted into a dark lane and tapped on Beatrice and Baldo Pacini's thin wooden door.

✝

Silence.

But then the door opened. A man of about twenty years with pale yellow hair peered into the alley, scowling in the light of a solitary candle. "What do you want?" he said, his eyes flickering in alarm when he saw the silver-eyed man in dark brown and black leather standing before him. In the youth's hand the candle, secured in a pottery saucer, wobbled. "What are you doing here?"

"I want to speak with Elena Veluti, your cousin."

"No! Just because that pig Orlando Niccolini is dead doesn't mean men like you can come sniffing around. Get back to the pile of shit where you belong."

Guid'Antonio pushed Baldo Pacini aside—surely this was the cousin Amerigo had mentioned. "I mean only to speak with her," he said, stepping past him into the house. "One way or another, I shall."

Carefully—he was not fingering his knife—he reached into his scrip and displayed the special license that allowed him to circulate in town at night. *Guid'Antonio Vespucci, Doctor of Law, Florence.* The license bore his signature and that of Chief of Police Palla Palmieri.

"I know who you are! Who doesn't?" Huffing his displeasure, Baldo Pacini stepped further back from the threshold. From the shadows a woman whispered, "Who's there?"

"Dottore Guid'Antonio Vespucci, sticking his nose where it doesn't belong."

Grudgingly, Baldo added to Guid'Antonio, "I am Baldo, and this is my mother, Beatrice Pacini. We've done nothing wrong." Baldo anchored his arms squarely over his chest, planting his rough bare feet on the packed dirt floor. His cotton shirt and hose, though plain, were reasonably clean, considering they probably were not often washed in the public well. A crude iron grille secured a solitary window, shuttered for the night, creating suffocating, smoky heat in the enclosed atmosphere.

"I didn't claim you had," Guid'Antonio said.

Baldo's mother set a candle alight, revealing a spinning wheel in one corner. A white cloth edged with an intricate design of birds, fruit, and flowers adorned the trestle. Beatrice Pacini could spin yarn all day, seven days a week, and never in her lifetime have the means to purchase such an ornament for her table. The cloth was a gift from Orlando Niccolini, most likely.

A wide-eyed girl peeked at Guid'Antonio from the edge of the wrinkled brown curtain strung across the room. Elena Veluti. Roused from sleep, and scared, as if ripped from a dream she could not now recall. A nightmare.

"*Buonasera, Signorina,*" Guid'Antonio said. "Forgive me for disturbing your rest. I'm Dottore Guid'Antonio Vespucci. Dottore Guid'Antonio to you." He made a smile, tipping his head.

"Elena, stay there!" Baldo snapped. "Dottore—what do you mean coming here like a thief in the night?" Baldo was all bluster, though his blue eyes were bright with fear.

"Would you have preferred I come when all the world could see?" Guid'Antonio gestured for Elena to emerge from behind the curtain. "I mean no harm, *Signorina*. I have a few questions about Ser Niccolini. Then, I'll slip away." He trailed his fingers through the air.

Baldo placed his candle—expensive beeswax, Niccolini, again—on the trestle, and the sapphire blue birds, scarlet roses, and purple plums embroidered along the hem of the tablecloth sprang to life. "We don't have to tell you *anything*," Baldo said.

"Oh, be quiet!" his mother snapped. "Elena, come out. Despite this man's sober appearance, I don't believe he means us grief."

Elena Veluti emerged into full view cradling her belly, protruding beneath her shift. "Yes, Dottore Guid'Antonio?"

she said in a shallow breath.

"Per favore, Signorina," Guid'Antonio said. "Sit." Easing one arm around her—careful, careful, he had little experience of this—he helped the girl ease beside him onto the trestle bench.

Baldo's eyes narrowed in a glare, but he kept silent.

"Orlando's dead," Elena said, her voice so faint, Guid'Antonio had to lean close to hear. "Killed by a wicked boy."

Guid'Antonio's first thought was which one? The Pacinis would have heard about Cesare Ridolfi, but now had they heard about Andrea Antinori, as well? He gave Baldo and Beatrice a questioning glance.

"That employee of his," Baldo said. "At Spinelli and Spinelli."

Guid'Antonio addressed Elena: "I am sorry about Orlando. I know this is trying. How did you meet him? When?"

Baldo slapped the table, and the candle flared. "What business of that is yours?" he yelled.

"Baldo!" Beatrice Pacini said. "Through me, Dottore! Ser Niccolini saw Elena here two years ago." With fingers whose joints were knotted and swollen, she gestured toward the spinning wheel. "Dropping off wool, picking up yarn. As a consequence—" She glanced at Elena's belly, sighing hard, as if to say, *You know the rest.*

"But Orlando was Spinelli's shop manager," Guid'Antonio said. "It wasn't his responsibility to make pick-ups and deliveries." No—a man of Orlando Niccolini's standing would have managed the shop, whose exquisitely dyed cloth commanded premium prices in the European markets. He would not have ridden with horse and cart from house to house in Florence, and certainly not here in Santo Spirito, making deliveries and collections, paying the women who worked for him on a piece-rate basis.

"The broker who usually came fell ill," Beatrice said. "So—"

She shrugged. "Ser Niccolini came himself. That one time. He said it was an emergency. After that there was a new broker, but Ser Niccolini returned unofficially to see Elena."

Of course he did. "Elena, do you know if Ser Niccolini had any enemies?" Guid'Antonio said. "In particular, I mean."

"No. Why would he?"

Baldo grunted. "How would she know something like that? She's an innocent girl! Why are you asking this? The apprentice is in jail."

Guid'Antonio gave the angry young man a long look. "I assume Orlando may have told your cousin things while they were . . . conversing . . . that he might not share with you and your mother."

High, hot color blotched Baldo's cheeks. He jerked away, giving his head a brisk shake, clearly smarting from Guid'Antonio's comment. "Elena is not my cousin, that's only what we call one another. She's my mother's ward, the child of my aunt's first husband. I asked why you're haranguing us, especially now the killer is in jail."

"Palla Palmieri is convinced of that," Guid'Antonio said. "Not me."

"You are one and the same," Baldo said.

Guid'Antonio smiled mildly. "Not always. How do you know about Andrea Antinori?"

Burning with indignation, Baldo said, "Do you think because we're poor, we're ignorant? Santo Spirito has town criers, too! Antinori confessed." Baldo made an ugly, slashing motion with his hands. *"Finito!"* The end. *And yet you are here*, his hateful look at Guid'Antonio said. *And I don't trust you.*

Tears leaked from Elena's eyes and down her neck. "I miss Orlando," she said. "He was better to me than anyone, except Cousin Baldo and Aunt Beatrice. Without them, I would be an orphan."

"Better to you how?" Guid'Antonio said.

"Elena," Baldo said, his tone not quite a warning but on the edge.

"He was kind! He loved me. And he meant to prove it," Elena said, gathering strength, smiling through her tears.

A look slid between Beatrice and her son. "Elena," Baldo said, more gently now, but entreating. "We are not to speak of that."

Ah. Guid'Antonio handed the girl his handkerchief. "She has the right to a voice. Prove it how, Elena?" he quietly asked. *Tell me, Elena, please, God, please.*

She chewed her lip, one hand caressing her belly. And then she flared, showing the fire in her veins, looking defiantly at Baldo. "Before he died, Orlando changed his will to favor me and our baby. He visited his notary before Saint John's Day. He wanted it done before leaving town."

Orlando's notary: banker Francesco Nori, again.

"Orlando changed his will," Guid'Antonio said. Of course: according to Niccolini's doctor at Santa Maria Nuova Hospital, Niccolini knew he was seriously ill. It stood to reason that if he meant to make changes in the document apportioning his worldly goods, he would do it before leaving for London. Here was something new. Something delicious that had not occurred to Guid'Antonio and would not have done in a million years. No wonder the young man standing before Guid'Antonio wanted him out of here: kill a rich man and collect his money, and who knew what else? Tentatively, he said, "Elena, to favor you how?"

She shook her head. "He did not say."

Guid'Antonio kept his face a mask of calm. However the new will favored her, these three had something to gain from the cloth merchant's death. Given that and the fact Baldo Pacini hated Orlando Niccolini for his relationship with his kinswoman, and *voilà!* as Francesco would say in French.

More than enough motive for murder. "Elena, at my *festa*, Orlando mentioned he was here with you before joining my table. Was he?"

"Yes. Why would he tell a falsehood?"

"Just . . . asking," Guid'Antonio said. So: on Saint John's Day, Orlando had been here in *Drago Verde,* then he had gone to Borg'Ognissanti, where he had soundly slapped Andrea Antinori across the face before proceeding to the meadow. A busy, angry man, Orlando Niccolini, with a worrisome cold riding astride a sick liver.

"This is cruel!" Baldo hissed. "Firing one question at my kinswoman nose to tail for absolutely no reason."

Guid'Antonio looked quietly at him. "Remember, Niccolini died at my table."

Baldo tightened his arms over his chest in a show of sullen aggravation.

"Elena, did you know Ser Niccolini was ill?" Guid'Antonio said.

"Jesus, Mary, and Joseph!" Baldo spat.

The girl shook her head. "To me he did not seem so."

"Dottore," Beatrice Pacini said, "it is the middle of the night. Truly, what do you want from our family? I'm tired of this." *Drago Verde*, Santo Spirito, the world. Him.

"As am I," Guid'Antonio said. He rose and took Elena gently by the hand to draw her up with him. Who knew what lay in store for the girl in the coming days? Death. Motherhood. Death. Survival and the benefits of a murdered man's last will and testament, mayhap.

Bitterly, Baldo said, "I know why you're here! To frighten us! To find a way to break the new will. You knew about it all along! You want to leave Niccolini's wife everything and us ashamed and poor."

"Nay. Until you mentioned it a moment ago, I knew nothing about a new will," Guid'Antonio said.

But wasn't Baldo's comment about Niccolini's wife interesting? If the cloth merchant had changed his will, and Guid'Antonio saw no reason for the Pacinis to lie about Niccolini's promise to do that, especially when it made them look guilty of *something*, where did things stand with Caterina, who believed she was sole heir to her husband's house? But: come to think of it, the dead cloth merchant had promised Andrea Antinori a written contract, and he had not followed through on that. Had he done so regarding his will? If he had not, Caterina Niccolini had naught to worry about.

Interesting! "Why haven't you—why hasn't Elena—come forward to make her claim regarding the will?" he said. "Whatever that claim may be."

Baldo hesitated. "I—we—knew if we did so too soon, we would be suspected of murder, accused of killing Niccolini for gain. Now you've a confession from this Andrea Antinori, we're free to do as we please and will do sooner than later, if only to alert the court we're here and have first claim."

"You could have done so early on, when my servant took the blame. Cesare Ridolfi."

"I know who he is," Baldo said, his sudden smile revealing a face blessed with pleasant features when he was not angry. "He wouldn't *accidentally* kill anyone. Everyone knows that. You should have known it, too. And so, we waited, trying to decide what to do and when."

Guid'Antonio spread his hands, granting Baldo this point, then glanced at the spinning wheel in the corner. "*Signora* Pacini, the wheel is yours?"

"It is. Or I should say Ser Niccolini purchased it and wrote a contract with us to make payments, so one day, it would be mine. Ours."

This was not unusual. Many workers within the cloth industry and without paid over time for the tools of their labor. "And did you actually see a contract?" Guid'Antonio said. "One signed by both Ser Niccolini and you?"

Beatrice shrugged. "Yes. But lately we had fallen behind—" She glanced at her son, who, according to Amerigo, had lost his job when his shop boss died several months ago. "We are deep in Ser Niccolini's debt," Beatrice said.

Or were, Guid'Antonio thought. People who could not pay their debts were prosecuted harshly, their bedding, kitchen utensils, and even their clothing, seized. If at any time Orlando Niccolini had taken the Pacini family to court for nonpayment, the authorities would have amputated Baldo's left hand. They would have thrown this little family of three—soon to be four— in the Stinche. They had been living under the merchant's fist, just like Andrea Antinori. And now? They had nothing to worry about—maybe.

"Has anyone taken Orlando's place?" Guid'Antonio said. He glanced at Elena, who had gone suddenly deathly pale, then quickly addressed Beatrice. "Delivering wool to you here, I mean."

"Yes!" Beatrice said, smiling. "There have been two deliveries since Ser Niccolini's death last week, praise God for that. For the deliveries," she added, hastily crossing herself. "And actually, he hadn't delivered wool since that first time when— you know. As I said, that was an emergency."

That, thought Guid'Antonio, careful not to look at Elena's belly, *was Fate*.

"I understand," he said, smiling all around. "*A dopo allora*, later, then. Sleep well."

†

Outside the hovel the wind moaned around every corner in *Drago Verde*, but not with enough intensity that Guid'Antonio failed to hear the sound of breathing accompanied by light footsteps following him as he made his way through the darkness of moldy, narrow lanes and stone archways. *Stay alert. Stay very alert now.* Fingering the hilt of his dagger, he hurried into a narrow warren of byways leading toward the open space around San Frediano in Cestello.

His pursuer kept pace.

Behind the church, Guid'Antonio stole into an alcove and waited. The soft slap of sandals came near, a stone dislodged as the bells in the church tower rang, pealing lauds. Barely breathing, Guid'Antonio looked around the corner. His pursuer, glancing left and right, stopped and peered through the darkness, flicking back his hood.

And then the man crept forward.

Deep set eyes, jutting hawk nose.

Guid'Antonio jammed against the church wall. The monk who had come for *Orsetto* had come for him. *Good!*

He stuck out his foot. The monk stumbled and flailed wildly, his sandals tangled in the folds of his robe. Off balance, he swiped his knife at Guid'Antonio, who slammed him against the church wall. "Who are you!" Guid'Antonio demanded, his voice a harsh whisper echoing against stone. All around them, doors and downstairs shutters were closed and bolted, the street deserted, except for Guid'Antonio and the man shadowing him with the intent to kill.

Eyes filled with fury, the monk hissed, "Better to ask where I'm from!"

"Volterra," Guid'Antonio said.

A hollow laugh escaped the other man. "You have it in one!" Fueled by bitterness and the desire for revenge, he lunged forward, breaking Guid'Antonio's grip. In an instant his knife blade sliced Guid'Antonio's neck, sharp as a razor. "Got you, you silver-eyed bastard!" the monk yelled, raising the stiletto for one deadly strike.

"Not yet!" Guid'Antonio flicked his blade toward the other man.

Down the street, the mastiff barked, rattling his chain, struggling hard for freedom.

"Who's there?" a voice called. *"Zanna!* Be still! This is the second time tonight, *cane pazzo*! Or should I unleash you now, my brave bear fighter? Who's out there, boy?"

Fang. Crazy dog. Bear fighter.

Guid'Antonio and his attacker stared at one another, eerily calm.

"I'll kill you!" the monk yelled before scuttling into the depths of *Drago Verde.* "I'll destroy everything you love!"

The sky split open, and thunder crashed all around, bouncing like cannon fire off the stones of Florence. Lightning flashed and rain pelted Guid'Antonio, half-blinding him as he made his way back across Ponte Carraia, woozy, his neck gushing warm blood. Descending the foot of the bridge, he found his way to Borg'Ognissanti, where he paused, touching his neck: his fingers came away, sticky with gore. Far down the thoroughfare on the right side of the street, high along the windows of his palazzo, the Vespucci family banners flapped and furled in the rain and wind.

Spedale dei Vespucci loomed closer, just ahead. Lightheaded, struggling to place one foot in front of the other, he reached the hospital entrance, touching the wall to keep from falling down. Fumbling in his scrip, he withdrew the key to the door and turned it in the lock. On the third try, it opened. Lena Barone lay on her pallet, snoring, dead to the world. From the basket just inside the portal, Guid'Antonio retrieved a candle and set it aflame from the brazier burning outside the patients' ward. The flame wavered, then flared into a tiny beacon of light. Of hope. Dottore Filippo Vernacci, he recalled, was in Castellina in Chianti, visiting a friend, but Maestra Francesca Vernacci was *here.* All Guid'Antonio needed to do was find his way across the pitch-black foyer and up the curving stairs to her door. Perhaps she would consent to saving his life, if he made it that far.

Thirty-One

VALERIANA

"Guid'Antonio—!" Francesca gasped, one hand flying to the front of her gauzy shift, her slender body framed by light cast by two tapers burning on the table by her bed. They were alone in the inky black hall a few doors from the hospital surgery, Guid'Antonio soaked with rain, his feet squishy in his drenched boots. "What in God's name do you think you're—"

She cut herself short, her stunned look turning to horror when she saw the dark stain at the collar of his tunic. "What happened?" she cried, stepping toward him, her feet bare on the stone floor. "Are you—you're bleeding!"

"Francesca. *Permesso*—" He reached for her but fell against the doorframe, the candle shaking in his hand.

She took the candle and held it tentatively toward him. "Guid'Antonio—?"

Too dizzy to speak, he shook his head.

Her cheeks, burning with heat, drew pale. "Hold onto me." She anchored one arm around his waist and helped him to a chair. "Can you sit?"

He slumped down, head spinning, as if at any moment, the tile floor might rise and slap him, hard. Blinking his eyes to keep them from closing, he eased his tunic away from his neck.

"Guid'Antonio!" Francesca drew a quick breath, her eyes wide with fear. "You've been cut." She touched his cheek, cupping it lightly with her hand, turning his head to inspect his neck. "It's a flesh wound, thank God. For the most part the bleeding has stopped." She lifted one finger. "Let's get you—no. Sit still."

He nodded, barely.

She returned in short order with a pitcher of water, clean cloths, and a shallow metal pan. The steel needle and length of thread she added to the other items on the shelf by her bed started alarm bells ringing in his head. "What are you doing?" he said.

"What do you think? This is a gash to be reckoned with. You'll need stitches once I clean your wound with wine and treat it accordingly."

"Oh, God," he breathed.

"It will sting, yes." Smirking, she departed again, returning now with a tray of pottery jars and pots and a glass vial in her hands.

He shied away. "There's more?"

"As you see," she said. "The cleansing wine, along with ointments and creams and a draught of *valeriana* to ease your fear."

Valerian. "I am not afraid," he said.

One brow lifted sardonically, Francesca grinned. "Of course not. Drink this." She handed him the glass vial. "Where was Lena when you came in? Did she give you entrance?"

The *valeriana* sedative tingled pleasantly in Guid'Antonio's chest. "I used my key. She was snoring so loudly, she wouldn't have heard the Arno rushing down the borgo, let alone me staggering across the floor. Too, there was the storm—" Beyond the bedroom window the violent rain sweeping town had lessened to a soft patter, and the moon threw silvery light into the room, chasing shadows into far corners. Francesca's hands were gentle, familiar, as she combed his damp hair back with her fingers, then gently washed his face.

Guid'Antonio felt a strange flutter in his rib cage. She was so close beside him, he could smell her familiar scent of jasmine and roses. Old memories. Roused feelings.

"Francesca—"

She cut him off. "Can you remove your vest?"

He fumbled with the buttons until she said, "Let me," leaning over him, her fingers nimble as she removed his *farsetto* and lifted the soggy tunic over his head. How odd to be naked in front of her again, if only by half. Exquisitely odd and pleasant. Their eyes slid toward one another, and away.

When she dabbed his neck with the wine, he gasped, his lips a tight line of pain. "What happened?" she said. "Why are you out on a night like this? In a raging storm."

He wanted to sink to his knees, both from the searing pain and the sight of his own blood mixed with the red wine as she swished the cloth in the pan and squeezed pink liquid from it. Then, amazingly, his body glowed, and the fog that had begun to envelop his mind lifted. "I went to Santo Spirito," he said, his tongue thick in his mouth.

"In the dead of night. Alone. Holy Christ, Guid'Antonio," she said in a chastising voice.

"It had—it had to do with Orlando Niccolini. I wanted to ask Elena Veluti—" His eyes were bleary, his lids heavy. "Do you know who she is?" he said, watching Francesca swipe her finger in one of the jars and lightly pat a bit of oil into the clean wound. "What is that?" he asked.

"Lavender oil from Assisi. The entire town knows who Elena Veluti is. She's the girl carrying Niccolini's baby, may the Lord protect her and her innocent child." Wiping the oil from her fingers, she began applying a second ointment to his wound.

"Another one?" he said, slurring the words.

"Yes, a cream made with Black Nightshade. So you won't feel the sting of the needle. Guid'Antonio, you act as if I've never treated your wounds before."

He nodded, the fog creeping in again. "Foolish, hmmm? I mean, I wished to ask Elena if she knows of anyone who might have wanted the cloth merchant dead. And also to—" To what? Oh, yes. To *feel* if her family somehow had something to do with Niccolini's poisoning from . . . whatever it was. And, anyway, how—

"Sleepy?" she said, looking down at him and smiling, her hand gently smoothing his hair from his face once again.

With an effort, he nodded.

"*Valeriana* is my sedative of choice," she said.

"You're not going to kill me, are you?" he asked.

She laughed. "No. I'm just going to mend your neck." She reached for her spectacles and poked the thread through the eye of the needle. "Ser Niccolini's killer is in jail," she said. "The boy named Andrea Antinori confessed, though, granted, everyone wonders how he could have sneaked the mushroom in one salad and made certain it was served to the person for whom it was meant. Anyway, that girl didn't attack you, surely. Do you know who did?"

"He didn't do it. Andrea, I mean." Guid'Antonio struggled not to go down into the pit. "She—Elena—lives in Green Dragon with her aunt and her cousin, Baldo Pacini. Her cousin by marriage."

"You are avoiding my question. Who attacked you?"

"I don't know."

"You're lying."

Yes. He sighed. "It has to do with—" With what? Politics.

Hatred. Revenge. She would want to hear none of that. "It has to do with Florence," he said.

She sighed, her thoughts loud and clear: *Of course it does.* "You could have been killed," she said. She met his gaze a moment too long, and her face turned pink. "Like so many other times in the past. You're always in the center of the web," she said.

"Yes. Francesca—" His eyelids drooped and, gently, he claimed her hand.

She fluttered her fingers away from his. "Hold still."

He tensed, catching his breath on a gasp of pain as she stuck the needle in his flesh, carefully drawing the thread through his skin like a tailor stitching the hem of a gown.

She looked at him carefully as she bandaged his neck. "There. That wasn't so bad, was it?"

"Not at all," he said.

"Oh, my Guid'Antonio." Laughing, she helped him rise and eased him onto the side of the bed. Her bed. "The effects of the *valeriana* will wear off soon. You may go home then, not before."

"My hose are drenched," he mumbled. "My vest. My tunic—"

She removed her spectacles. "Don't worry about them."

She pulled off his boots, and blissfully he sank into the mattress. There was something else he meant to say before his eyes closed from their own weight. "Andrea Antinori told me he came to you for medicine some short while ago—" He stopped, focusing his thoughts. "What was it?" he asked. "The medicine, I mean."

She cocked her head. "You know I cannot tell you that."

"It's me, Francesca," he said.

"That's neither here nor there," she said back.

"Then who was it for—his mother? Or his cousin Emilio? I'm trying to help him."

She hesitated. "He said it was for him," she answered. "For Andrea, himself."

Guid'Antonio smiled. "He lied." Breathing deeply, he prayed he would remember this confirmation of his suspicions when he woke tomorrow morning. Thursday. A lot to do then . . . but he could not remember quite what. "I'm sleeping," he said.

"I know." She looked down at him for a long moment before turning away.

"Where will you be?" He caught her hand. The rain had stopped, and a fresh breeze blew in the window. Beyond the tile roofs stretching across the Unicorn district, a blanket of stars stretched across Florence. The same blanket of stars he had witnessed on the nights he had spent in this bed with her an eternity ago.

"I'll be where I always am," she said. "Here with you."

All the weight dropped from his limbs as he sank deeper and deeper in their bed. He felt her draw down to him, her thin gown whispering to the floor, her breath warm on his skin.

She lay alongside him, trailing her fingers over his chest, twining the silver curls in her fingers. When she bit his nipples, he groaned with pleasure, shuddered, and groaned again. She scooted down, nipping his skin with her sharp little teeth. She unbuttoned his damp hose, and he felt the familiar tingling sensation in his loins. Rising over him, she arched her back and moaned, rocking, until, exhausted, she sank down beside him in the bed.

"I wish I could take you with me," he said, a cry so soft, no one but she ever would hear.

Turning toward him, one arm over his waist, she gazed at him with longing. "Guid'Antonio *mio*," she said. "*Ti amo*. I wish I could go. *Ti amo*."

†

Sunshine poured in the bedroom windows, where last night there had been a pale sheen of stars. Guid'Antonio emerged from sleep, the evening returning to him slowly, like a dream unfolding: Elena Veluti, the monk's attack in Santo Spirito, and then—hot, searing pain, *valeriana*, and Francesca ministering to him.

He sat up in bed so quickly, his head spun. Carefully, he touched his neck. The bandage remained in place. Francesca was gone, and he remained half-naked, his clothing hanging from a peg on the wall by the door. He reached down. The flap of his hose was closed and buttoned.

How long after he sank into oblivion had Francesca stayed? After denying themselves for so long, had they taken pleasure in one another again? The mere thought made his loins groan with desire and satisfaction such as he had never known . . . he cut off that ridiculous thought. W*hether she did everything with you, or merely pleasured you with her hands, that or nothing, it felt mighty good, you know it did*, whispered a demon in his ear. *Admit it and get it over with, go on your way, and say one thousand Hail Marys.*

He drew a ragged breath, suddenly feeling ill. Feeling like Adam and Eve in the garden, whether anything truly had happened with Francesca last night, or no. Yellow eyes closed to slits, *Gatto*, the cat, watched as Guid'Antonio pressed his hands on the mattress to steady himself. Fighting the wave of fuzziness washing over him, he stood and donned his soggy tunic and vest, then sank into the chair. Hands shaking, he pulled on his wet boots.

Nothing to do now but make his way to the surgery.

†

"*Mattina,*" Francesca said. "You look like anything but an esteemed lawyer, Dottore. More like something *Gatto* dragged in."

No more saying my name, *Guid'Antonio*, then. Deeply disappointed—oh, yes! Even with God watching, he had to admit it—he combed his fingers through his tousled hair. "To you, as well."

Standing at the surgery counter, Francesca closed the journal in her hands and faced him fully. "Any pain this morning?"

"No. Only—a little confusion." He locked eyes with her.

"Valerian sometimes has that effect. It will pass," she said.

"Will it?"

"Sit." With deft fingers she eased the soiled cloth from his neck, washed the wound with wine, and then applied ointment and a small strip of fabric to his skin. "Can you walk home? I could send a message. Have someone come here to assist you."

"That won't be necessary," he said. "Thank you for everything."

"*Prego.* Take this ointment. I made it from sweet briar rose. Have Maria or Cesare apply it to the wound and change the bandage daily. The lavender oil, also. A massage with it would fare you well."

"Maria and Cesare are in Peretola. For another few days, they will be there."

"You'll find someone to do it, I'm sure. Take care of yourself," she added as they moved toward the stairs and began a slow descent to the foyer. "You're still unsteady."

"I'm sorry I roused you in the middle of the night," he said. Two could play this game, correct?

"It was nothing," she said, a smile touching one corner of her mouth. He would swear to it. "Rest today. Stay home."

Not likely. "What will you do?" he said.

She lifted her shoulders lightly, one arm circling his torso as they continued down the stairs, her eyes going to the empty cot by the hospital door. "Lena's already out and about. Good. As for me, I'll walk to Santa Maria Nuova Hospital with Sandro and Luca. We have a guild meeting. Then I'll go to the Sign of the Stars with Luca to advise patients."

He nodded. Francesca, Sandro Botticelli, and Luca Landucci all belonged to the guild of *Arte dei Medici e Speziali*, the Guild of Doctors and Apothecaries, which included not only doctors and druggists, but painters, as well. "Your father isn't going?" he said.

"No, bless him. He isn't coming home until Sunday. Late afternoon, probably. I miss him. I need him here. And you?"

"The usual," he said. His court appearance in the matter of Jacopo Caretto was tomorrow.

Then there was Andrea Antinori, who would hang if Guid'Antonio did not prove his innocence, whether the boy wanted him to or not, and soon. As for the monk—he and Francesca, she because she had assisted in the aftermath of a crime, would report the incident to Palla, who would conduct a search, undoubtedly to no avail. Meanwhile, here he stood in Spedale dei Vespucci, foggy-headed, still sifting and sorting, and wondering about . . . everything. Lightly, he shook his head. Soon all would come clear. He was as good at stitching things together as Maestra Francesca Vernacci. Surely.

Carefully taking the last step to the door, his voice a whisper, he said, "Francesca. Last night. If anything—I'm not—"

She stared wordlessly at him, her gaze neutral, dispassionate.

He lost courage. "Thank you again."

Gently, she pushed him out onto the borgo. *"Buona giornata.* Be more careful the next time you venture into *Drago Verde,* Dottore. It can be dangerous there. Well—everywhere is when you skulk around in the dead of night."

✝

He unlocked the gate to his garden, the church bells all around him announcing terce, the third hour of this sunny, rain-washed morning. Head pounding, he ascended the steps to his bedchamber, his body crying for rest—just for a while—before he began the day, again.

In the corridor, hearing the sound of voices, he paused. "*Ciao?*"

Cautiously, he opened the chamber door. And was stunned to see Maria and Cesare unpacking their traveling trunks, Cesare humming a quiet tune. *Orsetto* bounded over, yipping, announcing Guid'Antonio's arrival. *Good Christ in Heaven*, he thought. *My goose is cooked.*

Cesare, turning, threw him a dimpled grin. Then his eyes went to the bandage on Guid'Antonio's neck. The lady's gown the boy had removed from one of the traveling chests slid from his hands onto the floor, and he gasped. "What's this?!"

"Guid'Antonio, where were you so early in the day?" Maria said, the hem of her traveling cloak whirling around her ankles as she turned to him with an elated smile. "We're home unexpectedly! I wanted to put the two of us in good order. To mend—" She paused, straightening her spine as she absorbed Guid'Antonio's startled expression and wet, rumpled clothing. "I wanted to surprise you," she said, her smile fading from her lips.

"And did," he said.

Thirty-Two

THIEF IN THE HOUSE OF LOVE
THURSDAY, 1ST JULY 1473

Maria came to him slowly, her fingers falling shy of his bandaged neck. "You're hurt."

"Not mortally."

"Mama mia!" cried Cesare Ridolfi. "I leave your side for one moment—!"

Guid'Antonio slumped on the edge of the bed, his head floating. The *valeriana*? Yes, and so much more. "I was working," he said.

"Working?" Maria removed her cloak, raising her brow questioningly, folding her arms stiffly over her chest.

"You're in disarray—and, and—damp!" Swiftly but gently, Cesare tugged Guid'Antonio's wet boots from his feet, removed his brown leather vest, and pulled his limp tunic over his head. "What happened to you?"

Guid'Antonio fell into the arms of the bed. "What happened is I need peace and quiet for a few moments. Cesare, please go."

"But—"

"Grant me this single wish, *per favore*."

Huffing a sigh of discontent, the boy settled a blanket over Guid'Antonio and closed the door behind him, but not before tossing a smart, "As you say!" over his shoulder.

Maria sat beside him, the worried look in her eyes undercut by distrust. "Working? You smell of salves and ointments."

Orsetto jumped onto the bed, licked Guid'Antonio's face, bounced around, and sailed back onto the chamber floor, where he grabbed a fabric cat and vigorously shook it, growling, all around the apartment. "Yes, I was," Guid'Antonio said, wondering at the dog's boundless energy after his frightening ordeal on Monday. The medicaments Francesca Vernacci had sent home with Guid'Antonio lay in the small bundle beside him, tied with string. "Why are you here now, Maria? I meant to join you—" *When? Tomorrow after court? Probably. Oh, yes.*

"I told you. I regretted the anger between us earlier this week. It plagued me. I missed you," she said, her voice tart.

"But you've only been gone three days. I need for you to do as I say, always." He must be in control. As often and as much as possible, else all would crumble to ashes, never to be regained. "Maria, I need you safe." The monk could have targeted—could still target—his wife and family. "Now you're here, under no circumstances are you to leave the house. Not until I say so."

"Where would I go?" she said. "And where have you been?"

"Working, as I said."

Her eyes strayed to his neck. "Who helped you? Praise them."

"The hospital."

"—Ours?"

"Yes."

Her thick lashes brushed her cheeks. "You sought Dottore Filippo Vernacci. I'm glad."

"No," Guid'Antonio said. "Filippo is in Castellina in Chianti. Maestra Francesca tended me in his stead."

Maria tensed visibly. "In the middle of the night," she said.

"It was either that or bleed to death. Now, tell me about your trip. Did Father Vittori enjoy the gifts?" Incense-holders, a candelabra, and a small crucifix in copper for the local parish priest.

"He did and sends his thanks," she said. "As for the rest, Silvio requests three additional casks of wine and two half barrels of vinegar and oil." Silvio Doffi, the farm manager. "She has stolen your heart," she said.

Guid'Antonio groaned to himself. On the day he and Maria were wed, he had stood in the presence of family and friends outside her house in Piazza Santa Croce in full view of her neighbors. As was the custom, Maria's father had taken her right hand in his left and placed it in the hands of the groom, Guid'Antonio di Giovanni Vespucci, who dutifully slid a ring on her finger. Guid'Antonio had received his own ring, too, and so—it was done. Proudly, he had escorted the sixteen-year-old, raven-haired girl with olive skin to her new home, Maria adorned in a gown of crimson silk velvet, her lengthy train swishing across cobblestones beneath balconies crowded with people on the long walk from the Ox to the Unicorn district. In her arms she had cradled the plaster Santa Margherita doll her mother had presented her, a sign of the flesh and blood babies Maria would carry in her belly sooner than later, please God and All the Saints.

That was not quite three years ago.

Aware of the hurt and confusion he knew his wife was feeling, summoning strength, he traced her cheekbone with his thumb. "Not stolen. Freely given. But never fully taken.

Just the opposite, and that was before I first spied your radiant beauty in the market. Lie down with me, Maria."

She hesitated. "You're not in love with her? Do you swear on the Virgin's head?"

His temper flared. "Maria, why do you always question me?" He forced himself to be calm. "Of course I swear it." He caressed her hand, her arm. "Yes."

After a moment, she did as he asked, curling beside him in her bulky gown, patting *Orsetto* absent-mindedly when the puppy jumped onto the bed again and made a nest in the blanket, turning in quick circles and sighing before settling down. "Did she have older sisters who commanded a marriage dowry? And then for her there was nothing? Why does she not have a husband to take care of her in her old age?"

Guid'Antonio lay very still. "Her mother and second stepmother died of plague before she was seven. All she ever has had is her father. She could have married had she had a mind to do so."

"Instead, she has our hospital."

"She does not have it," he said. He closed his eyes for a moment, his lids heavy. So much for resting. Still, quiet interest was better than a firestorm of anger. "Mona Caterina Niccolini told me of your kindness. Food, well wishes in the wake of her husband's death. Well done, Maria."

"I was happy to do it." She snuggled a little closer. "You went to speak with Mona Caterina?"

"After her husband's funeral, yes."

"How angry she must be."

Again, and again, and again. "Why do you think so?" he said.

"If I learned my husband had a mistress, I would be furious," Maria said. "A whore carrying his baby. She's a thief in Mona Caterina's house. She stole Caterina's husband, stole her love, and left her with no children. What is there for her now? I would kill the whore."

The poison issuing from Maria froze Guid'Antonio. Pure hatred, the opposite of love. "Those are harsh words, Maria." *Words I'm surprised you know.*

"They are sincerely meant," she said.

He opened his eyes and fixed them on her. *That*, he thought, *is no idle threat.* "Ah—Caterina knows about the girl?" he said.

Maria laughed without humor. "If not, she's the only one."

Had not Francesca said the same?

"Guid'Antonio—"

"Yes."

Her voice had lost its edge. "I should not have spoken with such . . . energy, neither now, nor the other morning. It's unseemly for a woman. Forgive me, *il mio amore*."

"You spoke your feelings," he said.

"Yet you never speak yours."

Her observation lay between them, a little brave, a little sad. And so he found himself telling her a bit about the Jacopo Caretto case and how in court tomorrow he must present his opinion regarding the man's fate. "The girl's family has filed for leniency," he said. "They want her grandfather freed."

Maria gasped. "She was as insignificant as that? How sad!"

His hand, stroking *Orsetto*, paused. No one—no one—had bothered to report the girl missing, not even when she had been gone four days. "Yes. It is," he said.

Maria settled against him again. "What will you tell the magistrates tomorrow?"

He made an ambivalent gesture. "I don't know yet," he said.

☦

Life was not much changed in Domenica Ridolfi's domain. Fresh *salame* and sausages of deep wine-red meat studded with white fat and black peppercorns hung from the wooden ceiling beams, and in the hearth, a low fire burned beneath a simmering kettle of some broth or sauce, no matter it was high, hot summer. *"Mio povero caro!"* Domenica said. "Show me your neck!"

Cesare rewarded Guid'Antonio's exasperated look in his direction with a wide-eyed, silent stare. *Did you think my mother would not notice that bandage, no matter how small? She who has tended you since you were a boy?*

Domenica exclaimed and fussed but in the end agreed Guid'Antonio likely would live. He had survived much the same, and more.

"Be careful when you go out, both of you," Guid'Antonio said, pulling up the collar of his fresh tunic. "Wicked men are about. Tell the rest of the house, *per favore.*"

Domenica cocked her head, she who had worked for Guid'Antonio and his family for almost thirty years. "When are we not? God will protect us."

They crossed themselves.

Cheese, wine, and grapes appeared on the trestle, selected and arranged by Cesare's deft hands. "And honey," the boy said, placing a comb dripping with fresh nectar beside a loaf of warm bread. "Now we make merry and celebrate the day." He did a jubilant dance.

"Why on earth would we do that?" Guid'Antonio ignored the food. His wooziness was lifting, but he did not want to tempt Fate with food and drink.

Cesare smiled beatifically. "Because according to my mother I've come home from Peretola to excellent news! What was once declared 'Death by Cesare' is now 'Death by Andrea Antinori.' *I* did not kill Orlando Niccolini, either accidentally or in any other way! I only wish I had been in town when Palla Palmieri brought the culprit in. I would have raced to the jail, looked in the sheriff's face, and laughed!"

No, you would not, Guid'Antonio thought. "At another man's misfortune," he said.

Cesare's right eyebrow rose. "No, for my good luck."

"Cesare—"

The boy frowned. "You're not happy for me?"

"Not yet."

Amerigo stepped in from the garden. "Everyone is saying Andrea Antinori will hang. Sooner than later, probably." His eyes on Guid'Antonio were eloquent: *If Andrea is innocent, as you believe, we must act fast.*

Guid'Antonio swiped his hand over his mouth. "Domenica, did you see the Antinori boy here—in the kitchen—on Saint John's Day?"

"I wouldn't know Andrea Antinori if he walked up and brained me," Domenica said, quaffing a large drink of the plum wine in her cup.

"Look at this, *per favore*."

From his satchel Guid'Antonio withdrew a paper with Andrea Antinori's likeness drawn in quick, sure strokes. Wednesday afternoon, after leaving the Red Lion with Amerigo, he had sent the kitchen boy, Poggio Bernini, to Verrocchio's workshop with a note asking Leonardo da Vinci to visit the jail and sketch Andrea Antinori for him. This Leonardo had done, then sent the drawing home to Guid'Antonio by the boy. "Domenica, Cesare, this is the youth in question, Andrea Antinori, fair face, fair curls."

Domenica squinted. "I've never seen him, though he is a pretty boy."

"Mama," Cesare said, "you know they are everywhere in Florence." Cesare snatched at the drawing, which Guid'Antonio quickly removed from striking range. "No," Cesare said. "Him, I would remember." He hesitated. "But wait . . . if he wasn't in the kitchen—mama! How did he do it?"

"How anyone did it is the question," Guid'Antonio said.

"But," Cesare said, "if *he* is innocent, people will glance back at me."

"Leave it, Cesare," Guid'Antonio said. "I'm working through this moment by moment."

"Yes! While the wheel of fortune keeps turning fast against me!"

Guid'Antonio returned the drawing to his satchel. Andrea Antinori had not been in the Vespucci kitchen on Saint John's Day; in fact, Andrea had not replied when Guid'Antonio questioned him about that. And the Pacinis? No. Any one of them would stick out in the Vespucci palace kitchen like a sore thumb.

"Domenica," he said, "who *was* here? While the rest of us were—" He twirled his finger, recalling the *festa* activity, the swirl of excitement and merry-making, while he had been seated at his table, thinking about the murdered girl. Or woolgathering, as Orlando Niccolini had said.

Domenica snorted. "Who wasn't? Besides family, there were musicians, vendors, servers, and children running in and out all day."

"Also, neighborhood friends enjoying my mother's plum wine," Cesare said. "Trumpeters, banner carriers—"

"In other words, a hive of activity," Guid'Antonio said. "But no out-and-out strangers?"

Domenica harrumphed. "Do you think I would allow such as that? Guid'Antonio *mio*, that wounds me deeply."

"Forgive me," he said, bowing his head like a guilty boy. No strangers: exactly as the kitchen girl, Livia, and Domenica's brother had told Amerigo when he questioned them. But that was the key, was it not? Surely, whoever poisoned the salad had been in the kitchen late last week.

"The man who killed Orlando Niccolini had to know the salads we were serving and how we would be seated," he said. "How did he, let's call him *Signore Death Cap*, manage it?"

"Five salads for five men seated just so at your trestle table in the drowsy afternoon heat, as I have pointed out at least once before," Cesare said, his hands planted firmly on his hips.

Guid'Antonio shrugged. "Yes, but how could our *Signore Death Cap* have known this?"

Domenica scoffed, her face rosy with wine and heat. "Orlando Niccolini had told everyone in the Unicorn district he would be there. I heard everywhere in the market how he bragged about his place at your table. Also, Cesare—"

"*Mama!*"

She held up her hand. "Also, my son, whose tongue wags from morning until night, had gossiped about the order of service. All your *Signore Death Cap* had to do was count the salad plates on Cesare's tray and then lace the merchant's plate with the poisonous mushroom. He knew the place settings and the company. Moreover, the fact the tray was rectangular is important. Had it been a round one our *Signore* would not have dared risk someone else receiving the salad with Death Cap in it. Unless he truly were desperate."

They all looked at her, blinking.

"That much is clear, isn't it?" she said, folding her arms beneath her bosom.

"It is now," Guid'Antonio said. He recalled then how in Piazza Ognissanti on Monday morning Giuliano de' Medici had said much the same about giving a poisonous mushroom to a hungry dog. *"Who would give a hungry dog a poisonous mushroom, unless in an act of desperation?"*

Amerigo glanced at him. "If Niccolini boasted about his invitation, and we know he did, Domenica is right about everything. He undoubtedly also bragged he would be seated in the place of honor between you and Giuliano de' Medici. As far as the mushrooms go, I'm sure all Florence knew our menu included them." He gave Cesare a pointed look. "And of course, Cesare, you were late with the salads. That must have given our killer pause."

Only if he were in the garden, thought Guid'Antonio. *Yes? No?*

Cesare rolled his eyes. "As I told Dottore Guid'Antonio and Palla Palmieri when they grilled me last week, everything must be perfect, and people were in my path. Moreover, since there were late-comers to our *festa*, when it came to serving the salads, I had time to spare."

Crossly, Amerigo said, "Time to spare? There was the little matter of the most important horse race of the year. The *palio* I almost missed, thanks to you, little man."

"Cesare, you mentioned late-comers," Guid'Antonio cut in. "Among them, there was Caterina Niccolini, arriving from the country where she had been visiting her ailing mother."

"Yes. However—" Cesare began, but Domenica said, "Everyone laughing and talking and a short while later her husband, dead. How gutted she must have felt. She wasn't expecting that."

"Who would be?" Amerigo said.

"The person responsible for killing him, obviously. Andrea Antinori, with an accomplice," Cesare said, making a bow.

†

In the garden, Amerigo said, "Absolutely not Andrea Antinori. Palla has the wrong man."

Guid'Antonio's neck bandage, slender as it was, chaffed his neck. "We knew this," he said, drawing in air to clear his head as he removed the sticky fabric.

"The fact everyone in our house agrees without question that Andrea was nowhere near—and so on and so forth—proves his innocence, I believe," Amerigo said, frowning. "What happened to your neck?"

Guid'Antonio told him, warning him to watch for the

monk when he was out and about.

Amerigo gasped. "That devil is still here? And he tried to kill you? Christ's Mother!" He crossed himself.

"Last night, yes. Gone now, who knows? I don't think he will rear his head again. He'll fear being caught and hanged. Regarding Andrea Antinori, remember, he confessed. Anyway, as long as Palla keeps Andrea in jail, Niccolini's killer believes he's safe, giving us time to hunt him down. Watch your back," Guid'Antonio said.

"I shall! But soon Andrea will go before the magistrates. They'll sentence him."

"One step at a time. Take this, please." Guid'Antonio handed his nephew his satchel and slipped the brown cloak he had left at the fountain earlier in the day over his shoulders. "Keep Leonardo's sketch of Andrea safe. Who knows when we may have further use of it. In fact, I have in mind making a habit of commissioning such drawings during investigations. One could have copies made and keep them handy. Have a file and hold it close at hand, just in case. Look for patterns, go from there."

Amerigo twisted his mouth. "Wouldn't that be encroaching—?"

"Not a problem," Guid'Antonio said. "Meanwhile, you've instructed everyone to keep the garden gate bolted from the inside from now on, no exceptions?" he said.

"Sì, mio Signore. E dove stai andando?" Yes, my lord. And where are you going?

"Lorenzo's," Guid'Antonio said. "Palazzo Medici."

"In mud brown?"

"As unassuming as a mouse," Guid'Antonio said. In insignificant brown during the day because he was not going straight to Palazzo Medici, no—he was making a detour, and he preferred not drawing attention to himself. Theoretically, anyway.

"Tell Giuliano hello for me. If he's home," Amerigo said.

"He will be. Also other representatives of *la banca dei Medici*."

Amerigo raised his brow.

"Imola," Guid'Antonio said, the thought of this meeting with Lorenzo filling him with dread. Referring to Pope Sixtus IV on Monday—a lifetime ago—Lorenzo had sworn he would find a way to stop the Pope from buying the town, or at least throw rocks in his path. *He thinks he can outplay me? Over my dead body.*

"*Buona fortuna,*" Amerigo said. "Oh, something else."

"As always," Guid'Antonio said.

"The town criers have news. Remember the fellow who sliced his wife's face during the holy week celebrations? Maurizio Maso mentioned the altercation Friday at the jail."

"Yes," Guid'Antonio said.

"The magistrates set him free."

Guid'Antonio absorbed this news slowly. "Their reasoning?" he said.

"The woman brought it on herself. She was wrong to provoke her husband," Amerigo said.

Thirty-Three

LEONE NERO ~ LEONE D'ORO

On the way to Palazzo Medici, Guid'Antonio walked deep into the Santa Croce quarter, where Chiara Caretto had lived with her grandfather, his object the concerned aunt who, according to Amerigo, had offered the girl a loving hand, only to be forestalled not only by her husband, but by the entire Caretto family. In Santa Croce, coins changed from hand to hand and ere long he found himself deep in the back alleys of the Black Lion district, where Chiara's uncle, the sausage-maker, Fenso Caretto, lived with his cowed wife, Battista. *I'm here to help, Signora. You have nothing to fear from me.*

It is not you I fear, but my husband. Please, go away!

I only want to talk with you, my lady. As for Fenso, surely he is not home but at the butcher's shop where he earns his daily wage.

Hushed voices, tears on the woman's part, anger rising to the boiling point on his.

Before emerging from *Leone Nero* into the hard white light of Piazza Santa Croce, he stopped to brush his fingers along his temples, removing the soot hiding the silver lacing his hair. Kept in his *studiolo* in a lidded jar, that black dust eased his way when he wished to go unnoticed here, there, everywhere. Perhaps he should have taken some to Imola last spring.

He drew a sharp breath, wiping his hands on the folds of his nondescript brown cloak. Eventually, the *signora's* words had spilled from her like water from a fount. Still, he felt no joy. What he had just learned from Battista Caretto did not surprise him, and yet as he strode across the sprawling, sun struck piazza, his skin felt cold.

Thirty-Four

THE FOX IN FLORENCE

Behind the Cathedral in Piazza del Duomo, Guid'Antonio's footsteps slowed as he gazed skyward, a small man eclipsed by the shadow of the dome. Beneath his feet, the ground tilted. He closed his eyes before slowly looking back up along the brick dome toward the bronze ball and cross atop the soaring church lantern. Brunelleschi's dome had been completed and consecrated in 1436, a few months before Guid'Antonio was born. Work on the marble lantern the architect had designed to cap the dome's vast opening had not begun until twenty-two years later. Another dozen-plus years had passed before the lantern was crowned by the bronze sphere and cross now just barely in Guid'Antonio's line of view. *Miraculous accomplishments take a little longer*, thought Guid'Antonio.

"Amazing, isn't it?" said a gentle voice.

He turned to see Leonardo da Vinci attired in a traveling cloak with a long leather cylinder slung over his shoulder. "It is, yes. *Ciao*, Leonardo." Guid'Antonio smiled a greeting. If Leonardo wondered about Guid'Antonio's plain brown cloak, he did not show it.

"You should be proud," Guid'Antonio said. The commission for the eighty-ton bronze ball and slender cross had been awarded to Verrocchio and Company, with Leonardo foremost among Verrocchio's workmen, who not only had collaborated on designs with the master, but also had helped devise ways to set the cross and ball atop the lantern high above Florence.

"I am pleased with it," Leonardo said, smiling.

In quiet companionship they stood with their necks craned, exactly as they had done two years ago. On that bright May morning in 1471, thousands of people had pressed into the piazzas and byways around the Cathedral, pushing against one another to see the ball set in place. Guid'Antonio marveled, remembering his arm snug around Maria. To position the ball's tremendous weight, working from the wooden platform circling the base of the dome 260 feet in the air, a team of men had used a swivel crane to lower the bronze sphere onto the lantern with a winch. When the ball finally settled, the spectators had burst into laughter and applause, their relief and pride of accomplishment immense. Atop the platform, the weary, exuberant, workmen had been rewarded with bread and wine all around. What an achievement for Verrocchio and Company! For Leonardo da Vinci, who had spent that morning on the ground sketching the buzz of activity, muttering happily to himself.

Three days later the town had gathered again, this time to see the cross set atop the bronze ball. What a glorious moment for the City of Flowers! Almost two centuries after workmen had begun digging the church foundations, with the God-given talents of Andrea del Verrocchio, Leonardo da Vinci, and all the architects and engineers, carpenters, and mechanics who had come before them, Santa Maria del Fiore was complete—the largest cathedral in the world—and Guid'Antonio was there.

"I'm pleased to see you, Dottore," Leonardo said. "At last, I'm bound for Vinci. I'm stopping by the bank for the traveler's checks I ordered, then by your house with the master's rent." Leonardo tapped the scrip at his waist. "Due today." Andrea del Verrocchio had rented workshop space in the Sant'Ambrogio parish from the Vespucci family for a long while, with payment due monthly.

Guid'Antonio thanked him. "You're riding out this late?"

"Vinci isn't far." Leonardo shrugged lightly. "And actually, I'm staying with friends along the way."

"Safe travels," Guid'Antonio said. "Thank you for the drawing of Andrea Antinori. Well done." Should he tell Leonardo that Domenico Ghirlandaio was the family's choice for the fresco in their chapel? Perhaps, but he hadn't the heart. Call him a coward, he would accept that label in this accord.

"*Prego*. Safe travels to you, as well, Dottore."

Safe travels to me? But I'm not going anywhere, Guid'Antonio thought, watching Leonardo go. *Except to Palazzo Medici. For now.*

Circling around the Cathedral to Piazza San Giovanni, Guid'Antonio found himself drawn to the tall column commemorating the memory of Saint Zenobius. There he touched the column as Giuliano de' Medici so recently had done. Yet again, no greenery burst miraculously into bloom, nothing living appeared. He smiled ruefully to himself. If the pillar had not blossomed for Giuliano the Beautiful when he brushed his fingers along its warm marble surface last Saturday morning, why would it blossom for Guid'Antonio now?

His boots clicked on stone as he strode past the wrought iron gates into the Medici family's arcaded loggia off Via Larga. In the bank's international office tucked in the loggia's southwest corner, accountants, secretaries, and clerks sat at trestles scratching figures in ledgers, perplexed, smiling, murmuring among themselves. Guid'Antonio continued straight into the palazzo's grassy inner courtyard, past Donatello's imposing bronze sculpture of Judith Slaying Holofernes and his magnificent little David—naked, save for boots and helmet.

A servant met Guid'Antonio at the entrance to Lorenzo's private apartment off the courtyard. "He is expecting you, Ambassador."

Guid'Antonio thought to correct the fellow's use of his title as an ambassador of Florence, but changed his mind in that regard. After all, he was here in that capacity. He had a say in all that transpired regarding Imola; or, at least, he had a voice. "I'll leave this here," he said, removing his brown cloak and folding it over a chair.

"Of course."

The hum of muted voices greeted him as he strode through the door into Lorenzo's ground floor apartment. Giuliano was present, also Francesco Nori in his role as head of the local Medici Bank office, along with Francesco Sassetti, the longtime, overall manager of the Medici banking empire, whose offices Guid'Antonio had passed on his way through the arcade. With a nod to the other men, he bent to pet the sleek greyhound who bounded toward him, ecstatically whipping her tail. *"Buon giorno, Aphrodite,"* he said, greeting Lorenzo's favorite dog.

Lorenzo rose from behind his writing desk, rubbing *Aphrodite's* head affectionately while gesturing Guid'Antonio toward a chair. "Good. You're here," he said, indicating the walnut sideboard set against one wall. Fruits, cheeses, *salame*, and more, much more, arrayed on silver trays flanked by decorative majolica platters, plates, and bowls. "Are you hungry? Would you like something to eat?" Lorenzo sat back down and ran his tapered fingers through his hair, holding its length from his face, which appeared troubled, yet set on a fixed course.

"No, *grazie*," Guid'Antonio said. "I'm late again? *Mi scuse*."

"No, no." Quickly rising to his feet, Giuliano squeezed Guid'Antonio's hands and kissed his cheeks before pouring wine into a cup and handing it to him, along with a hastily prepared plate of grapes and pecorino. "Please," he said. "You'll need your strength."

That sounded ominous.

Calmly accepting Giuliano's offering of food and drink, Guid'Antonio sat by the chamber's grated windows looking out on San Lorenzo, though he would have preferred pacing the room as he had so often seen Lorenzo do, like a lion, caged, here in the Golden Lion district of the San Giovanni quarter.

Lorenzo went straight to the point: "*Signori*, I swore I would think what to do about the Pope. After meeting with our government, privately, you know, I sent my reply to that fox down south in Rome."

"Not directly," Giuliano said. "Lorenzo wrote to our uncle Giovanni instructing him to inform the Pope that as much as it pains us to deny his request, we haven't the cash in hand to loan him forty thousand florins. We simply cannot do it." Giovanni Tornabuoni, manager of the Medici bank in Rome and Depositor General of the Apostolic Chamber. "We didn't say so," Giuliano went on, "but just as we discussed the other day, we can't place personal concerns before the concerns of Florence."

Even though Rome is the Medici Bank's most important account, thought Guid'Antonio.

His neck wound pricked, sharp as a bee sting. With an effort he resisted touching the cut beneath the collar of his tunic. Curiosity about it would only lead to questions whose answers he had no wish to reveal. The sacked town of Volterra was back down the road, his attacker, the monk, long gone. Of that, he was certain. Almost.

He took a small drink of wine. "And now?" he said.

Lorenzo shrugged. "We wait."

"Sixtus will know you're dancing around him," bank manager Francesco Sassetti said, frowning.

Lorenzo brushed this off. "Of course. And he will understand. He knows how this game is played. He plays it himself."

"And plays it well," Francesco Nori said.

Guid'Antonio kept his expression neutral. Sixtus would punish Lorenzo for denying him the loan. The question was how hard.

Divining his thoughts, Lorenzo said, "He will charge me like a mad bull, snorting and pawing the ground. Now, who knows if we'll ever see a cardinal's hat in our house."

"Did I wish to exchange my tunic for the crimson robes and skull cap of a cardinal?" Giuliano said, not quite under his breath. And louder: "No."

"But you would have done it for the family," Lorenzo said.

Guid'Antonio felt as if waiting for the Pope's response to Lorenzo's refusal was kin to waiting for a fireball to explode. "Lorenzo. You said you would make obtaining the funds difficult for Rome above and beyond declining his request yourself."

"And I have," Lorenzo said, smiling slyly, explaining how yesterday, acting on his own, he had approached every other banking family in Florence and asked them to say no to the Pope, if he approached them for the money. Going one step further, Lorenzo had asked the other bankers to keep his request private. A secret between them and Lorenzo. Under no circumstances should Pope Sixtus IV find out Lorenzo de' Medici had schemed against him. Should that happen—"The

Pope would have my ass on his horns," Lorenzo said.

Guid'Antonio glanced at Francesco Nori and Francesco Sassetti, who were exchanging worried glances. Apparently, like him, this was the first they had heard of Lorenzo's request to the other families. That Lorenzo had involved other bankers at all was dangerous in a town where trust was often undercut by betrayal in one form or another.

Guid'Antonio stared at Lorenzo. "You are inviting trouble. Do you believe the others will stay quiet?"

"Not for me, for Florence," Lorenzo said, his eyes tightening on the portrait of Duke Galeazzo Maria Sforza hanging near the hooded hearth. "I would like to put my fist through his face. Build a roaring fire and toss that painting in the flames."

"The Pollaiuolo brothers would not be pleased," Giuliano said beneath his breath. Antonio and Piero Pollaiuolo had painted Sforza's portrait a couple years ago, commemorating a visit by the duke to Florence. No one else said anything.

Guid'Antonio's throat felt thick. Someone would loan Sixtus the money, whether someone in Florence, or otherwise. With a sick feeling in his gut, he acknowledged to himself the Pope had won this round. Imola belonged to Rome. There would be no last moment signed contract for the town negotiated by Florentine Ambassador Guid'Antonio Vespucci in the spring of 1473. All he had gained for himself in that regard was the alarming attention of Pope Sixtus IV and his dangerous, grasping family.

"At least now we know why Sforza deserted us," Giuliano said, rising and leaning against the wall by the door.

We do? thought Guid'Antonio. He glanced at Nori and Sassetti, who shook their heads. Like him, they were in the dark. "Enlighten us, please," Guid'Antonio said.

"This arrived yesterday from one of our contacts in *Milano*." Lorenzo swiveled a document lying on his desk, indicating he would like Guid'Antonio to read it aloud. In a nutshell, when the Pope learned Florence was making a push for Imola, he had written Sforza warning him that if he did not sell Imola to him rather than to the Florentine Republic, he would not only annul the recent marriage that had taken place between their families, but also excommunicate him.

"Christ Almighty," Francesco Nori said.

"Exactly," Giuliano agreed.

Everything slid more firmly into place. Guid'Antonio—they all—had heard about the January wedding between Count Girolamo Riario and Duke Galeazzo Maria Sforza's natural daughter, Caterina Sforza, yet Lorenzo had believed the bond this created between Milan and Rome would be outweighed by the longstanding friendship between Milan and Florence. And perhaps it would have been.

But the threat of excommunication was the sharpest arrow in the Pope's quiver.

Excommunication meant no one within the walls of Milan or its outlying territories could marry in church. The dead would be buried in ditches and fields. Milan's trade would wither and die, like a rotting vine. The Milanese people would rise up in revolt, storm Sforza Castle, murder the duke and his family. In light of these threats, Galeazzo had had no choice but to bend over and sell Imola to the man in Rome.

And how had the Pope known Florence meant to have the town for herself?

"Rome has caught you here," the mayor of Imola had said that day not so long ago in the town square. *Rome, in the shape of the Pope's nephew, Count Girolamo Riario.*

Circles.

Chains.

"And so," Guid'Antonio said. "This is how it stands."

"For now," Lorenzo said.

✝

A light tap came at the door. Giuliano slid from the wall, casting a glance at the others, and called a greeting to Marsilio Ficino and Angelo Poliziano, who entered the *sala* escorted by the servant who had ushered them inside, their footsteps light on the marble floor. "Are we interrupting?" Marsilio said, his brow wrinkled, his intelligent eyes glancing all around. "Tomorrow, perhaps—?" The diminutive philosopher-teacher indicated the manuscript in his hand.

Come to wax eloquent about philosophy and poetry, thought Guid'Antonio, nodding a subdued greeting to them both. It was time to go. Had not all been said that could be said? But who knew what else might be hinted at, revealed? He settled himself to stay for awhile.

"No, no, Marsilio, you were invited," Lorenzo said, shooing *Aphrodite* from the hem of the little philosopher's robe. "I'm sick to death of government affairs," he added, sighing from his depths.

"As am I," Francesco Sassetti said. "The bank calls, and home." With a nod, he excused himself from the gathering.

Lorenzo sank back into his chair. "I despair for any girl in Riario's bed. Especially one so young as Caterina Sforza. Ugh."

"Tired of discussing this or no, my brother will have the last word," Giuliano said. "He is like a man whipping a dead horse."

"What girl?" Angelo, the poet, said.

"Ten-year-old Caterina Sforza," Giuliano said. "Girolamo Riario's bride."

"Bride? What a sickening notion," Lorenzo said, huffing a sour laugh.

Guid'Antonio remained quiet, swallowing his disgust at the thought of Girolamo Riario wed to Caterina Sforza and the circumstances surrounding their marriage. Riario had insisted on bedding ten-year-old Caterina on the day they wed, rather than wait until she was fourteen, as prescribed by law. Her father, the duke, had readily agreed to allow Riario to do so. That was how desperate the duke had been to unite the papal family to the duchy of Milan and reinforce the legitimacy of Sforza rule. And the Pope? Of humble origins and unsure of himself, no matter how many robes and rings he wore, Sixtus had wanted to secure the protection of Milan, the strongest state in Italy.

Devils, Guid'Antonio thought. He remembered with affection the vivacious little blonde girl who had visited Florence two years ago with her father and his flamboyant entourage—fourteen carriages decorated in silver and gold, two thousand cavalrymen wearing silk costumes in the Sforza colors of white and red, and more, more, more. At the time, Caterina had been eight years old. Guid'Antonio had seen her in Milan this past spring too, when, upon hearing he was at her father's court, she had ridden straight from the chase at the Sforza castle in Pavia to greet him, rushing to kiss him on both cheeks, her child-sized hunting knife bouncing at her hip.

A beautiful child, sparkling, but with a solid core, she had asked about Lorenzo and Giuliano and about Guid'Antonio's pretty wife, Maria, all of whom she had met during her delightful stay in Florence. Making inquiries, Guid'Antonio had learned the married countess would not live with her husband for several more years from now, so there was that, after all.

"Guid'Antonio," Marsilio Ficino said.

He came back to the conversation. "Yes?"

"I enjoyed Amerigo's visit to Fiesole last weekend. Such a bright young man." Marsilio gestured to Giuliano and Angelo. "Well, all his circle are. I want to express how saddened I was to learn of the cloth merchant's death at your door. And now people say he was murdered by an employee. A youth who has confessed. Andrea—?"

"Antinori," Guid'Antonio said.

"For money." Sorrowfully, Marsilio shook his head. "That fellow regrets his actions, surely."

"No matter," Giuliano said. "He will hang."

Into the silence, Lorenzo said, "Guid'Antonio has had a lot to contend with since Saint John's Day. His guest, as you say, dead at his table, and tomorrow he gives the court his opinion regarding the wool beater who killed his granddaughter."

"Apparently," Guid'Antonio said, his head beginning to throb.

Marsilio's eyes misted over. "When I was a boy, my brother was murdered."

Giuliano gasped. "How so?"

"His wet nurse smothered him. An innocent babe. And yet he was betrayed."

"Are you certain?" Guid'Antonio said. "Perhaps he was overlain." All too often hired nurses who took a newborn baby home to suckle rolled over the child in bed and accidentally smothered it to death.

Marsilio's lips trembled. "Who can say? With God's grace, I feel my brother with me every day. My thoughts of him make him immortal, and that brings me comfort."

"Benedetto is with me, always," Angelo Poliziano said. Benedetto was Angelo's father, murdered by opponents of the Medici family five years ago. "He is with me constantly, like all the angels and saints."

"There's a lovely thought," said Giuliano. "Those we love live forever in our hearts. God is good." He crossed himself.

Quietly, Marsilio said, "Guid'Antonio, what offers you peace, my friend?"

A still silence fell.

Memories of his dead father and mother? Of his lost wife, Taddea, and their baby boy? "Thinking," he said.

The others shared a startled look. "Much like you, Marsilio," Guid'Antonio said, slightly startled himself. "Thinking of your loved ones, of Plato. Much like all of you, in fact." *Though you write and discuss, while I act.*

"I collect pottery from Spain," Francesco Nori said, and they all laughed. "We know that, Francesco," Lorenzo said.

Beyond the barred window the marketplace around the church of San Lorenzo had closed a long while ago, when night began to fall. Now, bells all over Florence tolled the mid-evening hour. *Francesco*, Guid'Antonio mouthed. *Andiamo.* Let's go.

The other man rose, donning his cloak. "Lorenzo, Giuliano, thank you both. Marsilio, Angelo—*buona notte* to all."

At the *sala* door, Guid'Antonio swung around. "Angelo. Our Homer," he said.

"Yes?"

"How well do you know Caterina Niccolini?"

"Cat—the wife of Orlando Niccolini?" Angelo seemed puzzled. "Not well—in fact, as far as I recall, not at all. Why, Dottore?"

Because I remember you on Saint John's Day, seated on a stool with your back to the meadow, and the expression approaching alarm on Caterina's face when she noticed you at my table.

"She seemed surprised to see you at my *festa*," Guid'Antonio said. "You, particularly. I thought mayhap—" He shrugged. *"Non è niente."* It is nothing.

†

After Guid'Antonio retrieved his brown cloak, he and Francesco crossed the grassy palace garden in a wash of pale moonlight, then stepped together into the loggia, where torches burning in iron holders whooshed and flared, illuminating their faces in shuddering shades of yellow and orange. The arcade was wrapped in silence, the Medici Bank closed, the employees gone home long ago.

"Francesco—" Guid'Antonio said, glancing from the slender form waiting in the shadows beneath the book shop awning across the street on Via Larga. It was Amerigo, come to meet him tonight. In secret, since Guid'Antonio did not believe in allowing anyone to know his business. "—Neither you nor Sassetti knew Lorenzo meant to entreat the other families not to loan Sixtus the money."

"No! It came as a complete shock to me," Francesco said, leaning against the old Roman sarcophagus set against one wall. One of Lorenzo and Giuliano's ancient ancestors, Guccio de' Medici, had lain in that marble tomb for two centuries or more.

In all that time, what had Guccio heard? *Enough, no doubt, to make him uncomfortable even in death*, thought Guid'Antonio. "What would you have advised Lorenzo to do?" he said.

"What does it matter?" Francesco laughed dryly. "I think it was not a good move. Especially now we know that who would have Imola was decided weeks ago. We've been waiting in a void." He touched Guid'Antonio gently on the shoulder. "I'm sorry, *mio amico*. I know how much—" He trailed off.

Guid'Antonio shrugged, smiling slightly. "Sing and it shall pass."

Francesco pulled up his hood, gesturing toward the dark street and home. "Shall we?"

Guid'Antonio shook his head. "For me, the night is young."

"When is it not?" Francesco said.

"Almost never," Guid'Antonio said. "Francesco, before Orlando Niccolini died, did he change his will?"

Caught by surprise, Francesco Nori said, "Obviously, you know he did."

"Yes."

"How?"

"I spoke with the Pacini family."

"And it would do no good to ask why you did that, correct?"

"No," Guid'Antonio said.

"What did you learn from them?"

"Stop prevaricating," Guid'Antonio said. "Your client is dead. Murdered, in fact. Professional ethics no longer stand in your way."

"True," Francesco said. "And what a poor excuse for a man."

"You seem to bear him some special animosity. I noticed on Saint John's Day."

Francesco's mouth turned down at the corners. "Orlando Niccolini was a devil. No less so than when he changed his will to favor his mistress, rather than his wife, Caterina."

"He actually did that?" Guid'Antonio said. Hard to believe, no matter what the Pacini family had said.

"Yes."

Oozing anger, Francesco described the serpentine paths the cloth merchant's will had taken—a revised will, signed, sealed, and notarized by Francesco in his office. "If that villain had not died when he did, I would have quit business with him."

Appalling, the changes written into Orlando Niccolini's will. The man's duplicity, his cruelty, had known no bounds. No wonder Francesco Nori had comforted Caterina Niccolini last week in the meadow. Francesco knew her husband's secret in all its hatefulness and contempt.

"Have you told Caterina?" Guid'Antonio said.

Francesco shook his head. "The idea sickens me. So, no, not yet."

"I will do it," Guid'Antonio said. "I feel some responsibility in this."

Francesco gave a heartfelt sigh. "Thank you."

"You're welcome. One more thing," Guid'Antonio said.

Francesco hesitated. "Yes?"

"As far as you know, has Andrea Antinori ever made any monetary payments to Orlando Niccolini? Payments made and legally recorded, that is."

Francesco seemed surprised. "Not by me, no. Why do you think so?"

Guid'Antonio explained how Andrea had told him and Palla Palmieri that Orlando had promised to replace the money Andrea had pilfered from the wool shop coffers. "Andrea replaced one florin, but the other one, he had spent. Orlando promised Andrea he could repay him a few pennies back when and as he could, and Andrea had started doing that," Guid'Antonio said. "Apparently, though—"

"Niccolini took the naive boy's meager payments and didn't give him credit. And so, Andrea has no proof they had a business relationship," Francesco said.

"Not a shred."

"And yet I think you believe Andrea not guilty. Though hasn't he confessed? Yes," Francesco said, making connections and answering his own questions himself. "Well," he said, "wherever you are going in the dark this evening, take care, my friend."

"And you as well. I mean it, Francesco. God bless you."

✝

The moment the sound of Francesco's footsteps faded into the night, Amerigo hastened across Via Larga, through the Medici gateway, and into the arcade "I thought he never would leave," he fussed.

"Lower your voice, please," Guid'Antonio said, swirling his cloak around his shoulders.

"I've been waiting an eternity."

"So have I. Now, though, we begin the last leg of this journey."

"We do?" Amerigo paused for a moment. "Where to at this time of night?"

"Back across the river into the Santo Spirito quarter."

$\mathcal{T}$HIRTY-FIVE

LO ZOPPO

From Palazzo Medici Guid'Antonio and Amerigo slipped down Via Larga, then skirted the Cathedral through suffocating lanes and serpentine alleys, boots light on the ground, shadows pressing in as they crossed Ponte Trinita. "Come, Amerigo."

Quietly, Guid'Antonio led the way into the Santa Spirito quarter though close, twisting turns that opened into Piazza Santo Spirito, where *festa* banners drooped from iron poles fixed to the walls of workshops and fortified towers. In the moonlight illuminating the piazza, *ragazzi* lounged around the steps of the Church of the Holy Spirit. The young men stirred, eyes glinting at their nocturnal visitors in the flare of a torch here, a half-dead candle there. Silence crackled all around.

Amerigo lifted his hood. "Mama. I don't like it here."

"Put your hood back down," Guid'Antonio said.

"But everyone will know it's us."

"They already do," Guid'Antonio said. *"Navigare necesse est."* One must chart his course and sail.

Reluctantly, Amerigo pushed his hood back onto his shoulders. "Here's a den of unrest."

"It is also the home of three of our town's most popular festivals, festivals you enjoy immensely each year with your bravos."

The faint smell of smoke and dust teased Guid'Antonio's nose. Santo Spirito, that venerable old Augustinian church and monastery, had suffered ruinous damages from the raging fire ignited during the passion play staged there to celebrate Duke Galeazzo Maria Sforza's visit two years ago. Altars, crucifixes, panel paintings, manuscripts—all had gone up in flames. Now, ladders, wheelbarrows, shovels, and bricks lay scattered around the square, the duke and Lorenzo were at odds, and the duke's daughter, Caterina Sforza—therefore, Milan—was wed to Rome through that malefactor, Girolamo Riario. *Ah, Italia*, thought Guid'Antonio.

Senses prickling, he turned. Accompanied by a large dog, a figure limped toward him from the shadows at the far end of the square.

"Two nights in a row?" said the man standing before him.

"Two nights?" Amerigo echoed.

Faintly, Guid'Antonio smiled. "There is always so much happening here." Had it been only last evening he had passed haltingly from the Pacini abode located not far from this piazza to his hospital, wounded, with blood dripping from his neck onto the collar of his tunic?

"I wish I could take you with me."

"I wish I could go. Ti amo. Ti amo."

The peddler whom Guid'Antonio knew only as *Lo Zoppo*, The Lame, looked with amusement at Guid'Antonio, his face stark in the meager light of his torch. "You don't mean only the ongoing construction, do you?" he said.

"No." Reaching down, Guid'Antonio patted the dog, a sturdy *Cane Corso Italiano*, or mastiff, named Monica for Saint

Augustine's mother, the patron saint of difficult marriages, victims of unfaithfulness, and abuse.

Monica eyed the bone Guid'Antonio offered her and glanced at her keeper, who said, "You know it is safe if it is from him." Sinking to her haunches, the dog anchored the bone vertically in her paws and gnawed it with gusto.

"Now, what?" *Lo Zoppo* said, his eyes twinkling on Guid'Antonio.

"Mushrooms," Guid'Antonio said.

"Information," the peddler said. "And?"

"Death Cap."

"Ah. The dead cloth merchant. Also, *Cannella*, the girl's little dog."

"Yes," Guid'Antonio said.

Lo Zoppo's eyes searched his. "You believe Andrea Antinori is innocent," he said.

"Yes. I need to prove that and expose the true killer. Soon."

"Humph. You'll not find those mushrooms in this town. The old witch who supplied them lives outside the walls."

"A witch?" Amerigo said, his voice low and thrilled.

A woman provided them, then, thought Guid'Antonio. *Neither in Santo Spirito, nor anywhere in Florence.* "The woman's name?" he said, nodding to Amerigo, who slid a coin from his scrip. *Lo Zoppo* raised his brow. Rolling his eyes, Amerigo dropped another coin into the peddler's hand.

Leaning close, his breath a stench of garlic and fish, *Lo Zoppo* whispered the name and location in Guid'Antonio's ear, adding, "Also, the monk who took *Orsetto* and then accosted you last evening—"

"Yes?"

"—Rest easy. He has been persuaded to leave town."

"How?"

"We made him an offer he could not refuse."

With that, *Lo Zoppo* folded into the shadows, limping, with his dog.

†

"So! Our monk truly is gone. Good! But the witch who provided the Death Cap to Orlando's killer lives in the countryside," Amerigo said as he and Guid'Antonio crossed back over the Arno. "Wouldn't you know it? Not only the countryside, but a lengthy ride from here."

Walking toward the river from Piazza Santo Spirito just now, Guid'Antonio had noticed a weak light burning behind a grilled window in the Church of the Holy Spirit. One of the friars, restless in the dead of the night, reading, or saying prayers. "Anything to make this journey more difficult," he said.

Amerigo looked aghast. "You can't mean to ride out now! It's late, we need our horses—and it's raining again." Amerigo pulled up his hood, gathering his cloak close around his shoulders to protect himself from the light drizzle falling down on them now. "Why was *Lo Zoppo* so quick to give up this—this witch who deals in poisons? No honor among thieves, I suppose."

"Give the man some credit," Guid'Antonio said. "He has standards. As far as the countryside goes, we'll not go tonight. We'll leave at dawn tomorrow."

"But tomorrow's Friday," Amerigo said. "We don't have time to hunt Niccolini's killer with you expected in court with Jacopo Caretto."

"Before dawn, then. And we'll have to hurry," Guid'Antonio said.

Thirty-Six

THE OLD WOMAN IN THE WOODS
FRIDAY, 2ND JULY 1473

A mound of stones, three crosses fashioned from reeds, and beyond the crosses, a thin path leading into a dense forest of trees whose limbs bent across the passage, clinging to one another like lovers. "This is it?" Amerigo said, wide-eyed. "You're going in that tunnel of dark?"

Guid'Antonio flipped back his hood. "We are," he said.

On foot, with Guid'Antonio leading the way, they eased along the rain-soaked trail with their horses, Flora and Bucephalus, boots and hooves sucking the wet earth, Flora snuffling in Guid'Antonio's ear. They had not gone far when a hut materialized before them. Ramshackle, with a solitary white hen pecking the ground. Guid'Antonio handed Amerigo Flora's reins. "Stay here. Keep watch. Take care."

Don't worry, Amerigo's expression said.

Without preamble, Guid'Antonio opened the cottage door.

☦

A candle burned on the hearth. On a nearby stool, a bundle of cloth stirred. A woman lifted her head, staring at him, her eyes rheumy in the scant light. "Ah, Dottore," she said. "You want a healing potion. Something to ease your troubled mind and soul."

He stepped back, thrown by the intimacy of her words, by her familiar address. "No," he said.

She cocked her head. "I am no devil. And you need something soothing in your veins."

"Then, yes," he said. *I am not afraid.*

She gestured toward the pottery cup on the trestle. Reaching for it, Guid'Antonio drank the liquid down, pleasant enough, though bitter around the edges.

"Sit," she said.

"No."

Her eyes shone. "Death Cap."

"Yes."

"You believe I provided it to someone seeking poison."

"I know you did."

"I merely described it," the old woman said. "I never would sell it to anyone. Death Cap is dangerous. The name alone signifies that." She grinned.

"Described it?" he said.

"Yes. I don't keep poisonous mushrooms on hand."

The killer had not been familiar with Death Cap, then. "Described it how?" he said.

She regarded him as if doubting his wits. "Where and how it grows. Its nature and appearance. Its foul odor."

"So he could collect it and use it to kill someone," Guid'Antonio said.

Her gnarled fingers touched her lips, her eyes wide and innocent. "Is that what happened?"

"Save me from your dissembling," he snapped. "I don't have time for this."

Her gaze narrowed. "Save me from your arrogance! Why do you care, Dottore High and Mighty? Sometimes, people deserve to die. From what our killer said, that was never more true than in the case of your dead cloth merchant."

"Not when they are innocent," Guid'Antonio said, and told her about Andrea Antinori, who would hang if Guid'Antonio did not solve the mystery surrounding the cloth merchant's death. Now. Today.

"Ah! The fair-haired boy who lives nearby," the woman said. "Or he did until he moved to Florence. He's a good boy, or so I'm told. Yet set to hang for a crime he did not commit?"

"Yes. When did your visitor arrive at your door? What day?"

She stared at him, measuring her reply. Measuring him. "During the week of the celebrations for Saint John the Baptist," she said, laughing. "A short while before. Like you, sneaking through the forest."

"Describe him," Guid'Antonio said. "And why he was so angry. Angry enough to commit murder."

She cackled. "You ask me that? You, who know so little of love and so much of betrayal and loss?"

Guid'Antonio stared at her, speechless, his chest constricting in pain. So much for healing potions.

"Give me your hand," she said.

He did as she asked. "Know this. You will lose a beloved friend. More than one. Evil-doers will corrupt Florence. You, too, will have murder on your hands. That time is not far ahead. Shall I tell you when—?"

He snatched away his palm. *"Pazza!"* he hissed, withdrawing toward the door. "Crazy!"

"I told you things you do not wish to hear," she said. "And yet, you listened. Listen, now, as I say who came to me seeking information about poisonous mushrooms and other means of murder."

†

"What happened?" Amerigo said, jumping back as Guid'Antonio stumbled from the hut.

"Let's get out of here." Guid'Antonio hurried through the forest, swiping wet branches from his face, Flora's lips nuzzling his shoulder, as if the horse understood everything and sympathized entirely.

"Did she name our killer?" Amerigo said.

"She did," Guid'Antonio said.

"And?"

Guid'Antonio told him.

Amerigo gasped. "God's pants! Why—"

Love, loss, betrayal. "Everything," he said.

"But you have to prove it," Amerigo said.

"Yes."

"You don't seem happy."

"The truth sickens me," Guid'Antonio said. Both the motive and the deed. Also—the old woman's words had plumbed an ache in his soul, one that played a sad song in his heart.

They emerged from almost total darkness into a light mist beneath thick grey clouds. Tentatively, Amerigo said, "What's next?"

"We ride like the wind to Florence," Guid'Antonio said, swinging into the saddle and urging Flora into a gallop. "I want you to hasten to the jail straightaway and find Palla—no, go home first and fetch my crimson cloak, I need it for court later today—then go to the jail and tell Palla I want to speak with him at—" He checked the rainclouds lumbering across the sky, as if in pursuit of them as they rode. "—toward midday. He'll know where."

Amerigo drew a small, quick breath. "Why don't you go to the jail? Where are you going straightaway?"

"To church. To Ognissanti for peace and quiet in the presence of God and Giotto's Crucifix. To think." *For hope, Amerigo,* he thought. *For hope.*

Thirty-Seven

PONTE CARRAIA

From where Guid'Antonio stood on Ponte Carraia, the distant Apennines appeared hazy and low, not quite blue, not quite grey as the sun struggled to shine from behind a sea of ominous dark clouds. No rain yet, but rain was not far away. Behind him the bridge was alive with noise and movement, a courier on horseback clattering from Santo Spirito into downtown Florence, dogs barking at the boys dancing around barefoot, armed with slingshots, firing stones at the scantily clad men fishing from boats in the river far down below Guid'Antonio. Eyes wide and fearful, beside Guid'Antonio Flora pranced and jerked against her reins.

"Easy, there, *mia ragazza*," he said, gently patting the horse. "It's only another day in the life of this fierce old bridge." Two hundred years ago, Ponte Carraia had been destroyed by a flood and rebuilt. Later, the newer wooden structure had collapsed beneath the men, women, and children who had gathered there to celebrate spring by cheering the mock battles on the river. That day almost every family in

Florence had lost a loved one to drowning or flying debris. Once again, Ponte Carraia had been rebuilt. And rebuilt again following yet another devastating flood. And so here Guid'Antonio Vespucci stood on this early July day in 1473, arms resting on the parapet overlooking the Arno, with who knew what death and destruction lay ahead for the bridge, and for him.

"You will lose a beloved companion. More than one," the old woman had said. "Shall I tell you when?"

No! No.

"I'm here whenever you beckon," a voice snapped in Guid'Antonio's ear. "And this had better be good. Amerigo caught me dining but since it's *you*—" Holding a packet of cheese and bread in one hand, and Guid'Antonio's crimson cloak in the other, Palla Palmieri slid from his mount. Behind the chief of police, the boys scattered, slingshots hidden behind them. "So—what is this about?" Palla said.

"Andrea Antinori is innocent. I can prove it," Guid'Antonio said, packing his brown cloak in his saddle bag and adjusting the crimson one over his shoulders.

Palla huffed. "Amerigo mentioned nothing about that."

"He wasn't meant to," Guid'Antonio said.

Palla fixed him with a concentrated stare. "I'm confused."

Guid'Antonio told him everything, leaving nothing unsaid.

Palla was so astonished he nearly dropped the olive he had begun to lift to his mouth. He recovered at once, a wide smile of surprise spreading over his delicate, dark features. "Well, well. Never let your feet be left out of both stirrups."

"I wouldn't have put it quite like that, but yes. Or no, whichever is the case," Guid'Antonio said. "Did Amerigo explain the next step?"

"He did. I sent him riding to *Drago Verde* to detain Beatrice and Baldo Pacini until my men arrive and haul them to jail for the murder of Orlando Niccolini. This, on your word and your word alone. I amaze myself."

"And me, as well. But they are not to arrest Elena Veluti," Guid'Antonio cautioned. "The girl is innocent of any wrongdoing."

Palla bowed. "They were instructed to leave her behind. Your wish is my command."

"*Grazie ancora,*" Guid'Antonio said. Thank you again.

"You'll tell Caterina Niccolini the news?" Palla said.

In his mind's eye, exactly as he knew Caterina would do, Guid'Antonio envisioned Beatrice and Baldo Pacini in the prisoner's cart a week or so hence, bumping and rattling on wooden wheels along Via dei Malcontenti behind a tired old horse with worn hooves plodding toward the scaffold. Along the way, people would cheer and spit on mother and son, anticipating the noose tightening around their necks, their flapping hands and twitching feet.

"I will, after I give the magistrates my decision regarding Jacopo Caretto a few moments from now," Guid'Antonio said.

"And have you determined what the magistrates should do with him?"

"I have."

Thirty-Eight

CASE 421946

Foresto Gondi, Chairman of the panel presiding over the Court of Criminal Justice today, glanced up at the sound of boots squishing toward the table where he and the two other magistrates sat shoulder-to-shoulder. "Dottore?" Through his spectacles, Gondi measured with blurred astonishment Guid'-Antonio's soggy crimson cloak. The two men flanking Gondi appeared astounded, eyeing the moisture lifting off the lightweight wool in waves. The rain that had been threatening town and countryside suddenly had unleashed itself upon Florence. Now, beyond the windows that usually afforded the chamber illumination for the greater part of the day, silver lightning flashed, briefly lighting the sky. Thunder shattered the air, and the wind moaned around the courtyard beyond the chamber doors. A bit of fiery color reflected from candles and torches, along with the oil lamp chandelier attached to an iron chain hanging from the courtroom ceiling, stained the walls and licked the faces of the men in the chamber in streaks of red and orange.

"Dottore Vespucci, we do not often see you in such . . . disarray," Gondi said, with a tiny smile.

Guid'Antonio combed his fingers through his hair, curling at the temples. "Chairman Gondi, *Signori. Ciao,*" he said, then nodded briefly to Jacopo Caretto and his son, Salvatore, who eyed Guid'Antonio warily from a long bench placed against the courtroom wall.

"Better late than never," Chairman Gondi said. "And don't bother mentioning you were caught in the storm. It is obvious that is what happened." Eyeing Guid'Antonio, Salvatore Caretto shifted on the bench, muttering something beneath his breath, and he and his father laughed smugly.

"Prego," Guid'Antonio said.

"For the record, Dottore—" Chairman Gondi huffed a weary breath. "You are here to give your recommendation for punishment for—" The chairman paused, squinting toward the notary seated nearby, armed with paper, pen, and sand.

"Case 421946, Jacopo Caretto, wool beater, Black Lion district, Santa Croce quarter," the notary said. "On the night of his arrest Caretto confessed to defiling and strangling his kinswoman. Since then, he has offered no defense."

Salvatore snorted derisively, nudging his father. "Kinswoman?" he said.

Chairman Gondi ignored the comment. "Caretto has offered no motive?" he said, again addressing the notary, who shook his head. "No."

Gondi grunted, tapping his foot beneath the magistrates' table. Heavy around the middle and snowy-haired, Gondi was a good deal older than anyone else in the chamber. "Dottore. You've spoken with the accused?" he said.

Guid'Antonio nodded. "On two occasions. Yes."

"And your recommendation is?"

A sudden movement took Guid'Antonio's notice. Turning slightly, he saw Palla Palmieri leaning against the chamber door in brown boots, hose, and tunic. Palla arched an eyebrow. *And?*

Guid'Antonio faced the court. "Decapitation," he said.

"What?!" Salvatore Caretto scrambled from the bench so quickly, he slipped and had to fight to regain his balance. "We filed an appeal! My father's a good man!" In the dim light of the chandelier, Salvatore's face was a fury of purple and scarlet. "My father—"

"Sit down! Silence!" Gondi pounded the table with his fist. "*Guardia!*"

The burly fellow posted behind Salvatore and Jacopo slammed Salvatore down on the bench. "You heard the chairman."

Eyes bulging, Salvatore did as he was told. With his outburst diffused, Gondi yawned profusely, and his two bench mates followed suit, stretching the tiredness from their backs and necks. "Dottore Vespucci, you're aware the Caretto family has petitioned the court for leniency."

"I am," Guid'Antonio said.

Gondi glanced at the notary. "Andrelino. On what grounds have they filed?"

Andrelino glanced at his notes. "Again, Jacopo Caretto has no record of prior arrest. According to his employer and his neighbors, he is a hardworking, honest man who assists his family with a good portion of his wages. When the girl's parents died, he welcomed her with open arms, offering her a home and a bed. Meanwhile, lately the girl's behavior had been questionable. She was becoming increasingly disobedient."

"A home and a bed. How truly kind of him," Gondi said.

Guid'Antonio cleared his mind, seeking calm, aware he was walking on eggshells. There would be no sentence for Jacopo Caretto today, and the atmosphere in the court told him which way the wind was blowing. The magistrates seated before him would give Guid'Antonio half an ear and hurry home to an afternoon nap after a generous cup of wine and a plate of grapes and cheese. Next week, these same three men would convene with the additional five members of the Eight on Public Safety. Together, they would hand down sentences regarding the cases heard this week. The Eight, who were the watchdogs of Florentine justice, could accept Guid'Antonio's recommendation, modify it, or reject it entirely. They could fine Jacopo a few *lire* and possibly add another few *lire* for court costs, as described in the *Condempnationes et Absolutiones* Guid'Antonio and Amerigo had researched in the chancery office, and let him go.

Deliberately, Guid'Antonio coughed back a laugh. "A home and a bed. Yes. The bed where Jacopo raped Chiara from the time she was a child of six until she was ten or eleven. And then not quite two weeks ago, he choked her to death." Leaning slightly toward the bench, he added softly, "His own granddaughter."

The magistrates flinched, their distaste for his words plain. "Dottore Vespucci!" Gondi said. "I must protest—"

Salvatore squealed, his hands bunched into fists, as if willing himself not to spring to his feet. "What man has ever been executed for having his way with prick teasing girl?" He fawned on the magistrates: "*Signori*, you know how it is—she made my father wild! She did that to men. Flaunting herself, inflaming him." Salvatore's face twisted. *"Passione!"*

Keep going, thought Guid'Antonio. *Please*.

"Silence in the court!" Chairman Gondi said. Flustered, he addressed Guid'Antonio. "You needn't describe what happened so coarsely."

"Yes, I must," Guid'Antonio said. "Although I understand that rather than rape, you would prefer assaulted, ravished, interfered with, or taken by force."

For the first time, Banco della Casa, the magistrate at Gondi's right elbow, spoke. "Dottore, one day your inherently arrogant attitude—your complete lack of respect for this court—will land you in such trouble, your famous young friends on Via Larga will not be able to save you."

Inherently arrogant—me? Guid'Antonio glanced at Palla, who grinned slightly.

"Perhaps not," Guid'Antonio said neutrally.

"Where were we?" Chairman Gondi said, scratching his forehead.

Jacopo Caretto's lips drew back in a snarl, revealing the brown stubs of his teeth. "As you said when you came to my cell, Dottore, there are two sides to every tale."

"And what is yours?" Guid'Antonio said.

Jacopo's pocked face contorted in a hideous grin. "You heard my son! I'm a good man! Look in my file, and you'll find the kind words of my neighbors and friends."

"What else?" Guid'Antonio said, but Chairman Gondi, overriding him, raised his hand for silence.

"Enough," he said.

A hushed conversation between the three magistrates ensued. And then Chairman Gondi turned toward the court. "As stated by the accused's son, Salvatore Caretto, this was a crime of passion. We all know how certain girls blossom like hazel trees as they grow. It sets fire to a man."

"Yes!" Salvatore said. "My father is an *uomo virile*, a virile man." He shrugged, adding with a grin and a wink, "Despite his age."

The magistrates smirked along with him. "Dottore Vespucci," Gondi said, motioning at the same time for the guard to return Jacopo to his cell to await the court's final decision. "Your recommendation for punishment has been duly noted, along with the family's appeal."

"Wait," Guid'Antonio said.

✝

The three magistrates, in the middle of rising from the bench, froze. Through clenched teeth, Gondi said, "You have made your point, which is all you have been appointed to do, Dottore. You know the procedure—you present your *disegno* and then you leave." Gondi fluttered his fingers, as if ushering Guid'Antonio out the door.

Guid'Antonio collected his thoughts. When he was a boy, his father had taken him high atop Santa Maria del Fiore, the Cathedral in the heart of Florence capped with Brunelleschi's red brick dome. The biggest Cathedral in the world! He remembered climbing the spiraling stone corridor, up, up, up!—then flinging off his father's hand and sprinting in the open air to the edge of the wooden platform circling the dome beneath the marble lantern. He remembered slamming to a halt, wavering on the rim, his arms flailing as Piazza San Giovanni whooshed up from the ground far down below. He remembered watching himself, a frightened child, from somewhere in the clouds, remembered his terror and the crystalline understanding *this* was the defining moment of his life so far.

Nauseated.

Scared.

He remembered his father behind him saying in a soft voice, "Step back. Be still."

In the courtroom, he stilled his pounding heart. And then he flung his crimson cloak from his shoulders. "No."

"Guid'Antonio!" Gondi shouted. "You are out of order!"

"I mean to be," he said calmly.

"Holy Mary, Mother of God! If you were not who you are—what *is* it, then?" Gondi said, sinking with the other two magistrates onto the bench, motioning at the same time for the guard to remain in the courtroom with Jacopo and Salvatore Caretto.

"This is no longer the Jacopo Caretto case, but the case for his granddaughter," Guid'Antonio said. "With me as Chiara

Caretto's advocate, speaking in her name."

An exquisite silence took hold of the room.

"What?" Salvatore Caretto said in disbelief. "What the hell—"

"Silence!" Gondi yelled.

Beside Gondi, Banco della Casa said, "Dottore, you are supposed to remain *neutral*."

"In court-appointed cases, yes," Guid'Antonio said. "I'm moving beyond that in this instance." He addressed the notary: "Andrelino, please note this new case and number it however you choose: Chiara Caretto, age ten or eleven, versus her family."

"What?" Salvatore yelled.

Gondi stared at Guid'Antonio, stiffening his posture. "You mean to make a personal denunciation. An *accusatorial*."

"I do," Guid'Antonio said.

"I could postpone this, set another date, since it is another case." Gondi sighed. "But I would rather get it over with."

Salvatore Caretto let out a cry of exasperation. "A—a what? But why? No one cared about her! She was—she was—" Still standing with his father, Salvatore gestured helplessly around, groping for words.

"She was nothing," Guid'Antonio said, thinking, *Like the boy in the piazza, scalped and running for his life. Like the two apprentices whose abusive master was punished with a fine and fifty lashes, rather than with the death sentence, as called for by law. Like the slave woman whose rape warranted a fine, and nothing more, as long as she returned to her master, waiting there for her, with his bedchamber shutters drawn. Like the woman whose face would forever bear a razor scar, thanks to her husband.*

Guid'Antonio went on: "So much so, no one—not one person in her family—bothered reporting her missing. These last few days, I have found myself asking: Was Chiara Caretto so insignificant as that?" Those were Maria's words, yes.

Gondi blinked hard. "But decapitation? Jacopo didn't mean to kill the girl, clearly."

Didn't mean to? Guid'Antonio soldiered on. "And lose having her in his bed? No, probably not," he said.

Gondi squirmed. "When your servant, Cesare, killed a guest at your *festa* table, Palla Palmieri called it an accident, fined the boy, and set him free. *Killed*, Dottore." Gondi's eyes fixed on Palla, who stared back coldly, the smile flitting across his lips gone in an instant.

"Different circumstances surrounded the death of Orlando Niccolini," Guid'Antonio said. "But Salvatore," he went on, addressing Jacopo's son. "I have to ask—why do you protest so violently? What are you hiding?"

A flush infused Salvatore's face. "Me?"

"You," Guid'Antonio said.

"I only want justice for my father," Salvatore said, his eyes darting here and there. "Men were coming around her like she was a bitch in heat. She was ripe! Like a peach!"

Guid'Antonio locked eyes with him. "Were you using her, too? Were *you* inflamed, Salvatore? Or did you merely watch? In that case, I understand why you wouldn't rush to the authorities to report her missing. They might have turned their eyes toward you. Which, actually, is where we are now. Watching and wondering about you."

"Me? No!" Salvatore cried. "Tell them, Father—"

Jacopo ignored his son.

"*I* will tell *you*, Salvatore!" Guid'Antonio said, his voice thunderous in the courtroom. "Everyone in the Caretto family understood what was happening behind those doors. No one—almost no one—cared, so long as Jacopo shared his wages. Yours was a conspiracy of silence, making everyone in your family an accessory to rape and murder, whether or not you participated. Standing by, while Jacopo made Chiara his slave."

Whining, Salvatore said, "She owed him! She owed all of us for allowing her and that bitch dog she took off the street to share the food from my father's table and have a bed."

Guid'Antonio swallowed the bile rising in his throat. "That is where you are wrong. Chiara had one very important friend: *Cannella*, her little ginger dog. A loyal, bereaved dog who loved her mistress so much, she dragged what she could of Chiara home—a sad, torn sleeve. Except for *Cannella*, Jacopo would have gotten away with raping his granddaughter—your niece—for half her life and then choking her to death."

A vein popped out on Jacopo's neck. "She enjoyed it!" he screamed. "She bewitched me, singing like Eve in the garden with the smell of the Devil's blood between her legs!"

A shocked silence descended over the court. Guid'Antonio addressed the magistrates' bench, inhaling a long, quiet breath. "Yes. Chiara had started her courses. She had become a woman with all the accompanying allurements. This aroused Jacopo to the point of violence. Chiara was older now—as she matured, I believe she could and did resist him. That thrilled him even more. Probably, she threatened to go to the family, or even to the authorities. He—they—couldn't allow an investigation into the wickedness in their house. And so, he strangled her. Not in a fit of passion, but premediated. The family needed her dead."

Once again, the magistrates whispered to one another. "Guid'Antonio," a subdued Chairman Gondi said. "One question, *per favore*."

"Yes."

"You asked Salvatore why he is making such a protest. Of you we would ask the same."

Guid'Antonio regarded the magistrates for a long moment. And then he spread his arms to encompass the room, as if addressing the world, the universe, God. In a voice tight with emotion, he said, "Chiara was Jacopo Caretto's grandchild. He was bound by honor to provide for her as best he could. He was her protector, meant to shelter her from harm. Instead, he stole her innocence and her life, preying on her with the rest of his family like a pack of hungry wolves. Oh, yes. I believe it. They were thieves, stealing her love, her lifeblood. He had a child, and he destroyed her." Tears pricked his eyes. How could anyone do that?

"Jacopo, Salvatore," he said, turning to father and son. "Why bury Chiara in a hole in the ground? That was a fatal mistake, one that allowed *Cannella* to find her little girl's corpse. Why not throw her in the Arno with the other trash?"

Jacopo's expression dulled. "I loved her. As you say, she was my granddaughter."

†

"Well done," Palla said, walking with Guid'Antonio from the suffocating courtroom into the jail's wet, but airy, courtyard. The storm had rumbled off toward the west, and the *cortile* was quiet, the majority of lawyers, notaries, and messengers gone home for the weekend.

Guid'Antonio craned his neck. Overhead, the sky had transformed into a thing of beauty. Gone were the bruised, black thunderclouds, and there was the sun, casting pink and blue shadows on gossamer white clouds. Light. Warmth. "Well done? I fear otherwise," he said. "I should have hurled incest at them. I had it at hand."

Palla laughed. "I wish you had. Like Zeus casting thunderbolts at his enemies." Zeus, the god of the sky and thunder, the king of the gods, according to some.

Guid'Antonio allowed himself a smile. "I let my heart rule my head and so several good opportunities slipped away. I am no god. I'm weary of this. The killing, the cheating, the anger, the strife, but most especially, the betrayal."

Palla inhaled bracingly and slapped him on the back. "You are bristling with energy, my friend."

"That you think so gladdens me. Next week, the Carettos could issue another appeal. File a *bollettino*, requesting mercy. I fear Chiara will not see justice in this world."

"So," Palla said. "We wait and we do not surrender hope."

"Never," Guid'Antonio said.

"Tell me," Palla said, his dark eyes intense. "What—how were you so certain about the terrible things happening in that house?"

"A good woman told me," Guid'Antonio said. "Chiara's aunt by marriage. One light shining brightly in the darkness choking that family. But never breathe a word of that to anyone. There is no telling what her husband might do." Fenso Caretto, Jacopo's other son.

"Bless her," Palla said. "In the end, the reason Jacopo would not speak in his defense to you when you questioned him is clear. He feared he would give himself—all of them—away."

"Yes. Now I'm off to tell Caterina Niccolini who killed her husband."

"I don't envy you," Palla said. "First death by Cesare, then by Andrea Antinori, and now by Beatrice and Baldo Pacini. At the end of this day, Caterina Niccolini will feel as tired as you."

Before Guid'Antonio could make a reply, a familiar figure ran into the courtyard. Glancing hastily around, Cesare's violet eyes searched the *cortile*. "Dottore Guid'Antonio!" he cried, rushing forward. "Praise God I found you here! I saw Flora tethered outside, and—"

"Cesare! What now?" Guid'Antonio said.

"Dottore Filippo—" Cesare grabbed his chest, struggling for breath. On the verge of tears, his words came out brokenly. "Filippo Vernacci is dead!"

Francesca's father, Guid'Antonio's dear friend? His heart

stilled. "No, I just saw him—" When? When was that? On Sunday in Piazza Ognissanti, which seemed so long ago.

"What happened?" Palla demanded. "Are you sure? Tell us, boy!"

"He was killed!"

"Stop crying and explain yourself," Palla snapped, his voice trembling and urgent.

Cesare's words tumbled one over the other. "He fell in front of an oxcart at the door to the hospital. He struggled to rise, but stumbled. The beasts crushed him. And then—and then the wagon wheels." Tears streamed down Cesare's cheeks. "In another moment, he would have been home safely. He has always been nice to me."

Awkwardly, Guid'Antonio put his arms around Cesare and held him, this boy, this boy who was becoming less a servant to him and more like a son. Filippo Vernacci, *gone*. Not from his coughing sickness, but from an unfortunate twist of fate. And now Francesca, alone in the world. "Cesare," Guid'Antonio managed to say, patting the boy, prying him from him. "I have to go to the hospital."

"I'll accompany you," Cesare said, his voice high with sorrow.

"No, no. As you say, Flora is here. I'll ride fast and speak with Maestra Francesca."

He looked at Palla. "After that, Caterina."

†

Blood on the stones in front of Spedale dei Vespucci. People standing around, whispering among themselves. Several of Palla's police family, questioning them.

At the hospital entrance Guid'Antonio inhaled deeply, fortifying himself for the next few moments, for the sad days ahead. In a daze, he entered the foyer and nodded to Lena

Barone, who greeted him in silence, her expression grim. And then up the stairs he went, his body floating. What to say? *I am so sorry? I feel your loss deeply?* Empty sentiments, meaning nothing in the face of death.

His mind scrambled. Soon, the *beccamorti* would arrive. Eventually, the stones on Borg'Ognissanti would be washed, sparkling and clean. No: this was muddled thinking. There was no need for the *beccamorti*. Dottore Filippo Vernacci was already in the surgery.

At the door, he caught sight of Francesca bent over the stone table, her shoulders quivering beneath the fabric of her white gown. Weeping uncontrollably, heartbroken. "All those years ago, I chose you, Pippo," she whispered to the broken corpse of her father. "I chose you. And now—"

Guid'Antonio blinked. Yes, she did. All those years ago? It had been three years, only.

He stood rooted where he stood for what seemed to him a century.

Stay?

Or go.

Turning, he descended the stairs and walked out onto the blood soaked borgo to find Orlando Niccolini's widow, Caterina.

Thirty-Nine

LIMBO

Apprehension filled her eyes the instant she saw him on the lip of her threshold: damp hair, wrinkled crimson cloak. She recovered quickly, but that she was shaken by his second visit to her house was unmistakable. "Dottore Vespucci," she said. "It is you once more."

Like the plague. He nodded, recalling the words he had heard Francesca Vernacci utter over her father's corpse a few moments ago. *I chose you, Pippo. I chose you.* She may as well have added, *Instead of Guid'Antonio. Never him, not in a thousand years.* "In the flesh," he said.

Caterina's gaze flicked past him to the rain-soaked piazza beyond her door. Quiet surrounded the muddy, sunken graves in the children's cemetery, the only sound the soft swish of a priest's skirts as he entered the Church of the Holy Apostles, surrounding himself in darkness behind thick walls of centuries-old stone.

Guid'Antonio cocked his head. "Mona Caterina, may I enter, *per favore*?"

"Oh! Of course. Forgive me, Dottore."

As Caterina had done on the day of her husband's funeral, she gestured toward the wine in a silver pitcher on the credenza near the hearth. "Thank you," Guid'Antonio said, noting relief on her face when he accepted the cup and drank.

She cocked her head. *And?*

"We know who murdered your husband," he said.

Caterina's face was a study of confusion with a hint of impatience. "Yes. Palla Palmieri arrested Orlando's apprentice, Andrea Antinori."

"That has changed, *Signora*."

She fingered the jeweled cross at the neck of her black damask gown, folds of mourning engulfing her slender body. "Who, then?"

"Baldo and Beatrice Pacini."

"What?" Caterina stumbled back a step.

"A wool scourer and his mother, a wool spinner. They live in *Drago Verde*, across the river."

"I know who they are and where they live!" Caterina snapped. "In less than a year they have caused me a lifetime of humiliation and regret. People whispering, 'Poor Orlando Niccolini! He has no children, no family.' Because of me, they mean. Caterina!" She wrung her hands. "His whore is proof of that. He's with her for one moment, and her belly is as huge as Piazza Santa Croce."

"Caterina," Guid'Antonio said in a soothing voice.

She was not finished. "Oh, yes! I've seen him with her. I trailed him across the Arno and watched him stroll into that shack, smirking, one fat hand caressing her plump ass. I hope she rots in jail. I hope she hangs!"

"Elena Veluti hasn't been charged," he said. "Only Baldo and Beatrice."

Caterina's eyes closed to slits. "Where is she?"

"At home in *Drago Verde*." He shrugged. "I suppose. I

mean, presumably, she has nowhere else to go."

"Why would those people kill him? He was their bread and butter," she said, her voice hard.

"Because they discovered he was worth more to them dead than alive."

She hesitated. "How so?"

"You may wish to sit."

"I wish to stand."

"Before he died, your husband altered his will."

"Altered it? How?"

The truth of the matter as shared by Francesco Nori was shockingly cruel. In the event of Orlando Niccolini's death, his house—*this* house—and all its goods were to go to the mother of his child. "That is *if* the child is a boy and *if* Elena names him Orlando Niccolini," Guid'Antonio said. "He meant to adopt him."

Caterina gaped at him. "He had that written down?"

"He did. Signed and sealed by Francesco Nori."

"What was he thinking?"

"To have an heir."

"And if it is *not* a boy?"

"Give birth to a girl and Elena receives nothing."

"Nothing?" Caterina echoed.

"Nay. Not so much as a silver penny."

"What about me?" she said, her hand at her throat. "I was to have this house. He told me so! I made sure of it, also—"

In his mind, Guid'Antonio watched Caterina slip into her husband's *studietto* when he was away on business. Watched her fix the iron key in the lockbox with trembling hands and search his documents, then slip away, as pleased as a cat with cream on its lips. He said, "That was then, and this is now."

She looked directly at him through defiant eyes. "I don't believe it! This is too much!"

And yet it was not everything. "Why would I say so,

Caterina? Francesco Nori is—was—your husband's notary and privy to his will. Francesco amended the document for him. It is Francesco who told me about the will's revised contents."

She stared at him with hollow eyes. "Again, what about me if that whore lives or dies, bears boy or girl?"

Guid'Antonio ached for her. "You receive nothing in any case. Your husband stated you shall have—the convent you enter shall have—a set amount to sustain you for ten years." The stipend provided a pittance for soup and bread.

Caterina stood before him in stunned silence, then slowly looked around at the tapestries and paintings, the Turkey carpet leading to the curtained kitchen. Everything—*everything*—gone with one stroke of a heartless man's pen. Stolen. Given away. Her glance slid toward the painted wedding chest against one wall. Clearly, she was estimating the value of its contents. Under-gowns, shifts, sleeves, lace-trimmed handkerchiefs, perhaps even a pearl band for her hair. In a used-clothes shop, she might see good coin for personal items. So, too, Orlando had clothes and a horse she could sell . . .

Guid'Antonio shook his head. "Everything goes to Elena, in the event, and so on. Including your clothing and jewelry. I would suggest you tuck the cross you are wearing someplace safe."

Her lips tightened into a thin line. "He hated me that much." Rallying, she said, "You say if this Elena creature has a girl, she gets nothing. Who reaps the reward then? What about that child?"

Again, he shook his head. "In that case, everything goes to *Ognissanti*, All Saints."

"To Abbot Roberto Ughi," Caterina said, her voice dull and flat. "The church my *husband* and I attended for a dozen years."

"Yes."

"The nunnery," she said.

"But one of your choosing," Guid'Antonio said.

She let out a choked laugh, making cutting motions at her wrists with her hands. "Thank you, Dottore! Your words shall give me great comfort when I enter those dark doors. She stole my child. Now, she has stolen my life, as well."

Caterina's child. Yes. He had heard about that, although it was not Elena who had done the stealing. "I am truly sorry, Caterina," he said.

Her shoulders settled and a look of defeat commanded her face, her eyelids at half-mast. "Why did you come to tell me this?"

"Because, Caterina, he died at my house."

☦

He left her with her head bowed, careful to gently close the door as he stepped out into the piazza, smiling faintly when he heard the sound of pottery crashing in pieces on Caterina's tile floor. *Good for you*, he thought. His gaze swept the small graves made for lost souls, and he sobered, mourning the infants who died unbaptized in Florence, and everywhere in the world, his quiet footsteps leading him away from Piazza Limbo in the Viper district of Florence toward his home in Ognissanti.

Forty

GOD AND GUID'ANTONIO

That night a hooded figure makes its way across the river and into the Santo Spirito quarter, failing to notice the two men skulking in the shadows of shuttered shops and dark byways, trailing at a careful distance as they wind deep into *Drago Verde*.

"Zanna! Fang!" a man yells. "*Silenzio, per l'amor di Dio! Every night, it's the same thing! You have ghosts on the brain!*" The fellow curses the barking mastiff repeatedly before slamming the shutters with a loud bang. The neighborhood holds it breath, and the trio resumes motion.

On Borgo Friano, with the church of San Frediano on the right and the gate to Pisa straight ahead, the hooded figure pauses, glancing around before stepping into deeper darkness. The two men follow in time to see their quarry search the shadows again before reaching out, fingers turning the handle of a door that will not give. An exasperated huff of breath, another quick movement, a key unlocks the bolt, and the figure eases inside the Pacini family's humble abode.

"That's it, and it makes me sad," Amerigo whispers as the tail of Caterina Niccolini's cloak vanishes over the threshold.

"We trailed her from the Viper district," Palla Palmieri whispers in reply. "The answer is clear."

†

Inside the house, a solitary candle burns low. Slowly, carefully, Caterina approaches the curtained sleeping space near the hearth and eases back the cloth. There stands a narrow bed. The form beneath the thin sheet is that of a sleeping girl, one hand protecting her protuberant belly. Along with the latch key, Caterina has a stiletto. She creeps forward, gripping the hilt in a hand slick with sweat. In the light of the candle, the blade glints as Caterina plunges the weapon toward the girl's stomach, but catches herself back, the knife suddenly slipping from her fingers, clattering on the floor. "I can't!" she cries. "No!"

"Thank God," Guid'Antonio says.

"You!" She whirls as he steps from the shadows in his brown leather *farsetto*. Rich brown tunic, hose, boots.

He smiles sadly. "Always."

"I could have killed her!" Caterina screams. "And yet you stood by—" Anguish fills her voice, and she trembles uncontrollably.

"No," he says. "What you see on the mattress is a figure fashioned from straw. Anyway, you drew away at the last moment."

Sobbing uncontrollably, she says, "I am not a bad woman," and he takes her shaking body in his arms, patting her shoulder, listening. "I'm glad I killed *him*," she whispers emphatically through her tears. "I hated him! I wanted him to roast in hell."

"You admit you killed him?" he says.

"Yes! Moreover, I want all the world to know I poisoned him and why!"

Amerigo and Palla have slipped inside the house, and if they are astonished to see Guid'Antonio comforting Caterina Niccolini, they do not show it. She sees them, though. Stepping away from Guid'Antonio, hiccupping, she says, "You tricked me into coming here tonight, Dottore. You connived with these two companions of yours."

"I did," Guid'Antonio says. *And we connivers have just heard you confess.*

In a monotone, Caterina says, "How did you know it was me?"

"You told me, Caterina."

"How? she cries in disbelief. "When?"

Palla steps in, his expression grave. "We will continue this at the jail."

☦

"How did I tell you?" she said. "When?"

These were the same questions Caterina Niccolini had asked in Santo Spirito a short while ago. Now there was little emotion in her face, her voice. The *cortile* outside the cell where she sat on a cot with her hands clenched in her lap was dimly lit with torches whose flames paled from amber to ghostly pale yellow as they vanished in the darkness of the starry night sky far, far above. Just beyond the cell door a sergeant stood guard, slump-shouldered and snoring, his hand limp against the keys dangling at his belt. Jacopo Caretto's cell was not far away. All was dark and silent there.

"Once I suspected Orlando had been murdered, I watched everyone and listened to them with the utmost care," Guid'-Antonio said.

"You always do," Palla murmured, chiming in.

By the light of the oil lamp in the police chief's hand, Caterina's face was drained of all color. "When?" she pressed.

"Let us begin with you," Guid'Antonio said, sitting beside her on the cot.

Closing her eyes for a moment, breathing deeply, Caterina related how she had learned of her husband's liaison with Elena Veluti, and how desperately she, Caterina, wanted him dead. In the beginning, the thought of killing him was no more than a delicious product of her imagination, a version of living life as a free woman of means. A rarity in Florence, but it could be done. "Consider your Maestra Francesca Vernacci," she said.

Guid'Antonio's cheeks surged with heat, but he said nothing.

She offered him a nudge and a little smile. "Then here came Cesare Ridolfi bragging about your *festa* to everyone in the Santa Maria Novella quarter. The food, the music, the four men chosen to grace your special table. Orlando, the fool, couldn't believe his good fortune! The onset of his fever, the sneezing, the muddled thinking, infuriated him. He vowed he would sit at your table on Saint John's Day or die trying." A playful smile tipped her lips. "Ironic, don't you think?"

"Very," he said.

"I despised him!" she said. "Chicken soup from Santa Maria Nuova. Warm lemon water and honey at home, all manner of medicaments from the Sign of the Stars. I thought if I heard one more time how he would be seated between Giuliano the Beautiful and you, I would be sick myself! After the *festa*, he was setting sail for England. When he could no longer smell his own farts, I saw how I could get away with murder."

"That's cold," Palla said.

"You weren't married to him!" Caterina yelled.

Palla flinched, something Guid'Antonio never had seen

him do while questioning a suspect. But this was the formidable Caterina Niccolini.

"You need only lace Orlando's salad with poison," Guid'-Antonio said, addressing her. "And here's the key: here is the link that eluded me for far too long. A day or so after leaving Florence, Orlando would die aboard ship and be buried at sea. That should have made your plan foolproof: no one would know he had been poisoned. No one would know he was dead—not for a long while. You would have gotten away with murder. It was as simple as that.

"But then Angelo Poliziano's unexpected arrival in the meadow turned your plan on its head. From Cesare, you knew the exact seating order, and you had already laced the second salad plate on his rectangular tray with Death Cap, expecting him to serve the first plate to Giuliano de' Medici, the second to your victim, Orlando, the third to me, and on down the table to Amerigo and lastly, to Francesco Nori."

Palla, leaning against the door to the cell chewing on a bit of straw he had taken from his scrip, frowned. "Explain to me again the scenario in the meadow."

"Gladly. Just before Cesare arrived with the salads, Angelo Poliziano joined us—not at the table proper; there was no room. He sat on a stool facing us, instead. Shortly afterward, Caterina came off the borgo, her destination Maria's table, but when she saw Angelo, she froze—what if Cesare served Angelo Poliziano first on the stool where he was seated? And then went around the table to Giuliano?"

"Good God," Palla whispered, touching his breast. "Giuliano de' Medici would have died a day or so later."

"Quite likely," Guid'Antonio said. "Instead, at that exact moment my kinswoman, Simonetta Vespucci, invited Giuliano to dance. Of course, he did. Caterina, watching this play out, remained frightened—with Giuliano's seat vacant, now Cesare would serve Orlando first . . . and then me."

"You?" Palla said.

"Yes."

"The mind staggers."

"It does." Guid'Antonio regarded Caterina Niccolini. "But then with *another* turn of Fortune's wheel, Angelo Poliziano leaped up and took Giuliano's place. Now, Angelo would have the first plate, and Orlando Niccolini, the second, as planned. All this happened in the blink of an eye."

"Yet you noticed," Caterina said dully.

Guid'Antonio smiled. "Yes. With everything settled, shaken but relieved, you proceeded to my wife's table, where you ate my food and drank my wine."

Eyes glinting, Caterina said, "I would not have let you die! Neither you, Dottore, nor Giuliano de' Medici! It was Orlando I wanted dead."

"And you succeeded in killing him," Guid'Antonio said. "But now, misfortune plagued you. Following the law of the land, I ordered an autopsy, one that revealed not only Orlando's sick liver, but also the Death Cap in his gut. In the end, however, you could breathe easily: Palla questioned my little salad-maker and charged him with accidental murder. 'Death by Cesare Ridolfi'."

Palla sighed, wagging his finger. "Anyone can make a mistake. I'm not above admitting that in this instance, I did. And incidentally—if Cesare had served Angelo Poliziano first while Giuliano was still at the table—well, he probably wouldn't have served Angelo at all, would he? He had only five salads, after all. He would have had to have six—"

"Don't make this more complicated than it already is," Guid'Antonio said. "Up, down, and sideways. My mistake was blaming Cesare rather than facing the fact a guest had been murdered at my Saint John's Day celebration. It wasn't until the little dog at my *festa* died of Death Cap poisoning that I had to admit to myself we had a killer on our hands. Would

Cesare make the same mistake twice? No. In addition to the chopped Death Cap in Orlando's gut and the whole one Palla found in Cesare's kitchen basket, there always had been a third mushroom—the one that killed Chiara Caretto's unfortunate, but brave, little pet. Giddy Cesare may be, but he is not careless.

"Also, Caterina," Guid'Antonio went on. "Among the many things I observed on Saint John's Day was how *Cannella* tagged behind you and Francesco Nori as you departed the meadow, hastening on your heels. Before coming there, you had fed her the third Death Cap, and *Cannella* hoped you might feed her again. She believed you were her friend. Poor thing."

A red flush crept up Caterina's neck. "I didn't mean to harm the dog. I was desperate. The alley was empty when I tossed the mushroom away. Somehow, she found it."

Desperate—yes. Exactly as Domenica Ridolfi and Giuliano de' Medici had suggested this past week.

Palla raised his eyebrows. "Caterina was trapped in the kitchen," he said.

Guid'Antonio nodded. "Yes. Another mistake I made was not realizing that when I asked Domenica and Cesare whether or not there were strangers there on Saint John's Day, they replied there were none because to them Caterina Niccolini is not a stranger. They see one another often in the markets and at church. Domenica, Gaspare, and Livia, the kitchen girl—all I have heard about that day is how many people were in the kitchen, in the garden, on the borgo. Caterina would not have been noticed. Or at least, not remembered. Actually at one point, Caterina, Cesare almost gave you away.

"On Thursday, when I quizzed him and Domenica a second time, he mentioned late-comers to the meadow. I had noticed your late arrival, of course, but Orlando said you had been visiting your ailing mother. Cesare was about to say, 'However, she was truly late because she was in our kitchen, visiting', and so on. But Domenica cut over him to mention how everyone was laughing and a short while later, Orlando was dead. The point being, Caterina, you were in the kitchen, and had I paid closer attention, I would have known that and put things together much sooner than I did."

"Whew," Palla said. "And—"

"I am not finished," Guid'Antonio said. "Speaking of Livia, that was another thing, Caterina. When you mentioned it was Livia who delivered Maria's gifts to your house, you didn't say they were delivered 'by your kitchen girl', or even 'by your girl, Livia.' No. You used her name as if you knew her well."

He studied the woman seated before him. "Your turn," he said.

Caterina stared vacantly into the shadows as she told them how she had slipped into the Vespucci kitchen on Saint John's Day. Yes, mayhem reigned, grocers and bakers coming and going, musicians in the garden blowing their horns, servers preening—the latter including Cesare, who, having prepared his salad plates, fluffed his hair and stepped into the garden to alert the trumpeters the time had come to march to the meadow in a flurry of fanfare. Moving quickly, Caterina had added the chopped Death Cap she had brought with her to the second plate on the rectangular silver tray Cesare had earlier in the week polished to a high sheen.

"And the mushroom I found later in Cesare's market basket?" Palla said. "Why was it there? The mushroom that killed the little stray."

"Not a stray," Guid'Antonio said.

The growing regret in Caterina's eyes deepened. "When I heard Cesare flitting back to the kitchen, I still had two whole mushrooms in my cloak pocket. Foolish!"

"The traveling cloak you had on at the *festa*, correct?" Guid'Antonio said. "The one you wore to travel into the countryside supposedly to visit your ailing mother." Instead,

Caterina had gone to the old woman in the woods—Amerigo's "witch"—and learned where Death Cap might be found growing locally. That old herbalist had told Guid'Antonio the person in question was a woman, and now, here she sat.

Caterina tapped her foot on the cell floor, agitated, quick. "I was afraid! I couldn't risk having those mushrooms found on my person. After adding the Death Cap to Orlando's plate, I had time to hide one in the nearest basket, but then Cesare appeared from out of nowhere. By then, I was late to Maria's table. I hurried into the kitchen alley and tossed the last mushroom to the ground as I ran."

"Where *Cannella* gulped it down, thereby killing herself and her puppies," Guid'Antonio said.

Caterina swallowed hard. "That was the dog's name?"

"Yes." He did not mention the case he had handled regarding Chiara Caretto this week; what good could come of that? "A beggar could have consumed it," he said. "A hungry child. No matter how foul the smell."

A silence fell over the cell. Caterina broke it, clenching and unclenching her hands in her lap. "I had not considered that."

"At any rate," Guid'Antonio said, "*Cannella's* death told me most likely we had a cold-blooded killer walking the streets of Florence. Once again, you had a lucky twist. Palla discovered Andrea Antinori's fraud and arrested him for Orlando's murder."

"He confessed," Palla said. "Why, I wonder?" he added, knitting his brow.

"That comes later," Guid'Antonio said.

Palla noted this with a grunt of acceptance. "What is important here is that you believed Andrea Antinori innocent and kept hunting the true killer," he said.

"Yes."

Caterina looked directly into Guid'Antonio, and in her expression he saw a contorted jumble of emotions. Understanding. Hate. Respect. "You goaded me into going to *Drago*

Verde tonight. You told me about the changes in Orlando's will. You made me believe the girl's family had been arrested for Orlando's murder and implied she was home alone. You knew I would seek revenge."

"I hoped so," Guid'Antonio said.

Caterina straightened her shoulders. "But why *me* in the end?"

That same plaintive cry. Gazing at her, Guid'Antonio was transported to the feast of San Giovanni, only eight days ago. He told her how as time unfolded, he had begun remembering more about the events of last Thursday and stitching together the seams of the story. "A revealing slip of the tongue here, an unguarded look there. That is all it takes for killers to expose themselves."

"All it takes for you," Palla said.

"Concerning unguarded looks," Guid'Antonio continued, "there was your odd reaction to Angelo Poliziano. Arriving late, you saw him seated on a stool at my table. His unexpected presence terrified you, because, as we have said, this tossed the seating and serving arrangements to the wind. You raised your hand—in warning, I believe. But then Giuliano left with Simonetta, Angelo took Giuliano's place, and so on and so forth. I admit I wondered about your reaction to Angelo even then, but brushed it off as—well. That isn't important now.

"Also, as for slips of the tongue, I recalled your words in the meadow: 'I wasn't expecting this.' A sentiment reinforced by Domenica, who echoed the same sentiment to me when I spoke with her about that day. You certainly were *not* expecting it, Mona Caterina. No, as established, you expected Orlando to die aboard ship, emphatically depended on it. Then Maestra Francesca Vernacci's autopsy revealed Death Cap—and the cause of Orlando's immediate demise, his sick liver, which you did not know about, until you learned the results of the autopsy."

"Even if she had known about his liver, she wouldn't know that condition would cause immediate death in reaction to the Death Cap," Palla said. "Who would? Well, other than Maestra Francesca or another doctor."

Guid'Antonio nodded agreement. "The list continues, Caterina. Monday, when I came to your house to offer my condolences, you said, 'He would have died *anyway.*' Meaning you did not have to kill him. You could have just waited for the disease to do the deed. All that risk, all that fear was unnecessary." In her way, Maria had told him, too. *"Niccolini's girl is a thief. She stole Caterina's husband, stole her love, and left her with no children. What is there for her now? How angry she must be. I would kill the whore."*

Caterina regarded him with eyes filled with weariness and frustration. "Despite his liver, despite everything, I would have wanted to kill him because I loathed the sight of him and his sickening smell. Not just because of the girl and—"

"The baby," Guid'Antonio said. "You stopped when it came to knifing the straw figure you believe to be Elena Veluti. Why?"

Caterina's nostrils flared. "That girl—or so I believed—was just lying there! So innocent for all her betrayals of her body and herself. Of me! What a bastard my husband was! Such contempt for a baby girl, should she have a girl rather than a boy. Contempt for both Elena Veluti and me! I would love a daughter as much as a son. And have, if only for a day."

Palla raised his brow. Guid'Antonio glanced at him. *Not now.* "What Orlando wanted was a son," Guid'Antonio said. "No more, no less. Perhaps only another man would understand how he felt."

Caterina smiled knowingly at him. "You would adore a baby girl, Dottore. I know that as well as you."

Tears sprang to his eyes. He cleared his throat. "Would you have let Andrea Antinori hang? Had I—the court—accepted

Andrea's confession of guilt and let things lie, you would have gotten away with everything."

"The devil assists our plans," Palla said.

Caterina gave a throaty chuckle. "Don't give Satan credit. I planned everything myself. God watched over Andrea Antinori in the end." She crossed herself.

"God and Guid'Antonio," Palla said.

†

It had been a long night and before that, a long day. By the time Guid'Antonio and Palla walked from the jail onto Justice Street, morning was full upon Florence, the air fresh and clean, the sun glancing off clouds in shades of gold, purple, and pink. Guid'Antonio felt suddenly very tired. "What now?" he said.

Smiling slyly, Palla said, "Usually, everyone asks you that. Between Caterina Niccolini and Jacopo Caretto the axman shall have a busy few weeks. That is, of course, if the law works in good order."

Forty-One

TOWER OF STRAW
SIX WEEKS LATER ~ 24TH AUGUST 1473

The iron bolt moved smoothly as Guid'Antonio and Cesare stepped through the gate into the cool shade of the Vespucci family garden. Seated together at the fountain, Maria and Amerigo glanced up from their conversation, smiling. Maria shook back her freshly washed hair, damp tendrils clinging to the curve of her breasts. "At last, you're home from All Saints," Maria said, reaching out to Guid'Antonio, beckoning him forward. *Orsetto* dropped the ball Amerigo had tossed him and darted over, frisking at Guid'Antonio's heels.

"*Buona mattina di nuova*, Good morning again." Guid'Antonio rubbed the puppy's head and kissed Maria's cheek. Sinking down beside his wife on the circular stone bench, he inhaled the smell of the soap she had used for her hair, filling his nostrils with the pleasant fragrance of lemon verbena.

"You are a kind man," Maria said, nudging him with her shoulder.

He smiled. "I'm happy you think so. Cesare and I wanted

to honor Chiara. To show her the respect she deserves in our own quiet way."

"I feel almost as if the dead girl and I were kin. And we have given her rest," Cesare said. Rather than sit, Cesare remained standing, his hands clasped before him, his manner quiet.

Amerigo glanced from Cesare to Guid'Antonio, his expression curious, but he remained content to let it go. Within the shadows of All Saints Church, Guid'Antonio and Cesare had set flame to candles and placed on the altar the fresh pink roses Maria had gathered for the purpose earlier that day. Kneeling before the painting of the *Virgin Mary of Impruneta*, they had whispered a prayer for Chiara Caretto and for her little cinnamon-haired dog, *Cannella*. In the silence of that holy place, Cesare had wept. "I was careless! I didn't purchase the Death Cap that killed Orlando Niccolini, no, but I could have served it to anyone, including to Giuliano or you. I could have brought down the Florentine government. I'm a bad apple, all the way to the core."

"No, you are not," Guid'Antonio had said. "You are still learning, as are we all. Tell me your favorite color again."

Cesare slanted his eyes at him. "Violet."

"Yes, and everyone in Florence knows how that color is made," Guid'Antonio said. "With passionate reds and lustrous, cool blues. Like you. A harmonious balance. Beautiful, in fact."

"—You believe this?"

"I do."

Cesare had stunned him by taking his hand as they turned from the church altar to go home. "I understand if *Cannella* hadn't died, we may never have known the cloth merchant was murdered."

"Yes." The fact the little dog had belonged to the dead girl had been an amazing coincidence that brought events full circle. If Niccolini had not had a diseased liver, he would have died aboard ship, rather than in the meadow, and Caterina would have gotten away with murder. If Angelo Poliziano had not taken Giuliano's place at the table, if, if, if.

"I understand this, as well," Cesare said. "You did everything you could to preserve Chiara's honor. Oh, yes. People are talking about it in the street."

Pausing before Giotto's marvelous Crucifix, Guid'Antonio replied simply, "Good." The week following Jacopo Caretto's court appearance, the Eight on Public Safety had sentenced the wool beater and his son Salvatore to be decapitated in the jail courtyard. If Guid'Antonio truly had had his way, those two would have been castrated, drawn, and quartered, and the other men of the family investigated. That had not happened—yet. Still, he had the satisfaction of knowing that over the centuries, his words spoken for Chiara Caretto and the court's final decision regarding the circumstances surrounding her death as recorded in *Condempnationes, Vol. Three*—eventually!—would set the standard for future, similar cases in Florence, please God and Mary.

Moreover, he now had the answer to the initial questions he had asked himself on Saint John's Day while woolgathering, yes, about the case of the murdered girl from the Black Lion district. *Why this child? Why this dog? And, if only secondarily, why me?* Because God had had a hand in this affair, connecting him to Chiara; this, Guid'Antonio firmly believed. Another lawyer may or may not have pursued Jacopo Caretto to the extent Guid'Antonio had done. Leniency may have prevailed. As for *Cannella*, that loyal little dog not only had led him to Chiara's killer, she had been the foremost instrument in revealing Orlando Niccolini's killer. In effect, *Cannella* had solved both crimes Guid'Antonio had been investigating. She should be awarded a medal for valor.

"You saved my honor, too," Cesare had said as they departed Ognissanti. "I love you, and I shall remain with you until the end of your days, Dottore Guid'Antonio. You may rest assured."

"I shall take great comfort in that," Guid'Antonio had said, smiling. "You know you will always have a home with us, Cesare Ridolfi."

†

In the garden, Amerigo said, "By the way, while you were in church, something amazing happened."

"Again?" Guid'Antonio said, patting *Orsetto*, who had settled in Maria's lap.

"Yes. Caterina Niccolini escaped jail."

"No!" Guid'Antonio exclaimed. "When?"

"Now. Well, this morning."

"How do you know this?"

"The town criers," Amerigo said.

"Ah." While awaiting her court appearance, Caterina Niccolini had been held in Florence's thousand-year-old Tower of Straw, a former fortification that now served as the women's prison in Piazza Sant' Elisabetta, near the church of Saint Michael of the Trumpets and the Duomo. In that airless place, Caterina's only bedding had been a thin layer of straw on the stone floor, her food, cold soup and hard bread.

"You don't seem surprised," Maria said, easing *Orsetto* from her lap, tossing the puppy his fabric cat.

Guid'Antonio smiled. "No?"

"That isn't all," Amerigo said.

"It never is," said Guid'Antonio.

"Someone bribed Caterina's guard—well, that is the gossip—and provided her a horse. Moreover, before galloping thorough the Prato Gate, she rode to Innocenti and claimed a little girl she said was her own." The Hospital of the Innocents, the orphan's hospital in Santa Croce.

"The town crier didn't say all this, surely."

"Of course not, no."

"Claimed a little girl? I don't understand," Maria said.

How much to say? How much to tell? "It seems last spring Caterina went to the orphan's hospital and adopted—or at least took home—a baby girl to cherish as her own. Orlando would have none of it and ordered her to return the child to the wheel in the dead of night, when no one would see." Luca Landucci had told Guid'Antonio that sad story when Guid'Antonio took *Orsetto* to the Sign of the Stars for help earlier in the week.

"How terrible for Caterina," Maria said. "I'm happy she escaped."

"Apparently, she had at least one friend in this town. Rather like Chiara Caretto," Amerigo said, nudging Guid'Antonio with his elbow.

"Not exactly," Guid'Antonio said. "One of them was innocent."

Maria shivered. "No wonder to me Caterina hated that girl, Elena Veluti, and resented the fact she was with child."

From the look of her, that girl, Elena Veluti's, baby was due to arrive in late August, or so. Male or female? Having heard about the amazing stipulations in Orlando Niccolini's will, the entire town was wondering how this would play out. All or nothing for Elena and her family. Nothing for Caterina—except freedom and a little girl. Guid'Antonio smiled to himself.

"Jealousy is a cruel mistress who sets hearts aflame," Maria said, a blush rising in her cheeks.

Passione. Maria was thinking of Francesca Vernacci. Guid'Antonio had braced himself against Maria's full fury when, in light of the vacancy created by Filippo Vernacci's death, he had appointed Francesca the doctor of the house at Spedale dei Vespucci. From Maestra Vernacci to Dottoressa

Vernacci, thanks to Guid'Antonio Vespucci. At first, despite Maria's outward calm when he told her his decision, he knew by the tightness of her eyes that she—like everyone else in the Unicorn district—wondered what he would have from the dottoressa in return. Slowly, but surely, Maria had shown an air of calm. Guid'Antonio did not increase—as far as Maria knew—the frequency of his visits to the hospital. In fact, so far, he mostly had kept his distance. Particularly after Francesca had employed a handsome young man as her surgery assistant, one whose salary Guid'Antonio would pay. Ah, well. The assistant had removed the stitches from Guid'Antonio's neck skillfully.

"I'm happy for her," Maria had said before setting the topic free. "I believe she finally has what she wants."

Perhaps, Guid'Antonio had thought. *Perhaps not, Maria.*

At the fountain Amerigo stood and stretched luxuriously. "I'll never understand why Andrea confessed to a crime he didn't commit. Why would he do that?"

"You are full of questions," Guid'Antonio said.

"Like you. Always," Amerigo said, grinning.

"That shall remain a mystery," Guid'Antonio said, thinking, *Andrea confessed to the crime of murder because he wanted desperately to protect his lover, Emilio Barucci. Desperately, yes.* Guid'Antonio had guessed this early on. Had Andrea not confessed, Palla would have kept investigating and quite likely have discovered Andrea and Emilio's relationship—one punishable by death for both young men, at the whim of the Officers of the Night. That illegal relationship had been the sword Orlando Niccolini had been dangling over Andrea's head—a weapon Orlando could drop at any time, for any reason, keeping Andrea his puppet, his slave, much as Jacopo Caretto had done his granddaughter. As for the argument on the borgo, Andrea had hinted that Orlando Niccolini had wanted more from him than money to repay his debt to the wool shop. Andrea had refused and threatened to expose him to the Officers of the Night. And so, the slap.

A sodomite but no murderer, Andrea still was guilty of fraud. To that end, Guid'Antonio had paid his fine and wheedled Palla into pardoning Andrea to relieve crowding in the jail. Saint John's Day was one of several religious occasions deemed suitable for such leniency. Not surprised by Guid'Antonio in the least, Palla had at last said yes. "You amaze me."

"*Grazie.*"

Guid'Antonio had mentioned nothing to anyone about slipping into the Niccolini household and breaking into the cloth merchant's lock box where, as expected, he had found the sad contract bearing one signature, and one signature only, along with the money Andrea had paid the merchant. Money Guid'Antonio had given Andrea before the boy left town which, added to the rest of the coins in the box, made a tidy sum. "Take this. Go." He did not give a fig if Spinelli and Spinelli took a loss in their accounts.

†

"The world's a mysterious place, Amerigo," Guid'Antonio said, rising from the stone bench, grateful for the cooling spray of water issuing from the fountain as he placed his hand on Maria's back. "Where are you going, my darling nephew?"

"To Giuliano's house, where else?"

"I'll accompany you as far as Gianozzo's shop," Cesare said. "I hear he has some lovely silk in the delicious, rich blue violet called *pavonozzo*. I must have some for All Saints' Day."

"Of course you must," Guid'Antonio said.

"Will we have another *festa*?"

"No!" Guid'Antonio and Amerigo said, and Cesare laughed.

"Oh!" Amerigo turned as he and Cesare walked companionably to the gate. "Yesterday morning, I spoke with Leonardo. He showed me a sketch he made when he was in Vinci. It is lovely. He is pleased. So much so that at the bottom, he inscribed the date and a note, if you can imagine any painter doing that. It says, 'Fifteenth August 1473. *Sono contento.* I am content.'"

"As am I," Guid'Antonio said, starting up the narrow stone stairs to his apartment with his hands caressing Maria's supple waist and *Orsetto* scrambling at his feet.

With this life. With this day. With this moment.

*E*PILOGUE

GIULIANO
FIVE MONTHS LATER ~ 15TH JANUARY 1474

Guid'Antonio's heart knocked against his ribs as he climbed the steep stone passageway to the top of Florence Cathedral. As he moved up the steps, sucking cold winter air into his lungs, the walls squeezed in. What if this time, he were trapped? Every time he met Giuliano de' Medici up here, he wondered the same thing. Fighting the panic in his chest, he counted fifty steps, then two-hundred, and then, thank God, the four-hundred-sixty-third and final step out onto the circular wooden platform high above the city. Emerging at last into sunlight and falling snow, he glimpsed the silver ribbon of the Arno visible in the middle distance. Farther off, snowcapped mountains lay beneath a brushstroke of puffy white clouds.

"Guid'Antonio, *ciao*," Giuliano said, turning from the iron railing separating him from Piazza San Giovanni far down below. Cheeks rosy with cold, Giuliano tugged at the folds of his black velvet cloak, pushing his hood from his face, smiling as the crimson silk lining and thick velvet puddled around his shoulders. "Thank you for coming. You seem winded. Forgive me! This is one of the few places in Florence we may speak without risk. The only place, perhaps."

Guid'Antonio gulped frosty air. "I'm fine." He kissed Giuliano's bright cheeks, mustering a grin. The dome's two narrow passageways had accommodated the brick masons and other laborers who, during the construction of the dome, had arrived in Piazza San Giovanni before daylight on workday mornings to make the arduous ascent clutching chisels, trowels, hammers, and wine flasks, along with leather pouches containing their lunch of cheese and bread. There were two passageways so that some men could make their way up, even as others went down. Eventually, Filippo Brunelleschi had had a kitchen built up here to make things a bit easier all around. This steep journey on almost a daily basis for sixteen years. Guid'Antonio resisted glancing skyward at the bronze ball and cross high over his head. "So," he said. "What is this about?"

A shiver ran over Giuliano, and he rubbed his arms for warmth. "My brother's fight with the Pope and the growing animosity between Lorenzo and Franceschino de' Pazzi frightens me. The Devil is dancing, while my brother rants and rails."

Yes. A lot had happened in the last five months. Despite Lorenzo's plea for all the other bankers in Florence not to loan Sixtus the money to buy Imola, Franceschino de' Pazzi had betrayed Lorenzo twice over: not only had the Pazzi Bank made Sixtus the loan, Franceschino had whispered in Sixtus's ear that Lorenzo had asked everyone else to deny him the money and keep his interference a secret, lest he feel the furnace blast of Rome. Franceschino had fanned the flames of suspicion and hate, flipping his fingers at Lorenzo. With the funds from the Pazzi bank in the Pope's hands, the transfer of Imola to Rome had gone smoothly. In its wake, Sixtus had named Girolamo Riario vicar of the Holy Church of Imola by virtue of Girolamo's noble blood.

In Florence none of this had gone down well.

"'Noble blood'?" Lorenzo had shouted in a hastily-called meeting of his inner circle. "There's a laugh! Girolamo Riario is a count only by virtue of that miserable little hamlet his uncle bought him! And Franceschino de' Pazzi, that double-crossing, whey-faced rat! Not only did he hand Imola to Rome, thus betraying the Florentine Republic, he betrayed me, personally, as well! He will pay dearly for this," Lorenzo had said. "May God help me see it done."

Lorenzo de' Medici, embarrassed, made a fool by Franceschino de' Pazzi, a man Lorenzo considered his inferior in every way.

Lorenzo de' Medici made an enemy of Rome.

Now, as Guid'Antonio stood high in the frigid air above Florence, Sixtus IV suspected private citizen Lorenzo de' Medici of plotting to block his quest for power and glory in every regard. Which was true, of course. In retaliation for Lorenzo's "disloyalty," Sixtus had done exactly what Lorenzo had feared he might do and transferred his personal financial account from the Medici Bank to the Pazzi Bank in Rome.

A powerful slap at Lorenzo.

A sweet pat on the ass for Franceschino, currently considered a traitor to Florence and excluded from the business of the city. How dangerously angry he must be.

Could the situation be any worse?

Yes.

According to a missive recently delivered to Palazzo Medici, the Pope's *second* favorite nephew, twenty-eight-year old Franciscan Archbishop Pietro Riario, had suddenly collapsed and died while traveling south from Venice to Rome. Poisoned, some said. Within the space of a few days, Pietro's brother, the ubiquitous, noxious Girolamo Riario, had stepped into Pietro's velvet slippers as the Pope's chief financial and diplomatic advisor. Now, in addition to acting as commander-in-chief of the papal armed forces and lord of Imola, Girolamo, that one-time grocer and clerk from Savona who had had the amazing good fortune to marry Caterina Sforza, Girolamo was the *padrone della barca vaticana*, the Captain of the Vatican Ship of State.

When Guid'Antonio remembered Girolamo in Imola last spring, gloating and posturing in the town square, when he remembered Franceschino in Via Larga, taunting him, when he remembered the monk, who he knew remained in the world, waiting and watching him—them—he wanted to howl. But he could not do that. He must remain steady for them all. For God. For Florence.

Moreover: Giuliano de' Medici had asked him here today for comfort, for some beacon of light to shine through the darkness. Giuliano had every right to be frightened because, yes, he had the Devil's attention. They all did.

I won't forget you, Dottore.

And yet—

"We have only to take each day as it comes," Guid'Antonio said. "God is on our side, not theirs. Never forget, we have survived challenging times before. We shall survive this." Survive—but at what cost? That same question, over and over again. For now, he let it lie.

Giuliano's pensive features eased, and he smiled that gloriously innocent Giuliano de' Medici smile, one for the ages. "Yes! Let's not forget the good things that have happened. I'm not a cardinal! Thank God and all the saints, now I never shall be, given the Pope's hatred for all things Medici. But I am a new uncle. Also, people are saying Verrocchio's monument for our father and uncle in San Lorenzo is one of the most beautiful tombs ever made." Lavish porphyry, marble, and bronze, with lion's paws and tortoises supporting the tomb's hefty weight. "There's a lot to celebrate in our beloved Florence," Giuliano said. "It is no wonder to me other cities and states are mad with jealousy."

Guid'Antonio smiled back. In late July, Clarice Orsini and Lorenzo de' Medici had welcomed a healthy baby girl into the world and named her Maddalena. Now, Lorenzo, who had celebrated his twenty-fifth birthday just two weeks ago, was the father of three children, two girls and a boy. Good for him. As for the tomb for Lorenzo and Giuliano's father, Andrea del Verrocchio wasn't the only craftsman in town with reason to celebrate. Perhaps because of his assistance on the tomb, Leonardo da Vinci had received the coveted commission to paint sixteen-year-old Genevra de' Benci on the occasion of her marriage—the wedding was happening later today, in fact, in Palazzo Benci on Via degli Alberti. This would be the first portrait Leonardo had painted. Or his first commission for one. Was he fearful? Probably. But also eager to perform admirably.

Closer to home, Domenico Ghirlandaio had begun preparing the fresco at the entrance to the new Vespucci Chapel in All Saints. So far, work on the *Annunciation* was proceeding according to schedule. And what of Elena Veluti? In early September that young woman had given birth to twins, a boy and a girl, thereby depriving Abbot Ughi of Orlando Niccolini's worldly goods—or not. Guid'Antonio had heard the sour old abbot meant to fight in court for the right to the proceeds of the dead cloth merchant's will, since one of the babies was a *girl*. This possibility delighted Guid'Antonio. One day soon, he might square off with the abbot in Elena Veluti's name and that of her new husband, her distant kinsman, Baldo Pacini. He certainly had enjoyed winning the case for Sister Piera against her in-laws and her immediate family. The money Sister Piera now would have from her mother's dowry would go a long way in making much-needed repairs to her convent.

As for his hospital: the Physician's College had accepted

Dottoressa Francesca Vernacci's recipe for the *Recettario fiorentino*. Francesca had told Guid'Antonio this recently, when he encountered her and her assistant on their way to yet another meeting of the *Arte dei Medici e Speziali*, the Guild of Doctors & Apothecaries, adding that, of course, the *Recettario* would not be complete for years to come. For a long while Guid'Antonio had watched her and her assistant go, their heads bent close as they talked.

He wanted to feel optimistic in the face of . . . everything. Despite the wicked machinations of the Pope, Girolamo Riario, and Franceschino de' Pazzi, all was not lost. Thanks to the influence of his close Medici connections, this past autumn Guid'Antonio had once again been elected a Lord Prior of the Florentine Republic. His two-month term was now over, but he believed he had his finger firmly in the pie of Florentine politics and, perhaps, even its history. He would do what he could to keep his friends and family safe. Though he still had no child, he had Maria, he had *now*, he had today, and he believed God meant him to do good in the world.

†

Giuliano walked across the icy platform to the iron railing, where he leaned out, peering at the snow-covered workshops and palaces sprawled far down below. A rope of fear tightened in Guid'Antonio. "Giuliano, step away from there. You could slip." In fair weather and foul, during construction of the dome, workers had fallen forty stories from the platform to their deaths in Piazza San Giovanni, far down below.

Blinking snowflakes from his eyelashes, Giuliano turned, reaching out his gloved hand.

Guid'Antonio grasped his fingers and together they made their way down the narrow, spiraling staircase, past the sanctuary altar, and across the Cathedral floor to the front doors, the sound of their boots echoing up the walls, until the sound faded and was lost in the vault high above their heads, whispering, *Go peacefully for now, go, Giuliano.*

From the church, they stepped out into a silent world of white, entirely alone. Extracting a small stone from the pocket of his cloak, Giuliano kissed it softly and handed it to Guid'Antonio. "From our garden. Add it to your collection, Guid'Antonio *mio*. Keep it with you. In this way, you and I shall always be close."

"Thank you," said Guid'Antonio, his eyes stinging with emotion.

After a brief farewell, Giuliano pulled up his black velvet hood and disappeared onto Via Larga toward the warmth of the Medici Palace, while Dottore Guid'Antonio Vespucci strode, shivering, in his dark brown leather *farsetto* and brown cloak through a white whirlwind of swirling snow toward the Unicorn district, alone.

5th July 1473. "A wool beater was condemned to death and was beheaded. He had committed the crime of violating a girl of about twelve-years-old in such a way that she died; and then he had buried her body outside the *Porta alla Giusticia*. Later her body was discovered, as the dogs raked it up . . . When captured, he confessed having committed the outrage."

Luca Landucci, *A Florentine Diary From 1450 to 1516*

> "Avarice, envy, pride,
> Three fatal sparks, have set the hearts of all on fire."
>
> Dante Alighieri, *The Divine Comedy*

> "Don't you see that a woman who has no children has no home?"
>
> Niccolò Machiavelli, *Mandragola*

GUID'ANTONIO VESPUCCI

The historical Guid'Antonio Vespucci (1436-1501) was the oldest son of Antonia Ugolini and Giovanni Vespucci. By the time of Guid'Antonio's birth, the Vespuccis ranked among Florence's leading families, with holdings in rental properties, vineyards, olive groves, silk shops, and wool. Like the sons of all wealthy Florentines, Guid'Antonio would have been educated in Latin, arithmetic, and logic. As a young man at the universities of Bologna and Ferrara, he studied civil law, rhetoric, and poetry, the latter two deemed essential for the Renaissance practice of diplomacy. For his profession, he chose Doctor of Law.

As Guid'Antonio once said, he believed in the maintenance of legal order and the utilization of the abilities of the cities' most able citizens. Thus, from the first days of his career, like his father before him, he supported the Medici family in its private administration of the democratic Florentine government. When he was in his early thirties and Lorenzo's father, Piero de' Medici, was the *de facto*, or unofficial, ruler of Florence, Guid'Antonio served as one of the Florentine Republic's nine Lord Priors, the state's highest-ranking council. When Piero died in 1469, Guid'Antonio immediately aligned himself with Piero's two young male heirs, Lorenzo and Giuliano de' Medici. His close bond with them saw him serve the Medici family and the Florentine Republic in myriad ways, including traveling to Imola in early 1473 on an official government mission to secure that desirable little town for

Florence—a mission destined to fail.

When Guid'Antonio was about thirty-four, he married his second wife, Maria del Vigna. As implied in our story, families lived close by one another in Florence, often in the same household and, certainly, in the same parish. Thus, he would have encountered Brother Giorgio and Nastagio Vespucci (Amerigo's "other" uncle and his father) on almost a daily basis. Of all his nephews, Guid'Antonio seems to have been particularly close with Amerigo, who eventually sailed west and into the pages of history, while Guid'Antonio played his part as one of the most influential and powerful personages of his time until his death on Christmas Eve in 1501 at age sixty-five.

Together, Guid'Antonio and Amerigo lived when educated Italians already spoke of the "rinascimento," an era in which a new spirit of rebirth in life, art, and literature prevailed. Nowhere was this more evident than in Florence, at this time a city of about 50,000 souls. Within the town's walls, Guid'Antonio and Amerigo rubbed elbows with their neighbors Sandro Botticelli, Leonardo da Vinci, Paolo Toscanelli, and many other Renaissance luminaries, while at the heart of Florence there stood the controversial, charming, and brilliantly talented poet and statesman, Lorenzo de' Medici, the untitled prince of the city known to history as "Lorenzo the Magnificent."

AUTHOR'S NOTE

Many of the people in *The Hearts of All on Fire* are real, and the story draws on major events in their lives. While it is hard to believe the conflict between Florence and Rome over the purchase of a small town in northeastern Italy led to a plot designed to murder Lorenzo and Giuliano de' Medici in Florence Cathedral, that is what happened. Guid'Antonio Vespucci did go to Imola in early 1473 as the representative from Florence. As described in *The Hearts of All on Fire*, the Florentine Republic lost the coveted town when Pope Sixtus IV (Francesco della Rovere) threatened Milan with excommunication, among other things, unless the duke of Milan sold Imola to him. As Imola's new owner, Sixtus could name his favorite nephew, Girolamo Riario, the town's lord, thereby establishing a toehold in the area for the combined Rovere-Riario families. When the duke bowed to the Pope's threats, Sixtus requested a loan from the Medici Bank to seal the deal. Though conflicted—Lorenzo did want a cardinal's hat for his brother, Giuliano—he said, "No," while also asking other Florentine bankers to deny the Pope the money, as well. Dear Reader, you know the rest.

All the artwork and most of the architecture mentioned in *The Hearts of All on Fire* may still be seen in Florence today (with the exception of the painting known as the *Virgin Mary of Santa Maria Impruneta*, which is in the Cathedral of S. M. All'Impruneta, a short distance away). In our story, Guid'Antonio compares his house, church, and hospital on Borg'Ognissanti, All Saints Street, as "strung along the west bank of the

Arno like beads on an expensive chain." After six centuries and counting, that row of massive stone buildings is still there. While Guid'Antonio's *palazzo* and hospital are no more, visitors to Florence quick on their feet can peek inside the entrance of the former Spedale dei Vespucci, with its large foyer and broad winding stairs, where Dottoressa Francesca Vernacci would have practiced medicine.

Today inside Guid'Antonio's family church (All Saints) you may see the *Annunciation* Domenico Ghirlandaio painted for the Vespucci family chapel. The fresco includes likenesses of both Amerigo and his uncle, Brother Giorgio Vespucci. Giotto's *Crucifix*, dating from the early 1300s and so admired by Guid'Antonio, also is in All Saints, manifest in all its radiant glory after being found in a church closet, identified, and restored in the early 21st century, an endeavor of about ten years.

Readers familiar with Florence will notice how in some instances I have used present-day names for buildings and streets, while in others they retain their 15th century names. Palla Palmieri's police headquarters and jail today is called the Bargello, and I have used that designation. Now a national museum, the Bargello houses primarily Florentine Renaissance sculpture, with rooms dedicated to the works of Michelangelo, Andrea del Verrocchio, and many other artists, including Donatello, featuring his saucy little bronze sculpture of *David*, naked but for hat and boots. Donatello's imposing *Judith & Holofernes* is in Palazzo Vecchio (the City Hall called in Guid'Antonio's day Palazzo della Signoria).

Lorenzo and Giuliano's ancestor, Guccio de' Medici's, tomb is in the Baptistry directly across from Florence Cathedral in Piazza San Giovanni. The centuries-old marble column dedicated to the memory of Saint Zenobius stands outside in the piazza. With the assistance of Leonardo da Vinci, Verrocchio did complete Piero and Giovanni de' Medici's magnificent marble tomb in 1473. The tomb is in the San Lorenzo Church complex, a short walk from the Cathedral. In the summer of that same year, Leonardo sketched with lightning speed a pen and ink drawing of the valley of the Arno, near his hometown of Vinci. He inscribed the drawing with the words, "Day of St. Mary of the Snows, August 5, 1473," adding, "*Sono contento.* I am content." The drawing, housed in the Uffizi Gallery in Florence, is considered the first study dealing wholly with landscape in Western Art.

For an introduction to the Medici family, interested readers might begin with Christopher Hibbert's *The House of Medici: Its Rise and Fall* and Miles J. Unger's *Magnifico: The Brilliant Life and Violent Times of Lorenzo de' Medici.* For my research on the Vespucci family, as always I drew heavily on *Amerigo and the New World* by Germán Arciniegas, and then on materials gleaned from Italian Renaissance scholars, whose work has been invaluable to me. Ross King's *Brunelleschi's Dome* has been a steady resource, along with *Dressing Renaissance Florence* by Carole Collier Frick; *The Renaissance Man and His Family: Childbirth and Early Childhood in Florence, 1300-1600* by Louis Haas; *The Pazzi Conspiracy: The Plot Against the Medici* by Harold Acton; and all books on the Italian Renaissance by Gene Brucker.

A deep bow must be given, as always, to apothecary Luca Landucci and his wonderful personal work, *A Florentine Diary from 1450 to 1516*. Luca—where would I be without your amusing observations, frustrations, and your sharp and forthright comments about everything happening around you, my dear friend?

For *The Hearts of All on Fire* in particular, the court cases studied by Guid'Antonio and Amerigo in the Chancery in the Bargello in downtown Florence and the overall attitude about crime and punishment in 15th century Florence are drawn from a number of sources, including *Criminal Justice and Crime in Late Renaissance Florence*, John Brackett; *Lawyers and Statecraft in Renaissance Florence*, Lauro Martines; *The

Criminal Law System in Medieval and Renaissance Florence, Laura Stern; *The Laboring classes in Renaissance Florence*, Samuel K. Cohn, Jr.; and *Forbidden Friendships: Homosexuality and Male Culture in Renaissance Florence*, Michael Rocke.

John Henderson's *The Renaissance Hospital: Healing the Body and Healing the Soul* and Katharine Parks' *Doctors and Medicine in Early Renaissance Florence* were my door to the world of 15th century medicine in Florence, specifically to the role women played therein.

Here is even more . . .

To his credit, apparently Pope Sixtus IV was dismayed by his nephew, Girolamo Riario's, demand that he be allowed to "bed" ten-year-old Caterina Sforza on the day they were wed—and even before then. At age fourteen, Caterina moved with Count Girolamo from Rome to Imola. Many books have been written about this amazing woman. One excellent title is *The Tigress of Forlì* by Elizabeth Lev, with its depiction of Caterina's later blistering encounter with Cesare Borgia.

Regarding the church of Santi Apostoli, tradition holds that the three flints used to light the lamps in Jesus's tomb were acquired by a Pazzi family ancestor who was among the first Christians to scale the walls and lead to the capture of Jerusalem during the First Crusade in the 11th century. Today, the flints are linked to the ceremony of *Lo Scoppio del Carro*, The Explosion of the Cart, and the lighting of fireworks after a celebratory mass. Santi Apostoli still houses the flints in Piazza Limbo.

Prego.

READER'S GUIDE

Questions for Discussion

In *The Inferno*, Florentine poet Dante Alighieri wrote, "Avarice, envy, pride, three fatal sparks, have set the hearts of all on fire." How does that relate to this story?

Do you consider Guid'Antonio a religious man? Why or why not?

Guid'Antonio believed in government by the best and the brightest, sometimes with no political holds barred—do you agree with that? Do you consider him a good man?

What do you think of Guid'Antonio's relationship with Francesca Vernacci, the doctor at his hospital near his home?

Does Guid'Antonio love Maria? What do you think of their often tense relationship?

In *The Hearts of All on Fire*, coincidence plays a significant role. What do you think of coincidence in our lives—how often have you experienced it, and in what ways?

Consider Guid'Antonio's relationship with Lorenzo de' Medici and also with Lorenzo's brother, Giuliano. Do you consider Guid'Antonio and Lorenzo friends? How about Guid'Antonio and Giuliano?

Does angry Little Francesco de' Pazzi have the right to feel slighted by and jealous of the Medici boys? Could the Medici and Pazzi families ever have stood side by side in Florence?

Would you want to live in Renaissance Florence? Why or why not?

In Guid'Antonio's day, women wore hoods and cloaks to keep them covered in the eyes of the public. How does that compare to the present day, generally speaking, from one country and religion to another? Have you ever considered this question before?

Children and the need for them is important to this story. Guid'Antonio is quietly desperate for an heir. How is this different from today—if at all?

Dogs play important roles in this story. Did this surprise you? Could you relate to Guid'Antonio's relationship to *Orsetto*, his Little Bear? Why does he dote on *Orsetto* as much as he does?

ACKNOWLEDGEMENTS

As I often have said, my life has been blessed by libraries, and I would be remiss if I did not express my heartfelt gratitude for their calm and constant presence. In difficult times, libraries have been my safe place, my haven. In my childhood, they provided me with books—free. Later, they opened up the world of the Italian Renaissance as I began exploring that colorful and complex time in history. God bless the Nashville Public Library and Interlibrary Loan for making it possible for me to place my hands on books written by scholars of the Italian Renaissance, present and past, whose work otherwise would not have been available to me.

I want to thank the members of my former writing group, the Nashville Writers Alliance, for many years of camaraderie and support, particularly friend and author Mike Coleman, who offered invaluable suggestions regarding *The Hearts of All on Fire* in the early stages. Huge thanks to Blake Leyers at Blake Editorial and author/writing coach Jaden Terrell—both women are book editors extraordinaire, whose insights kept me on track when I was in a dark wood wandering. Also to author and friend, Tinney Sue Heath, whose love for everything medieval shines forth in her books. Tinney, your sharp eye for details and your encouragement in the final stages were a blessing to me. Add the friendship and razor-sharp wit of Lynette Ingram, with whom I have shared many hours of serious conversation and much-needed laughter about writing—who, what, and, for goodness sakes, when? Where would

I be without the Historical Novel Society, a balm to my soul since the first HNS conference in Salt Lake City, Utah? So many writerly talks, so much camaraderie. Sarah Johnson, you are amazing. Sarah's popular blog, "Reading the Past," is a must-read for lovers of historical fiction everywhere. Once again, a special thanks goes to Sally Schloss, author and friend, who introduced me to Atmosphere Press and its creators, Nick Courtright and Kyle McCord, and to all the lovely staff.

ABOUT ATMOSPHERE PRESS

Atmosphere Press is an independent, full-service publisher for excellent books in all genres and for all audiences. Learn more about what we do at atmospherepress.com.

We encourage you to check out some of Atmosphere's latest releases, which are available at Amazon.com and via order from your local bookstore:

Dancing with David, a novel by Siegfried Johnson

The Friendship Quilts, a novel by June Calender

My Significant Nobody, a novel by Stevie D. Parker

Nine Days, a novel by Judy Lannon

Shining New Testament: The Cloning of Jay Christ, a novel by Cliff Williamson

Shadows of Robyst, a novel by K. E. Maroudas

Home Within a Landscape, a novel by Alexey L. Kovalev

Motherhood, a novel by Siamak Vakili

Death, The Pharmacist, a novel by D. Ike Horst

Mystery of the Lost Years, a novel by Bobby J. Bixler

Bone Deep Bonds, a novel by B. G. Arnold

Terriers in the Jungle, a novel by Georja Umano

Into the Emerald Dream, a novel by Autumn Allen

His Name Was Ellis, a novel by Joseph Libonati

The Cup, a novel by D. P. Hardwick

The Empathy Academy, a novel by Dustin Grinnell

Tholocco's Wake, a novel by W. W. VanOverbeke

Dying to Live, a novel by Barbara Macpherson Reyelts

Looking for Lawson, a novel by Mark Kirby

A LETTER FROM ALANA

Author Photograph by Maddux Imaging

Dear Reader,

I want to say a huge thank you for choosing to read *The Hearts of All on Fire*. If you did enjoy it and want to keep up to date with all my latest releases, just go to my website at www.alanawhite.com.

I hope you loved Guid'Antonio in *The Hearts of All on Fire* (and, quite possibly, in *The Sign of the Weeping Virgin*). If you did I would be very grateful if you could write a review. I would love to hear what you think, and it makes such a difference helping new readers to discover one of my books for the first time.

Stay with me kind reader! I enjoy hearing from you—you can get in touch on my website, my Facebook Author Page, and also through Twitter and Goodreads. As well as participating for many years in the Historical Novel Society, I am a longtime member of Mystery Writers of America, Sisters in Crime, the Authors Guild, and the Women's National Book Association.

Thank you,
Alana White

Facebook: Alana White, Author
Twitter: @Alanawhite1480

Website: Alanawhite.com
Insta: Alanawhiteauthor
Pinterest: Alana White, Author
{For lovely images of the real-life people and the artwork in the Guid'Antonio mysteries.}

CPSIA information can be obtained
at www.ICGtesting.com
Printed in the USA
LVHW031646180423
744574LV00004B/86